MISS YOU

Kate Eberlen grew up in a small town thirty miles from London and spent her childhood reading books and longing to escape. She studied Classics at Oxford University before pursuing various jobs in publishing and the arts. Recently, Kate trained to teach English as a foreign language with a view to spending more time in Italy. Kate is married with one son.

Kate Eberlen

Miss You

MANTLE

First published 2016 by Mantle
an imprint of Pan Macmillan
20 New Wharf Road, London N1 9RR
Associated companies throughout the world
www.panmacmillan.com

ISBN 978-1-5098-1994-2

1 3 5 7 9 8 6 4 2

A CIP catalogue record for this book is available from the British Library.

Typeset by Ellipsis Digital Limited, Glasgow
Printed and bound by CPI Group (UK) Ltd, Croydon, CR0 4YY

*In memory of my lovely Gran,
who made ordinary things wonderful*

PART ONE

1

August 1997

TESS

In the kitchen at home, there was a plate that Mum bought on holiday in Tenerife with a hand-painted motto: *Today is the first day of the rest of your life*.

It had never registered with me any more than Dad's trophy for singing, or the New York snow dome my brother Kevin sent over one Christmas, but that last day of the holiday, I couldn't seem to get it out of my head.

When I woke up, the inside of the tent was glowing orange, like a pumpkin lantern. I inched the zipper door down carefully so as not to wake Doll, then stuck my face out into dazzling sunlight. The air was still a little bit shivery and I could hear the distant clank of bells. I wrote the word 'plangent' in my diary with an asterisk next to it so I could check it in the dictionary when I got home.

The view of Florence from the campsite, all terracotta domes and white marble towers shimmering against a flat blue sky, was so like it was supposed to be, I had this strange feeling of sadness, as if I was missing it already.

There were lots of things I wouldn't miss, like sleeping on the ground – after a few hours, the stones feel like they're

3

growing into your back – and getting dressed in a space less than three feet high, and walking all the way to the shower block, then remembering you've left the toilet roll in the tent. It's funny how when you get towards the end of a holiday, half of you never wants it to end and the other half is looking forward to the comforts of home.

We'd been Interrailing for a month, down through France, then into Italy, sleeping on stations, drinking beer with Dutch boys on campsites, struggling with sunburn in slow, sticky trains. Doll was into beaches and Bellinis; I was more maps and monuments, but we got along like we always had since we met on the first day at St Cuthbert's, aged four, and Maria Dolores O'Neill – I was the one who abbreviated it to Doll – asked, 'Do you want to be my best friend?'

We were different, but we complemented each other. Whenever I said that, Doll always said, 'You've got great skin!' or 'I really like those shoes,' and if I told her it wasn't that sort of compliment, she'd laugh, and say she knew, but I was never sure she did. You develop a kind of special language with people you're close to, don't you?

My memories of the other places we went to that holiday are like postcards: the floodlit amphitheatre in Verona against an ink-dark sky; the azure bay of Naples; the unexpectedly vibrant colours of the Sistine Chapel ceiling, but that last, carefree day we spent in Florence, the day before my life changed, I can retrace hour by hour, footstep by footstep almost.

Doll always took much longer than me getting ready in the mornings because she never went out without full make-up even then. I liked having time on my own, especially that morning because it was the day of my A-level results and I was trying to compose myself for hearing if I'd done well enough to get into university.

On the way up to the campsite the previous evening, I'd noticed the floodlit facade of a church high above the road, pretty and incongruous like a jewel box in a forest. In daylight, the basilica was much bigger than I'd imagined, and as I climbed the grand flights of baroque steps towards it, I had the peculiar thought that it would make the perfect setting for a wedding, which was unlike me because I'd never had a proper boyfriend then, let alone pictured myself in a long white dress.

From the terrace at the top, the view was so exhilarating, I felt an irrational urge to cry as I promised myself solemnly – like you do when you're eighteen – that I would one day return.

There was no one else around, but the heavy wooden door of the church opened when I gave it a push. It was so dark inside after the glare, my eyes took a little time to adjust to the gloom. The air was a few degrees cooler than the heat outside and it had that churchy smell of dust mingling with incense. Alone in God's house, I was acutely aware of the irreverent flap of my sandals as I walked up the steps to the raised chancel. I was staring at the giant, impassive face of Jesus, praying that my grades were going to be OK, when suddenly, magically, the apse filled with light.

Spinning round, I was startled to see a lanky guy about my own age, standing beside a box on the wall where you could put a coin in to turn the lights on. Damp brown hair swept back from his face, he was even more inappropriately dressed than me, in running shorts, a vest and trainers. There was a moment when we could have smiled at one another, or even said something, but we missed it, as we both self-consciously turned our attention to the huge dome of golden mosaic and the light went out again with a loud clunk, as decisively and unexpectedly as it had come on.

I glanced at my watch in the ensuing dimness, as if to imply that I would like to give the iconic image more serious consideration, perhaps even contribute my own minute of electricity, if I wasn't already running late. As I reached the door, I heard the clunk again, and, looking up at Christ's solemn, illuminated features, felt as if I'd disappointed Him.

Doll was fully coiffed and painted by the time I arrived back at the campsite.

'What was it like?' she asked.

'Byzantine, I think,' I said.

'Is that good?'

'Beautiful.'

After cappuccinos and custard buns – amazing how even campsite bar snacks are delicious in Italy – we packed up and decided to go straight down into town to the central post office where I could make an international call and get my results so that wouldn't be hanging over us all day. Even if the news was bad, I wanted to hear it. What I couldn't deal with was the limbo state of not knowing what the future held for me. So we walked down to the *centro storico*, with me chattering away about everything except the subject that was preoccupying me.

The fear was so loud in my head when I dialled our number, I felt as if I'd lost the ability to speak.

Mum answered after one ring.

'Hope's going to read your results to you,' she said.

'Mum!' I cried, but it was too late.

My little sister Hope was already on the line.

'Read your results to you,' she said.

'Go on then.'

'A, B, C . . .' she said slowly, like she was practising her alphabet.

'Isn't that marvellous?' said Mum.

'What?'

'You've an A for English, B for Art History and C for Religion and Philosophy.'

'You're kidding?' I'd been offered a place at University College London conditional on my getting two Bs and a C, so it was better than I needed.

I ducked my head out of the Perspex dome to give Doll the thumbs-up.

Down the line, Mum was cheering, then Hope joined in. I pictured the two of them standing in the kitchen beside the knick-knack shelf with the plate that said *Today is the first day of the rest of your life*.

Doll's suggestion for a celebration was to blow all the money we had left on a bottle of *spumante* at a pavement table on Piazza Signoria. She had more money than me from working part-time in the salon while she was doing her diploma and she had been hankering for another outside table ever since Venice, where we'd inadvertently spent a whole day's budget on a cappuccino in St Mark's Square. At eighteen, Doll already had a taste for glamour. But it was only ten o'clock in the morning, and I figured that even if we stretched it out, we would still have hours before our overnight train to Calais, and probably headaches. I'm practical like that.

'It's up to you,' said Doll, disappointed. 'It's your celebration.'

There were so many sights I wanted to see: the Uffizi, the Bargello, the Duomo, the Baptistery, Santa Maria Novella . . .

'You mean churches, don't you?' Doll wasn't going to be fooled by the Italian names.

Both of us were brought up Catholic, but at that point in our lives Doll saw church as something that stopped her having a lie-in on Sunday and I thought it was cool to describe myself as agnostic, although I still found myself quite often praying for things. For me, Italy's churches were principally places not so much of God but of culture. To be honest, I was pretentious, but I was allowed to be because I was about to become a student.

After leaving our rucksacks in Left Luggage at the station, we did a quick circuit of the Duomo, taking photographs of each other outside the golden Baptistery doors, then navigated a backstreet route towards Santa Croce, stopping at a tiny artisan *gelateria* that was opening up for the day. Ice cream in the morning satisfied Doll's craving for decadence. We chose three flavours each from cylindrical tubs arranged behind the glass counter like a giant paintbox.

For me, refreshing mandarin, lemon and pink grapefruit.

'Too breakfast-y,' said Doll, indulging herself with marsala, cherry and fondant chocolate, which she described as orgasmic and which sustained her good mood through an hour's worth of Giotto murals.

The fun thing about looking at art with Doll was her saying things like, 'He wasn't very good at feet, was he?' but when we emerged from the church, I could tell she'd had enough culture and the midday city heat felt oppressive, so I suggested we take a bus to the ancient hill town of Fiesole, which I had read about in the *Rough Guide*. It was a relief to stand by the bus window, getting the movement of air on our faces.

Fiesole's main square was stunningly peaceful after Florence's packed streets.

'Let's have a celebratory *menu turistico*,' I said, deciding to splurge the last little bit of money I'd been saving in case of emergencies.

We sat on the terrace of the restaurant, with Florence a miniature city in the distance, like the backdrop to a Leonardo painting.

'Any educational activities planned for this afternoon?' Doll asked, dabbing the corners of her mouth after demolishing a bowl of spaghetti *pomodoro*.

'There is a Roman theatre,' I admitted. 'But I'm fine going round on my own, honest . . .'

'Those bloody Romans got everywhere, didn't they?' said Doll, but she was happy enough to follow me there.

We were the only people visiting the site. Doll lay sunbathing on a stone tier of seats as I explored. She sat up and started clapping when I found my way onto the stage. I took a bow.

'Say something!' Doll called.

'Tomorrow and tomorrow and tomorrow!' I shouted.

'More!' shouted Doll, getting out her camera.

'Can't remember any more!'

I jumped down from the stage and made my way up the steep steps.

'Shall I take a picture of you?'

'Let's get one with both of us.'

With the camera positioned three steps up, Doll reckoned she could get us in the frame against the backdrop of Tuscan hills.

'What's the Italian for cheese?' she asked, setting the timer, before scurrying down to stand next to me for the click of the shutter.

In my photograph album, it looks like we are blowing kisses at the camera. The self-stick stuff has gone all yellow now, and the plastic covering is brittle, but the colours – white stone, blue sky, black-green cypresses – are just as sharp as I remember.

With invisible crickets chattering in the trees around us, we waited for the bus back to Florence in uncharacteristic silence.

Doll finally revealed what was on her mind. 'Do you think we'll still be friends?'

'What do you mean?' I pretended not to know what she was asking.

'When you're at university with people who know about books and history and stuff . . .'

'Don't be daft,' I said confidently, but the treacherous

thought had already crossed my mind that next year I would probably be holidaying with people who would want to look at the small collection of painted Greek vases in the site museum, or enjoy comparing the work of Michelangelo and Donatello, and the other Ninja Turtles (as Doll referred to them).

Today is the first day of the rest of your life.

There was a little twist of excitement and fear in my tummy whenever I allowed myself to think about the future.

Back in Florence, we made a small detour for another ice cream. Doll couldn't resist the chocolate again, this time with melon, and I selected pear which tasted like the essence of a hundred perfectly ripe Williams, with raspberry, as sharp and sweet as a childhood memory of summer.

The Ponte Vecchio was a little quieter than it had been at the start of the day, allowing us to look in the windows of the tiny jewellery shops. When Doll spotted a silver charm bracelet that was much cheaper than the rest of the merchandise, we ducked through the door and squeezed inside.

The proprietor held up the delicate chain with miniature replicas of the Duomo, the Ponte Vecchio, a Chianti bottle and Michelangelo's *David*.

'Is for child,' he said.

'Why don't I buy it for Hope?' Doll said, eager to find a reason to spend the rest of her money.

We were probably imagining, as we watched the man arrange the bracelet on tissue in a small cardboard box stamped with gold fleurs-de-lys, that this would be something my sister would keep safely in a special place and that, from time to time, we would all unwrap it together and gaze upon it reverently, like a precious heirloom.

Outside, the light had deserted the ancient buildings and the noise of the city had softened. The mellow jazz riff of a busker's clarinet wafted on the balmy air. At the centre of the bridge, we waited for a gap in the crowd so we could take photos of each other against the fading golden sky. It was weird to think of all the mantelpieces we would appear on in the background to other people's photos, from Tokyo to Tennessee.

'I've got two shots left,' Doll announced.

Scanning the crowd, my eyes settled on a face that was somehow familiar, but which I only managed to place when he frowned with confusion as I smiled at him. It was the boy I'd seen in San Miniato al Monte that morning. There was a red-dish tinge to his hair in the last rays of sunshine, and he was now wearing a khaki polo shirt and chinos, and standing awk-wardly beside a middle-aged couple who looked like they might be his parents.

I held the camera out to him. 'Would you mind?'

The perplexed look made me wonder if he was English, then, his pale, freckly complexion flushing with embarrass-ment, he said, 'Not at all!' in a voice Mum would have called 'nicely spoken'.

'Say cheese!'

'*Formaggio!*' Doll and I chorused.

In the photo, our eyes are closed, laughing at our own joke.

With a six-berth couchette to ourselves, we lay on the bottom bunks, passing a bottle of red wine between us and going over our memories of the holiday as the train trundled through the night. For me, it was views and sights.

'Remember the flowers on the Spanish Steps?'

'Flowers?'

'Were you even on the same holiday?'

For Doll, it was men.

'Remember that waiter's face in Piazza Navona when I said I liked eating fish?'

We now understood that the phrase had another meaning in Italian.

'Best meal?' said Doll.

'Prosciutto and peaches from the street market in Bologna. You?'

'That oniony anchovy pizza thing in Nice was delish . . .'

'*Pissaladière*,' I said.

'Behave!'

'Best day?'

'Capri,' said Doll. 'You?'

'I think today.'

'Best . . . ?'

Doll drifted off, but I couldn't sleep. Whenever I closed my eyes, I found myself in the little room I had reserved in the university halls of residence which, until now, I hadn't allowed my imagination to inhabit, excitedly placing my possessions on the shelves, my duvet cover on the bed, and Blu-Tacking up my new poster of Botticelli's *Primavera* which was rolling gently from side to side on the luggage rack above me. Which floor would I be on? Would I have a view over rooftops towards the Telecom Tower, like the one they'd shown us on Open Day? Or would I be on the street side of the building, with the tops of red double-decker buses crawling past my window and sudden shrieks of police sirens that made it feel like being in a movie?

The air in the compartment grew chilly as the train started its climb through the Alps. I covered Doll with her fleece. She murmured her thanks but did not wake, and I was glad because it felt special to have private time to myself, just me and my plans, travelling from one stage of my life to the next.

I must have fallen asleep in the small hours. I awoke with the rattle of a breakfast trolley. Doll was staring dismally at viscous raindrops chasing each other down the window as the train sped across the flat fields of Northern France.

'I'd forgotten about weather,' she said, handing me a plastic cup of sour coffee and a cellophane-wrapped croissant.

*

It wasn't that I was expecting bunting, or neighbours lining the street to welcome me back, but as I walked up Conifer Road after leaving Doll outside her house on Laburnum Drive, I couldn't help feeling disappointed that everything was exactly the same. Our council estate was built in the late sixties. It was probably the height of modernity then with its regular rectangular houses half pale brick, half white render, and communal lawns instead of front gardens. All the streets were named after trees, but apart from a few spindly flowering cherries, nobody had bothered to plant any. Some of the right-to-buy households had added a glazed porch at the front, or a UPVC conservatory to the through-room downstairs, but the houses all still looked like the little boxes in that song. With a month's distance, it was clear to me that I had outgrown the place.

Mum only had a rough idea of when I'd be getting back, but I was still slightly surprised that she and Hope were not positioned by the window or even sitting on the front lawn, waiting for me. It was a lovely evening. Maybe Mum had filled the paddling pool in the back garden? Perhaps there was too much splashing for them to hear the bell?

Eventually, a small, familiar shape appeared on the other side of the frosted glass.

'Who's there?' Hope called.

'It's me!'

'It's me!' she shouted.

It was never quite clear whether Hope was playing games or being pedantic.

'It's Tree!' I said. 'Come on, Hope, open the door!'

'It's Tree!'

I could tell Mum was responding from somewhere in the house but I couldn't hear what she was saying.

Hope knelt down to speak through the letter box at the bottom of the front door. 'I get chair from kitchen.'

'Use the one in the hall,' I instructed through the letter box.

'Mum said kitchen!'

'OK, OK . . .'

Why didn't Mum come down herself? I was suddenly weary and irritable.

Eventually, Hope managed to open the door.

'Where is Mum?' I asked. The house was slightly chilly inside and there was no warm smell of dinner on the air.

'Just getting up,' said Hope.

'Is she poorly?'

'Just tired.'

'Dad not home yet?'

'Pub, I 'spect,' said Hope.

I manoeuvred my rucksack off my back, then Mum was at the top of the stairs, but instead of rushing down delighted to see me, she picked her way carefully, holding the banister. I put it down to the slippers she had on under the washed-out pink tracksuit she wore for her aerobics class. She seemed distant, almost cross, and wouldn't catch my eye as she filled a kettle at the sink.

I looked at my watch. It was after eight o'clock. I'd forgotten it stayed lighter in the evenings in England. I started to think I should have found a phone box and rung home after getting off the ferry, but that didn't seem a serious enough offence for Mum to give me the silent treatment.

I noticed Mum's hair was unbrushed at the back. She had been in bed when I arrived. Just tired, Hope had said. She'd had four weeks of coping on her own.

'I can do that,' I offered, taking the kettle from her.

I felt the first whisper of alarm when I noticed the collection of dirty mugs in the kitchen sink. Mum must really be exhausted, because she always kept the place spotless.

'Where's Dad?' I asked.

'Down the pub, I expect,' said Mum.

14

'Why don't you go back upstairs and I'll bring you a cup?'

To my surprise, because nothing was ever too much trouble for Mum, she said, 'All right,' then added, as if she'd only just remembered I'd been away, 'How was your holiday?'

'Great! It was great!'

My face was aching with smiling at her and not getting anything back.

'The journey?'

'Fine!'

She was already on her way back upstairs.

When I took the tea up, my parents' bedroom door was open and I caught a glimpse of Mum's reflection in the dressing-table mirror before I entered the room. You know how sometimes you see people differently when they're not aware you're looking at them? She was lying with her eyes closed, as if some vital essence had drained from her, leaving her insubstantial, like an echo of herself. For a couple of seconds I stared, and then she stirred, suddenly noticing me standing there.

Her eyes, bright with anxiety, locked on mine, telegraphing, *Don't ask in front of Hope.* Then, seeing I was alone, closed again, relieved.

'Let's sit you up,' I said.

She leaned against me as I plumped up the pillows behind her, and her body felt light and fragile. Half an hour before, I'd been walking up the Crescent, hating how familiar and ordinary it was, and now everything was shifting around me like an earthquake and I desperately wanted it to go back to normal.

'I'm poorly, Tess,' she said, in answer to the question I was too scared to ask.

I waited for her to say, 'It's OK, though, because . . .' But she didn't.

'What sort of poorly?' I asked, giddy with panic.

Mum was diagnosed with breast cancer when she was pregnant with Hope. She hadn't had the chemo until after

15

Hope was born, but she'd recovered. She'd had to go regularly for a check-up but the last one, just a few months ago, had been clear.

'I've got cancer of the ovary and it's spread to my liver,' she said. 'I should have gone to the doctor before, but I thought it was a bit of indigestion.'

Downstairs, Hope was singing a familiar tune, but I couldn't work out what it was.

My brain was trying to picture Mum before I left. A bit tired, perhaps, and worried, I'd thought because of my exams. She was always there for me: in the kitchen at breakfast time, keeping Hope quiet as I raced through my notes; and when I came home, with a cup of tea and a listening ear if I wanted to talk, or if I didn't, just pottering around washing up or chopping vegetables, a quietly supportive presence.

How could I have been so selfish that I didn't notice? How could I have even gone on holiday?

'There was nothing you could do,' Mum said, reading my thoughts.

'But you were fine at your last scan!'

'That was in my breast.'

'And they don't check the rest of you?'

Mum put a finger to her lips.

Hope was on her way upstairs. The nursery rhyme was 'Goosey Goosey Gander', except she was singing 'Juicy Juicy Gander'.

'Upstairs, downstairs, in my lady chamber . . .'

We forced ourselves to smile as she came into the room.

'I'm hungry,' she said.

'OK!' I jumped up from the bed. 'I'll make your tea.'

If I'd needed further evidence how bad things were, it was the empty fridge. Although there was never a lot of money in our family, there was always food. I felt suddenly angry with my father. In our house the division of labour was very traditional: Dad was the breadwinner, Mum was the homemaker, but surely he could have stirred himself in these circumstances? I pictured him in the pub milking the self-pity, with his mates buying him pints. Dad was always moaning about the hand life had dealt him.

I found a can of Heinz spaghetti in the cupboard and put a slice of bread in the toaster.

Hope was staring at me, but my mind was so full with trying to take it all in, I couldn't think of anything to say to her.

The spaghetti began to bubble on the stove.

I slopped it onto the piece of toast, recalling the bowl of perfectly al-dente pasta we'd eaten in Fiesole the day before, with a sauce that tasted of a thousand tomatoes in one spoonful, and Florence in the distance, the backdrop to a Leonardo painting, so far away now, it felt like another life.

The dictionary confirmed that 'plangent' means resonant and mournful. It comes from the Latin *plangere*: to beat the breast in grief.

2

August 1997

GUS

I took up distance running after my brother died because it was an acceptable way of being alone. Other people's concern was almost the most difficult thing to deal with. If I said I was OK, they looked at me as if I was in denial; if I admitted I was finding things pretty difficult, there was no way for them to make it better. When I said I was training for a charity half-marathon to raise money for people with sports injuries, people nodded, satisfied, because Ross had been killed in a skiing accident, so it made sense.

At optimum speed, the rhythmic pounding of shoe on road delivered a kind of oblivion that had become addictive. It was what made me get out of bed every morning, even on holiday, although in Florence, the uneven cobbles and sudden, astonishing encounters with beauty, made it difficult to maintain a pace that made me forget where or who I was.

On the last day of the holiday, I ran along the Arno at dawn, crossing the river in alternate directions at each bridge, then looping back on myself to mirror the route, with the pale gleam of the sun in my eyes one way and its warmth on my back the other. With only an occasional road-sweeper for company, it felt as if I owned the place, or, perhaps, that it owned me. At the level of cardiovascular exertion that freed ideas to float across my mind, it occurred to me that I could come back to Florence one day, even live here, if I wanted. In this historic city, I could be a person with no history, the person I wanted to be, whoever that was. At eighteen, the thought was a revelation.

On my third crossing of the Ponte Vecchio, I slowed to a walking pace to cool down. There was no one else around. The glittering goldsmiths' wares were hidden behind sturdy wooden boards. There was nothing to indicate that I hadn't been transported back in time five hundred years. Yet somehow it felt less real than it had the previous evening, heaving with tourists. Like a deserted film set.

I suppose I'd hoped to find the girl there again. Not that I'd have known what to say to her any more than I had on the first two occasions. Handing back the camera, I hadn't even been brave enough to make eye contact, then, given a third chance, I'd blown that too.

Standing in the queue for ice cream beside the bridge, I'd felt a tap on my shoulder, and there she was again, smiling as if we'd known each other all our lives and were about to go on some amazing adventure together.

'There's this brilliant *gelato* place just down Via dei Neri where you can get about six for the price of one here!' she informed me.

'I don't think I could manage six!'

My attempt at wit had come out sounding pompous and dismissive. I wasn't very practised at talking to girls.

'Honest to God, you would from this place!'

Why don't you show me where it is? Great! Let's go there! None of the responses I'd like to have given had been available with my parents standing right beside me. Instead, I'd stared at her like a moron, with sentences jostling for position in my

19

head as her smile faded from sparkling to slightly perplexed before she hurried off to catch up with her friend.

On the north side of the river, Florence was beginning to wake up to the mechanical clatter of shutters as bars opened up for the day. As I entered the Duomo square, the sun's rays lit up the cassata stripes of the Campanile and the air was suddenly full of bells. Florence was a kind of heaven on earth and I thought it would be impossible to be unhappy living here.

I joined my parents in the lobby of our hotel on their way in to breakfast.

'The loneliness of the long-distance runner!' my father remarked.

It was what he always said when he saw me after a run, as if it meant something, when it was actually just the title of a film he'd seen in his youth.

I always felt prickly with my parents, like a Pavlovian reaction to their company.

I knew, from overhearing conversations at school, that a proper Tuscan holiday meant renting a villa with a pool, if you didn't actually own one yourself, surrounded by olive groves and views of rolling hills. My father had instead booked us into this expensive hotel in the centre of Florence. I was never sure how the done thing got established, but I was aware from quite an early age that there was a done thing and that my father often got it slightly wrong. Not having been to a private school himself, but now able to afford to send his sons to one, he would turn up to sports days wearing a blazer and tie, whereas the cool dads, who went to the Cannes film festival, or held offshore accounts in the Cayman Islands, wore jeans, polo shirts and loafers with no socks, as if vying for a most-casually-dressed award. As a liberal-minded sixth-former, I upheld the right of anyone to dress as they wished; as his son, I was mortified.

'Who on earth wants cheese at this time in the morning?'

My father inspected the buffet table. He was the sort of man who made loud statements, as if inviting the room to agree with him.

'I think it's what Germans eat.' My mother spoke in a low voice so as not to be overheard.

'You never hear about the German rates of colonic cancer, do you?' Dad mused. 'All that smoked sausage too . . .'

'Where are you off to today?' I asked, as we returned to the table with laden plates.

Included in the price of the Treasures of Tuscany package were excursions to the other principal tourist cities of the region. Since having to stop the coach twice to throw up on the first trip to Assisi, I now spent the days in Florence alone, visiting the galleries and churches at my own pace, enjoying the wonderful feeling of weightlessness that came from getting away from my parents.

'Pisa,' my father said.

As someone who didn't quite believe in travel-sickness, he couldn't disguise his irritation at my failure to get full value from the holiday and the tour company's refusal to refund a proportion of the cost.

The city centre was filling with groups of tourists following dutifully behind the raised umbrellas of their guides, but it was easy enough to peel away down a shadowy side street. I'd walked so much in the past week, I had the map of Florence in my head. The covered market near San Lorenzo, its cool air infused with the smoky scent of delicatessen, was my first daily pilgrimage. Some of the stallholders recognized me now. At the fruit stall, the old man's practised thumb roamed over a pyramid of peaches to select a perfectly ripe fruit. At the *salumeria*, the friendly mamma paid serious attention to my search for a filling for my single bread roll, offering little slivers of different salamis for me to taste or sniff like fine wine. As it was my last day, I treated myself to *un'etto* of expensive San Daniele pro-sciutto. She carefully arranged the wafer-thin translucent slices in overlapping layers on a sheet of shiny paper.

'*Ultimo giorno*,' I told her, attempting a few Italian words. It's my last day.

'*Ma ritorno*,' I added – but I'll come back – as if voicing it would make my intention more real.

I had bought a sketchbook, covered in hand-printed Florentine paper, to take with me to the art galleries because drawing made me look more closely at the paintings and feel less self-conscious about it. Art had always been my best subject at school, if you considered it a subject, which my father didn't. The more I studied the art in Florence, the more I wished that I had summoned the courage to apply for Art History at uni-versity. It wasn't just the skilful application of paint to canvas or fresco, it was what the artist was thinking that fascinated me. Did they believe in the religious stories they made so human, with saints and apostles dressed like Florentine bur-ghers, or were they just doing it to make a living?

I'd been steered towards Medicine, because it was 'in the family', as my sixth-form tutor put it, as if it was some kind of genetic mutation. As everyone always said, I could look at pic-tures in my spare time. Now, inspired by this city where art and science had flourished side by side, I wondered if there was even a way of combining the two. Perhaps I would come back to the Uffizi one day as a visiting professor in Anatomy? At least as a doctor, I'd have the means to return. There was no money in Art, my father always said. 'Even Van Gogh couldn't make a living out of it!'

I ate my *panino* sitting on the steps of the Palazzo Vecchio, occasionally tapping my foot to the music of a guitar-playing busker to make it look as if I was doing something. Time on my own seemed to pass very slowly and I was pathetically shy about striking up conversations with strangers. I wondered if I'd have been any better at it if my friend Marcus had been there. We were supposed to be Interrailing together, but he'd got off with a girl from our sister school at the end of school prom, and had naturally chosen sex in Ibiza over trailing round Europe with me. Neither of us had any real experience with girls and I think had both assumed that sex was something that wouldn't happen until university, so I had a grudging admiration for Marcus, but it had left me with the unwelcome decision to cancel our holiday or go it alone.

Around the same time, one of my father's patients, who'd broken a crown on a slice of panforte, expressed astonishment that my father had never been to Tuscany. The inferred criticism had stung Dad into action.

'What do you think?' he'd asked, pushing a brochure across the kitchen table one morning, as I was shovelling down cereal before cycling to my summer job at our town's new gastropub.

'Great idea!' It had been good to see him focusing on a plan again.

'Want to join us?'

'Really?' Somehow, through a mouthful of Weetabix, I made dread sound like surprised enthusiasm.

Being a dentist, Dad never expected much more than a slight nod in answer to his questions, so, by the time I arrived back from work, the holiday had been booked and paid for.

I'd told myself that it would be churlish not to accept my parents' generosity, but the truth was, I was a wuss.

Scanning the crowds of tourists taking photos with the replica statue of Michelangelo's *David*, I began to wonder if I would actually recognize the girl if I saw her again. She was tall, and her hair was longish and brownish, I thought. There wasn't anything particularly memorable about her features, except that when she smiled her face was suddenly full of mischief and intimacy, as if there was a thrilling secret that only she knew and was about to share only with you.

Via dei Neri was a narrow street winding towards the Piazza Santa Croce and I missed the *gelateria* on the way down. It was just a single door with a dark interior. For my first cone, I chose *nocciola* and *limone*, because that was what the Italian man in front of me ordered, the delicious creaminess of the hazelnut perfectly complemented by the refreshing citrus tang. I walked back down to Santa Croce eating it, then returned and ordered another, pistachio and melon, and loitered in the cool shade of the shop, glancing at each new customer in the hope of seeing the girl again.

In the heat of the afternoon, I made my way through the crowds on the Ponte Vecchio to the Boboli Gardens. The numbers of tourists dwindled the higher I climbed, and, on the top terrace, I found myself completely alone beside the ornamental lake. The sun was still very hot but invisible now behind a veil of humidity that muted the view of the city like the varnish of age over an old master. Distant thunder rolled around the hills and the air was thick with imminent rain. Opening my sketchbook, I recorded the smudgy outline of the Duomo.

Suddenly, a bright beam of light broke through the unnatural yellowish twilight, giving surreal definition to the trimmed box hedges, lighting up the greenish-blue water. As I raised my camera, a white heron, which I had perceived as a static element of the ornate marble fountain in the centre of the lake, took off, startling me. It flew across the water, the flapping of its wings the only sound or movement in the still air.

It occurred to me that I had not given Ross a thought since breakfast.

For a moment, I saw my brother's face glancing back at me through a cloud of thickly falling snow, his teeth white, the flakes settling on his dark, swept-back hair, his eyes hidden behind mirror ski goggles.

'They should sort out their queuing system,' my father announced, from which I gathered that they had not been able to climb the monument, and could not therefore deem it a mission accomplished.

- THE LEANING TOWER OF PISA.
  Photographed but unclimbed.

It was not an entirely satisfactory conclusion to the holiday.

'There are lots of other buildings,' said my mother.

'Cathedral and whatnot. Jam-packed with tourists, obviously.'

Nothing in their description gave me a reason to say that I'd like to go one day, and if I had, it would only have reminded my father of the wasted place on the coach, so I said nothing.

'Ah, yes, *buona sera* to you too,' said my father when the waiter arrived to take our order. 'We're going to have the Florentine beefsteak.'

The best place to sample this 'most famous typical dish' had been a project from the start of the holiday. Dad had sought the advice of the driver who met us at the airport on our first night and all the receptionists at the hotel. We were now sitting in the restaurant recommended by a majority of five to one.

Priced by the kilo, a *bistecca alla Fiorentina* was not just a meal, it was a spectacle performed on a raised platform within the dining area of the restaurant. First the rib of beef was held aloft by a chef in a tall white hat; a large knife was sharpened with swift, dramatic strokes; then a very thick slice of meat, a chop for a giant, was severed and weighed before being placed on a trolley and wheeled over to the table for approval. My father swelled with satisfaction as the other tables oohed and aahed obligingly at each stage of the ritual. I didn't begrudge him this small pleasure, but my insides squirmed with embarrassment.

'What did you get up to?' my father asked, as the meat was

trolleyed off to the kitchen and we had to talk to each other again.

'Walking, mainly. I went to the Boboli Gardens.'

Silence.

'I saw this heron, actually.'

'Heron? We're too far inland, aren't we? Sure it wasn't a stork?' said my father.

'It was kind of weird, because I thought it was part of the statue at first, then it just took off, as if the stone had come alive.'

My parents exchanged glances. 'Fey' was the word my mother sometimes used to describe me. 'Airy-fairy' or 'arty-farty' were my father's expressions. In the shorthand descriptions that parents give to their children, I was the one with my head in the clouds.

I made the mistake of extemporizing.

'It was the sort of thing that might make you think you'd seen a vision, you know . . . I mean, maybe all those visions of St Francis actually have a neurological explanation? Maybe there was something different about his brain . . .'

I realized, too late, that 'brain' was one of the words we didn't say any more. Certain words triggered inevitable associations. Over the last few months our family's spoken vocabulary had shrunk dramatically.

Now my parents were both staring into the middle distance.

My carelessness had got them thinking about the side of Ross's head, the thickness of the bandage unable to disguise the fact that there was a bit missing.

Had some of my brother's brain spilled out into the snow? I wondered. Had the rescue party covered it up with more snow? And when the snow melted in the spring, were there still fragments of skull on the mountain?

If this holiday was an attempt to move on, it hadn't been a great success. The last time we were on holiday, Ross was with us. A winter holiday, so very different from the sticky heat of Florence, but a family holiday nonetheless. When you remember holidays you think about the sights and the weather, but somehow you always forget the confinement of being together, meal after meal. Ross used to dominate the conversation, bantering with my father and joshing me while my mother gazed at him adoringly. Now, his absence made him seem almost more present.

You know that expression, 'the elephant in the room'? You're the elephant, Ross!

I thought he'd quite like that description. Occasionally, I found myself speaking to my brother in my head even though we hadn't had that kind of relationship when he was alive. I was surprised in retrospect how much we'd had in common just by virtue of being in the same family. Ross was the one person who would have understood how pitiful my parents were in their grief, and yet how annoying they still managed to be.

'You have to deal with reality,' said my father eventually. I wasn't sure whether it was intended as a reprimand to me or an instruction to himself. 'You have to get to grips with what's in front of you.'

What was in front of him now was the giant steak, charred and leaking blood onto the wooden board on which it was presented.

My father looked up at the waiter.

'We'd like Chef to cook it for us if that's not too much trouble!' he barked.

I pictured the chef's face as the waiter returned to the kitchen. During my summer job I'd learned that customers who sent their steaks back to be well done were even further down the hierarchy of contempt than pot washers.

When the steak was returned to us, it was pale brown all

the way through, as if it had been given ten minutes in a microwave.

My father doled out the leathery slices.

'How many for you, Angus?'

'Just one.'

'One?'

'Angus has never had a huge appetite,' my mother reminded him.

Ross had an enormous appetite. Was it over-sensitive of me to hear an unspoken comparison?

I was completely different to Ross. My brother was dark, handsome and built; I had inherited my mother's willowy height, and, although my hair wasn't orange like my father's, I had enough of his freckly complexion to be called a ginge at school.

Ross had been captain of the rugby and rowing teams and Head Boy; I enjoyed football and had never been considered for the prefect body. Ross's summer job after leaving school had been a lifeguard at the local open-air swimming pool. Being a lifesaver was something to boast about, unlike being a kitchen boy. Not that Ross ever actually saved a life, although plenty of girls pretended to be struggling in the hope of being man-handled by him. Ross had starred in his own version of *Baywatch*. In Guildford.

I was never sure whether the truth was that my parents weren't very good at disguising their obvious preference, or that I was in fact pretty mediocre compared to Ross. It wasn't something you could talk about without sounding like a whinger, so I never did, except occasionally to Marcus, who knew what Ross was really like. Was it Ross's sporting prowess that had made the teachers at our school so willing to turn a blind eye to his other activities, we'd sometimes speculated, or had they too lived in fear of him? Perhaps Ross and his acolytes kept a record of punishable offences committed by the staff as well as the lower-school boys? I'd never know, because nobody said anything remotely critical about him now that he was dead.

We sat in silence, chewing our steak.

'I expect you're itching to get to uni . . .' my mother said.

Was my discomfort so obvious?

The truth was that although I was counting down the hours until the claustrophobia of the holiday would be over, I was also feeling pretty nervous about what was coming next. I thought I'd probably be OK at Medicine because I was good at Biology and interested in how people worked.

'Which makes you sound like an agony aunt!' Ross had needled, just the previous November, which now felt like a lifetime ago, because, in a way, it was.

In spite of his ridicule, or maybe because it had made me think harder, I'd performed well at the interview and been offered a place conditional on achieving three As at A level. But I'd always felt uneasy about following in my brother's footsteps. Over that Christmas holiday, I had actually made up my mind to ask if I could defer a year and use the time to decide if Medicine was what I really wanted to do.

Then the accident happened.

When I returned to school the deadline for acceptances was looming. My father had been so proud at the thought of both his sons becoming doctors. Doing Medicine, or at least, not *not* doing it, was the only small way I could begin to make it up to him.

Only the previous day, calling the school to get my A-level results, with my parents hovering in the hotel corridor just outside the door, a tiny part of me had still been hoping to be granted a reprieve. But my grades were good enough.

I realized I hadn't responded to my mother.

'Yes, really looking forward to it now,' I assured her.

At least there would be sex. If Ross's experience was anything to go by, medics were at it all the time.

3

September 1997

TESS

On Hope's first day of school, she was surprisingly amenable to getting dressed in her little grey skirt, white polo top and blue sweatshirt. She ran into Mum's room to get a goodbye kiss.

'Take a picture, Tess,' Mum said.

We'd decided that Mum wouldn't even try to come, because then it would become one of Hope's routines. Hope seemed to accept that I would be the one to go with her. Perhaps it seemed natural to her, as it wasn't long since I'd been the one going off to school every morning. I'd been bracing myself for screaming and crying, but as we left the house, and Mum called down, 'Bye then!' it was her little voice that was feeble with tears.

Mum and Hope were inseparable. Mum was forty-three when she had her. 'An afterthought,' was the way she put it, because she would never have said Hope was an accident. With all the rest of us practically grown up, Mum had had the time to do things like reading library books and baking fairy cakes together. Most people considered Hope spoilt. She'd been a pretty little baby, with a froth of blonde curls, and, with five big people in the house, six if you included Brendan's girlfriend Tracy, she'd got a lot of attention. We all loved holding her and

32

jiggling her to make her smile. People said that's why she was a bit late with walking and things, because everything was done for her. Mum had tried taking her to nursery school but Hope wouldn't be left. She could count to a thousand by the time she was four and could sing all the nursery rhymes, which was probably more than most children of that age.

She walked with me happily enough and marched over to stand in line with the other tiny children in the playground. I waited by the gate with my fingers firmly crossed, praying that everything would be fine, and that school would be her protection from everything that was about to happen.

The perfect silence of those first few seconds after the whistle blew, felt like a gift, a miraculous gift from God who I should not have abandoned. Then a familiar sound tore it apart.

Mum used to say Hope's carrying-on was what drove my brothers away. I was never sure whether she was joking because she'd always add that it was about time they spread their wings. Mum had a sharp sense of humour. I think it was because of her being intelligent but not very confident, so she'd put something out there, then make out she was joking if she got the wrong reaction.

Kevin was the first to go, to London when he got his scholarship, then America. He and Dad had never seen eye to eye, especially when Kevin refused to go into construction. So it made things easier at home, really. Then Tracy got pregnant, and Brendan dropped the bombshell that they were emigrating to Australia. He'd always felt in Kev's shadow; this was going one better. So Hope had got her own room, instead of sleeping in mine, but it was still noisy. I used to spend as long as I could in the library at school. Dad used to spend as long as he could at the pub. People said Mum had the patience of a saint.

It was natural for a child to be unsettled, Mrs Corcoran, the head teacher at St Cuthbert's, told me, when there was so much worry at home. She thought the best idea would be if I came along to school with Hope to reassure her. I could help out with the little ones. The Reception class's teaching assistant was on maternity leave, so they could do with an extra pair of hands.

I welcomed the distraction. With a class of thirty small children, there was no time to think about anything except getting coats, hats, gloves, painting aprons and gym clothes on and off, tracking lost shoes, monitoring trips to the toilet, making sure hands were clean, and handing out slices of apple at break time.

At home, Mum was sleeping a lot because of the morphine. You'd think that if you knew someone was going to die in a few weeks, or days, you'd try to say everything there was to say, but it wasn't like that. It was almost like we didn't want to make it over before it was over and were afraid of getting everything ready and then having nothing to do except wait.

I did tell Mum that I loved her. I told her every day, and then I started saying it every time she went to sleep, or I had to leave the room to cook Hope's tea or something, until it started sounding a bit silly. You wouldn't think 'I love you' could become meaningless, would you?

Course, I said other things too, like, 'You mustn't worry about us, because we will cope.'

To which Mum replied, 'I know you will.'

We never really talked about what that coping would entail, because I didn't want it to sound like *I* was the one with the problem.

On one occasion, Mum held my hand and said, staring me out to show she meant it, 'You must go to university.'

'I will, don't worry.' Leaving it vague meant that neither of us had to confront the glaring question of how.

I helped Mum make a memory box for Hope. It was a shoebox that we covered with pink gingham offcuts from the

34

curtains Mum had made when the boys' bedroom was turned into Hope's. Mum embroidered 'Hope' on the rectangle we cut for the top with yellow silk thread from her sewing box. I pasted and stapled the fabric on. The box looked really good; the difficulty was knowing what to put into it. There wasn't a lot of physical evidence of Mum's time with Hope. Parents take a lot of pictures of their firstborn, but the novelty seems to wear off with the subsequent children. We did find a lovely photo of her with Hope as a smiling baby. And Mum dictated her recipe for Hope's favourite trifle. Using the microphone and Hope's Fisher Price cassette recorder, Mum recorded a message for her. Finally, she took off the gold cross she always wore and asked me to put that in.

'You wouldn't want it, would you, Tess?'

I wasn't sure whether it would make her happier if I said yes, or if she had the consolation of it going to Hope. The cross went in the box. But then Hope noticed Mum wasn't wearing it and Mum wasn't going to tell her why before she needed to know, so the cross came out again, and the box went back in its hiding place under the bed. On a couple of occasions, Mum said, 'Can we think of anything more for the box? How about a CD? ABBA's *Greatest Hits*? She loves that one with the children singing . . .'

I wished in a way that we'd never started on it, or chosen a smaller box, because the few items rattling around were such inadequate tokens of Mum's love.

One of the questions I did ask, while we were stitching and stapling – like Victorian ladies, Mum said – when it was easier to talk because we were both engaged in another activity, was this: if there was an afterlife, could Mum please find a way of giving me some kind of sign, so I'd know.

That made her laugh.

'I can't give you faith, Tess,' she said. 'It's a step you have to take yourself, and then everything follows.'

'But could you try, please? Just a little sign?'

'If you'd put the imagination you spend doubting into believing . . .' she said, in that mildly exasperated way she had that made criticism sound like a compliment.

Brendan and Kevin arrived from different ends of the world in suits. Brendan, hefty with success and lurching between the show-off swagger of a prodigal son and the crumpling confusion of imminent disaster; Kevin, toned and dapper, in light brown pointy brogues and tight grey trousers showing his calf muscles through the slightly shiny fabric, and a lot of talk about issues – his own that is, not Mum's.

After visiting Mum at the hospice, Dad took them down the pub, and there was something strangely jolly about the three of them rolling back home late and smelling of beer.

'Like the old days,' Dad said, with an arm draped around each son, recalling a happy tradition that he'd have enjoyed, but had never actually happened.

It was just me by the bed with Mum at the end. I don't know if she wanted it like that, or if she ran out of time to do all the individual goodbyes. It was almost like she'd waited to see all her children, then was in a hurry to go. Perhaps she was thinking about the boys' needing to get back to their jobs. Mum always put others before herself.

The curtains around the bed gave a false sense of privacy and we could hear everything the others were saying just on the other side.

Brendan's 'Have I time for a coffee, do you think?'

I should probably be grateful to him for the gift of her last flash of smile, conspiratorial – would you listen to him!

One moment she was there, then the light in her eyes went out.

I thought I was prepared for her leaving, but when I realized she was dead, I felt as shocked as if it had happened without warning. I sat holding her hand until it no longer seemed right not to share her with the others.

The men cried immediately. I did not. All their hungover heaving and blubbing felt like blows against my shell of numbness.

Hope didn't like it either and shouted at them to stop.

'Sssh!' she said, finger to her lips. 'Mum trying to sleep!'

I told her to give Mum a kiss, and then I took her to the hospice cafe for sausage and chips, and, to her astonishment, a whole bag of Haribo.

When I put Hope to bed that night, she asked what time we were seeing Mum the next day (we were doing telling the time in Reception class), and I told her that Mum had gone to heaven.

'Why?'

'To see the angels,' I improvised.

'And Jesus,' said Hope.

'Yes.'

'And Nana and Granda and Lady Di and Mother Teresa . . .' Hope listed all the people they'd recently prayed for together.

I had never seen the point of heaven but now I could. Was that a sign?

I waited for the lull that told me Hope was asleep, then began to creep towards the door.

'Tree?'

'Yes?'

'When Mum coming back?'

What was I supposed to say?

'She's not, Hope. She still loves us though.'

'She'll never stop loving us,' said Hope.

Even though it was dark in the room, I could tell she wasn't crying. For Hope, it was a simple statement of fact because Mum had said it, and would say it again and again on the cassette tape.

A lot of the relations made the journey from Ireland that they'd never made while Mum was alive. Her leaving for England with Dad in the seventies had been resented by her siblings because, as the older sister, she was supposed to be the one who looked after their father after their own mother had died young. I knew my uncles, aunt and cousins only vaguely from sitting in chilly front rooms drinking tea from the good china that was brought out for guests, on the boring part of childhood holidays in Ireland that Mum and Dad had called 'Doing the rounds'. None of them had met Hope before, but still they claimed the right to pat her on the head with tear-filled eyes, or scoop her up in great hugs, which she didn't like at all.

'That enough kissy stuff!' she shouted, making herself all stiff.

'She's a character, isn't she?' said my mother's sister, Catriona, adding, in a loud, doom-laden whisper, 'You'll have to watch her, now, Teresa, and yourself as well, because they say it runs in families. It's a terrible thing for us all to have hanging over us.'

Even with Mum dead, I felt she was still trying to blame her.

I didn't think Hope should go to the funeral, but Dad and Brendan wanted her to and Kev said nobody ever took any notice of his opinion anyway, which was a good way to get out of giving one. So that was a kind of majority. Except I was sure that Mum wouldn't have wanted it either.

'Did she tell you that?' my father demanded.

'No.'

It was one of the many things I should have asked her. It

was so stupid. All that time we'd had and I'd never dared ask what she wanted for her funeral.

'Well, then,' said Dad.

Hope was fine, swaying along to the organist's slightly slow and tentative interpretation of ABBA's 'I Have a Dream', as we walked in. She stood between Dad and me as we sang 'How Great Thou Art' which was Mum's favourite hymn. We all said the Lord's Prayer and Hope said that too, with Dad glancing over the top of her head at me as if to say, *Told you!*

I don't think she even noticed the coffin until Brendan got up to read his poem.

With hindsight, Kev or I should have stopped him. I think we were both so shocked by the idea of Brendan, of all people, writing a poem, that neither of us thought to ask if we could read it first. In fact, we both probably felt a little bit ashamed for not writing one ourselves.

If you look in the local newspaper at the memorial section, you'll see that just because something rhymes, doesn't make it profound, except to the author. It was Brendan's couplet that had 'Always there to wash my socks' with 'Now, you're lying in a box' that caught Hope's attention.

'In a box?' she echoed, her voice ringing through the hush.

'Sssh!' said Dad.

'Tree, is Mum in that box?'

'You have to be quiet now, Hope, we're in church.'

It used to work when Mum said it, but there wasn't enough conviction in my voice.

'Mum is in heaven with Jesus!' Hope declared.

Father Michael came creeping across to us.

'Your mother's body is in the box, Hope, but her soul is gone to heaven,' he whispered, breathing his halitosis over her.

The screaming was piercingly loud as I carried Hope flailing from the church. How could such a little person possibly understand about the separation of the body and the soul? I should have trusted my instincts. A funeral was no place for a child. I'd known it. Worst of all, I felt I'd let Mum down.

It was one of those breezy late-September days, with a few white clouds racing across a blue sky and the trees just beginning to turn copper, too beautiful a day for something so sad. Hope stopped screaming as soon as we were out of the church and started struggling to get down from my arms. The tarmac path had little bits of confetti trodden onto it, pink horseshoes, white butterflies, lemon hearts. Hope skipped away from the church, chasing occasional falling leaves. I stood watching her, thinking that if she caught one, it would most definitely be a sign. Of course she didn't. Autumn leaves have a habit of darting away when you think you're on to them and Hope's coordination was never the best. Before frustration could turn to fury, I took her down the road for a McFlurry.

So we missed whatever trite words Father Michael had to say about Mum being a dutiful mother and wife, and Charlotte Church singing 'Pie Jesu' on the CD player, and the coffin going into the ground, which you're supposed to see for closure. I wonder whether that's why Mum still sometimes appears in my dreams, and I wake up with this lovely moment of relief – I *knew* it couldn't be true! – before my brain cells reorder themselves back to reality.

Mum was a popular member of the community and her friends took it upon themselves to organize the wake in the church hall. The small kitchen beside the stage was a production line of women in aprons turning out platters of sandwiches and mini quiches, scones and home-made cakes, great plastic bowls of crisps and trays of piping-hot sausage rolls, while others wielded the big metal pots of tea they used at the Christmas Fayre and poured glasses of sherry for the women and whiskey for the men.

It wasn't long before the atmosphere shifted from sombre to

animated, and people started telling their stories. Mum's sister Catriona talked about how when she'd heard Mum had passed away she went to the room in the house that had been hers and she'd smelled a powerful scent. Didn't they say that when people returned, they sometimes brought a fragrance with them? She'd been sure for a moment that Mary was there, before she remembered that she'd put an Autumn Breeze air-freshener plug in the room because it was a bit musty from lack of use.

Dad regaled anyone who'd listen with the anecdote about how they'd met. He'd gone back to his home town in Ireland for his grannie's funeral and he'd spotted my mother across a crowded room and the light of love was in her eyes.

That phrase, 'the light of love', made me think of Mum's eyes just before the end. It was a good description. Dad could surprise you like that. You'd be looking at him and wondering what it was that had drawn someone as gentle and intelligent as Mum to him, and then you'd get a glimpse.

'We met at a wake, and now we're saying goodbye at one!'

His closing line became more tearily indulgent as the evening went on, and people clutched his arm and said wise words like 'The cycle of life, Jim,' or 'You've a lot of happy memories to see you through.'

'Ach, she was a wonderful wife to me!' he told them, which was true, although I'd never heard him say it to her.

I didn't think he'd been nearly a wonderful enough husband to her, but Mum had never complained.

'Your father's got a lot on his mind,' or 'Your father works very hard to put food on the table,' were the usual excuses for why he was more often at the bookie's or down the pub than at home. Not that any of us hankered for his presence because there was always an aura of threat hanging around Dad.

'It's the drink, not the man,' Mum had even defended him after the terrible night it came out that she had secretly been

41

paying for Kev's ballet classes with the housekeeping money, and Brendan had to leap on Dad's back, kicking his calves to hold him back, and I'd run down the street shouting at the neighbours to call the police because I thought he was going to kill them.

By the time it got dark outside, there was quite a party atmosphere, with that fug of alcohol and exaggerated emotion that you often get at weddings with family members who haven't seen each other in a while.

Kev pushed the piano out on the stage, and played his party piece, 'Danny Boy', which he'd probably sung a few times in New York on St Patrick's Day because it's an even bigger deal there than it is in Ireland. Kev's singing was never as good as his dancing, but he could hold a tune well enough and the performance brought a stunned silence to the room before people started clapping and telling him how proud his mother would have been.

'Will you give us a song, Jim?' someone called.

After only a moment of protest, my father said, 'Ach, go on then,' and made his way to the stage, where he stood, leaning against the piano, and, with Kev accompanying him, sang the Fureys' 'I Will Love You'.

There wasn't a dry eye in the house after that. For me, it wasn't the words so much as seeing Kev and Dad together, and knowing how happy that would have made Mum. At the end, a moment of reflective silence was broken by a small voice, surprisingly loud and clear next to me.

'Twinkle, twinkle, little star, how I wonder what you are. Up above the world so high, like a diamond in the sky. Twinkle, twinkle, little star, how I wonder what you are!'

There was something about the seriousness on Hope's face and her stout little frame, with her fingers doing the twinkling

42

actions she'd learned at school, that would have made it comical if it hadn't been so moving.

When she finished, everyone clapped, but unlike Kevin and Dad, Hope didn't bask in the attention. She didn't actually seem to notice it.

'What about you now, Teresa?' my aunt Catriona called out. 'We haven't heard anything from you.'

To be fair, she probably only meant to give me the opportunity, but she made it sound like I didn't want to contribute.

'I can't sing,' I protested.

'That all right, Tree,' Hope chimed up. 'Everyone has things they're good at and things they're not so good at.'

Which sounded so much like Mum that everyone except Hope laughed.

'OK. This was Mum's favourite poem,' I said, wondering why I hadn't thought of suggesting it for the service.

'"The Lake Isle of Innisfree".

I will arise and go now, and go to Innisfree.

And a small cabin build there, of clay and wattles made.

Nine bean rows will I have there, a hive for the honey bee,

And live alone in the bee-loud glade.

And I shall have some peace there, for peace comes dropping slow . . .'

As I spoke the words, slowly and evenly, trying to keep the wobble out of my voice and do her proud, I wondered whether Mum had yearned for peace and solitude away from the constant noisy chaos of our family. And as I looked around the faces of her friends and relations, I thought that we were all perhaps thinking that the poem described a kind of heaven for her, which made us feel calmer about the whole injustice of it. That's probably why people talk about the consolation of poetry.

When I'd finished, the room was quiet.

'Bedtime,' I said to Hope, taking the opportunity to say our goodbyes before the singing inevitably started up again, along with more drinking and the potential for the mood to switch from affection to umbrage in a single sentence.

Hope spotted the butterfly in the corner of the bathroom window when I was giving her a bath. One of those white ones with a tiny black spot on each wing. Cabbage White.

'Want to get out,' she said.

So, without thinking about it really, I opened the window, and the butterfly flew into the dying light.

It was only when I knelt down again and started lathering Hope's hair that I wondered how the butterfly had got in. There was a buddleia in the back garden which attracted butterflies in the summer, but usually those were orange, and I'd never seen one in the house before. Wasn't it a bit late for butterflies anyway? Perhaps it had come in to get warm?

Or perhaps the butterfly was the sign I'd asked Mum for, and all I'd done was let it out into the cold.

The morning after, while Dad was still snoring upstairs, and Hope was watching *Teletubbies*, Brendan came over from the Travelodge and reported that Kevin had already left for the airport.

Apparently there'd been a big row in the church hall a couple of hours after we'd gone home, when Kevin got up the courage to announce that Shaun, the man who was sharing his room at the hotel, wasn't in fact a colleague en route to a business meeting, but his partner of two years, a partner, he'd shouted tearily, who he couldn't even introduce to his own family at his own mother's funeral!

The fact that Kevin was gay didn't come as much of a shock to me or Brendan (or in truth, I suspect, to my father, who'd always been suspicious of the dancing) but to come out at a funeral, Brendan said, well, it just wasn't on, was it?

Dad, now twice the mawkish victim, had wailed to Father Michael, 'I've lost my wife and my son on the same day!'

So that had given Kevin the opportunity to list all the resent-ments he had harboured since adolescence. Ironically, it was Shaun who saved the day, arriving in a taxi and scooping Kev off back to the Travelodge after hearing his belligerent meander-ings on the phone.

He seemed like a decent enough fella, Brendan said.

It did cross my mind afterwards that maybe Kevin had, consciously or unconsciously, created the opportunity for a dramatic exit – he's always been theatrical – to relieve him of any familial duty. Or perhaps it never even crossed his mind, as it didn't seem to cross Brendan's, that there were three of us with a sister about to be only five years old and a father who was a drinker.

'I wanted to talk to you about what's going to happen with Hope,' I said, trying to broach the subject.

'She'll get over it sooner than you think,' Brendan said. 'Kids do.'

He was a father with two little ones of his own now so he knew about these things. And he lived on the other side of the world. What did I ever think he was going to do? But it would have been nice if someone had just asked if I was OK.

I left it to the last minute to cancel my university place. Not because I forgot, or was distracted, but because I think I was hoping for some kind of miracle.

I waited until Dad and Hope took Brendan to the airport, so I was on my own in the house.

The woman in the accommodation office was brusque. 'It's terribly short notice.'

'My mother died, so I've been busy with the funeral,' I told her.

'Oh. I'm sorry.'

I hadn't yet worked out how to respond to people saying that. 'It's all right,' didn't do it. 'So am I,' sounded impertinent.

'It's not your fault,' I said. Which wasn't right either.

There was an embarrassed pause.

'I'm afraid we won't be able to refund the deposit unless we find someone else to take the room,' the woman finally said. 'Which I have to say is very unlikely at this point. Obviously, I'll inform you if the situation changes.'

'Thank you.'

I put the phone down and that's when I cried. Great, wracking sobs. Sounds selfish, doesn't it? But it wasn't just the end of my dream. It was Mum's dream too. Going to university had been our project.

I don't know how long I wept, sitting in the kitchen that felt so empty without her, until I finally stopped and found myself staring at the plate that said, *Today is the first day of the rest of your life.*

It says in all the books about bereavement that when a small child loses a parent, the worst thing you can do is change things. You'd think that a fresh start or a change of scene would be a good idea, but it says not. The child's had enough change. What they need is a bit of stability. I suppose that's how it was for Hope with the plate.

I put it away in a cupboard, but Hope noticed as soon as she came in and demanded its return. So it remained on the knick-knack shelf in the kitchen. And sometimes it made me rueful, and sometimes it made me depressed, and other times I felt so angry I wanted to smash it on the floor, which are all stages of grief, according to the books.

4

September 1997

GUS

It's difficult to look cool with your mother trailing behind you carrying armfuls of items she's purchased for your student life, like scatter cushions, a first-aid kit, a desk tidy and a toilet brush in a ceramic holder.

When my possessions were finally heaped in the centre of the room, the three of us stood for a moment at a loss for anything to say. It was just a room, with a single bed, a built-in wardrobe and a desk, the last but one along a corridor of similar rooms, all with open doors awaiting their new occupants. It was on the second of four floors, so didn't have as much of a view as the showroom in the prospectus, but it was at the back of the building, away from the road. My father and I stood looking out of the window, staring at the branches of two large trees whose leaves were just beginning to turn brown.

'At least you're not on the ground floor,' my mother said. 'Let's get this lot put away, shall we?'

My father and I exchanged a rare moment of understanding.

'I expect Angus wants to arrange things his own way,' he said, with a gentle but determined shove of my mother's arm.

'Oh!' Her eyes were suddenly watery as she realized the time had come, sooner than she'd anticipated, to say goodbye. 'Shouldn't we at least buy him lunch?'

The finishing post kept moving away. My heart sank at the prospect of trawling around the locality peering at menus, with my father taking out his glasses and reading the dishes out loud. But I said nothing. Another hour or two of embarrassment was preferable to parting with the lingering guilt of not behaving properly.

My father checked his watch. 'We've only got another twenty minutes' free parking.' The car was parked underneath Sainsbury's.

'Well then.' My mother stood on tiptoe to peck my cheek, holding me at arm's length for a moment, as if making an assessment. As usual, I felt I had been judged slightly in-adequate.

Over her shoulder, I noticed a girl with pink hair and a ruck-sack stop outside my door, look at me, then at the number on the door, then at the piece of paper in her hand, before moving on.

I was expecting my father to shake my hand like one of his golf-club cronies, when, out of nowhere, he produced an orange plastic carrier bag. 'You have to spend a fiver to get the free parking . . .

I pulled out a bottle of champagne.

'But that's . . .' Much more than a fiver, I was about to say. Of course it was. '. . . very generous!'

'Don't drink it all at once!'

Seeing him beaming with the success of his surprise, I remembered that he was once a person who was capable of having fun.

We all went down to the front hall together.

'Got your keys?'

'Yes!'

'It's the start of a new future for you,' my mother began,

then trailed off and I knew she was actually thinking about Ross's future, which had been taken away.

'Work hard!' said my father.

'I don't think I'll have a choice about that!' I replied, which seemed to please him.

I stared at their backs as they strode away, her camel coat and his blazer marking out their class and provenance against the backdrop of urban graffiti. Then I went back up to the room, feeling strangely empty. Freed from the suffocation of my family's grief, I'd been hoping to create a new identity for myself, but, strangely, it felt as if there was nothing at all inside me.

The girl with pink hair was Sellotaping a piece of paper to her door that said *Nash's Room* in large, bold handwriting.

'Bit institutional, isn't it?' she said, throwing open the door to show me her room, which had an extra window because it was on the corner of the building. She'd already hung up a mobile type of thing, with mirrory bits that caught the weak rays of autumn sunshine and made a fluttering pattern of lights across the grubby beige carpet.

'I've lucked out, right?' she said. 'Didn't even have a room yesterday but someone dropped out at the last minute. Nash, by the way. Short for Natasha.'

I nodded at the notice on her door.

'Duh!' She tossed back her pink hair in a dramatic way that made me wonder if I was supposed to remark on it.

'Angus,' I said.

'Seriously?'

Was it such an amusing name?

'It sounds Scottish,' she said, explaining, I suppose, that she hadn't detected a Scottish accent.

'My father's originally Scottish.'

'So what shall I call you?'

Clearly Angus wouldn't do.

At school we knew each other by our surnames. I was Macdonald, so people shortened it to Mac, or sometimes Farmer. I wasn't going to tell her that.

'How about Gus?' she suggested. Nobody had ever called me Gus. I quite liked it. My new identity had a name.

'Gus, absolutely,' I said quickly, offering my hand to seal the deal.

'How tall are you?'

People think it's OK to ask that question even though they'd never dream of asking how much a fat person weighs, or even how short a short person is.

'Six foot four.' I couldn't think of a question to ask her.

'I would offer you coffee,' she said. 'If I had any coffee.'

'Do you drink champagne?' I heard myself asking.

'What a ridiculous question!'

My father would be horrified at the idea of me opening the bottle before six, and drinking it warm from china mugs off the wooden cup tree my mother had supplied, but that made it taste even better.

'Divinely decadent, darling!' said Nash.

She was a bit like Sally Bowles in *Cabaret*. Not that she looked like Liza Minnelli, in her baggy black parachute suit and plimsolls without laces, but there was something of the same self-conscious eccentricity. It crossed my mind that she might see me as the innocent, possibly gay, Michael York character just arrived in the big city.

'What are you studying?' I asked, wincing at the prosaic quality of my conversation.

'Guess!' she said, lying back on her bed, which she'd already made up with black sheets and a red duvet cover. There was a poster of Che Guevara just behind her head.

'Politics?'

She looked surprised.

'English and Drama, actually.' She peered at me intently. 'Psychology?'

I was flattered if that was how I appeared to her. I liked the idea of looking like a 'Psychology' sort of person. 'Medicine.'

'Oh. You must be clever.'

'Not especially.'

'I'm going to be an actor,' she announced.

Perhaps wanting to appear a little mysterious, I said, 'I'm not sure what I want to be.'

She laughed.

'What?'

'You're going to be a doctor, obviously!'

Hearing it from someone I'd only just met, at the beginning of my new identity, the inevitability depressed me.

I poured out the rest of the champagne, knocking it back like lemonade.

'Do you think we ought to get something to eat?' Nash said, suddenly the less drunk, sensible one.

The nearest restaurant was Greek. It wasn't serving food until six, but the waiter said we could sit and have a drink. Nash, who had been to Greece, said we should order retsina. The sour pine taste was like the air in the school shower room after the cleaners had been in.

Nash was very direct. 'How did you vote?'

Born in 1979, we were Thatcher's generation. We had known nothing but Conservative government, but this May, change had swept across the country.

'I'm not very political.' I tried to duck the question because I hadn't actually voted.

'You're a Tory then,' said Nash. 'If you're not prepared to challenge the status quo . . .'

I'd never thought about it like that. I'd been brought up to think it rude to ask about someone's politics.

'Football or rugby?' she demanded.

'Football and running.'

'So you're a minor public-school boy who didn't quite fit in,' she deduced, with a flap of her napkin and a wave in the direction of the waiter who was setting up a big table.

I winced at the accuracy of her summation.

'I bet your dad's a doctor.'

'He's a dentist.'

'A failed doctor then. Even worse!'

It had never occurred to me that maybe Dad's desire for both his sons to become doctors had in fact been about his own ambition. Had he not quite made the grade himself? Was Nash very perceptive, or just very rude?

'What shall we have?' she asked, browsing through the menu. 'I'm vegetarian, by the way.' Her statements came out like challenges, as if she was expecting me to argue with her.

Apart from a dish called moussaka, which was pretty much indistinguishable from all the other sloshy trays of mince they'd served us at school, I'd never eaten Greek food before so I let her order. The waiters brought us little plates of oily dips, slabs of fried rubbery cheese, and baskets full of warm pitta bread that sank comfortingly to my stomach, soaking up the pine aftertaste, and allowing me to agree that a carafe of house red would be a good idea.

My memory of the evening is hazy. There was sparring, and laughter, and crying too. Nash's parents were divorced, her father twice remarried, her mother now living with another woman. She seemed to have a lot of half-brothers and half-sisters in various countries around the world. Nash referred to her father as a bastard, but clearly longed for his affection. A sense of relief washed over me when I realized that this woman, who came across as so sophisticated, was also insecure.

'So what about your family?' she asked me.

'Nothing to tell.'

'Very mysterious!'

'Or very ordinary?'

'Any brothers or sisters?'

A second elapsed.

I saw Ross's face glancing back at me through the thickly falling snow, his teeth white, his eyes hidden behind ski goggles.

'No,' I said.

It's not really a lie, Ross.

'Look,' I added quickly. 'I'm not interested in being defined by where I come from or who my parents are. I've always felt like an outsider in my family and at my school. Now I'm free to be who I really am.'

'So, who's the real you?' she asked.

'Haven't a clue.'

Nash mistook my answer for wit.

I woke up the following morning fully clothed, but feeling fine, almost sparklingly alert, until I went to get up and discovered my skull had been replaced by a rigid steel box that bashed against the tissue of my brain with every slight movement. I weighed the alternatives of ducking back under the duvet, or running off the remains of the alcohol.

Among the still-unpacked possessions lying on the floor, I located my sports bag and pulled on shorts and running shoes. After a panicky search for my key, I saw that I had sensibly left it in the door when I locked it, although I couldn't remember doing so. I couldn't actually remember returning to the room, although, as I stepped out into the rain and splashed along at a slow jog, a mental video of the previous evening began to spool through my mind, freezing randomly on single frames of searing embarrassment. Had my hair really become entangled in the plastic vine that decorated the Greek restaurant ceiling when I stood up to go to the toilet? Had we really smashed plates and danced in a frantic circle with the wedding party?

The city pavements were slippery with a dirt soup that

splashed my legs and soaked into the mesh of my white running shoes, but the rain felt cool and cleansing, flattening my hair, cascading down my face when I tilted back my head.

The streets were fairly empty, with only an occasional bus sloshing past. I had no idea where I was running to, but decided to turn left when I reached a major crossroads, into a more well-to-do area with estate agents, a pub with tables outside and baskets of bruised red geraniums swinging in the damp breeze, and a newsagent which was just opening up. Flipping through an A–Z, I saw that I'd come three quarters of the way around a squarish circle. My hall of residence was less than a mile away. I bought a pint of milk. The rain was beginning to ease as I pounded back, and my hangover was gone.

In the male shower room, a big, bluff kind of guy was towelling down ostentatiously just like the rugby players did at school to make sure you clocked the size of their muscles and their dicks.

He stared at my mud-bespattered legs.

'Got wrecked last night. Been out to run it off,' I said, and saw I'd gone up in his estimation.

Back in my room, I found a brand-new kettle in a box marked *Kitchen* along with a big jar of premium-quality instant coffee, a canister of Coffee Mate creamer and some tins of baked beans. My mother had thought of everything and I now regretted my reluctance to let her help me unpack and tidy everything away as she would have liked.

With two mugs of coffee in my hands, I was about to give Nash's door a sharp kick, when I had another flashback.

Did we kiss? We did. Right there outside her door. A peck, then a Frenchie and then, looking at me with heavy-lidded eyes, she'd asked if I wanted to come in, and it was clear that we could have had sex, but I'd muttered something about it not being a good idea.

Nash wasn't really my type. I hadn't even known I had a type until then.

I drank both cups of coffee, then set off to the Medics' introductory talk.

There was an almost tangible buzz of nerves among the crowd of strangers congregating outside the lecture theatre and a ripple of laughter when the student who was standing nearest the big wooden door tried the handle and discovered that it was open.

'Your first step on the way to becoming independent learners,' the professor remarked acidly from the lectern, as we filed into the tiers of seats, casting surreptitious glances around to see if others were taking off jackets, or taking out notepads.

Along the rows, I recognized a couple of faces from the interview day. A boy with glasses soberly acknowledged my nod of recognition; a girl wearing a headscarf looked away shyly.

'Which one of us is going to faint, do you reckon? There's always one, apparently, at our first sight of a cadaver . . .' the guy next to me whispered.

I unfurled a forefinger to point at the shiny blonde bob of a girl sitting right in front of us, who suddenly turned, as if she'd detected the slight movement in her direction. She was classically pretty in an appley, English kind of way. Her eyes held mine for a moment and I could feel the colour spreading over my face.

Her name was Lucy, my neighbour discovered when we broke for coffee and ended up sharing a table in the cafe. His was Toby.

If I'd been a moment later arriving outside the lecture theatre, or squeezed onto the end of a row of seats instead of starting a new one, I would probably have spent my training with different people. Or doesn't it work like that? Were Lucy and I always destined to meet and have coffee together? If I'd sat next to Jonathan, the guy with glasses, would I have passed my university years playing chess, and would I, too, have gone on to be a renowned oncologist? We think we choose our friends, but perhaps it's always just a matter of chance.

They took us into the anatomy lab during the first week. I suppose the idea was to confront it straight away. In the corridor outside, everyone was talking loudly, but silence descended as we trooped in. The air was thick with chemicals.

I had tried to prepare myself by imagining all sorts of different people when the bag was opened up, but the faces I had envisaged were old. This was a young man, the side of his face disfigured where his head had hit the pavement as a lorry turned left into his bike.

Next to me, Toby fainted. I helped carry him out of the lab, lying him on the floor with his legs up on a chair, and sat with him, pretending to be the calm one, until he thought he was up to going back inside. By that time, the other students at our table had been allowed to touch the body, and shown how the organs would be accessed in a surgical procedure. Anatomy teaching would not start in earnest until the second term, our tutor reassured us, by which stage we'd have had several opportunities to get used to the experience.

'Are you OK?' Lucy asked me as we stood in the refectory queue afterwards.

The concern on her face made me wonder if she'd observed my own struggle in the lab. She was so sweet and so pretty that for a moment, in a cynical attempt to make her like me more than Toby, I was tempted to tell her about Ross. But I held back because I couldn't bear the idea of my new friends being all sympathetic or limiting their vocabulary around me.

I've spent my whole life in your shadow, Ross. I'm not doing that any more.

5

December 1997

TESS

Hope was the little donkey in her first nativity play. Nobody thought she'd do it after the fuss she made about not being allowed to be an angel. To be honest, I didn't see why she couldn't be an angel, there were enough of them, but Mrs Madden, the Reception class teacher, said people weren't doing Hope any favours bowing to her will all the time. To be fair to Mrs Madden, I don't think it was because Hope didn't look or behave like an angel, I think she was just tired of all the questions.

Christmas was a confusing time for Hope.

'Is Mum with the *herald* angels?' she would ask, making them sound like some chapter of bikers. And, 'The Virgin Mary looks just like Our Lady.'

'Because she is the same, Hope.'

'Why is she called Virgin?'

'It's just another name.'

I made her a cardboard donkey mask just in case she changed her mind, and when at the dress rehearsal Mrs Madden pointed out, in a last-ditch attempt to include her, that the little donkey was the only one apart from baby Jesus who had a carol just about them, Hope decided she would go on stage after all, on all fours, taking her role very seriously and getting very cross when the other children joined in to *her* song. In the end, a compromise was reached where Hope sang the first verse herself and the rest of the class were allowed to come in for the chorus of 'Ring out the bells tonight, Bethlehem! Bethlehem!'

Hope had sat out watching so many rehearsals, she knew where everyone should stand. You could hear her telling the camel that he wasn't in the right place in between verses of 'Away in a Manger'. Several of the mothers came up after to tell me how Mum would have been proud, their fixed smiles meaning they'd let it go this time.

Hope wasn't popular, even with the other kids. You'd think that four- and five-year-olds would be too young for that, but they're not. On playground duty, I would watch her charging around and around the painted lines on the tarmac in some determined pursuit of her own, praying that one of the kids would ask to be her friend. Hope didn't seem to notice, but it broke my heart.

When I mentioned Hope's isolation to Dad, he just came out with the usual stuff about Hope being spoilt and mollycoddled. If people just left her alone, he said, she'd soon sort herself out, missing the point that people were leaving her alone, but you didn't challenge Dad like that.

Brendan rang from Australia every fortnight, but he wasn't much help when I told him my concerns about Hope.

'I expect you'd be lonely, if you were five years old and lost your mammy,' he said. 'You worry too much!'

'I expect you'd worry if you were eighteen and you'd been landed with your little sister to look after,' I wanted to say to him. But that would have been childish.

At lunchtime on the last day of term, Mrs Corcoran sent

word she wanted to see me. Waiting on a hard chair outside her office, I was sure she was going to issue a warning about Hope's behaviour, or worse, but when she called me in, she told me that the school was about to advertise for a teaching assistant, but if I wanted it, the job was mine.

'A mutually beneficial arrangement,' she called it.

'You might as well get paid for all the work you do,' said Doll, as we sat watching *Sleepless in Seattle*. She'd got into the habit of coming round with a takeaway and a video every Friday night when Dad was out at the pub, usually choosing something romantic on the basis that we'd both be able to have a good old cry. 'Just until Hope settles,' she added.

We all used that phrase a lot. When Hope settles. As if it was just a temporary arrangement. I borrowed books from the course reading list from the library, so I wouldn't be behind if some miracle allowed me to slot back into university.

I suppose I had kind of been expecting Doll to put up an argument, but we both knew I didn't really have a choice. Dad had to go out to work so he couldn't look after Hope, even if he'd had the capacity or inclination to deal with a young child. Any other alternative was unthinkable.

'I know how much you wanted to go to university, so I'm sad for you, but I'm happy for me,' Doll said, picking up a triangle of pizza. 'Do you think that makes me a good friend or a horrible selfish person?'

'A horrible selfish person, obviously,' I said, with a hollow little laugh.

We both sat staring at the television screen for a while.

'Do you believe in The One?' Doll finally asked.

'Depends what you mean by The One,' I said, with that unintentionally surly voice you get when you're trying to hold back tears, not because of the romance on the screen, which I wasn't paying much attention to, but because it felt like we'd finally confirmed I was stuck here for the foreseeable future.

'As in, there's one person out there who's destined for you?'

'Seems unlikely, doesn't it?'

'Why?' asked Doll, attempting to deal prettily with an infinite string of mozzarella.

'That there's only one person out of the whole of mankind? I mean, what if your person happens to live in the Amazonian rainforest, or speak Arabic, or something? And how would you ever know anyway, because if you think somebody is The One and he's not, then you might have given up your chance of meeting The One who is . . .'

'What about Mr Darcy, then?'

Like everyone else, we'd both had a big crush on Colin Firth in the television series of *Pride and Prejudice*.

'That was the eighteen hundreds,' I said. 'You didn't get to meet as many people.'

'You're so unromantic!'

My mind wandered through the great romantic pairings in literature. Had they really met because they were meant for one another, or simply because they lived in close proximity? Cathy and Heathcliff shared the same house, Romeo and Juliet were both in Verona. Wasn't The One more to do with the fact that the emotion we called love, which I had yet to experience, was so powerful it made you believe that this was the only person in the world for you? Wasn't it more a matter of definition than of destiny?

On screen, Meg Ryan and Tom Hanks finally met at the top of the Empire State Building.

'She could do better, don't you think?' Doll said over the closing credits. 'I mean, he's a good actor, but he's just not sexy, is he?'

'Sorry, which one of us was the unromantic one?' I asked.

60

'So, if it was anyone in the whole world, right now, who would it be?' Doll wanted to know.

It was the sort of conversation we used to have as we walked home from school. In those days, it was all Robbie Williams, although I'd always assumed that if our paths had crossed, he would have chosen Doll, because Doll was petite and blonde and boys liked her.

'George Clooney?' I offered.

ER was the programme the teaching assistants at St Cuthbert's talked about. Lusting after George Clooney was something I had in common with a staffroom of sympathetic middle-aged women, where conversation often centred on topics like varicose veins and the menopause.

'A bit old for you, isn't he?' said Doll.

'I'm never going to meet him, am I?'

'You always did have a thing for the older guys,' Doll mused.

'How d'you work that out?'

'*Little Women*, remember? You didn't mind when Jo got that old professor bloke instead of nice Laurie. It's the one book I've read all the way through,' she admitted when she saw me looking at her, astonished. 'Only 'cause you made me.'

'So who would it be for you?' I felt obliged to ask.

'If we're talking a famous person, Tom Cruise.'

'Yeah, he is pretty gorgeous.'

'He's too short for you,' said Doll immediately, as if I was planning to snatch him from her.

She got up and removed the video cassette from the machine.

'What about blokes we know?' she asked.

I was about to say that men hadn't been uppermost in my mind for the past few weeks, when I heard Dad fumbling with his keys at the front door, so jumped up to tidy away the pizza debris. You could never tell what mood he'd be in after the pub.

A cloud of curry entered the room with him.

'So you girls had yourselves a pizza, did you?' he asked, seeing the box on the table.

'We did.'

'None left for me?' He lifted the lid of the box, in a twinkly rather than menacing way.

'Sorry!'

'How much does one of these takeaway pizzas cost, then?'

'Doll paid,' I said quickly.

'You've got yourself a job, have you?' Dad asked her.

'I have, Mr Costello. I'm working full-time at the salon now.'

While I was in the sixth form, Doll had been at the local college, doing her diploma, but she'd always worked evenings and weekends at the town's poshest hairdressing salon since she was thirteen, graduating from the girl who swept the floor all the way up to junior stylist.

'There now,' said Dad, giving me a look.

'I've been offered a job as well,' I heard myself telling him, my heart sinking at the inevitability of accepting Mrs Corcoran's offer. 'I'm going to be a proper teaching assistant on the staff after Christmas.'

'You'll be getting the pizza in then,' said Dad.

Not well done, or anything like that. Dad hadn't forgiven me for choosing university rather than work, even though I hadn't gone.

Doll and I exchanged glances.

'Well, I'll be off,' said Doll.

'I'll walk you,' I said, hoping that Dad would have fallen asleep by the time I got back. You would have thought with Mum dying we'd have got along better together, but if anything, Dad seemed more cantankerous than ever. Perhaps it was one of his stages of grief.

The cool air was refreshing after being indoors all evening.

'Oh, I forgot! Mum said you're to come for Christmas,' Doll announced.

'Seriously?'

'All of you.'

I almost wept with gratitude. I'd been so worried about Christmas. I hadn't been able to decide whether to get the tinsel tree down from the loft, or decorate the lounge with paper chains, in case it seemed disrespectful. Whenever I tried to speak to Dad about it, he'd say, 'Christmas? Doesn't it get earlier every year?'

And there'd be some excuse – the pub, the snooker, the match – as to why we wouldn't talk about it yet.

The cards we'd received were piled up on the hall table, except for the one Hope had made at school in the shape of a Christmas tree, so loaded with glitter and glue it never properly dried. That went up on the knick-knack shelf in the kitchen and each morning while she was eating her Coco Pops, Hope gazed at it, saying, in rather a good impression of Mrs Corcoran's Irish lilt, 'That's really very good, Hope, isn't it now?'

I'd dreaded tackling the Christmas lunch. My cooking skills were non-existent. It was fortunate that they served a hot lunch at school, because in the evenings all I ran to was toast with beans, toast with spaghetti or toast with Marmite. Occasionally, when Dad was flush from a win on the horses, he'd arrive home with a big bag of fish and chips, but usually he ate at the pub, or at the Taj Mahal after closing time.

One Sunday, I'd tried to make us a roast dinner, Hope's favourite, chicken with little sausages, but I got the timings all wrong, and omitted to remove the plastic tray under the chicken before putting it in the oven. The custard for the trifle was sweet scrambled egg, and I over-whipped the cream, so instead of being all floaty, it was fatty and impossible to spread. After that, Dad started taking us to the Carvery on Sunday where it was all you could eat for £4.99 and kids went free, including an Ice Cream Factory which Hope went backwards and forwards to, until Dad decided value for money was one thing, but enough was enough. The Carvery wasn't open on Christmas Day.

Christmas shopping in London was something I'd always done with Mum before Hope was born. We'd rarely bought anything but we used to look at all the Christmas windows of the department stores, sometimes venturing inside to take a surreptitious squirt of Chanel Nº5 – 'If you marry a rich man, Tess, that's the scent he'll buy you!' – while the perfumery assistant's back was turned. I knew it was a risk taking Hope, but I thought she might enjoy all the decorations and the change of scene.

It was a mistake to stop outside Hamleys. When I tried to move us on, Hope literally stuck herself to the pavement, the force of her will making her much heavier than she really was. Inside, she immediately spotted the mountain of soft toys.

'You can touch them very carefully and nicely. Nicely, Hope! Gently. Now put it back, please, Hope . . . put it back!'

I ended up having to buy the giraffe who was on the point of losing his tail by the time we got it to the till. I couldn't believe the price. Dad had given me a twenty-pound note to have ourselves a good time, but there was only enough left for a Happy Meal for lunch. At that point, it would have been more sensible to go home, but it was already 23 December and I hadn't yet got gifts for Mrs O'Neill or Doll, and I wanted to buy them something in Selfridges.

After Doll and I turned fifteen, we were allowed to go up to London in the holidays if we saved enough money from our Saturday jobs. We loved walking round the city, discovering all the different little villagey areas and fantasizing about sharing a place there one day. Doll fancied a modern flat overlooking Hyde Park; I preferred the idea of one of the little houses at the top of Portobello Road which were all painted a different bright colour. The dream was that I'd be a librarian or work in a book-shop and Doll would be one of the women in Selfridges' perfumery who wear a clinical-looking white uniform and offer you a demonstration facial.

Oxford Street was crammed with last-minute shoppers. You just had to keep moving along with the crowd, which was tiresome enough for someone as tall as me but much worse for Hope. When she couldn't stand the crush and the noise any longer, she stopped dead.

'Come on, Hope. It's not far now.'

The columns of Selfridges were just up ahead.

'Hope! We're holding everyone up.'

Initial glances of sympathy changed to disapproval as the screaming started.

'Hope! Come on now! What would Mum think of this behaviour?'

I'd vowed never to use Mum's memory as a threat, and as soon as I said it I wanted to take it back, but the question had distracted her for the second I needed to scoop her off her feet and carry her. She started fighting and kicking me.

'Put me down!'

'Only if you'll promise to behave.'

'Put me down!'

The screams were getting louder, her face was all hot and wet with tears, and then suddenly, she stopped, cocking her head to one side, like a robin. My ears searched the rumble of traffic and detected the noise of a band playing 'Silent Night' somewhere in the direction of Selfridges.

We must have stood there for half an hour listening to the

carols, Hope's face lighting up as she recognized each familiar tune. She knew all the words to 'Away in a Manger' and 'We Three Things', as she called it, and sang them completely unselfconsciously. When the band stopped for a break, I gave her fifty pence to go and put in the collection box.

'Aren't you the little angel?' the Salvation Army lady said.

'I'm the little donkey,' Hope told her.

Selfridges was packed inside, and all the cosmetic counters were just a little too high for Hope. When I tried to interest her with a squirt of perfume on the back of her hand, she started coughing in a silly exaggerated way. I quickly chose a box of guest soaps with beautiful floral wrappers for Mrs O'Neill and a gift pack of Rive Gauche *eau de parfum* and body lotion, Doll's current favourite fragrance.

'I'd like them in separate bags, please,' I told the assistant when we eventually got to the front of the queue.

The whole point was the bright yellow Selfridges bags.

'That's twenty-eight pounds, madam.'

Delving around in my bag, I could feel the line behind me growing impatient and had a horrible sinking feeling that some clever pickpocket had stolen my wallet in the crush of shoppers. Finally, I felt it at the bottom of my bag.

'Here!'

Thrusting two notes at the assistant, I was suddenly aware that Hope was no longer holding my hand, nor was she standing next to me.

'Hope?'

No sign of her.

My chest tightened, as if I'd forgotten how to breathe. Keep calm. She must be around somewhere. I scanned the crowds. There were hundreds, maybe thousands, of people on the ground floor of the shop. Where had she gone? People were packed onto every step of the escalators going up and coming down; and everywhere there were mirrors reflecting more people. But no Hope.

'Hope?'

With the cash still in my hand, I started moving through the crowd peering over the tops of the shiny glass counters looking for her. Perhaps she was hiding? But it would be so unlike Hope to hide. Whenever I tried to play hide-and-seek with her, she didn't get the idea.

'. . . nine, ten, coming to get you!'

'Here I am!' Hope would call out from behind the curtain.

Had she run away? Hope never ran away. She wriggled and kicked, but she didn't run.

It was like a nightmare, except instead of shouting and nothing coming out of my mouth, I was shouting and nobody was paying any attention.

Someone must have taken her! Please God, no! Don't let someone have taken her!

The revolving door was whirling people into the street. Did someone have a car outside waiting, a car with black windows? Surely people would have seen her being taken? But I'd had all the disapproving glances and nobody had asked, 'Is that child yours?' Everyone was too busy shopping.

Please God! I will believe in you, if you just bring her back to me!

As I started saying Hail Marys in my head, I suddenly had a flash of inspiration. *Aren't you the little angel?*

Outside, I dodged this way and that, not caring who I bumped into in my haste to get back to the Salvation Army band.

An ambulance siren screamed nearby. Please God, don't let her have tried to cross the road and gone under a big red bus!

Calm down. She'll be standing by the litter bin where we listened to the band.

She wasn't! I'd lost her! I really had lost her! And it was

stupid to leave the shop because if she was looking for me, she wouldn't find me now!

The band started a new carol.

'Little donkey, little donkey, on the dusty road . . .'

In my panic, I hadn't seen Hope standing right next to the conductor. She was adamantly refusing to hold the hand of the worried-looking woman with the collection box.

'Stop that huggy stuff!' Hope shouted, as I squeezed her ever so tightly in my arms. 'Stop it, I said.'

She fell asleep on the train home, a picture of innocence, her hand clasped around the giraffe's neck, his soft face next to hers. When I thought about it calmly, it was astonishing that she had found her way through the store and back to the band. Didn't that just prove that she was as intelligent as any other child, if not more so? That would be something to tell Mrs Corcoran.

Or not. Because that would involve admitting that I'd lost her.

A middle-aged woman sitting opposite us with her Christmas shopping nodded and smiled.

'Bless her!'

'You should have seen her earlier,' I said. 'Screaming blue murder!'

'You don't ever want to criticize your own,' she admonished me. 'There'll be plenty of people in life who'll do that for you.'

Normally, I'd have explained that I wasn't Hope's mother, but those cataclysmic seconds, minutes – I don't even know how long it was – without her, had made me realize that Hope was so much more important than anything else. It was suddenly clear as an epiphany that I had a choice: I could either go on thinking life was unfair and getting all bitter and resentful, or just get on with looking after her. It was actually a relief. And it was true what Brendan said the last time I'd had a bit of a moan on the phone. Not studying English Literature didn't stop me reading books, did it?

I thought of something Mum often used to say. *If you do something with a happy heart, it will bring you joy.*

Or as Doll put it, because she was the only person I ever told about the incident:

'You lost Hope, but then you found it again.'

6

December 1997

GUS

As the days grew shorter, I began to feel as if London was my home. Autumn sharpened the experience of living in the city. We came out of our afternoon lectures into darkness, with street lights sparkling in the rain and the air steaming with appetizing wafts of spicy food. Shivering throngs at dripping bus stops were cheerfully united in suffering. In summer, it felt more like being a tourist; if you were there as winter approached, it was because you had to be.

On Bonfire Night Lucy, Toby and I joined the crowds of people trudging up Primrose Hill and gazed over the vast, illuminated map of London spread out below us. As we oohed and aahed at the firework display, it was obvious that Toby and I both fancied Lucy. There was an unspoken competition between us, which she pretended not to see.

On the first day of the holidays, most of the students loaded up with dirty washing and headed out of town. Lucy was eager to see her family, Toby to be reunited with his school friends; Nash was flying off to see her father. Everyone else was looking forward to the thing I was dreading: Christmas at home.

I kept finding reasons not to leave, spending mornings studying in the library for the January exams, and afternoons in the National Gallery, working my way from the Renaissance to fin-de-siècle Paris. When I discovered that the National Theatre had a batch of cheap tickets available on the day for the evening performance, I headed south instead of north on my morning run, crossing the steely grey Thames as the first commuters began to spill across the bridge, and standing in the box-office queue, with the cold river air slicing through to my bones.

The day before Christmas Eve, it occurred to me that I hadn't yet bought any presents, which provided an excuse to delay my departure for another few hours. In the past, my mother had always bought our presents for us: from me, after-dinner mints for her and liqueur chocolates for my father. From Ross, a collection of guest soaps and a set of golf balls. The theory was that we paid her back out of our pocket money, but we never did. We were responsible for wrapping, although paper, scissors and Sellotape were thoughtfully placed on our beds beside the gifts, and on Christmas morning she would feign surprise as the parcels were opened. This year, I was determined that my mother would be genuinely delighted when she opened her gift from me, even though I didn't have the slightest idea what to buy her.

I made my way to Selfridges, where we used to be taken to see Father Christmas as children. Afterwards, my father, Ross and I would tuck into generous salt-beef sandwiches with lashings of mustard and gherkin at the Brass Rail, while my mother sought advice about face creams and tested lipstick colours on the back of her hand in the perfumery department. Then we'd drive down Regent Street, Ross and me in the back seat, craning our heads to see the lights.

The old-fashioned revolving door at the centre of the store triggered a memory of Ross pushing as fast as he could to whirl unsuspecting shoppers off-balance. One section of the ground floor was a sturdy, masculine kind of place where I found a range of gifts for men and bought a matching tartan-covered hip-flask and scorecard holder in a faux-wooden box. On the more feminine side of the store, I chose a Yardley boxed set of talc and bath oil tied with lavender ribbon and stood in the line for the till.

In front of me, there was a tall woman with a fidgety little girl in one hand and a couple of boxes in the other. Her gift sets looked much more sophisticated than mine and I became a little anxious about the Yardley. She was talking to the child so patiently that I was about to pluck up the courage to ask her opinion, but then it was her turn at the till, and, as she delved into her shoulder bag, the little girl shot off through the legs of the shoppers.

I was suddenly at the front of the queue.

'Can I help you?'

I picked up the black, blue and silver box the woman had abandoned and weighed it against mine.

'Girlfriend or mother?' demanded the shop assistant.

I could feel the colour spreading across my face and burning the tips of my ears.

'Mother,' I murmured.

A small, knowing smile completed my humiliation.

'Probably safer with the Yardley, then,' she said, taking it from my hand.

For a moment, I was tempted to buy the other box out of sheer defiance. Perhaps my mother was younger and trendier than she assumed? Perhaps I would give it to Lucy? We'd made tentative plans to meet up between Christmas and New Year. But I had no idea what perfume, if any, she used.

My father picked me up at the station, leaning across the passenger seat to open my door.

'They're saying it might snow.' He was something of an amateur weather forecaster and there was a mahogany barometer in our hall, but the statement was freighted with deeper layers of meaning.

'Let's hope not,' I said.

We both sat in silence, staring straight ahead as if to face down any stray snowflakes for the duration of the short drive home.

There was the usual wreath of holly and tartan ribbon on the door and a real Christmas tree in the hall, but the Blue Peter advent crown that Ross and I had made the winter we both had measles had been retired. My mother emerged from the kitchen in her festive apron. Her hands were covered in flour, so we air-kissed, and then she looked me up and down as if she was expecting me to have changed.

At supper, in our rarely used dining room, my father was eager to catch me out with questions about the working of organs and glands. I remembered him behaving in a similar way towards Ross early on in his training. Perhaps Nash was right about him being a failed doctor? Ross had been more combative than me, unafraid to challenge him. My reticence simply made my father more persistent. And yet, when my mother said, 'For goodness' sake, leave him alone, Gordon!' I almost wished he would keep going, because the silence in the room was so acute, it was like an inaudible scream of pain.

The dining table was polished to a high shine, the glasses and cutlery twinkled. With all her attention to cleanliness and propriety, my mother had made the place as sterile as my father's surgery.

'More wine?' asked my mother.

I had barely touched my glass, but hers had been filled and emptied three times. The neck of the bottle tinkled slightly against its rim. My father stared at it. She put the bottle carefully down and picked up her glass. Then, the doorbell rang.

'Who on earth?' said my father.

'Probably carol singers!' My mother seemed almost feverish at the distraction. When she opened the front door, the sound that filtered through to the dining room from the hall was not a song, but an exaggerated squeal of delight.

'What a lovely surprise!' Her voice became louder as she walked down the hall towards the dining room. 'Guess who, Gordon? Angus?'

Ross's girlfriend Charlotte followed her into the room. She was wearing a long lilac coat with a shawl collar that on anyone less elegant or slim might have looked like a dressing gown, but made her look like a film star. She was holding a cube wrapped in incongruously cheap and cheerful wrapping paper.

'Please don't get up!' she said. 'I don't want to disturb your supper.'

'You're not!' I blurted, ridiculously grateful to her for changing the dynamic.

'Let me get you a drink!' My father clicked into the jovial-host mode I'd forgotten he was capable of.

The dining room felt nice, normal again.

'Something soft.' Charlotte put down the parcel and slid off soft black leather gloves. 'I'm in my car.'

'Your own car? How exciting!' said my mother.

'It's just a little Peugeot.'

My father opened a bottle of tonic water. Ice cubes cracked in the glass as the fizz frothed over them and a faint, bitter aroma drifted across the table. 'Peugeot, eh?'

With a shrug of Charlotte's shoulders, her coat hung itself over the back of her chair, revealing a slippery satin lining. Underneath she was wearing a plain black polo neck and black jeans. Her long hair was so black and shiny, it almost looked blue; her complexion was flawless. In the photo of her and

Ross on the living-room mantelpiece, dressed up as the Addams family for a Halloween ball, there was something almost vampiric about her beauty, but now, with her lips pale from the cold, she was like a model shot by David Bailey in the sixties: stunning, and somehow a tiny bit vulnerable.

'So you're a houseman now?' said my father. 'Or am I meant to say "houseperson"?'

The pale lips formed a thin smile.

'Any areas you're keen to specialize in? General practice?'

'Cardiac surgery,' she replied, evenly.

For some reason, I let out a little snort of laughter.

I'd been in awe of Charlotte from the first time Ross brought her home the summer at the end of his second year. My dad had just built the hot tub on the decking. Charlotte had worn a tiny white bikini. I'd never seen a woman wearing so little before. She'd been tantalizingly aloof. I couldn't even tell if she'd noticed me behind her film-star sunglasses.

'How are you enjoying Medicine, Angus?' she asked.

'Fine. Hard work, obviously,' I mumbled, thirteen years old again.

'Not as hard as being a heart surgeon,' my mother said. 'Goodness! I should think that's the most difficult—'

'It's a competitive area,' Charlotte acknowledged.

'I wonder . . .' my mother began.

Her eyes had the watery, unfocused look that meant she was thinking about what path Ross would have chosen.

'Anyway,' said Charlotte, taking a sip of her tonic water. 'That's for the future.'

'Good to have ambitions, nevertheless,' said my father. It didn't sound as though he rated her chances. 'So, you're going home for Christmas?'

Her mother's house was just a few miles from ours, though Charlotte and Ross had met at uni.

'I've fucked women on five continents,' he'd told me once,

as he shaved before a date. 'When the finest fuck lives five minutes down the road.'

'Just today and tomorrow. I'm working Christmas Day,' Charlotte replied.

'Welcome to real life!' said my father.

I could think of only one Christmas when he had been called upon to prescribe antibiotics for an abscess.

'And New Year?' my mother asked quietly.

'Yes, New Year too.'

'Probably just as well,' said my father.

'Yes,' said Charlotte.

The silence seemed endless.

'How lovely of you to come to see us, though! Gordon, isn't it lovely?'

Charlotte pushed the parcel towards my mother.

'Just a little something,' she said.

'You shouldn't have! But how lovely!' said my mother. 'I must go and get yours.'

From the length of time she was out of the room, I wondered if my mother really had purchased a gift for Charlotte, or whether she was wrapping something up that she had bought on the off-chance that, even with all her meticulous Christmas lists, she had overlooked someone.

'Where are you living?' I asked Charlotte, to break the silence.

'Battersea. Do you know it?'

'No.'

'It's quite convenient.'

'I've been to the National Theatre.'

To produce this howling non-sequitur, my thought processes had jumped from Battersea to the only place I knew south of the river.

Charlotte regarded me disdainfully.

'Lucky you,' she said, with a thin edge of irony.

'You can get cheap tickets on the day,' I said, for the benefit of my father, who was looking perplexed. 'I run,' I added.

'I run too,' said Charlotte.

'Perhaps you'll run into each other!' my father tried to join in, but his attempt at a joke simply closed the conversation down.

My mother returned with a soft parcel and handed it to Charlotte.

'Shall I open it now?' Charlotte asked.

She tore the paper to reveal a red knitted glove and scarf set from Marks & Spencer.

'Mmm,' she said, draping the scarf around her neck. 'This will keep me nice and warm!'

She pointed at the cube on the table, which my mother unwrapped to reveal a box with a pink amaryllis on it.

'You plant the bulb and it shoots up a lovely flower,' Charlotte said.

'I've always wondered if they work,' said my mother doubtfully, turning the box over and peering at the instructions.

'Of course they work!' I said, dismayed to see that Charlotte was slipping her narrow shoulders into the satiny sleeves of her coat. The knitted red scarf looked as discordant against her outfit as the parcel had when she came in. I wondered how far she would drive down the road before taking it off.

'Well, I must be getting going,' she said.

Charlotte air-kissed my mother, then, after holding out her hand to be shaken, stiffly allowed my father to give her a hug.

So that there was no question of looking as if I was expecting a kiss or hug myself, I rushed to the front door to see her out.

'Thanks for coming,' I said. 'Cheered them up no end.'

Charlotte looked up at me. Her eyes, I noticed, were a greeny colour, like a cat's.

'You've grown so tall, Angus,' she said. 'Goodness, I think you're bigger than Ross now.'

'He'd hate that!'

It just came out and I was immediately ashamed that I had made the only reference to him irreverent.

Charlotte's forehead was furrowed with a small frown, as if she was considering the truth of the proposition, and then, to my great relief, she smiled, a genuine smile, as if remembering something pleasant.

'You're absolutely right! He would!' she said, and gave my arm a tiny squeeze before stepping out into the cold.

Although it was just the three of us, my mother was up before dawn on Christmas Day to put a huge turkey in the oven. I hadn't slept well and went downstairs as soon as I heard the clanking of baking trays. The kitchen was already swathed in a warm mist of offal from the giblets she was boiling for gravy. I drank the cup of tea she put in front of me, and told her I was going for a run.

'Blow away the cobwebs,' she said.

Outside, the air was opaque with freezing fog, the pavement laced with frost which stuck slightly to the soles of my trainers. With zero visibility, I found myself jogging slowly, as if some primal instinct had kicked in, causing my brain to think me blind and in need of protection from obstacles that might loom in my path. I couldn't get up to the precious speed where thought left my body and nothing mattered but the pounding rhythm of feet hitting the ground.

Suddenly aware of another person's steps, I slowed to a halt.

Perhaps you'll run into each other!

A man I didn't know ran past. He must have eaten garlic the night before. The acrid odour hung in the still whiteness as his laboured breaths receded into silence.

*

There was a smell of burning when I returned to the house. My mother was standing over the kitchen sink scrubbing at the blackened giblet pan. She didn't look round as I stood in the doorway, but from the angle of her shoulders, I could tell she was crying.

I showered for a long time, enjoying the hot water streaming over my cold face.

When I came downstairs, my father was sitting at the kitchen table in his usual Christmas mufti: thick tweedy sweater over checked shirt and corduroy trousers.

I'd noticed a slight air of impatience about him since my return, like a man waiting beside a motorway for the RAC to turn up.

My mother brandished one of her Christmas platters. 'Smoked salmon and champagne?'

'It's a bit early, isn't it?' he said.

'Some of us have been up for hours!'

I had heard the same exchange every Christmas morning for as long as I could remember.

'Well, you only live once!' was my father's standard reply. But obviously he wasn't going to say it this year.

Previously, I had been allowed only half a glass of champagne, but at eighteen, it appeared I could have as much as I wanted. It slipped down my throat like cream.

'It hardly seems worth lighting the fire in the living room,' my mother was saying.

For the last few years, that had been Ross's job. I couldn't decide whether she was hinting that I should do it this year, or indicating that she would be happier not to go in the living room where we'd be surrounded by photos of him.

'Why don't we have our presents in the kitchen?' I suggested.

'Nice and warm,' said my father immediately.

79

'Why ever not?' My mother seemed almost excited about the break with tradition.

She had bought me a pair of pyjamas, a voucher for ten driving lessons at the British School of Motoring, and, from my father, a pedometer.

'Let's have a look,' he demanded, making it clear that it was the first time he had seen it.

'It counts how many paces you've done!' said my mother.

I would never use it, but I recognized the thought that had gone into the gift. I could almost hear her saying to her WI friends, 'I can't think of a thing for Angus. All he does these days is run!'

My father appeared satisfied with his gift from me, but there was something about the way my mother said, 'Oh! Lavender!' when she unwrapped hers, that made me realize that she didn't like the fragrance. She turned the pretty box over and over in her hands.

'Ross always used to buy me Yardley guest soaps,' she whispered, throatily.

A barb of resentment stabbed through the cotton-wool cocoon the champagne had spun around me.

'*No, he didn't!*' I wanted to say. '*You did! Why does he have to be a saint?*'

The clock ticked on the wall. The turkey spat and sizzled in the oven.

'Good Lord, is that the time?' my father suddenly said. 'I said I'd have nine holes with Brian!'

'Why don't you take Angus along?' my mother suggested.

I sensed a slight hesitation.

'Would you like to come?'

I knew that he would have preferred me to say no, but my mother seemed equally keen for me to go.

I waited in the hall for him to come downstairs jangling his car keys amid a powerful waft of some cologne I'd never smelled on him before.

We drove several miles to his golf club. There were a few diehards in the club lounge, and a lone woman sitting at a table by the log fire. As I pushed open the door, she glanced up expectantly, then down again when I was not the person she was waiting for.

'What'll it be?' My father put an arm around my shoulder, ushering me towards the bar.

I asked for a half of bitter knowing he wouldn't hesitate to voice his thoughts about lager drinkers to anyone who would listen.

'Two halves of your best!' he said loudly to the bartender, then turned to me. 'Don't think we've had a proper drink together, have we?'

'I don't think so.'

We both knew we hadn't. My eighteenth birthday in April had come and gone without anyone really noticing it.

'Pubs in London any good or are you more of a wine-bar man?' he asked.

'I haven't been to that many.'

'Cheaper at the Union, eh?'

I wasn't sure if he wanted me to be a hearty drinker or whether it was a trap.

'I suppose so!'

'He supposes so!' said my father, as if to invite the others at the bar into our manly tête-à-tête.

There were a few smiles but no takers.

He drained his glass.

'Another?' I asked.

'Better not,' he said. 'Not when I'm driving. Look, while you're finishing up, I just need to point Percy.'

I stood at the bar, trying to ignore the drainy taste of the warm ale as I gulped it back.

My father returned with the woman I'd noticed when we came in.

'Angus, would you believe it! This is Samantha, my new nurse at the practice!'

'Not that new!' she said with a little laugh, looking at him, not me, as we shook hands.

Like most dental nurses I had encountered, she was pretty, in a clinical sort of way, with short hair, good teeth and sensible little stud earrings. She was wearing tight, clean jeans tucked into leather boots, and a pale blue fluffy jumper. A silk scarf with a navy border and a pattern of gold buckles was draped around her shoulders, slightly at odds with the rest of her outfit. I imagined it was his Christmas present to her. She wasn't yet the age for silk scarves.

'How long is it now?' my father was asking her.

'Seven months,' she said.

'Is it really? So, you're a member here, are you?' he asked, as if anyone was going to believe that she was the sort of girl who would nip out on her own to practise her swing on Christmas morning.

'Daddy is,' she replied. 'I'm spending Christmas with my parents.' She caught my eye for the first time, as if we both knew what a pain that was. 'I really should be getting back.'

In the car on the way home, I couldn't decide what I felt, if I felt anything at all. If Samantha was the way he had found some comfort, then good for him. I guessed she wasn't the first. My mother probably suspected – she had been his nurse herself – so perhaps her suggestion that I accompany him had been mischievous? One thing I was clear about was that she would not want to be told by me.

'Samantha seems nice,' I ventured, with a hint of complicity.

'What? Oh, yes, she's not bad at all,' my father replied, keeping his eyes focused on the road.

There was a yellowy glimmer of impending snow in the fading light.

As we turned into our drive, my father suddenly remembered his alibi.

'I don't know where Brian got to!' he exclaimed.

'We were rather late,' I said.

My father turned and gave me the kind of blokey smile I had only ever seen him give to Ross.

'That must be it!'

'A girl called to speak to you,' my mother announced as the two of us walked into the hall.

'Oh?' said my father.

'Not *you*, Gordon. Angus! A girl.'

'A girl, eh?' My father smiled at me again.

'Did you get her name?' I asked.

'Did you get her name!' he echoed, delightedly. In a sentence I had gone from being the son he was unsure about to Casanova.

'It wasn't a good line. She said she'd call again later. I hope not while we're eating.'

The phone rang as my mother was offering me custard, cream or both with my Christmas pudding.

'It's for you!' said my father, giving me a wink as he passed the handset over.

I took it in the hall, my heart racing a little as I cleared my throat before speaking. But it wasn't Lucy, it was Nash.

'So, how's things? Are you having a good one?'

'Fine,' I said. 'Pretty quiet. How about you?'

'Bloody disaster! I've only been here two days. Dad's new girlfriend is a bitch. I don't know a soul! Look, Dad says he'll pay for a friend to fly over for New Year . . . ?'

'Where are you, exactly?' I asked, thinking New York,

Brussels or one of the many other cities where Nash's father owned property.

'The chalet in Val d'Isère,' she said. 'You ski, don't you?'

'No,' I lied. 'So I wouldn't be the best—'

'Oh, come on, Gus. Think croissants, good coffee and oodles of red wine. Please, pretty please?'

'Sorry . . . I just can't, Nash. Thanks for the offer . . .'

I put down the phone, and stared at the bunting of Christmas cards festooning the hall. Snow on churches, snow on trees, snowy Bruegel scenes of skaters, a snow-encrusted branch with a robin perched on it, glittering snow on the roof of the nativity stable – did it actually snow in the Middle East? – a cute Labrador puppy with a red bobble hat, skidding in snow. Row after row of soft, white images twinkling their snowy greetings. Had no one thought?

I saw Ross's face glancing back at me through the thickly falling snow, his teeth white, his eyes hidden behind mirror ski goggles. There were flakes settling on his dark, swept-back hair.

'What offer's this then?' my father asked when I returned to the table.

My mind replayed the conversation with Nash, in case there was anything else they'd overheard that I was going to have to explain.

'Nothing,' I said.

'Nothing, eh?'

I hated the idea of the two of us being men with secrets.

'Look, do you mind if I save this for later? I'm stuffed . . .'

He shot me a wounded glance. Our bubble of matey bonhomie had been fragile, and now I'd popped it.

In my bedroom, I stared at the snowflakes falling past the window, thinking of this time one year ago.

*

84

The snow had started to fall as the light faded. It wasn't safe to ski off-piste, but it was sheer madness if you couldn't even see where you were going.

'Why did you come up, if you didn't want to ski down?' Ross demanded.

My brother's strategy was always to make me feel stupid first.

'I thought you wanted to go down the usual way . . .'

'We've done *"the usual way"*,' he whined, mocking me.

'Not in these conditions. It'll still be fairly dangerous . . .'

'*"Still be fairly dangerous"*!' Another mocking echo, then the inevitable taunt that never failed to spur me into doing things I didn't want to do. 'God, you're such a fucking wuss!'

Ross looked down the slope. I looked down the slope. Then he looked at me, his eyes gleaming with the challenge.

'Last one to the bottom gets the drinks in!' He pulled his goggles down and was off, straight to 'Go!' when I was still at 'Ready!' just like every race we'd ever run.

I almost followed. I almost followed. But I did not follow.

I'd heard the taunts so often, they'd lost their power. I didn't even ski down the marked run. The little wave of triumph ebbed away as I stood alone in the bubble, drifting slowly down through the dense fog, as if I'd finally accepted defeat.

Back at the hotel, I sat in the window of the bar, staring out into zero visibility.

After a few minutes, Mum and Dad found me. She'd been in the spa all afternoon and was looking rather pink and shiny; he'd called it a day after the snow came in and had already showered and changed for dinner.

'Where's Ross?'

'He wanted to ski down. I'd had enough.'

I didn't tell them about Ross going off-piste. Didn't see the point in worrying them unnecessarily.

After about an hour, Mum started getting fidgety and look-ing at her watch every few minutes.

'He's probably bumped into someone and gone for a drink,' I suggested.

'He's probably gone back to the room to dry off,' said Dad.

'It seems to be clearing up now,' said Mum. 'Perhaps he took shelter and waited for it to pass over?'

We were all keen to imagine possible scenarios that would explain the unnatural delay.

I think perhaps all of us were frightened of Ross. My mother didn't dare to be thought of as a worrier; my dad revelled in his older son's courage and prowess and didn't want to be seen to be questioning that; my own growing anxiety was com-pounded by not having told them the full facts.

'Do you think we should alert someone?' I finally asked. 'It's just that I think he was planning to ski off-piste . . .'

'What? Why the hell didn't you say before?'

My father had already decided to blame me.

By the time we'd ascertained what we were supposed to do in the circumstances and the rescue team had set off, three hours had passed since I'd last seen my brother. They found him at nine o'clock that night, still alive but hypothermic, with a shattered arm and catastrophic head injuries. It appeared that, just a minute or so after we'd parted, Ross had skied into a tree at speed. They were able to pinpoint the time because the watch on his broken arm had stopped. I always pictured him hurtling through the whiteness, glancing back over his shoulder to see if I was catching him up, losing the crucial split second he needed to avoid the suddenly looming obstacle.

'Why did you let him go . . . ?' my mother screamed at me when she saw the stretcher.

'. . . alone?' added my father.

They must have known that I couldn't have stopped him,

but they needed someone to blame and they couldn't blame Ross, because Ross was clearly going to die. And those who die young must always be heroes.

7

December 1997

TESS

On Christmas morning, I woke up to the distant clatter of saucepans. Leaping out of bed, I ran downstairs in my nightie and bare feet. In the kitchen, Mum was crouching down to look at the progress of the turkey through the glass door of the oven. She turned and smiled up at me. 'How was Midnight Mass?'

'I knew it couldn't be true!!' I was bursting with joy as I ran towards her, arms outstretched. Then I woke up, the cocoon of exquisite happiness shattered by crushing disappointment.

The room was dark, the blankets and pink candlewick bed-spread heavier than my duvet at home. The warm aroma of roasting turkey and distinctive clatter of someone cooking fil-tered up from the kitchen below. The O'Neills' guest room, I remembered.

I wondered how long my dream had lasted. Was it a few minutes, or just a second? How did the brain do that? How did the sleeping consciousness manage to construct a story to interpret the smells and sounds around it? And why did I have to wake up so soon? I closed my eyes tight, trying to conjure Mum back, but she'd gone.

Was this the sign? I suddenly thought.

Mum could have said anything, but she'd mentioned Mass.

Hope was sleeping in the twin bed an arm's length from mine.

'Happy Christmas, Tree!' she said, opening her eyes. 'Christmas Tree!' she repeated, delighted.

I don't think I ever saw Hope being sad. Obstinate, yes, angry for no reason, yes, but she'd always been like that. Sometimes I looked at my sister and I wondered whether she missed Mum at all. I didn't ask, because I wasn't going to introduce unhappiness if there was none. Sometimes I asked myself, if a five-year-old child can get over it, why can't you?

'How was Midnight Mass?' Mrs O'Neill said as we gathered in their living room to open presents.

'Same as usual,' said Doll, straight out.

She'd always been much better at lying than me, keeping it simple, gambling on getting away with it, rather than making up a narrative to explain our absence in case any of the congregation reported back on us.

I wondered if it was my guilt for going to the pub the previous evening instead of going to church that had subconsciously put the words into Mum's mouth? Her presence still felt so strong, I was strangely disorientated.

'Which ones are my presents?' asked Hope.

With money Dad had given me, I'd got Hope a CD player from him. I'd bought her a carol compilation. Santa Claus had got her a selection stocking, although he didn't actually visit our house or the O'Neills' because we didn't have chimneys: Hope was very literal-minded and the idea of a big man with a beard sneaking around at night frightened the life out of her.

I'd got Dad some Homer Simpson socks from Hope and a bottle of Jameson's from me, because that was the whiskey

Mum always used to buy him. Dad seemed pleasantly surprised, as if he hadn't expected anything.

Then it was my turn to open the gift of dangly earrings from Accessorize that I'd bought from Hope for me.

'Where's your present for Tree?' Hope asked Dad.

I probably should have realized I was meant to buy myself something from him too. I felt like an idiot for believing Mum's exclamations of surprise when she opened his gift of cheap perfume each year.

'Well now,' said my father, uncomfortably. 'I didn't really know what to get you, Tess, so you'll be better off getting something for yourself.'

He stood up, took the money clip out of his back pocket and peeled off first five, then, aware of Mrs O'Neill watching him, a further five ten-pound notes, which was generous, but I'd have preferred it if he'd thought of buying me a gift.

Mum always got me a diary, a normal A5 page-a-day from WHSmith which she customized with a fabric cover she embroidered with my name and the year. It was the first Christmas I hadn't received a diary since I was ten years old.

At lunch, there was a box of twelve crackers, which we never had at home because of the cost. After the shock of the initial bang, Hope became obsessed and went around the table insisting on pulling every single one, collecting up all the little gifts in the pink handbag Doll had bought her, but allowing us, after a small debate, to keep our tissue crowns.

'It's what Christmas is all about, children, isn't it?' Mr O'Neill remarked, on several occasions, as if to remind himself.

Mrs O'Neill made turkey with all the trimmings, with extra little sausages for Hope, and, for dessert, her very own Ice Cream Factory, which was a tub of soft-scoop Cornish and a selection of Smarties, jelly beans and chocolate buttons, because Mrs O'Neill had had enough little ones of her own to know that they didn't always like Christmas pudding.

In the afternoon, Dad and Mr O'Neill went to the pub and Hope settled down with Mrs O'Neill in front of the big TV to watch the Disney film. After Doll and I had done the washing-up, she suggested we go for a walk.

There was a pale, silver path across the water towards the wintry sun. When the colours were mistily muted like this, you could see why the town had attracted artists in its heyday, including Turner himself. Nowadays, most of the Victorian villas where well-to-do Londoners used to enjoy their holidays had become old folk's homes, or hostels for what everyone referred to as 'Care in the Community', a motley collection of addicts and people with mental-health problems who wandered around the town during the day. Dingy loops of tinsel hung in joyless windows.

There were a few other people out and about, walking off their lunch. Without the usual bleep and rattle of slot machines from the amusement arcades, my ears tuned into tiny snippets of conversation.

'Sad for those boys . . .' an older woman in a wheelchair said to the younger woman who was pushing her along.

'A tragedy . . .'

Were they talking about a bereavement of their own, I wondered, or the Royal Family's?

I guessed the two men in their thirties walking towards us were brothers who'd come home for Christmas. Or perhaps a gay couple? As they approached, one of them clocked Doll. So not gay. The other one was talking.

'. . . that's the thing about living the dream . . .' From the look of him – cheap jeans and a leather jacket the colour of diarrhoea – I didn't think things had worked out the way he'd hoped.

'What do you think the dream was?' I asked Doll.

'What dream?'

'Never mind.'

I'm always listening in to other people's conversations and making up stories in my head to explain their history. Mum was the same. We'd go for a cup of tea in a cafe on the seafront and we'd be having this perfectly normal chat, but when the couple at the next table left, we'd immediately start discussing everything we'd overheard: 'He's feeling guilty about something . . . I didn't believe him when he said he was sorry, did you? Do you think she was his bit on the side . . . ?'

Doll didn't really do that, because she usually had a lot to say herself.

We went down onto the beach. The tide was out and the sea was very calm, with waves no bigger than ripples of silk breaking over the flat, wet sand.

'Lapping with low sounds by the shore . . .'

'You what?' said Doll.

'It's from Mum's poem.'

'Oh.'

Was there a time limit on grief? Three months? Six? Even Doll wouldn't be patient for ever. Wasn't it time I 'came to terms with' or 'got over' it, or were these just phrases clung to by those who had never suffered a loss?

'In Italy, you visit your dead relatives on Christmas Day,' said Doll. 'There are flower stalls outside the cemeteries. It's kind of a nice idea, don't you think?'

I thought of Mum's grave, at the end of a row in the cemetery. Apparently, you had to let the earth settle before you put a headstone up, so we hadn't done that yet. I hated the thought of her lying there with people she didn't know, under a litter of dead flowers and rain-soaked teddy bears. On the next grave along there was a shiny black heart-shaped headstone bearing the message *All ways in our heart's* which Mum would have hated because she was very particular about spelling and punctuation. I should have gone today, I thought. It hadn't even occurred to me, because I didn't have any real sense she was there.

'. . . Fred says it's like including them in the party,' Doll continued.

'Fred?' I tuned back in.

'Fred Marinello. His dad's Italian.'

'Duh!'

What I was asking, and she knew I was asking, was, how come you're suddenly so familiar with Fred? I should explain that Fred had been the captain of the football team and the coolest boy in our year at school. At sixteen, he'd been given a contract by a local semi-professional football club, their young-est ever signing, and recently, it was rumoured, been scouted by Arsenal. The story had been front and back of the local newspaper under the banner *Fred for the Premiership?* Fred was the nearest thing the town had to a celebrity and every girl in our year fancied him.

Now that I thought about it, he'd been in the Crown the previous evening with a crowd of lads and I'd noticed Doll exchanging a few words on the way to the ladies and pointing back at me, as if to say, 'We're sitting over there.'

'He comes to the salon for a leg wax,' she said, breezily. 'Some of the Premiership players have them, apparently, for the aerodynamics.'

'Or a wind-up!' I laughed.

Doll didn't. She took her profession very seriously. She had wanted to be a beautician since she was five and got a doll for Christmas with hair that grew when you cut it. Being the baby of her family and the only girl, she'd been allowed to experi-ment with Mrs O'Neill's old stubs of lipstick and dried-up pots of eyeliner. On one occasion, when we were about seven, Doll had used me as her model, horrifying my mother, and causing our families to sit in different rows at Mass for several weeks.

'As a matter of fact,' Doll said, 'he's invited us to a New Year's Eve party.'

'Fred? Us?'

'Well, me, but I said could you come too.'

'Thanks, but no thanks,' I said.

'Oh, go on. If you're there, we'll be able to stay as long as we like. You know how my mum is.'

My mum had been slightly wary of Doll's influence on me, whereas Mrs O'Neill had always encouraged our friendship because I was the one who read books and knew what home-work we'd been given, and what you were supposed to bring in for cookery classes, that sort of thing.

'What about Hope?' I said, searching for an excuse. 'Dad's bound to want to go to the pub.'

'She can stay at ours, can't she?' Doll said.

'But I don't have anything to wear.'

'Now you sound like Cinderella.'

'So it's all arranged, is it?' I said.

'You shall go to the ball,' said Doll.

It was only when Fred Marinello opened the door on New Year's Eve that it clicked. Fred's smile like a sunlamp. He'd had crooked teeth as a child, but they'd recently been knocked out in a goal-mouth clash, so now he had a full row of even white caps.

His eyes travelled up and down Doll's body.

Then, as if he'd only just seen me behind her, 'Tess!'

I was as tall as Fred even in flats, and men like him didn't quite know how to deal with that.

'Sorry to hear about your mother,' he said. 'She was a nice lady. Your hair suits you like that, by the way.'

Usually I tied my long curly hair back to keep it under con-trol, but this afternoon Doll had insisted on straightening every strand and parting it at the side so that half of it fell across my face. When I moved my head, I could still detect a slightly scorched smell.

'Doll did it,' I said.

'Talented as well as beautiful . . .' Fred kissed Doll on the lips.

I felt pretty stupid. I was good at making up stories about the lives of people I'd never met, but I'd missed my best friend's first big romance. Recalling the conversation we'd had recently about The One, and all that stuff about Italian families, it had been obvious really.

'How long?' I asked Doll, in Fred's parents' bedroom where we left our coats and checked our teeth for lipstick smears in the dressing-table mirror.

'I wasn't sure if it was serious,' was Doll's excuse for not telling me.

'It's serious?'

'He calls me Maria D!'

'And you like that?'

It was what she was called when teachers took the register. To distinguish her from Maria Lourdes who was Maria L.

'I think it sounds more grown up,' said Doll, smoothing down her clinging black-lace dress.

I stared at my reflection. Standing next to Doll seemed to emphasize my height, because she was petite and perfect. On social occasions, I always felt self-conscious beside her, like a slightly censorious chaperone instead of a best friend. I was wearing black jeans and a red velvet top with a floppy kind of neckline at the front that made it look a bit fifties, and matching Ruby Gem lipstick from the palette of lip colours that had been Doll's Christmas gift to me. I sometimes felt I'd been born into the wrong era as far as fashion was concerned. With long legs and slim hips, I looked good in jeans or trousers, but my top half was two sizes bigger. A swimmer's build, my mum used to say, after one of the medallists at the Barcelona Olympics became a bit of a pin-up and went on to advertise cosmetics.

I couldn't work out whether the funny feeling I had was because I was jealous that Doll was moving on without me – not that I fancied Fred myself, and even if I had, he was way out of my league – or whether I was just annoyed with her for not telling me straight out. Was I acting so pathetic that my best friend didn't dare tell me she was going out with her dream boyfriend?

The people at the party were mostly from our school year, although there were a few additions who looked like they were probably footballers. As far as I was concerned, they divided into three basic groups. Those who knew about Mum, who mostly smiled at me, or said, 'How ARE you?' to which the only answer was 'Fine.' Then there were the people who didn't know about Mum, who asked how I was liking university, so I had to tell them, even though I didn't want to keep bringing it up. I decided that 'Thank you' was the best response when people said they were sorry, but that sounded like they'd said, 'I like your top,' or something. Then there were new people, but I wasn't confident enough to introduce myself to them.

My peers mostly had proper jobs now and were aspiring towards a mortgage and an interest-free dining suite, whereas I'd gone backwards, so far backwards that I was spending my days at the primary school we'd all been to.

'God, Mrs Corcoran, I was always terrified of her!' said Cerise McQuarry.

'I still am!'

We were drinking rosé cava in the kitchen. It was all cava in those days. Nobody had even heard of Prosecco.

'Lucky old Doll, eh?' said Cerise. 'The One Most Likely to Marry a Millionaire . . .'

'That's assuming Fred becomes a millionaire and they get married,' I said.

Cerise gave me that look I used to get a lot at school. She had been The One Most Likely to Be a Model, which is probably why she'd mentioned the yearbook, but for the time being, she was working behind the No 7 counter in Boots.

I'd been The One Most Likely to Be a Teacher, I suppose because I was a bit swotty and pedantic. Being a teacher was what Mum had wanted for me, but I'd never been sure. Even less so, now. The staffroom at St Cuthbert's was divided by a strict hierarchy. We teaching assistants sat together to eat our sandwiches, while the teachers sat up the other end moaning about the National Curriculum and the amount of work they had to do at home. It didn't sound like much of a life.

I've never been great at parties. If you're tall and shy, it's worse than being small and shy because when you're tall, people approach you with the assumption that you must be confident, so then if you're a bit tongue-tied, they think you're stand-offish. The other problem is that a lot of men are quite short, so they say things like, 'You're a big girl, aren't you?' which puts me on the defensive.

There was one guy here, however, who was so tall he had to duck when he moved from one room to another. Our fingers touched as we both went for the last sausage roll and then did this kind of 'You, no you, no really' thing. I wasn't even hungry, but looking at the food made it seem like I was doing something rather than just standing there on my own.

'Fred says you're Maria's friend?'

It took a moment.

'I call her Doll,' I said. 'Dolores, rather than the children's toy. Did you know Maria Dolores means "Mary of the Sorrows" . . .' I prattled on.

'Doesn't look very sorry now!' he said, glancing into the living room. 'I'm Warren, by the way.'

'And your connection is?'

'What? Oh, I'm the goalie.'

We had a dance and it was kind of nice to feel a great meaty hand round my waist and to get a proper kiss when the bongs went. Warren was so tall and built, he made me feel almost delicate and petite in his arms.

'Come on, get your coat!' he murmured into my neck.

'I don't think so, thank you very much!' I shrank away, prim as a nun.

'Did he honestly think that I was going to have sex with him after one snog?' I asked Doll on the way home.

Her silence spoke volumes.

'Oh my God, you and Fred? You're . . . ?' I said, feeling suddenly very sober. The reason I'd felt isolated at the party was nothing to do with Mum dying. They were all having sex. And I was still very much a virgin.

'Sorry, Tess,' Doll said.

She meant for not telling me.

I remembered when we'd first started thinking about boys we'd taken it in turns to practise our kissing technique on the mirror in Doll's bedroom, which was odd when you think about it, because something cold and flat was never going to approximate human lips, and you kept your eyes open to see how you were doing, which people in romantic clinches don't normally do.

Since then, Doll and I had both gone on dates, but nothing more serious than a milkshake on the seafront, or a movie. We'd always shared the extent of the physical contact, comparing love bites and how far we'd gone on a scale from one to ten, although, since neither of us had actually been 'all the way' it was sometimes difficult to calibrate the experience. What seemed like a five one year only felt like a two the next.

Now Doll had got to ten, and I probably wasn't even at six,

because I wasn't keen on boys touching my breasts, let alone down there.

'Is it nice?' I asked.

'It's bloody fantastic. Much better than I thought.'

'Do you love Fred?' I asked, feeling about twelve years old again.

'I think so,' said Doll. 'I can't believe it sometimes. Fred Marinello!'

It was a cold night. Our breath made clouds and our footsteps pinged on the pavement. I looked up at the dome of stars.

'Isn't it weird that there are thousands of couples who'll meet for the first time tonight?' I said. 'And some of them will last two weeks and some of them will still be together in twenty years' time, but none of them know right now . . .'

Doll looked at me as if I'd lost it.

'Warren's all right,' she said. 'He's in telesales.'

I wasn't thinking about Warren. I wasn't even thinking about me. It's just that sometimes when I'm looking at a clear night sky, with all those stars, the universe seems so vast and random, it's strange to think how our tiny little moments down on earth can hold so much significance.

'He's got a company car,' said Doll, as if that clinched it.

'Look, I know you think I'm choosy,' I said, 'but when Warren said, "Come on! Fred says you're in need of a good seeing-to!" it wasn't the most seductive line I'd ever heard.'

'Oops!' said Doll. 'Sorry!'

'I'm really happy about you and Fred, though,' I said, because I thought I was supposed to. 'I'm just a bit sad that I won't see so much of you. Which probably makes me a horrible selfish person!'

'That's two of us then!'

We laughed and, for a moment, we were back to normal, then we both went quiet again because it wasn't really as symmetrical as that.

*

You could hear Hope from down the street. Dad and Mr O'Neill had gone to the pub and Mrs O'Neill hadn't wanted the CD on again with Big Ben coming up.

'She does like her carols, doesn't she?'

Mrs O'Neill had brought up four boys as well as Doll, but I'd never seen her looking as worn out as she did after an evening with Hope.

'Shall I just take her home?' I suggested.

'At this time of night?' said Mrs O'Neill. 'When the guest room's all made up?'

I said Hope could have the CD player on in the bedroom, if she stopped carrying on and brushed her teeth and got into her pyjamas first. Just to make sure she behaved, I got into the other twin bed straight away, instead of having a Snowball with Doll and her mum.

The CD played all the way to 'In the Bleak Midwinter' before Hope finally fell asleep.

I lay on my back thinking about New Year's resolutions.

When I was young, I used to write them out in my best handwriting and tie them into little scrolls with coloured thread from Mum's sewing box, then hang them from the knobs on the chest of drawers in my bedroom.

I will always do the washing-up.

I will help Mum more.

I will save my pocket money.

I'd long since stopped writing them out, but I still made them in my head – everyone does, don't they? – but now I couldn't think of any.

A year ago, Mum and I had seen in the New Year together, with the silver tinsel tree twinkling, Jools's *Hootenanny* on the box and a small glass of Baileys. My resolutions had been pretty straightforward: to revise really hard for my A levels in order to get the grades for university; to save enough money

100

from my Saturday job at the One Stop to go travelling in the summer.

'What are yours?' I remembered asking her.

'Mine's always the same, Tess,' she'd replied. 'To be happy with everything I have.'

To be honest, I'd been exasperated with her, because I thought if Mum hadn't been so saintly, she could have made a bit more of herself. She was an intelligent woman, such a fast reader that she got through two or three library books every week. She could answer all the questions on *Who Wants to Be a Millionaire?* She could have done something better with her life.

Now, it occurred to me that I might have missed her meaning.

Did the fact that Mum had to *resolve* to be happy mean that she wasn't *actually* happy?

Had she not felt fulfilled in life?

Why hadn't we talked about all these things?

Why hadn't she told me what she was thinking, instead of giving me that infuriating smile that said, *You'll find out soon enough*?

Why, when she could have said anything, did she ask whether I'd been to Midnight Mass?

And what was I supposed to deduce from a bloody butterfly?

I turned my face to the wall in a silent howl, my shoulders heaving as hot tears cascaded down my cheeks. Curled up like a baby, my legs scrunched up to my chest, I sobbed and sobbed, until I could almost feel Mum bending over me concerned, like she did when I was little and had a temperature.

In *Truly, Madly, Deeply*, which Doll had rented one Friday mistaking it for a straightforward romcom, Juliet Stevenson had cried so hard that Alan Rickman came back from the dead to be with her.

But there was no cool, damp flannel for my forehead, no soothing 'There, there! You'll feel better soon, I promise.'

In the slight chill of a room where no one usually slept, I yearned for Mum so much, my heart literally ached.

'It's not that I can't cope,' I told her silently. 'It's just that I miss you being there when we come home from school because the house feels so empty. I miss talking to you in the kitchen and I miss not talking because we're both eavesdropping. I just miss you so much, Mum! It's not the same when you're not here . . .'

I suddenly thought how sad she would be to see me like this, crying my eyes out and making Mrs O'Neill's pillows all wet.

'I'm sorry, Mum,' I said.

And I could almost hear her reply: 'I'm sorry too, Tess. It's not what I wanted either, you know.'

8

December 1997

GUS

Ross died at midday on New Year's Eve.

The decision was etched on my parents' faces that morning, though they didn't tell me. If I'd asked, would they have allowed me to be in the room? I didn't because it felt like something private between them and him. They'd brought him into the world and spent five years with him before I ever came along. I would only be in the way. So I didn't get a chance to say goodbye, because nobody wanted to face up to what was about to happen. 'Passed away' is so much easier than 'switched off'. It would have been an empty farewell anyway, since he was brain dead. The only difference I could detect when I was called in was that the machines had stopped whooshing and bleeping. The room was totally silent. I was glad he'd gone while it was still light, rather than just before midnight with fireworks going off and cars sounding their horns in the street outside.

We all flew home a couple of days later in a plane full of hungover skiers except for the one empty seat next to me. Following long deliberation, my parents decided to cremate what was left of his body after the organs had been donated, and scatter the ashes at sea. Ross had always loved the sea.

He'd always talked about trying to set a record for rowing the Atlantic.

Exactly a year later, on New Year's Eve, my parents and I set off to Lymington to catch the ferry to the Isle of Wight. We were silent, the beating of the windscreen wipers marking time as the tyres sloshed through the surface water on the M3. Next to me on the back seat lay a large bouquet of white lilies.

Dad had it in mind that we'd row out into the bay in the little clinker boat that came with the coastguard's cottage we always used to rent for the summer, and drop the flowers in the same area of the bay that we'd scattered the ashes the previous spring. But when we stopped outside the cottage, it was raining so hard and the wind was so strong, it felt as if someone was throwing giant buckets of water at the car, rocking it with the force of the gusts. Through the steamed-up windows, it was impossible to distinguish where the meadow ended and the sea began.

Midday passed with us all hoping for a sudden miraculous break in the weather. Nobody said anything. After waiting for a good hour with no sign of it letting up, my father suddenly turned on the ignition and drove us back to Yarmouth, his fury at the failure of the mission as overpowering in the confined interior of the BMW as the scent of the lilies.

'How about we drop them over the side of the ferry?' he finally suggested as we approached the town.

'Why don't we go to the little jetty by the pub instead?' said my mother, glancing round to enlist my support. 'Where you used to go crabbing?'

As we made our sorry little procession down the slippery boardwalk under a golf umbrella that didn't cover all of us, I wondered why Ross couldn't have a normal grave in a place that was already sad instead of turning this whole island, with its sunny childhood memories of sandcastles and ice cream, into a rainy place where we could never be happy again.

At the end of the jetty, Mum struggled with the crackly florist's cellophane on the lilies before finally ripping it off and passing it back to me to hold while the two of them performed the flower throwing.

'One, two, three!'

Their eyes were closed as they hurled, as if they were making a wish. The bouquet plopped onto the water. We stood watching it bob about, pelted by the rain. I found myself willing it not to sink, because that would somehow feel wrong, and yet not be washed inshore by the swell in case we had to go through the whole ritual again. After a couple of minutes, I thought perhaps it would be better if it did sink, because we were never going to leave unless something happened.

My mother finally sighed and said, with a fond smile in her voice, 'I bet he's gone twice round the world already.'

'I bet he has!' my father agreed heartily.

Even Ross's ashes were adventurous and heroic.

They both turned and stared at me as if they'd forgotten I was there.

They'd have preferred it to be me, Ross.

Of course they would.

We drove home in silence.

My mother went straight upstairs. My father poured himself a Scotch and switched on the Hogmanay celebrations.

In my room, I lay staring at the black window, remembering how I used to listen to the murmur of grown-ups at my parents' cheese-and-wine parties downstairs, or my father's sporadic guffawing at Ross's stories as they shared a single-malt whisky or two. Now, only the splashes of canned laughter from the show on television blotted my mother's stifled sobbing in Ross's room next door.

I opened the window, sticking my face out into the cold, still air, amazed at how dark and silent it was now that the rain had stopped. In London, it never got properly dark; there was always a fine orange gauze over the night sky. I thought about Bonfire Night and Lucy's face all golden as she gazed up with child-like wonder at shimmering palms of iridescence in the sky. In London, it was never completely quiet. There was always the rumble of an Underground train or the nerve-jangling shriek of a car alarm.

As my ears adjusted to the silence, I became aware of the slight reverberation of party music from some distant home. It stopped for the countdown to midnight; a faraway crowd of strangers shouting, 'Five, Four, Three, Two, One!' amid a dis-cordant blast of party hooters; a confident first line of 'Auld Lang Syne' trailing away into the base thump of dance music.

The sky was now clear. There were probably millions of people in the world gazing up at the twinkling universe, fixing resolutions on the stars.

Closing the window, I rifled through my bag until I found the piece of paper on which Lucy had written her number, then I ran downstairs and dialled it before I could change my mind.

'Who's calling?' the woman asked.

I could hear a buzz of people celebrating in the background.

'Gus,' I said, trying to keep my voice as quiet as possible, so there was no chance of my parents overhearing.

I thought I heard her say, 'It's him!' Then Lucy was on the line.

'Happy New Year!' I said.

'Happy New Year!'

There was a slight pause, then we both spoke at once.

'You know we said about meeting . . .'

'Look, d'you fancy meeting . . . ?'

Nervous laughter.

'OK if I come tomorrow?'

*

The familiar shape of Lucy's duffle coat and her beaming face when she spotted me walking down the platform towards her brought life streaming back into my blood. I'd told my parents I'd decided to go back to London early so that I could revise. It felt satisfyingly rebellious, as if I was running away from home.

Lucy drove us to the seafront. It had only been two weeks since we had seen each other, but she was full of news. Bright, happy, normal news about going to a school reunion to pick up her A-level certificates, and shopping with her sister at the sales in Bluewater, and the pantomime they'd taken her little niece Chloe to at the Winter Gardens in Margate, where they'd had to leave at the interval because the child was terrified by the dame.

I told her about my trips to the National Theatre, which seemed a long time ago now.

'On your own? Wasn't that a bit strange?'

'I suppose so,' I admitted. 'Maybe we could go together sometime?'

'Definitely,' she said.

We parked in one of the narrow little streets that led down to the beach. She handled the car with enviable confidence, backing into a tight space right next to the kerb.

'So how was your Christmas?' she asked.

I didn't have any funny stories like her Granny Cynthia, who apparently suffered from mild dementia, pouring the water jug over the Christmas pudding to put out the flames.

'Quiet,' I said.

It wasn't like the seaside I knew. On the Isle of Wight, there was fine pale sand, like caster sugar, but here it was coarse and dark, like builders' sand, and shelved so steeply into the Channel that it was a struggle to keep a footing. We had to dig in the edges of our trainers to stay upright. The first time Lucy slid away from me down the slope I grabbed her gloved hand to pull her back up and let go as soon as she was stable again. The second time, I kept her hand in mine as we climbed up to the promenade high above the beach.

'Let's get a coffee!' I suggested as we passed the window of a retro Italian cafe.

The steamy warmth inside relaxed the tension.

'This place is famous for its ice cream,' Lucy said, then ordered a hot chocolate for herself.

'I'll have a Knickerbocker Glory,' I told the waitress, then saw Lucy was laughing. 'What? I love ice cream!'

'You're so . . .' She searched for a word.

'Stupid?'

'Original.' Lucy chose the word carefully.

'Is that all right?' I asked.

'It's lovely!' she reassured me, then blushed, as if she'd said too much.

'You're lovely,' I heard myself saying.

My hand stretched across the pink Formica table. She had taken her gloves off but her fingers felt cold. I kneaded them gently in mine, releasing her hand quickly when the waitress returned with our order.

Lucy sipped her tall glass mug, then replaced it on the table.

'What's wrong?'

'The cream on top is fluffy, but the liquid underneath is boiling . . .'

'Did you burn your mouth?'

'A little.'

'Have some ice cream.'

I gouged out a quenelle of vanilla and offered it across the table on the long spoon. She hesitated before opening her lips for it. I felt a twitch of arousal in my groin as she took the whole spoonful and dabbed at the corners of her mouth with a paper napkin.

'Better?' I asked.

'Yes, thank you, doctor!'

The silence that followed was charged with unspoken thoughts as I delved and swallowed and she stirred her drink, spoon clinking occasionally against glass.

'We could go back to my house, if you like,' she said.

'OK,' I said, cautiously, wondering if jeans and a checked shirt were suitable for meeting her family.

'My parents are taking Granny Cee back to Rye.'

'Rye?' I repeated.

'She's in a home. Just outside Rye.'

'That's quite a drive, isn't it?' I wasn't really talking about the distance.

'About an hour and a half. They'll stay for tea.' Nor was she.

Lucy carried on stirring her hot chocolate.

'Why don't I put some more ice cream in that? Cool it down?'

She giggled. 'You're funny . . .'

I knew I wasn't very funny, or original, for that matter, but in her company, I felt as if I was all right, as if my frozen emotions were gradually beginning to thaw.

The family home was in a leafy private estate on the outskirts of town. A large detached house with mock-Tudor features, half-timbered gables and a stained-glass crest in the front door, it was built in an era when land was plentiful and people who could afford places like this expected a decent garden, front and back. There was a Volvo parked on the semicircular drive as we pulled in, making me fear that something had prevented her parents from going to Rye. Lucy read my mind. The car was her mother's, she told me. They'd gone in her father's Audi. The Renault Clio we were in was shared with her middle sister.

'How many sisters do you have?' I asked, finding it increasingly difficult to make small talk in the anticipation of what might be about to happen.

'Two. The oldest, Helen, is married and has Chloe and a

baby on the way. The middle one, Pippa, is in Canada at the moment.'

'Are you close?'

'We're all very different, but we get on quite well. I can't imagine what it's like being on your own . . .' Lucy gave me such a searching look that I wondered if she'd guessed.

I'd never directly lied to her about Ross, but I knew this was an opportunity to correct the mis-impression, possibly the last chance that I would have and still get away with it.

I said nothing.

Ironically, Ross used to say I was a hopeless liar because I couldn't come up with excuses quickly enough. Back then, my silences had given me away. Now they seemed to make me a little bit mysterious and unknowable.

'No wonder you're so . . .' Lucy searched for the right word.

I hoped she wasn't going to say 'spoilt'. That's what only children were usually called, wasn't it?

'Self-contained.'

The spacious hall was littered with bright plastic children's toys. A ride-along yellow horse with a blue mane towered like a giant over the scattering of much smaller farm and zoo animals.

'Mum looks after my niece two days a week,' Lucy said. 'So Helen can work part-time.'

'What does Helen do?'

'She's a GP.'

Lucy's father was a GP, her mother a health visitor, one sister a GP, the other training to be a physiotherapist. I imagined how eager my father would be to impress in this set-up.

'Coffee?' Lucy asked.

I followed her into a large kitchen diner, which, unlike ours, was filled with all the paraphernalia a happy family generates – unmatching fridge magnets with lists, taxi cards and children's drawings; opened boxes of cereal on the table; a bowl of cat food and one of water on the floor.

'Excuse the mess,' she said. 'I didn't know you'd be coming back.'

'I like it.'

She looked at me as if I was joking. The whoosh of water filling the kettle seemed inordinately loud.

I jumped as I felt something furry around my legs and looked down to see a large ginger cat.

'That's Marmalade. He doesn't normally like strangers! Do you have any pets?

'I had a guinea pig when I was little, but a fox got him.'

'Oh!' Lucy's face fell and I kicked myself for putting a downer on things.

We seemed to have gone back to square one. Or maybe even further than that, as if we had just met and were struggling to make conversation.

'Coffee or tea?'

'Coffee. Please.'

The jar of instant coffee on the counter had only one serving left. Lucy stretched to get another from the cupboard above.

'Here, let me . . .'

One moment I was behind her, my arm reaching for the jar, the next, she had turned to face me, and we were kissing, and, with my eyes tight closed, all I could hear was the bubbling of the kettle as the water heated to boiling point, and then clicked off.

She tasted of chocolate. All I wanted to do was kiss and kiss her again, cupping her face in my hands, inhaling the lemon scent of her shiny hair. At first, she stood with arms passively by her side, but as I drew away to look at her, she placed her hands softly on the small of my back at the precise spot that made me squirm and harden with pleasure.

Then she took my hand and led me out of the kitchen.

I wanted to kick aside the toys and do it on the parquet floor of the hall; on the carpeted stairs, the edges pressing into our backs; on the landing, the two of us reflected in the full-length mirror on the wall.

'I haven't got any . . .' I stuttered, as she opened a door with a little painted china plaque saying *Lucy's room*.

'It's OK. I'm on the Pill,' she whispered.

The statement was so clinical and unexpected, the spontaneity vanished, along with my erection.

All sorts of questions were racing around my head as I watched Lucy undress, folding each item in a neat pile on the stool of her dressing table. I had assumed that, like me, she was a virgin, with no one to compare me to. Had she planned this, and if so, for how long? And why hadn't I known? Or had she been having sex with other people? Not Toby, surely?

When she was down to a bra and panties, she lifted the corner of her duvet and got into bed and then I wished that I had undressed with her, because now she was looking at me. I turned away, took off my shirt, jeans and socks, and got into bed with my boxers still on. It was a single bed. There was no way we could lie without touching, but neither of us dared move.

My feet were sticking out. She was completely motionless. How weird we would look if someone walked in now! Had she changed her mind? Or was she waiting for me? In the kitchen, my need had been so urgent, I could barely hold myself together. Now, I didn't know how to begin.

'Nervous?'

'Yes.'

I wondered why we were whispering. We were the only people in the house.

'Have you ever done it before?' she asked.

'Not really . . .'

112

'What does that mean?'

'It means no,' I admitted.

Her laughter loosened the grip of my fear.

'Me neither.'

'We're medical students,' I said. 'We should know about anatomy and stuff. Tell you what . . .' I propped myself up on my elbow, '. . . shall I examine you?'

'OK . . .' she agreed, uncertainly.

'Just relax, and tell me does this hurt?' I kissed her ear.

'No!' She laughed again.

'How about this?' I kissed her shoulder.

'No!'

'And this?'

I kissed the top of her breast.

'That's nice,' she sighed.

'Let's have a better look.'

I pulled the duvet down an inch to expose the lacy edge of her bra, then kissed her there. She smiled and closed her eyes.

I burrowed under the duvet, my tongue travelling down the centre of her belly towards the elastic of her panties, and I kissed her there just above the line of her pubic hair.

Suddenly her arms and legs were around me, her mouth on mine, as we grappled to get naked. As I closed my eyes and felt her opening for me, I remembered her face in the light of the bonfire, all golden with wonder, and fireworks started exploding in my head.

Afterwards, we lay in each other's arms, skin against skin, breathing each other's breath. My eyes took in the neatness and girliness of her room. The curtains had a pattern of old-fashioned pink roses, the white dressing table matched the white fitted cupboards; on the pink carpet, there was a pair of oversized slippers in the form of two fluffy grey rabbits.

Lucy followed my gaze. 'Christmas present. Actually, they're really warm!'

'Hope they don't breed . . .'

She giggled.

'How long have you been on the Pill?' I asked, before I could stop myself.

'Two months.'

Two months! I tried to think back. November. Bonfire Night.

'Helen said if I wanted to, I should be prepared.'

She'd discussed it with her older sister!

'With me?' As soon as I asked, I realized that there was no way she was going to say, 'No, with someone else.'

'Of course with you, silly!'

'I wish I'd known!'

'Did you want to?'

I smiled and gave her a squeeze.

'Sure did.'

'When?'

'From the first moment I saw you,' I told her, which sounded like the sort of thing Ross would have said.

Was it true, I wondered, as we started kissing again? Or had I just said it to make her happy?

Our second time was more exploratory and sustained, and left us in a dreamy drift of satisfaction, unaware of time passing.

When we suddenly noticed that it had become dark outside and her parents would soon be back, it was a race to get dressed and out of the building.

Lucy drove me to the station and I had to run for the train to London.

Tomorrow, we decided, breathlessly, between kisses, she would come back too. We would revise for the January exams together.

She ran along the platform as the train pulled away, holding my hand for as long as she could, before letting go and waving.

'I can't wait to do some more *revision*!' I called.

From then on, it would be our special code word.

I sat in the carriage staring out into the night, the heater blowing ineffectively around my feet. I could still smell Lucy on my skin and feel her in my groin, and when I closed my eyes, I could still hear her sharp little breaths. In the rattling, draughty compartment, life suddenly felt bearable. The reflection of a face in the window smiled at me, and, for a moment, I didn't recognize myself.

PART TWO

9

1998

GUS

'You've struck gold!'

My friend Marcus and I, sitting at an outside table in the beer garden of the Gloucester Arms, watched Lucy, in a denim miniskirt and pink vest, disappear inside the pub to get another round.

For some unfathomable reason – Marcus didn't say this, but I knew it was what he was thinking – this near-perfect example of femininity had fallen for me. His undisguised approval made me even prouder of my girlfriend, not just because of her pretty face and great body but because of the attentive way she'd been drawing him out about his course and his life in Bristol, where he was reading Law. His university experience seemed to have a lot to do with debating societies and drinking. The tongue-tied boy I knew had become almost chatty in response to her questions.

After depositing two more pints in front of us, Lucy left us to spend the evening together. She'd arranged to go to a movie with a couple of her girlfriends.

'I'm sure you've got lots of catching up to do,' she said.

We both watched her walking away, her hair bright gold in the early-evening sunshine.

Inside the pub, the World Cup semi-final was on a big screen, the air suddenly full of cheering. We craned our necks to see who had just scored a goal. One all.

'Do you think it'll go to penalties?' Marcus asked.

'It's a possibility.'

'Brazil have to win, don't they?'

'You'd think so.'

Our friendship was founded on shared reticence rather than conversation. Both more naturally inclined to observe than participate, we'd met at the back of the dinner queue our first day at boarding school, sized each other up and discovered that we were both Arsenal supporters, although we'd quickly learned not to celebrate that allegiance in public. At our school, football was for chavs and wusses; real men played rugby. On the field, my speed and Marcus's skills helped us avoid the worst of the mauling. In the dormitory and showers, we looked out for each other and weighed in on each other's behalf. The fact that my big brother was Head Boy that year had offered me no protection from random violence. Ironically, Ross was always an enthusiastic proponent of the what-doesn't-kill-you-makes-you-stronger philosophy. As in most male friendships, there was always an element of friendly rivalry between Marcus and me. Assessing him with the benefit of a year's distance, I suspected I'd grown up more than he had. As sixth-formers, we'd envisaged wild student parties where females would roll into bed with us and roll out again in the cold light of morning when they saw the mistake they'd made. Now I started sentences with 'we' and knew about clitoral stimulation, and not just from my textbooks. I gathered that Marcus's Ibiza relationship hadn't been a great success, and though he'd slept with a couple of girls since, he had yet to find a serious girlfriend and still called sex 'shagging'.

Medics are renowned for playing as hard as they work, but Lucy and I were ridiculously middle-aged. Almost every Saturday morning, I awoke to find her handing me a mug of coffee before squeezing back into the narrow bed and giving me a kiss that tasted of toothpaste. Lucy did sex like she did most things, with a lot of thorough research. All the magazine articles she had read on the subject advised talking openly about what you liked, so we had become fairly expert at giving each other pleasure. Occasionally, Lucy asked if I had any fantasies, and I always said I was happy with things just the way they were because I was sure that was the correct answer.

Obviously, I didn't tell Marcus any of this.

For his second year, Marcus had made plans to rent a house with a bunch of guys from his hall; Lucy and I were going to be sharing a flat.

'So, it is lurve?' Marcus asked a little wearily.

Lucy and I called sex 'making love'. We were allowed to say things like 'I love how that feels' or 'I loved this evening' or even 'I love you when you're funny/silly/serious'. However, the words 'I love you' on their own remained unspoken, as if they had the power to cast an irrevocable spell on us. Once, I thought I heard her breathe the words over a particularly undulating orgasm, but I wasn't sure and could hardly ask for clarification.

'Whatever "lurve" means!' I replied, trying to show Marcus that I was cool about it.

The truth was that I didn't know if I loved Lucy. I liked her enormously. She was very easy to be with and cared about me much more than anyone else in my life ever had, noting things I said, even tiny inconsequential things like preferring crunchy peanut butter to smooth. Perhaps that was a girl thing? I didn't know because she was my first girlfriend. I felt constantly surprised and fortunate that she was interested in me. Was that

121

love? In the ensuing silence, Marcus and I both took long, serious gulps of our lager.

'I haven't told Lucy about Ross,' I suddenly confessed.

I couldn't work that one out either. Was it really because I didn't want her to get all sympathetic and insist on talking about it? Or was I harbouring some irrational fear that Ross still had the power to ruin the things I treasured, like my selection as Lower School goalkeeper, which I'd had to relinquish when he dislocated my shoulder, and Toffee, my guinea pig, whose hutch he'd 'accidentally' left open.

Marcus considered the statement for so long I was beginning to wonder whether he'd actually heard. Then he finally said, 'No reason to, I suppose.'

The relief was immense.

'A new chapter for you.'

'Yes.'

'Ross was such a psycho,' said Marcus. 'RIP, obviously.'

The match had gone to penalties.

Conversation was suspended while we watched Brazil go through to the final.

'You still playing squash?' I asked.

'Yup. You still running?'

'Every morning.'

My usual route – and it was important to have a usual route so that thinking didn't intrude on the meditative vacuum that running delivered – took me down through the grimy main streets of Camden, up Parkway, and through the gate into the quiet paradise of Regent's Park. In winter, frost on the grass, a pinkish tinge to the dawn sky, the delicate structures of trees, blurred by my misty breath, gave the landscape the feel of an Impressionist painting. In spring, I found myself noticing smaller-scale beauty like the stone urns, spilling over with tulips, in the formal Italian gardens near the Euston Road, and the wax-like petals of magnolia blossom. Summer brought swags of roses on the pergolas of the Inner Circle, which my route circumnavigated before a long straight sprint across the fields, past the giraffe houses of the zoo, over the canal and back across the lower slope of Primrose Hill.

On sunny days, cafe owners would be setting out tables and chairs along the wide, curving street which took me back to the railway bridge. It was one of those chichi areas of London where traditional businesses could no longer compete with the demand for coffee and fresh, delicious food. Over the course of the year, I'd watched a launderette being gutted, renovated and reinvented as an Italian canteen.

One day the owner, who'd done most of the work himself, was struggling on a ladder as I passed. I stopped and offered to help steady the sign, which said *PIATTINI*. Since then we'd exchanged a friendly *buon giorno!* as he chalked up the day's specials on a folding blackboard. The descriptions were unadorned – *polenta con funghi trifolati, salsiccia al finocchio, granita alla mandorla* – the smells filtering out from the kitchen, mouth-watering.

The day I noticed the words *WAITER REQUIRED* above the menu, I ran past, as usual, then stopped, turned, and ran back. Salvatore gave me an evening's trial after which he paid me for the hours I'd worked and asked if I'd like a job. I think I was probably prouder of that achievement than I was of passing my first-year exams.

'So you're staying in London for the summer?' Marcus asked.

'That's the plan.'

The flat Lucy had found for us became available at the end of the academic year, and now that I had a job, I wouldn't have to go home at all.

'How are your parents doing?'

'OK, I think.'

I called them every fortnight or so. Since I was last home, my father had re-tiled the downstairs cloakroom and installed a movement-sensitive security system, both projects, I suspected, designed to keep his mind from thinking about more intractable problems. My mother had taken up quilting. When they asked me if everything was going well, I said yes. The only way I could imagine of giving them any small pleasure was to qualify as a doctor. A photo of me in a mortar board on the living-room mantelpiece would be something to show their friends. Left to my own devices, I probably would have foundered under the pressure of the course, but Lucy made sure we both stuck to the work, nagging me to keep my portfolio up to date, and helping me with my reflections on practice.

'It's not a philosophy essay,' she said, when I was making a meal of it. 'All they want to know is what you could have done better. You're training to cure sick people, not change their lives.'

'What about you?' I asked Marcus. 'Do you have any plans?'

'I was thinking of Interrailing,' Marcus said, with a shrug that made me realize that was why he'd come to see me. For a moment I was tempted by the thought of going back to Italy, enjoying the holiday we hadn't managed the previous year. But the need to earn my own money was more pressing. Though my parents never mentioned the cost of my education, I was determined to be as independent as I could.

Lucy gave Marcus a hug when we saw him off at Paddington station. As he turned to offer me a formal handshake, I half-wished men were allowed to hug too. I had male friends at college, like Toby, although we'd seen each other less since Lucy and I got together, and Jonathan, the serious guy I'd met on the interview day, who I sometimes went for a drink with when he wasn't playing chess, but there was no one who knew me like Marcus. Nash was the closest I got to a confidante, but my friendship with her made Lucy uncomfortable. The most critical thing I ever heard Lucy say about Nash was that she was 'a bit much'; Nash was far more explicit, especially when drunk, accusing me of settling for the easy option of someone who didn't challenge me, to which my answer was, 'And your problem with that is?'

Which riled her all the more, although, somehow, we always ended up laughing a lot.

The flat was on the seventh floor of a big block on a council estate between Camden and Euston Road. The location, only ten minutes' walk from the hospital, was convenient, and we had a view north and eastwards over the mainline out of Euston, and beyond towards Camden, Gospel Oak and Hampstead Heath. At first, the grim, graffitied, concrete wasteland felt forbidding, but once we became familiar with the routes in and out, it didn't feel quite so much like a war zone.

Lucy and I took one of the bedrooms, her friends Harriet and Emma, the other two. Until university, I'd never been exposed to the company of women, but found it generally more agreeable than the all-male environment at school. There, my reluctance to join in initiation rituals, such as tea bagging, where you took another man's scrotal sac in your mouth, had been condemned as effeminacy; in the flat, I only had to be watching *Final Score* on Saturday afternoon to be considered unequivocally male.

We all shared household duties, with me volunteering to take the rubbish down (before learning how often the lift would be broken) and do the communal shopping once a week. I took to the role, searching out the cheapest places for staples like milk and toilet rolls, trawling Inverness Street market for bargains on Saturday afternoons when the stalls were packing up.

Under the tutelage of Stefania, Salvatore's wife and the chef at Piattini – where I continued working at weekends – I developed an interest in cooking.

125

'How many tomatoes can four people eat?' Lucy asked when I'd arrived back with a crate that cost me a pound.

But she had to admit that roasted with a little olive oil they made a delicious pasta sauce, especially with a little Parmesan cheese grated over the top.

I began to look forward to the methodical rhythm of washing and chopping vegetables, stirring, sipping, tasting and creating something delicious, like *ribollita*, from a few raw ingredients. It was a good way of winding down at the end of a day of hospital rounds, cheaper and more nutritious than buying ready meals or takeaways, and it was something I could do for all my flatmates to compensate for their efficiency with all the other household chores, like hoovering and cleaning the bathroom, which were done before I'd got round to noticing they needed to be.

In October, when my parents, who were curious about my 'living arrangements', announced that they were coming up to London for the day and asked me to book a restaurant for Sunday lunch – 'somewhere decent, you couldn't afford yourself' – I surprised them by instead serving *porchetta* stuffed with fennel, chilli and garlic, accompanied by rosemary-roast potatoes, and a crisp salad.

'This is really very good, Lucy!'

My father was doing that embarrassing-dad thing of trying to flirt with her.

'It's all down to Gus,' she told him. 'I'm useless in the kitchen!'

'Gus?' said my mother. 'Well, this is a surprise. A lovely surprise!'

It wasn't clear whether she meant my name, the evidence of my heterosexuality, or my cooking. The swell of childish pride I felt in finally demonstrating a talent Ross had never displayed, was immediately followed by a wave of dread that she would make the comparison out loud instead of inside her

126

head. She didn't. The day was a success. But not one I wanted to repeat.

'Your parents are nice,' Lucy said afterwards.

Your parents. I'd introduced them as 'my mother' and 'my father' rather than Caroline and Gordon. I wasn't even sure whether Caroline and Gordon would have been acceptable to them.

'Do you think they liked me?' Lucy asked.

I didn't know if they even liked me.

'I'm sure they did. They're just not the type who express affection very much.'

I'd never really thought about why that was. Perhaps, as only children themselves, they hadn't needed to; perhaps as people who had risen to the middle class from fairly ordinary backgrounds, they weren't sure how they were supposed to behave.

'You're not like them,' Lucy said.

'That's a relief,' I said, glad that her curiosity had been satisfied without the need to take her home to our chilly, lifeless house.

Lucy's parents were used to their daughters having boyfriends and treated me with exactly the right balance of fondness and suspicion. Lucy's mother, who instructed me to call her Nicky straight away, was warm and hospitable. When cooking, she always made a point of asking my opinion about how much spice to put in a curry or how long to give a piece of meat. When I jumped up to help clear the table, she'd say how nice it was to meet a man who didn't think that washing up was putting the saucepans in the sink and leaving them there to soak. Lucy's father, on the other hand, never told me to call him Bill. His circumspect frown always made me behave slightly clumsily, trailing my sleeve in my cereal bowl or tripping over a rake when I was helping him clear the leaves from the lawn.

Theirs was a more informal household than I was used to, where you could sleep in on Sunday if you wanted and make yourself toast at any time of day. When Nicky asked me if I'd like to join them for Christmas, I leapt at the invitation with almost unseemly enthusiasm, telling my parents that I was working in the restaurant until late Christmas Eve making it impractical to visit them, which was actually true, although I probably could have got the time off.

Lucy's family did a jokey Secret Santa before lunch. My gift was a pair of those huge soft-toy slippers in the shape of Gromit; the one I picked out for Lucy's older sister Helen, after much deliberation, was a soap-bubble-making machine, which delighted her little girl, Chloe. Helen was the sister I was least keen on. She had that cool, detached GP's way of appraising you that made you feel as if she'd seen symptoms she didn't much like the look of. When I'd told her once, only half-joking, that I didn't think I'd want to be a GP because I couldn't see myself sitting on my own and being confident enough to diagnose even a common cold, she informed me, humour-lessly, that most colds are caused by a virus and there isn't much you can do about them except advise the patient to keep well hydrated until their immune system does its job.

'But what about the one in a thousand cases that might turn to meningitis?'

'We all worry about that.'

'The thing is,' I said, 'I can't see myself ever able to make a decision about the nine hundred and ninety-nine—'

'You will when you've got thirty of them sitting reading dog-eared copies of *Hello!* in the waiting room,' she said, briskly. 'Never a good idea to over-think these things.'

The middle sister Pippa was much more fun: slightly flus-tery and inclined to take offence, but also quick to show affection. Compared to the other two, she was a bit of a rebel. Having suffered from bulimia in her teenage years – in a family full of doctors, this is the sort of thing they talked about at table – she now kept herself stick-thin by smoking surreptitious cigarettes at the end of the garden. She was the 'needy' one, according to those labels families often hang around their children's necks.

'What does that make Lucy then?' I'd asked Nicky when I felt our relationship was well enough established to get involved in such conversations.

'Lucy's the no-trouble-at-all one,' she told me.

'Probably because I've always had everyone looking after me,' Lucy said.

'See what I mean?' said Nicky.

In truth, Lucy could be a bit needy too. For instance, when I recounted anecdotes about the customers at Piattini, she'd always say, with a little moue, 'I think you like that job better than being a medical student.'

And I'd have to assure her, no, I like being a medical student (code for: I like being with you); it's just that, in a restaurant, you get a glimpse into the lives of all kinds of people with all kinds of different stories.

'You do in hospital,' she pointed out.

'Yes, but they're all ill!'

Lucy often thought I'd said something funny when I hadn't actually intended to.

We ate our Christmas lunch in the middle of the day with paper crowns on our heads, passing gravy and bowls of vegetables up and down the table, helping ourselves to cranberry sauce straight from a jar. I pictured my parents in the silent dining room dutifully eating their smoked-salmon starter with the correct cutlery and felt a horrible pang of guilt.

After lunch, the adults sat in the living room around the roaring fire opening our proper Christmas presents. After a lot of indeterminate searching, I'd found what I thought was the perfect gift for Lucy. We'd been to the Christmas fancy-dress party at the Union dressed as Sandy and Danny from *Grease*. Lucy looked great with her hair pulled up into a ponytail, wearing a fifties dress with a white plastic belt that she'd found in a charity shop. Everyone said so. When I saw a real fifties handbag on the arm of a mannequin wearing a similar dress in the window of a shop selling American vintage clothes in Neal Street, I'd paid more than I'd budgeted for it.

Without the dress to give it context, however, the white handbag looked more junk than vintage, the purse clasp at the top slightly rusty, the plasticized fabric brittle and cracked at the corners. As I struggled to explain my thought process, Pippa was unable to contain a little burst of laughter and Helen looked at me as if I'd brought in something nasty on my shoe.

'I love it!' said Lucy, loyally, carefully returning it to its wrapping and handing me the heavy package with my name on the gift tag.

Inside was a sketchpad, some drawing pencils and a wooden box of watercolours.

It was a gift that exactly reflected her generous and practical nature. Lucy wasn't interested in art herself – at the couple of exhibitions we'd been to together, she'd very quickly started glancing at her watch – but she knew I liked painting and was keen to encourage me.

'Gus wanted to be an artist when he was little,' she announced to the family.

'I can't imagine Gus being little,' said Helen.

'I can, he's got a very boyish face,' said Pippa.

'Who's Gus?' asked Granny Cee.

'Come on, then, draw something!' Pippa challenged me.

So, with the whole family watching, albeit in a friendly rather than a critical way, I sketched Marmalade, who was asleep in front of the fire.

'But that's really good!' Lucy exclaimed, when I turned the sketchpad round.

I wasn't sure whether to be flattered or a little bit offended by her surprise.

I tore the page off and gave it to her.

'I'm going to frame it!'

'Can you draw people?' Pippa asked.

'I've never really tried.'

'Try now!' she said. 'Go on!'

Keeping the sketchbook almost perpendicular to my thigh to stop anyone seeing my efforts, I did my best to capture Lucy's face. I noticed that there was a stillness about her expression that didn't change very much whether she was tired or bored or happy. I'd never seen that before I tried to draw her, but once I had, I could see that in all the photographs on her family's mantelpiece, Lucy always looked more or less the same. The equivalent photos of me on the mantelpiece at home caught me with all sorts of expressions, from pissed off to totally moronic.

When I allowed the family to look at the drawing, they seemed pleased. I was quite proud of the way I'd caught her aura of contentment.

'It makes you look like one of those dolls that goes to sleep when you tip it back,' said Pippa, peeping over her sister's shoulder. 'Which is actually how you do look, as a matter of fact! Maybe you should have been an artist, Gus!'

'There's no money in it, though, is there?' I said, with what I thought was the appropriate amount of modesty.

'Even Van Gogh never sold any paintings in his lifetime,' said Lucy.

It was one of two statements that people who knew nothing about art always trotted out. The other was that contemporary art which sold for a lot of money wasn't really art at all. But I didn't want to spoil the jollity by getting into a debate about sheep carcasses or unmade beds.

'Sorry about Pip,' said Lucy, as we lay curled around each other in her single bed that night.

'No, I like her. She's fun.'

I immediately regretted the word when Lucy said, 'I should probably be more fun.'

'You're *great* fun,' I assured her, hoping she wasn't going to ask me to put it on a scale of one to ten as she sometimes did with adjectives.

'In a week's time, it'll be a year,' said Lucy.

It took me a moment to realize she was talking about us. Did I have to buy a card? Or flowers? Or both?

'Yes,' I said.

'Does it seem longer or shorter to you?'

There was probably a correct answer involved, but I didn't know which it was. Time was supposed to go quicker when you were having fun, so I thought I should probably say shorter, but I wasn't completely sure. I'd never thought about it like that.

'It feels like about a year,' I said, uncertainly, feeling fraudulent when she laughed as if I'd been trying to be witty.

10

1999

TESS

The pink party dress that I'd bought Hope said 7–8 on the label but it was already very tight on her, and the stretchy, sequinned fabric emphasized all the wrong bits. Hope wasn't fat, exactly, but her body was kind of barrel-shaped and her legs were sturdy and a bit knock-kneed. I'd had her thick dark hair cut quite short after an outbreak of head lice in the class and it was all standing up with static from pulling the dress over her head. Hope regarded herself in the mirror.

'Don't you look as pretty as a picture?' she said. Which were the exact words Mrs Corcoran used when she wore the dress to the last non-uniform day. Hope had stopped saying the things Mum used to say. All her comforting little phrases had been replaced with Mrs Corcoran's observations, almost as if Mum had relinquished her.

'Have you got a pound for breast cancer?' Hope asked, as we left the house to walk to school.

'Yes,' I assured her, patting my handbag. 'But it's not really *for* breast cancer, Hope, it's *against* breast cancer.'

I don't know if I was the only person who found it a bit disturbing when all the little girls in the school shouted

'Yippee!' after Breast Cancer Research was announced as the charity the school was supporting on mufti day so they could wear pink. The choice of charity wasn't just for Hope and me, by the way. When you've lost someone, you discover that almost everyone else seems to have a friend or relative who's been affected. You'd think that would put your own suffering in perspective, but it doesn't really.

Hope didn't do chit-chat like most children her age, so on our walks to school, we played games like the counting game, where we'd have to choose a category like flowers or animals, and we'd spend the walk up to the main road spotting, and the bit with all the traffic listing. Usually Hope's list was much longer than mine because she'd have seen all the little purple flowers growing out of a wall, or the dandelion clocks and daisies on a lawn.

Hope's favourite was the silence game, where we'd do the first part in complete silence and then tell each other all the sounds we'd heard. Hope always won that because she'd hear not just a car door slamming and the wheels on the gravel of the drive, but the indicator ticking and the snatch of song on the car radio, which she could usually identify.

'Hands up everyone who's brought their pound for breast cancer,' Hope's class teacher asked, when she'd got them all sitting on the carpet in front of her.

'It's not for breast cancer, it's against breast cancer!'

'Thank you for that correction, Hope. Now, would you like to volunteer to collect up all the pounds for me?'

'No.'

A ripple of laughter went around the class.

Hope's being a bit different showed more than it had in Reception, when a lot of them were still doing their own thing. Even the star girls – there are always one or two of them in a class, usually the tallest and brightest, with nice mums who've

134

had a word with them about some children finding things more difficult – had given up trying to include Hope in their games of families or hospitals because she refused to cooperate or perform the role she was assigned.

For the first few terms, Hope had been invited to other children's birthday parties, but that had tailed off now that they were doing things in smaller friendship groups, like cinema trips or going to the waterslide park. Asking Hope meant asking me too, and that was a bit awkward with me not being a child and not being a mum either, and the children calling me Miss Costello.

On the plus side, we saved money on the presents, and it was more comfortable keeping a professional distance. You're in a privileged position as a TA. In the course of the day, you pick up a lot of personal stuff about the children's home life like Chantelle's sixteen-year-old sister having a baby so she could get her own flat, and Kaylie's mum thinking someone in the family was a 'fucking waste of space' (the phrase that rang out from the Wendy house whenever it was Kaylie's turn to be mother in Golden Time).

Hope didn't seem to notice she was being excluded, but I got a feeling of anguish each time I was stuffing the going-home post into the children's folders and there was no little pastel envelope with her name on it.

It was the same at the school disco, which was a bit mad, really, because there was nothing Hope loved more than music, but she was dancing by herself, as if there was an invisible fence around her that kept the other children at a distance.

The usual DJ was Bryan Leary, who did the socials at the church, playing songs like 'Magic Moments', but this time, Mrs Corcoran's secretary had had to find a different guy – the Music Man, it said on his poster – because Bryan had a problem with his waterworks.

The new DJ was much younger. He started off with 'I am a

Music Man', producing musical instruments from under the decks, a bit like Mary Poppins and her carpet bag, then went straight into the first bars of 'Hit Me Baby One More Time', causing a few raised eyebrows among the senior staff.

Lowering the volume, the Music Man spoke into his mic. 'Who knows how to play Musical Statues?'

Hands went up. The music went up.

'Oh, baby baby . . . !'

Hope loved the song, but she didn't really get the idea of the game. Her reaction to him cutting the music was to look cross rather than stop moving.

I said a silent prayer that the Music Man wouldn't make her first out.

'OK, kids,' he said. 'That was just a practice. This time, when the music stops, you stop, right?'

The instructions couldn't have been clearer, but Hope was in her own Britney world. I think the Music Man must have seen the look of panic on my face as I crept around the back of the hall to be close to Hope when she was called out.

'This time, you're going to have to listen up real careful . . .'

The music stopped; four children didn't. Emma and Kaylie sat out of their own accord, Patrick had to be tapped on the shoulder.

'You've got to sit out now, Hope,' I whispered.

There was a chorus of 'Hope's cheating!'

I looked despairingly at the DJ. He put the music on and cut it almost immediately, so the whole year was out.

'Who wants another game?' he asked. 'Make some noise! You call that noise? I can't hear you! Who wants another game? Make some noise!'

It was such an unlikely command, some of the brighter children glanced at Mrs Corcoran for confirmation before shouting, 'Meeeeeeee!'

'We're going to have a dancing competition. Who knows this song?'

The opening bars of 'Tragedy', by Steps.

Hope's hand shot up along with almost every girl in the room.

'Who's going to dance to this song?'

Hope's hand stayed firmly in the air.

'OK then. Get dancing. And remember! I'm watching.'

As Hope began performing an elaborate sequence of steps and mime to the music, I noticed that a few of the other girls were trying to do the same routine, but none of them was hitting the beat like Hope. The teaching staff started to nudge each other, and point at her. Squashed like a sausage into the gleaming pink dress which was riding up her thighs almost to knicker level, Hope was totally unaware that anyone was looking at her.

'I'm a fantastic dancer,' she announced to Dad that evening.

'Is that right now?'

'The Music Man said.'

'The Music Man, is it?'

'She really is,' I told him. 'She won a sweetie in the dance competition, didn't you, Hope?'

'Where did you learn to dance?' Dad asked.

'On *Top of the Pops*,' Hope explained.

'*Top of the Pops*, is it now?'

Dad never really listened. His way of communicating with us often constituted simply repeating the ends of our sentences.

'Like a bloody budgerigar,' Mum used to say.

We were eating from the chippie, which probably meant he'd had a win on the horses.

'Perhaps Hope could go to a ballet class?' I ventured. 'Some of the other girls are full of their shows.'

'Ballet?' said my father. 'Would you look at her, Tess?'

I kicked myself for using the word. In his eyes, ballet had been Kevin's downfall.

'It's more about moving to the music at their age,' I told him. 'Honestly, Dad, you should have seen her dancing.'

'Ballet class!' my father dismissed the idea. 'Do you think I'm made of money?' he added, with that semitone of threat in his voice that hinted at worse and we both knew better than to oppose him.

When Hope had gone to sleep, I went back into the bathroom, to clean the bath and tidy up. I picked up the pink dress off the lino floor where she'd discarded it.

Pink was such a happy, upbeat colour for breast cancer. If you'd asked me to associate a colour, I'd have chosen black or very dark grey.

I suppose the idea is to empower. The language people use about cancer is all about fighting and battling and being brave, as if it's an external threat that you have to vanquish. But if it was just about having the right attitude, most people would survive, wouldn't they?

I envisaged cancer more as a covert sleeper cell that I had to outwit. I'd read enough articles in magazines to know that I had to examine my breasts regularly. In the months following Mum's death, I'd convinced myself that I'd discovered several bumps and suspicious thickenings, then felt like a time waster when they'd disappeared by the time I got a GP appointment.

On the third visit, I got the new female GP.

'Breasts are very prone to hormonal fluctuations,' she told me. 'So it's best to stick to once a month. A few days after your period is normally a good time. Can you show me how you examine yourself?'

'In bed,' I said, lying back on the examining table, my hands hovering above my breasts, unwilling to touch them in front of her.

Being brought up a good Catholic girl, the combination of trepidation and shame was bad enough in the dark, under my duvet, surreptitiously feeling around with Father Michael's grave warnings from our confirmation classes about 'the pleasures of the flesh' echoing faintly through my brain.

'I think you'll find it easier standing up,' said the doctor, matter-of-factly. 'What I do is stand in front of the bathroom mirror, so I can do a visual check for any difference in appearance, pigmentation or puckering, then I examine each breast methodically.'

It was reassuring to know that she did it too. Made it more clinical somehow.

'But you know what you're looking for,' I said.

She smiled.

'Actually, Teresa, you're in a better position than me, because you know your own breasts. Or you should do. You'll get more confident as you go on. Do you think you can try that?'

Armed with her advice, I'd managed to reduce the slightly obsessive checking to once a month, but, since it was Breast Cancer Awareness Day, I now locked the bathroom door and stripped down to the waist.

I'd always been a bit self-conscious about my chest since I developed very quickly, aged twelve, going from nothing to an E-cup in less than six months. I still found myself taking a deep breath before touching, my pulse rate increasing with dread as I felt around each breast, pressing in a spiral until I reached the nipple, then raising my arm and checking my underarms too. There were no changes I could detect. I breathed out a long sigh of relief. Another month over and Hope was growing up all the time. If I could just manage to tick off one hundred and thirty-five more months to get her to the age of eighteen, then it wouldn't matter so much if I got cancer and died.

I wondered if everyone who was responsible for a young child worried all the time. Or was it just me? Worry's difficult to admit to, isn't it? The last thing you want is other people worrying about you worrying, so you tend to keep it to yourself, which probably makes it all build up.

On the final afternoon before the summer holidays, Hope and I were the last to leave school after hunting for a missing plimsoll. As we walked across the deserted playground, our footsteps echoing in the sudden silence that falls when four hundred children depart for the summer, I was happy that another year was over. We'd managed to get through it without too many setbacks. The disco had done wonders for Hope's self-esteem. The weather was hot. Things were definitely looking up.

'The Music Man!' Hope noticed him first.

'Hey, Hope!' he said, squatting down to give her a high five, but hitting thin air, because Hope didn't do high fives.

'It's the Music Man, Tree!'

'Tree?'

'Short for Teresa. I'm her sister,' I added, to explain why Hope didn't have to address me as Miss Costello.

'I didn't think you were one of them,' he said.

His smile made me smile too.

'Well, I am one of them, but thanks anyway.'

'I was hoping to catch you,' he said.

'Why's that?'

'I think I left something in the hall.'

'Oh, right. What was that?' I asked.

He looked awkward.

'Forget that last bit.'

'You didn't leave something in the hall?' I clarified, sounding like a teacher.

'I was just hoping I'd see you.'

It dawned on me suddenly that he was chatting me up.

Doll would have known what to do, fluttering her eyelashes, maybe touching his arm for a second.

'Why was that then?' I sounded as frigid as a nun.

'Wondered if you fancied going for a coffee sometime?' he asked.

'Hope would have to come,' I blurted.

'Fine by me, Tree,' he said.

'Tess,' I told him. 'Tess is what people call me.'

'Who's the hunk?' Doll asked.

She was waiting for us outside the gate in her pink Volkswagen Beetle with the sunroof down and a Mister Softee ice cream in her hand for Hope.

Was he a hunk? The Music Man – I was so flustered I hadn't even asked his name – was about my height, with short brown hair and clean-shaven like someone responsible who might wear a uniform, a fireman or a paramedic, not really what you'd think of as a DJ.

'He's the Music Man,' said Hope.

'I see!' said Doll, stretching the word 'see' to three syllables and giving me a knowing look as I strapped Hope in, as if I'd been keeping him secret.

'Wondered if you fancied going for a coffee sometime?' Hope repeated his exact words and intonation.

'I see,' said Doll again, as she switched on the ignition.

It's really not like that, I was going to say, but didn't, because it did feel special meeting someone new and a bit older, a man rather than a boy, who had a semi-glamorous job. If Doll hadn't seen him, I thought I'd probably have kept it secret, for a while, just until things were a little further along. But I was probably getting ahead of myself.

Doll's pink Beetle was a present from Fred on their first anniversary. Fred was now a Premiership footballer, and the two of them were about to move into a brand-new house that they'd bought off-plan.

The gates bleeped when Doll pointed the keys, and opened very slowly.

'The garden's still got to be landscaped,' Doll said. 'What do you think?'

Two tall white columns supported the porch, like the front of a temple.

'Amazing!'

Mrs O'Neill often remarked that it was a miracle how well Fred had done if you'd seen him at primary school.

'I thought you'd like the Roman theme,' said Doll. 'There's a hot tub and a plunge pool in the gym.'

'It's got a gym?'

'Well, it's a room with mirrors at the moment, until they install the machines. There's still so much to do!'

The hall was two storeys high with big Hollywood staircases going up to a balcony.

'Hope, why don't you go and explore?' Doll suggested.

Hope ignored her.

'Can Fred really afford this?' I asked.

I knew Fred's income had rocketed after the rumours about him being picked for the World Cup in France the previous summer. It was a good time to be a photogenic young English striker. Even so, the house must have cost a fortune.

'I bloody hope so,' said Doll. 'His agent does all the finances. It's cheaper than buying in London and he says it's great for Fred's image that he still loves his home town, and his childhood sweetheart, obviously. We've got *Hello!* magazine coming in two weeks! I've got my work cut out getting everything ready!'

'What's happened to your proper job?' Since she'd been with Fred, Doll and I spoke on the phone more than hanging out. I couldn't remember the last time she'd mentioned the salon.

'I just don't have the time any more, Tess, with all these premieres and charity auctions. Have you seen the pink diamond Fred got me for breast cancer?'

She pulled the fine gold chain away from her throat to show me the sparkly stone.

'*Against* breast cancer,' said Hope.

Doll shot her a look.

'I have to wear a different dress for each occasion, leg waxes, you name it, so I still spend half my life in the salon!' she continued. 'Should I get a couple of dogs, do you think? They always have those little white dogs in *Hello!*, don't they? Or a baby. I wouldn't want them crapping on the floor, though. Marble absorbs stains, did you know that? The interior decorator only told me after it was down, otherwise I might have gone for stripped oak. No red wine. Not downstairs, anyway.'

'A baby would be tough to organize in a fortnight . . .' I said, wondering whether she'd dropped that one into the conversation to get my reaction.

'We're not going there. Wouldn't it kill my mother? Bad enough Fred and me moving in together. When she saw the brochure, she said, "Well, there's five bedrooms anyway." She tells herself we're waiting 'til we're married.'

'Are you getting married?'

'Fred's agent says to wait for the England call-up. That way, we won't have to pay for the wedding!'

'Fred's agent decides?'

'Don't worry, he's my number one fan, Tess. Doesn't want Fred mucking around in clubs with kiss-and-tell slappers.'

I nodded discreetly in Hope's direction. You never knew what she would repeat.

'Oh my God! Hope!' Doll yelled.

Hope's ice cream was running down her hands.

'Stop dripping on my marble!' Doll shouted.

On another occasion, we would probably have giggled at the silliness of the words, but one of Hope's moods descended. It was literally like a dark shadow coming down over her face. She stood scowling at us. I think I preferred the screaming.

'Is there something wrong with her, do you think?' Doll whispered.

My protective hackles rose at her talking about my sister in the third person.

'You bought her the bloody ice cream!'

'I'm only saying what Fred says.'

'Fred's a paediatrician now, is he?'

I saw from Doll's face she thought I was accusing him of something much worse.

'It means children's doctor.'

'You and your big words!'

I hated it when Doll said that, trying to make out she was thick, because she wasn't at all. It was actually just a way of making me feel bad.

'She's got to learn,' said Doll.

'Learn what – that marble absorbs stains? It's not on the National Curriculum. You didn't even know until your bloody decorator told you!'

'I didn't mean—'

'It's only vanilla,' I said, getting out a tissue. 'Look, you can't even see it.'

I was on my knees, dabbing at the floor, close to tears.

Doll suddenly saw it had all got out of proportion. 'Sorry, Tess . . .'

*

What had happened to Doll? It was as if she'd lost sight of the important things in her new world of polished-granite work surfaces and underfloor heating. Or maybe she was really moving away from us, I thought, and not just to a new house.

'I don't like Doll,' said Hope, as we walked back to the estate.

Is there something wrong with her? Doll's words kept repeating in my head. I knew it was what some people thought. Sometimes I thought it myself, but Hope was so clever in lots of ways, there couldn't be anything wrong with her, could there? She knew all the lyrics to the CDs in our house. We all did now, including the funny changes Hope made if she didn't understand a word. I'd even caught Dad singing 'Chicken Tikka' to himself in the bathroom mirror while he was shaving. His face went all bashful at me through the bright white foam beard.

It's a funny word, 'bashful', isn't it? You'd think it should be 'bashless' really, but the dictionary says it's from the old word 'abash', which means to cause to feel embarrassed, not from the usual kind of bash.

Mum always used to say, 'Hope's just who she is.'

And, 'Wouldn't the world be a boring place if we were all the same?'

But I sometimes wished I could just ask her, honestly, if she'd worried too.

The Music Man rang that evening. I liked it that he put his cards on the table. It was much more grown up than playing those leaving-it-a-couple-of-days-in-case-he-looked-too-keen kind of games. His name was Dave Newbury and he was a plumber by trade, I learned. So no problem with Dad, I thought, getting ahead of myself again.

When we met under the clock tower the following afternoon, it occurred to me that I'd never been on a date, if that's what it was, with anyone I hadn't known since primary school.

I was very nervous and uncharacteristically out of ideas for conversation. I tried to imagine what someone looking at us would think. Did we look like a couple or was it obvious that we didn't really know each other?

'You look nice in that dress,' said Dave.

It was a hot day, so I'd gone with a sleeveless printed dress that I'd got in Principles' sale, but the fact that he'd remarked made me instantly wonder if I should have stuck to jeans. Or did he mean that I didn't look nice in the trousers I wore for work? What was I supposed to say? 'You look nice in that shirt' might sound like I was taking the piss. He did, though. It was short sleeved with broad blue-and-white stripes that made his eyes look bluer than I remembered. It looked like someone had ironed it carefully. I wondered if he still lived at home and let his mother do his washing, or whether he had a place of his own.

'Hope loved the dance competition,' I said, as we walked on either side of my sister, who had a giant lollipop Dave had bought her in one hand and the string of a dolphin-shaped helium balloon in the other.

'You're a big S Club 7 fan, aren't you, Hope?' said Dave, launching into the chorus of their recent hit 'Bring it all Back' and doing all the moves alongside her.

In the split second before Hope's arms stretched into the air, I foresaw what would happen, but wasn't quick enough to pre-vent it. Freed from the tether of Hope's hand, the balloon soared into the sky. We all watched it rising and then, as if she suddenly realized it wasn't going to turn round and come back, Hope started jumping up and down with her hands in the air, wailing at her inability to retrieve it.

'Don't worry,' Dave tried to soothe her. 'We'll get you another.'

'No, really, it's fine!' I told him.

It had been over-generous of him to buy her two things in

the first place. I didn't want him paying for a third, but now that Hope had heard the offer, she did her gluing-herself-to-the-pavement thing, which was bad enough when it was just the two of us, but so much worse with someone we hardly knew. Now people really were looking at us because Hope was too old for that kind of behaviour. Worse still, the balloon-seller didn't have another dolphin and Hope was not prepared to be appeased with a fish, a pirate ship, or even My Little Pony.

'Hope, stop it! Just stop it!' I was fed up with her, and embarrassed in front of Dave, who, having offered a twirly windmill, a stick of rock, even a beach ball in a net, was now standing a little way away from us with Hope's giant lollipop in his hand and defeat on his face.

The only thing that worked with Hope was distracting her, so I crouched down next to her on the promenade.

'You know where I think that dolphin's going . . .'

Hope stopped instantly, in the expectation of a story.

'I think he's going to the zoo. He was probably lonely being a dolphin all on his own with all those My Little Ponies, so he decided to go back home.'

'Dolphins don't live in a zoo,' Hope pointed out.

I looked up at Dave who shrugged, as if to say, 'She's got you there!'

'You know what, Hope, you're right,' I said, dredging my brain for dolphin facts. 'Dolphins don't live in a zoo. Where do they live?'

'In the sea?' Hope offered.

'That's right. Did I ever tell you that I met a dolphin once? It was in a place called Dingle, in Ireland, and there's a dolphin who lives in the bay, and his name is Fungi and he likes to swim with people. I was too small to swim with him, but I saw him from a boat. Perhaps your dolphin has gone off to see Fungi?'

Hope was still suspicious.

'Is my dolphin really a dolphin, or is he a balloon?' she asked.

'Well, he's actually a balloon dolphin. Which is quite rare, because instead of swimming, like most dolphins, he flies instead. What's his name, by the way?'

'Balloon Dolphin,' said Hope.

She was like that with names. The giraffe we'd bought in Hamleys was called Raffe.

'So where do you think Balloon Dolphin is going?' I asked.

We both looked up. I could still see the glint of the sun on the shiny surface far up in the sky. Would he keep rising until he got to space, I wondered, like one of those weather balloons you sometimes see them sending up on the local news?

'Heaven?' Hope suggested.

I pictured Balloon Dolphin's smiling face alongside the trinity of Princess Diana, Mother Teresa and Mum, who Hope prayed for every night.

'He was heading towards Herne Bay,' said Dave.

The balloon was actually going in the other direction, but I didn't mention that.

'What's Herne Bay?' Hope asked, calm enough now not to notice being pulled to her feet.

'Along the coast. If you like, we could follow Dolphin Balloon in my van,' Dave said.

'Balloon Dolphin,' I corrected him.

Hope sat in the passenger seat and I sat in the back on the floor, which was probably illegal, but Dave was a careful driver, and with the windows open and *Now That's What I Call Music!* turned up loud, Hope appeared to forget about Balloon Dolphin.

I looked at Dave's face in the rear-view mirror as he concentrated on the road and occasionally joined in a few bars of the chorus of a song with Hope. Had he known that playing music

148

would solve the problem, or was the suggestion of driving somewhere instinctive? Either way, it had worked. Suddenly aware of his reflection smiling at me, I felt myself blush, as if he'd caught me secretly checking him out.

Herne Bay is one of those faded English seaside resorts that has suffered badly from cheap flights to warmer places – I mean, given the choice, why would you opt for pebbles and the cold dirty water of the Thames estuary? – though some, like Whitstable just along the coast, were becoming fashionable weekend retreats for trendy Londoners.

'People say Herne'll be next to come up,' Dave said, as we walked along the seafront.

'No sign of Balloon Dolphin,' said Hope, despondently.

'Maybe Balloon Dolphin decided to go to France instead,' I said, thinking on my feet.

'Where's France?'

'Across the sea.' I gestured in the general direction. 'There's a beautiful city there called Paris. Maybe Balloon Dolphin wanted to see the Eiffel Tower, or fly over the rooftops of Notre Dame.'

'Or Euro Disney,' Dave joined in.

'Can I go to France?' asked Hope.

'One day,' I said, because it was wiser not to say no to her.

I found myself thinking that Balloon Dolphin's escape might be an opportunity rather than a setback. We could make up Balloon Dolphin stories at bedtime and maybe Hope would learn a bit of geography along the way. Balloon Dolphin could visit the Pyramids when her class did the Egyptians. He could go to Rome or even Florence. The adventures of Balloon Dolphin might wean Hope away from *James and the Giant Peach*, which we were currently reading for the fifth time, because Hope was intrigued about Kev living in New York, and that we might go and see him one day – in a plane, though, not a peach.

There were a couple of children's roundabouts near the entrance to the pier.

'How about a ride in the fire engine?' Dave suggested. 'I'll be back in a mo.'

I assumed he was going to the loo.

The ride was designed for children smaller than Hope and she sat wedged in the vehicle, very still and suspicious as it started moving, frowning at me as I urged her to ring the bell each time she passed.

'The Music Man found Balloon Dolphin!' she suddenly shouted, seeing Dave jogging towards us.

This time, he tied the balloon ribbon twice round Hope's wrist to secure it.

The sun was beginning to set, and the sky was layered coral and turquoise and grey. Hope was trotting along happily ahead of us, with the new Balloon Dolphin floating above her.

'Nowhere better on an evening like this,' said Dave.

The expression jarred slightly because it was what my dad always said to get out of taking us on a real holiday. If I ever hinted at another package to Tenerife, where we went the summer after the boys left home, he always said, 'What's the point of all that travelling, when we live a mile from the beach?'

At first I'd thought that maybe money was tight, but he'd spent two years as a site manager on the construction of a new out-of-town shopping centre, so I realized that the last thing he wanted to do was be away for a fortnight with just the two of us.

'Where did you find Balloon Dolphin?' I whispered to Dave.

For a moment, he frowned at me like I actually thought he'd found the original one, then cottoned on that I was continuing the pretence just in case Hope overheard.

'I was called to fix a leak at a party shop last week. I remembered they sold balloons, so I figured they all get them from the same supplier, don't they?'

He was lucky, I thought. But wasn't that what we needed, a bit of luck?

'Who wants fish and chips?' he said, capping off a perfect afternoon for Hope.

We ate our piping-hot supper out of paper sitting on a bench on the promenade under a string of coloured lights. It felt like a real holiday thing to do.

Hope fell asleep in the van on the way home. In the darkness, with the volume on the CD player turned down low, the atmosphere was suddenly intimate.

'You have a great smile, you know,' Dave said softly, glancing at me in the rear-view mirror.

'People usually say that if someone's fat or plain,' I said.

'What are you like?' he laughed. 'You're not fat, are you? And you're lovely-looking, but I'm still saying it . . .'

'Oh . . .'

'You should smile more often.'

Of course, then I couldn't stop.

We told each other our stories.

'You're great with her,' he said, after I'd described how I came to be looking after Hope.

He was four years older than me and came from the Isle of Sheppey just along the coast. Both his parents were alive and he lived with them, although he was saving a deposit for a flat. He'd got the idea of being a DJ from childhood holidays in Butlin's, and he was hoping to do it full-time when he'd built up a regular clientele. He had two older sisters who both had kids.

'That must be why you're so good at it,' I said, returning the compliment.

In his spare time, Dave went to the gym and played golf twice a week.

'Gets me out of the house,' he said. 'What about you?'

151

'I read,' I said. 'Gets me out of the house. In a different way, obviously . . .'

'Travel books, that kind of thing?' Dave asked.

'Novels, mostly,' I told him.

The one bit of the day I looked forward to was closing my bedroom door when I'd got Hope to bed and the house was all quiet, being transported to Victorian London, or Hardy's Wessex, or Ireland in the 1960s. Edna O'Brien was Mum's favourite novelist and reading *The Country Girls* trilogy made me wonder if that's how she'd felt about friendship and men and stuff when she was my age.

Dave had a nice smile himself. I'm not just talking about his mouth. With Fred, it was all those ultraviolet white teeth, but with Dave it was his eyes. He had nice, kind eyes.

'Forget your tall, dark and handsome,' Mum used to tell us, when Doll and I were mad for Robbie Williams. 'What you need to find is someone who understands who you are – a kind man, a gentle man.'

And then she used to sigh. We all knew my father was not one. He was a good-looking man, or at least he had been in his youth. He was a charming man who could be great fun when he was on form and was capable of having a really good time – craic, he called it. But I don't think I ever saw him do any-thing kind. With Dad, it was always about himself. When Kevin got a job with a dance company in New York, it was all about Dad's sorrow and nothing to do with well done to Kev. When I got my offer for university, it was all about how much that was going to cost. Mum used to tell us that was just his way of saying he was proud, but we knew that was her kind-ness, not his.

When the doctor said her cancer was stage four, which meant terminal, Dad's reaction was, 'Dear God, what have I done to deserve this?'

*

152

When Dave pulled up outside our house, he kept the engine running. I didn't know if that was because he was in a hurry to get away or waiting for me to invite him in. The house was dark, so Dad was probably out, but I wasn't going to risk him rolling in the worse for wear and making assumptions. Or being charming, because Dad was that unpredictable. Him making a mate of Dave was almost a worse prospect than him throwing Dave out.

'This has been the best day we've had in ages,' I said, first to break the slightly nervous silence that had fallen over the chugging of exhaust, and immediately thinking that sounded too keen.

Dave had probably had enough of us. In my head, I was preparing for the let-down, so when he did speak it took a second or two to understand what he was asking.

'You wouldn't be up for helping me out next Saturday, would you? I've been booked to do a wedding, one of those marquee-in-the-garden type of jobs – and it would be great to have you along, you know. Help set everything up.'

'I couldn't bring Hope to something like that.'

'No,' he said.

I realized I'd made it sound like I didn't want to go.

'I'll ask my friend if she can look after Hope, shall I?' I said quickly.

'Great!' Dave said. 'I'll call you in the week . . .'

If I'd been in the front seat, I sensed he would have leaned across and given me a kiss but it was awkward with me sitting in the back. Dave switched the engine off and came round to let me and Balloon Dolphin out.

'Come on, Hope. Time for bed . . .' I patted her gently to wake her up.

'I'm not tired!' Hope declared, as soon as her eyes were open.

'I'm sure Balloon Dolphin wants to go to bed,' I said.

'Balloons don't go to bed, Tree!' she said crossly.

'A wedding, eh?' said Doll.

'It's not like that,' I said.

After a lot of trying on, we decided that the most appropriate thing for me to wear would be black jeans and a white shirt, but Doll lent me a pair of earrings, two big single pearls, 'to lift the outfit', so I looked quite smart. She also bought a present of lacy underwear, which didn't show, obviously, but felt a tiny bit sexy.

On the Saturday morning she came round early to do my hair, straightening and smoothing it back from a middle parting into a long sleek ponytail, which made me look severe, before she applied pale pink pearly lipstick that totally softened the look.

Doll stepped back and assessed her work. 'Businesslike, but alluring.'

The person in the mirror didn't look at all like me.

'You don't think it's a bit much for this time in the morning?' I asked.

'Wow!' Dave said, when I got into the van.

It felt a bit strange, sitting in the front seat, occasionally looking at the side of his face as he concentrated on the road, and neither of us speaking, except when I gave him directions from the map. Maybe it wouldn't work without Hope there to keep things moving along?

I finally thought of a question. 'How did you get this job, then?'

'One of my mates knackered his Achilles heel,' he said. 'So he's chatting to the physio and she's telling him that she's got her wedding all planned, but the DJ's let her down, and so he told her about me. It's my first wedding.'

154

He was nervous too, I thought, which is probably why he'd invited me along.

'You'll be fine,' I said. 'Much better than Bryan Leary.'

'High praise!' he said.

We both laughed, and the atmosphere in the car was easy again.

Even though it was only a few miles from where I lived, I'd never been down this narrow bit of coast road before because it wasn't on the bus route.

'I think this is the place,' I said, spotting the entrance to a private estate.

There were big bunches of heart-shaped silver helium balloons tied to the gates of one of the large detached houses. A couple of florist's vans were parked up outside and a team of caterers were unloading piles of white crockery from another.

'How the other half lives,' said Dave.

11
1999

GUS

'Can someone get that?' Nicky called from upstairs.

I was waiting in the hall while the women got themselves ready, but I wasn't sure if 'someone' included me. There had been deliveries arriving all morning: ten large, round tables and eighty chairs; a bale of white tablecloths; the cake, heavy tiers in separate boxes that were now being stacked into a tower in the marquee; and flowers, so many flowers, all white and trailing ivy, pedestals of lilies, yards of garland that scented the air with jasmine, and shallow crates containing cushions of white roses for each table. I knew the drill, but it wasn't my house and, as I hesitated, Helen came running down the stairs in a dressing gown, her hair in large rollers.

'Side gate and through to the back,' she instructed the people on the doorstep. 'Our planner will meet you there.'

She closed the door and shouted, 'DJ's here, Pip!'

'What? Oh, thank God!' came a muffled cry from upstairs.

'Bit early, isn't it?' I said to Helen.

'Better early than late,' she said, running up the stairs again.

I took the comment to be a reference to my arrival that morning instead of the previous evening when I should have been there for the family dinner. Friday nights were the busiest in the restaurant and I'd had to work late in order to get Saturday off. By the time we'd finished polishing and setting up, it was one in the morning, and after that, though I hadn't mentioned it to Lucy, I'd gone round to Nash's because she'd just been dumped by an actor she'd met at the Edinburgh Fringe and needed a shoulder to cry on. It had taken most of the night to get her smiling again and I'd only managed to grab a couple of hours' sleep on her sofa. I'd had to leg it to Moss Bros that morning to pick up my suit before getting my train.

Despite this, I was now showered, shaved and dressed when none of them were ready. The service was due to start in forty minutes and there was a lot of walking around upstairs, but still no sign of the bride or bridesmaids. I felt a bit of an idiot standing idly in the hall, but I didn't want to sit down and read the paper in the living room because I'd never worn a morning suit before and wasn't sure what to do with the tails.

'Awright, mate?'

A stocky figure in a white T-shirt printed with the words *The Music Man* was standing in the door to the kitchen with a wheel of electric cable over his arm.

'Any idea where I plug in?' he said.

'I think there's a wedding planner in the marquee?' I said, anxious not to cause a breach of protocol.

'No one there except florists, mate!'

'Hang on . . .'

I called Helen.

'Oh, for heaven's sake!' she said, clattering down the stairs, in silk shoes the same pale blue as her dress. She hurried out through the kitchen with the man, returning a couple of minutes later.

'I don't know why we even bothered with a planner if I have to do everything!'

'You're brilliant at it,' I said. 'That's the problem.'

157

It was the kind of remark that would have worked if I'd said it to Lucy, but with Helen it just sounded ingratiating and priggish at the same time.

Helen peered through the small window in the front door.

'The bloody florists are going to have to move their vans before the cars arrive,' she said.

'Should I tell them?'

She gave me her GP's stare.

'Aren't you supposed to be an usher?'

'I think I am.'

'Shouldn't you be at the church, then?'

'I assumed I'd be going with Lucy.'

'There'll be no room for you in the car with the bridesmaids. And you can't go in with Pippa. I'm sure you should have gone with Dad and Granny Cee,' she said.

'I'll walk then, shall I?'

'It's quite a long way . . .'

'I'll be fine,' I assured her, not wanting to cause any more trouble, but realizing, when Pippa's vintage Rolls drove past me, that I'd completely underestimated the distance.

It's difficult not to draw attention to yourself when you're six foot four sprinting along in a morning suit with a top hat in your hand, and when I finally arrived at the church, Lucy and Helen were glaring at me, but Pippa was laughing.

'Very thoughtful of you, Gus,' she said. 'To give me something to worry about and take my mind off things!'

'I'm so sorry,' I stammered. 'You look gorgeous, by the way.'

I wouldn't normally have said 'gorgeous' to Pippa, because it sounded a bit personal for the sister of your girlfriend, but I was so out of breath, I wasn't really thinking. And it was true.

Inside the church, the dim coolness made me conscious of the beads of sweat trickling down my temples and I could feel my white shirt sticking to my back under my jacket. I spotted Nicky agitatedly beckoning me to the front, then the organ struck up the 'Arrival of the Queen of Sheba' and I suddenly realized that Pippa and her father were poised behind me and I was in the way. With everyone in the congregation now staring at me, I dived into a pew at the rear.

As the procession passed by, Pippa looked fragile as she gripped her father's arm very tightly; Lucy's glance was more dismayed than amused; Helen wasn't even prepared to look in my direction. In their high-waisted ice-blue dresses, with their father leading them, I thought they looked like a family of sisters from a Regency television drama. At the altar stood Greg and his twin brother Jeff, who had come over to be his best man. The two of them together were as wide as they were tall. For a moment, I wondered where there was going to be room for Pippa, but then Jeff stepped aside.

The general view in the family was that Greg would be good for Pippa. She'd met him on her training semester in Banff. Ruddy and robust, he was the kind of man you could imagine wrestling a bear, I'd said to Lucy, after the engagement dinner a few months back. It was clear that Greg doted on Pippa, in a puppy-doggish kind of way, which seemed to charm her, although I suspected that if his ogling admiration had come from an equivalent Englishman, she would have thought him a bit of a wally. I assumed he must be great in the sack.

'Don't you like him?' Lucy had asked me.

'He's not really my type,' I replied, putting on a camp voice, which made her giggle.

Apparently, all Pippa's previous boyfriends had been bastards – one of them had even been a drug addict – so there was huge relief that she'd ended up with someone reliable who would look after her. But as I heard her saying her vows with a slight laugh, as if the portentousness of the familiar words was a bit silly, I couldn't help thinking that she was going to wake up the next morning next to the hulk and wonder what on earth she had done.

159

I managed to nip down the side aisle to join Lucy while the bride, groom, best man and both sets of parents went to sign the register.

'Wasn't it beautiful?' Lucy whispered, her face morphing suddenly from dreamy to alarmed. 'You haven't got a button-hole!'

The bells started ringing, the organ struck up Mendelssohn's 'Wedding March', and the whole thing, which had taken months to plan and rehearse, was over. Except it wasn't, because the photographs needed to be taken, a whole album's worth of compulsory poses.

First, the bride's family, which was slightly awkward for me because neither Lucy nor I knew whether I was included or not. Helen's husband, James, was there with their daughters, obviously. After a few shots had been taken without me, Nicky called me in.

'Come on, Gus! Can someone please lend him a button-hole?'

Next, the groom's family, with the four of them taking up as much space on the church steps as the nine of us had; then the bridesmaids; the bride with bridesmaids; the bride with the grown-up bridesmaids with her dress hitched up to show her 'something blue' garter; and finally, the ushers in morning suits throwing their top hats into the air in a completely contrived act of spontaneity.

'Why?' I asked James, who gave me a lift back to the house.

'I suppose it's a use for the top hat,' he said.

There was champagne on the front lawn while the bride and groom had their photographs taken with the cake.

I couldn't help noticing that I was the object of interest for Lucy's assembled relations, who appeared at regular intervals to size me up.

'So, this is Gus! Goodness, you're tall, aren't you?'

'Almost seven foot in a top hat!'

'And you're a medic too?'

'I am, yes.'

'How exciting!'

No one actually asked if we would be next, but I sensed calculations going on behind the appraising smiles.

In the marquee, we were seated at the top table. Glasses of white wine had been poured for us. I downed mine, then Lucy's, before following her to the buffet table. I had that hungover kind of hunger that comes from alcohol on top of lack of sleep and I continued to slake my thirst with wine, when it probably would have been sensible to switch to water. By the time it came to the speeches, I was well on my way to being drunk.

Lucy's father talked about Pippa being the least predictable of his daughters. If it was a warning to Greg, it seemed a bit late in the day. Greg's speech was all about Canada, and how he was looking forward to showing his wife everything his country had to offer. Both he and his brother were wearing little maple-leaf pins on their lapels, a bit like American Presidents wear a badge of the Star-Spangled Banner.

'Why do they do that?' I whispered to Lucy. 'It's not as if we're going to forget where they're from.'

'Sssh,' she said.

'Where I come from,' Greg was saying, 'you can swim in the sea in the morning, and ski in the mountains in the afternoon.'

'It's about the last place I'd want to go,' I murmured.

'I think it sounds nice,' Lucy countered irritably.

Jeff got up, his broad face only distinguishable from his brother's by the helpful addition of a moustache.

'Are there two of them?' Granny Cynthia asked.

'Do you think Jeff grew the moustache for the occasion?' I asked Lucy.

'Stop it . . .'

He told a rambling anecdote about going fishing with Greg

when they were boys. Apparently, Greg had tried every ruse to catch a fish but never got one. Now it looked like he'd landed the biggest catch of the season!

'Poor Pippa,' I whispered to Lucy in the enthusiastic applause after the toast to the bride and groom.

'Why do you say that?'

'Not only is she big, but she's a fish. She's a big fish!'

'He just meant she's a catch,' said Lucy. 'You're getting a bit loud. They'll hear you on the video if you don't watch it.'

A cameraman was prowling the room. I'd noticed him earlier zooming in on the elaborate lacy pattern of mayonnaise on the poached salmon. Perhaps he would edit it into the fishing anecdote?

Greg's mother, who was seated a couple of places down from Lucy, tinkled her fork against her glass, but, when everyone in the room obediently looked in her direction, she became flustered.

'Don't worry, I'm not going to make a speech!' she said.

'That's a relief!' I murmured.

'Could you please just zip it?' hissed Lucy.

'In North America, when you tinkle, the bride and groom have to find each other and kiss wherever they are in the tent!' Greg's mother informed us.

Greg and Pippa, who were at that point still sitting next to each other, obliged.

Everyone clapped.

It was time for the cutting of the cake. Bride and groom got themselves into position with a big silver knife for some more photos. Greg's father tinkled his fork against his glass, so they had to kiss. Then the bottom tier of virgin cake was ceremonially pierced before being whisked away by catering staff to be portioned up into tiny cubes.

As guests returned to the buffet table to help themselves to dessert, Greg and Pippa circulated the room greeting their friends and family individually. The tinkling-glass thing was quite fun if you waited until they were at opposite ends of the marquee, but the third time I did it, I over-hit my glass, causing it to smash instead of tinkle. Fortunately, the only person who noticed was a tall girl with a ponytail dressed in a white shirt and black trousers. Her face broke into a wonderfully mischievous, almost conspiratorial smile.

'Do you think you could get me another glass?' I asked.

'I'm not a waitress,' she said.

'I am a waiter,' I told her nonsensically.

'You'll know where to find a glass then,' she said, smiling again.

For a moment, our eyes held each other's, our expressions puzzled. Did I know her from somewhere?

'Who are you?' I heard myself asking.

And then Lucy was standing next to me with a dustpan.

So people *had* noticed.

'I think I need some air,' I said.

'Very good idea,' Lucy said crisply.

It was already dark outside and the cool evening air was heady with the scent of tobacco plants. With '*La Vida Loca*' bouncing around the dark, empty garden, I was dimly aware that my grasp on time and space had become tenuous. I found myself sitting on the swing seat, which creaked gently as I rocked. Across the lawn, the glowing tent and thump of bass seemed far away.

When I woke up, my head was throbbing and my face was cold against the striped cushion. The clue that hours had passed was in the music. Robbie Williams was singing 'Angels'. I could see the shadows of slow-dancing couples on the sides of the marquee.

A flap of tent opened, throwing a triangle of light over the lawn. I recognized the tall silhouette of the waitress who wasn't a waitress. The triangle of light closed behind her. In the dark stillness, I could just about see her shadowy outline and I could tell, somehow, that she was thinking about something sad.

A shaft of light fell across the lawn again as a man came out of the tent.

'You awright?' he asked.

'I am,' she said.

'Couldn't have done this without you,' he said.

'I didn't do anything,' she told him.

He took a step closer to her.

'You're not like other women,' I heard him say.

'How do you work that out, then?'

'You've got this brilliant smile, but there's all this stuff going on in your head.'

'Now you're making me sound a bit mad!'

'Mad enough to be my girlfriend?'

A long moment of silence.

'Lot of stars, aren't there?' he said, placing a tentative hand on her shoulder.

Then she turned towards him and he kissed her, and I stayed very still, praying that someone wouldn't turn on a light in the house and reveal me there witnessing their moment.

'Where on earth have you been?' Lucy asked as I let myself into the living room through the French doors.

'Fell asleep in the garden.'

'Honestly!'

'Have I missed much?'

'You missed Jeff teaching me to salsa. Pip's about to go away. Jeff and I have tied all the silver balloons to the car.'

'You and Jeff, eh?'

'You know what they say about the best man and the chief bridesmaid?'

'Wasn't Helen the chief bridesmaid?'

'We both were!'

'Jeff got lucky!'

Lucy gave me a playful slap on the arm.

'Should I be worried?' I gave her neck a quick nuzzle.

'I don't know,' she said, shrugging me away. 'Should you?'

'Probably not with the moustache,' I said.

Another slightly less playful slap, then Pippa was standing at the top of the stairs, wearing a flimsy summer dress with a jeans jacket over it. Greg followed close behind in pressed chinos and a polo shirt. His hair was wet from showering. They looked as if they'd just had vigorous sex.

On the drive, a white Jaguar was waiting to take them to the airport hotel. As Pippa was about to get into the car, Helen rushed up to her with the small posy of white roses Pippa had carried into the church. I saw Pippa glance at Lucy, who shook her head imperceptibly, so instead Pippa threw the bouquet over her head in the direction of her best friend from school, who shrieked as she caught it.

'What was that all about?' I asked Lucy, as we waved the car away.

'The person who catches the wedding bouquet is the next one who's going to get married,' she said.

I wasn't stupid enough not to know that. I'd meant the silent little exchange between the sisters, which Lucy clearly thought I'd missed. Had I pissed her off so much she was losing interest in me? I'd never quite understood what she saw in me in the first place.

'We haven't had a dance,' I said, leading her back into the marquee.

Westlife's 'Flying without Wings' was playing. At first, Lucy was a little stiff in my arms, but as I drew her closer in, she relaxed against my chest and I felt I'd been forgiven.

'I love you,' I heard myself whisper into her hair.

She took a step back from me to look at my face.

'Do you?'

She looked so delighted, I thought perhaps I did.

12

2001

TESS

'Asperger syndrome?' Dad repeated, as if he had the slightest idea what that was.

For the first time in my life, I felt a tiny stab of pity for him because he'd been so stubborn in his refusal to believe that there was anything wrong with Hope, it must be humiliating to be told there was, especially in front of me. I was careful not to look at him, but I could sense the authority seeping from him, making his presence in the consultant's room seem smaller, somehow.

'So it's not autism, then?' Dad asked, which made me think he'd been more concerned than he'd let on.

The consultant regarded us over the top of his glasses. There was a chilly, dispassionate air about him, more what you'd think of as a bank manager than someone who specialized in children. The room was clinical, with no personal touches except for a silver frame on his desk, which was turned towards him so I couldn't see the photo.

'Asperger syndrome is classified as being on the autistic spectrum. But as Hope doesn't appear to have any significant learning disabilities, we would say that she is at the less severe end.'

'So it's not autism exactly?' Dad pushed.

'If you want to put it like that.'

'So, what is Asperger syndrome?' I was determined not to go home without information because of Dad getting into a stand-off about the terminology.

It had taken months to get a referral to the children's unit in London, and a whole morning of tests. Hope was currently in the waiting area outside with a student doctor who'd mistaken me for Hope's mother – she was only about my age, herself, so God knows how dreadful I must have looked – and Dad had promised Hope a trip to the zoo if she behaved herself, but there wasn't an endless window of opportunity to ask all the questions we couldn't ask with her there.

Nowadays you'd look it up on the Internet, wouldn't you? But not everyone had a laptop then. Google hadn't become a verb. I went to the local library every week to get our reading books, but the selection of non-fiction was very limited, and even though I'd read the entry on autism in the medical diction-ary, I'd never seen a reference to Asperger syndrome.

'It's characterized by difficulties in social communication, social interaction and social imagination,' the consultant ex-plained.

The words would mean even less to my father than they did to me.

'Could you give us some examples, please?' I asked.

'Each person is different, clearly. Some might have perfectly good language skills, but they won't understand that people often say things they don't mean. They may find it difficult to make friends. They may only want to talk about one thing that they're interested in . . .'

'That's Hope with her CDs, isn't it, Tess?' Dad exclaimed.

His recognition felt like a giant step forward.

'They may like routines or playing the same game,' the consultant continued. 'They may have some problems with physical coordination. They may also suffer from anxiety or depression . . .'

Which would account for the moods.

I wondered if he had picked out all the symptoms that applied to Hope just to prove the point to Dad, or whether Hope was a textbook case.

There was a wedding ring on his slim, bony hand. Was it a picture of his wife in the silver frame? Or his children? If there was ever anything wrong with one of them, was he the first or the last to see it?

'What causes Asperger syndrome then?' Dad asked.

'It only became a distinct diagnosis fairly recently, in the nineties. We're still not sure about the exact cause.'

'We've had a lot of sorrow in the family with my wife dying,' Dad said. 'My Tess does her best, but she's young, you know what I'm saying, doctor?'

I couldn't believe he'd said that! Though I'd given up everything to look after Hope, while Dad's life had hardly changed at all, I was still somehow to blame for her difficulties! A ball of fury rose in my throat and I had to consciously purse my lips and grip the chair to keep myself seated instead of getting up and walking out there and then. That wouldn't do Hope any good, would it?

'It's not a matter of upbringing at all, Mr Costello,' said the consultant.

I wanted to rush round the desk and give him a hug.

'This is something Hope was born with, I'm afraid. And it'll be with her all her life.'

No cause for hugging then.

'There's no cure?' said Dad, sounding so bewildered that I started feeling sorry for him again.

169

'What we can do is help Hope and the people involved in her life with some strategies.'

'Strategies!' my father shouted. 'You've brought us all this way for strategies! Have you any idea how much we're paying for the parking?'

On the way to the zoo, we stopped off at the children's play area in Regent's Park and Dad bought us ice lollies from the kiosk. I think we all felt exhausted from being inside such a long time, breathing hospital air, being told things that affected our lives profoundly by people who didn't know us at all. Neither Dad nor I were saying anything, but you could almost hear the levers in our brains cranking to reconfigure the implications.

I was relieved to have a diagnosis, because that meant we'd be able to get a statement of medical need so that Hope could get some funds allocated for a trained helper, but there was also a drumbeat of guilt for insisting on having her assessed. If nothing was really going to change, Dad was right, what was the point?

There was also this strange, empty feeling of loss, because now I'd never again have the comfort of telling myself it might be nothing.

I watched as Hope tried to negotiate her way up to the top of the climbing frame, knowing the determination on her face would turn to anger when she got stuck. Wasn't anger an emotion? Why was she capable of that, but not of affection, or empathy, or any of the ones that would make her life easier?

'Come on now, darling,' said Dad, lifting her high above his shoulders and placing her at the top of the slide so she could whoosh down like the other kids. The diagnosis seemed to have knocked the stuffing out of him, softening him, for the moment. 'We're going to the zoo, zoo, zoo . . .' he started singing.

'You can come too, too, too,' Hope sang back.

I thought it might be an idea to leave them together.

'Would you mind if I met up after?' I asked Dad.

'What will you do?' he asked, immediately suspicious.

'Just have a bit of a wander, you know . . .'

'You'll be outside the zoo entrance at four, or we'll get caught up in the rush hour,' Dad warned.

'What is the rush hour?' Hope asked.

'From five o'clock to around six-thirty there's terrible traffic because of all the people going home from work,' Dad explained.

'Five o'clock to six-thirty o'clock is one and a half hours,' Hope pointed out.

'Clever girl,' said Dad, with a bit of a gulp in his voice. 'She's clever to work that out, isn't she now, Tess?'

Dad, Doll, even Dave would have thought I was mad walking into University College quad just to stand there imagining what my life would have been like. Groups of students were sitting on the grass eating their lunch, some lying on their backs reading, books aloft to shade their eyes from the September sunshine. I thought they looked a lot younger than me now, with a casual confidence that allowed them to wear cut-off shorts and flip-flops on a weekday, whereas I was dressed in smart navy trousers and a blouse for the hospital. I was aware of quizzical glances, which made me feel like I shouldn't be there at all, but they were probably only wondering what this crazy person was doing staring up at the grand colonnaded portico like it was some kind of shrine.

What I love about London is the complex jigsaw of neighbourhoods, each with its individual character: the elegant Georgian squares of the university district; the solid Ionic pillars of the British Museum; the narrow cobbled streets around Seven Dials, lined with shop windows displaying items you

171

think would somehow change your life if only you could afford them, like pretty boxes of tea, Florentine writing paper, or a vintage bikers' jacket slung over a 1950s dress patterned with giant yellow roses.

I wound my way down to the river and stood in the middle of Waterloo Bridge, looking at the panorama, my hair blowing in the dazzling breeze, and water churning below, the colour of coffee with milk. I'd forgotten that feeling of sheer exhilaration I'd always had when Doll and I used to come up to town as teenagers to explore and fantasize about our future.

The Millennium had changed the skyline. The London Eye was like a giant, incongruous paddle-steamer wheel stuck onto the South Bank. To the east, new skyscrapers were going up in the City, mirror windows glinting in the sunshine. Just down the river they'd converted an old power station into the Tate Modern.

I looked at my watch. There wasn't time to go today, but what was to stop me coming back? Dave always claimed he didn't like London, but he'd only ever been once on a school trip to the Natural History Museum. We wouldn't *have* to do museums, or art galleries. I could show him all the little villagey bits that Doll and I had discovered, or explore some new ones. Kentish Town, Pimlico, Swiss Cottage, even the names were intriguing. Dave had never even heard of Portobello Road, but what was not to like about pubs and antique shops and market stalls piled with pyramids of luscious tropical fruit?

I got on a 168 bus to Chalk Farm. When we were teenagers, I'd insisted on learning the Tube map and the major bus routes. I used to test Doll on the train journey up.

'I'm at Charing Cross. What's the quickest route to Holland Park?'

'Why do we have to do this?' Doll always moaned. 'There's a map in every station, isn't there?'

172

'But we won't look like Londoners if we're reading the map, will we?'

The bus crawled back up through Bloomsbury and across the Euston Road to Camden Town. I got off at the final stop and walked across the railway bridge to the street that curved around towards the bottom of Primrose Hill. People were sitting at cafe tables, leisurely drinking coffee, with their children running around the wide pavements, like they did in Italy. The appetizing scent of charcoal grills and frying garlic drifted out of restaurant doors, the evening specials chalked up on boards outside.

What must it be like to live somewhere where you could choose to eat Greek, Italian, or even Russian food and see a different film or play every night of the week? Somewhere nobody knew who you were, so you had the freedom to discover the person you were meant to be?

I had to run the last couple of hundred yards to get to the zoo on time.

Dad was looking up and down the street, then at his watch.

'The lion was sleeping, Tree,' Hope informed me as we walked towards the car.

'There were hundreds of other animals, though, weren't there? All of them awake!' Dad's voice had that edge of someone unused to spending three hours with Hope.

'The lion was sleeping,' said Hope.

I started humming the tune of 'The Lion Sleeps Tonight'.

'Will you get a move on, now!' said Dad, increasing his pace so we had to run to keep up. 'At this rate, I'll miss the karaoke.'

'Karaoke?' said Doll, the following Sunday.

Fred's team were just back from pre-season training in the Emirates. She and I were in the back seat of Fred's Range Rover, with Fred driving and Dave in the front passenger seat.

It was supposed to be a nice lunch for the four of us, but

with Doll making the arrangements, it wasn't just lunch. When she'd read about the facilities at the hotel, she'd booked us girls a programme of treatments in the spa, and the boys a round of golf to make a day of it.

'Dad used to sing before he got married,' I said. 'His voice is OK, to be fair. He practises "Islands in the Stream" in the bathroom. What with him and Hope . . .'

'She's Kylie at the moment,' Dave told Fred. 'Puts a sheet round her head and writhes around singing "Can't Get You Outta My Head". Sounds exactly like her, though, doesn't she, Tess?'

I didn't quite like Dave talking about her like that to Fred, although I wasn't sure why, because Dave and Hope had a great relationship. His knowledge of pop songs was encyclopedic and he could do things like tell you every track on an album in the right order and how long they were, right down to the second. Sometimes when we were driving somewhere, Hope would get his CDs out of the glove compartment and read out the number of the tracks to test him; he'd test her on her collection when he came round to our house. For her ninth birthday, he'd bought Hope her own personal CD player that she wore round her neck like a giant medal, and which had earphones, that improved everyone's lives. There's a limit to the number of times most of us can listen to ABBA's *Greatest Hits*.

'So, who's your dad's Dolly Parton, then?' Doll asked me.

'How do you mean?'

'"Islands in the Stream", duh! It's a duet, isn't it?'

It was so obvious now that she'd said it. Dad had been paying much more attention to his personal hygiene recently. He'd even bought himself a couple of new shirts, but the idea that there was a woman in his life simply hadn't occurred to me, and I wondered now whether that was what had made him so reluctant to babysit Hope today.

I pictured Dad and some woman with big hair singing at each other with microphones in front of the dartboard. How long had it been going on? And was it serious? Should I prepare myself for sharing the house with her? How would she react to Hope? And Hope to her? Were the three of them even now sitting at our usual table in the Carvery?

In the front of the Range Rover, Fred and Dave were talking about who they'd buy in the transfer window if they were football managers.

Before they met, I'd wondered how the two of them would get along. Dave was so impressed when I first told him, because he was a lifelong supporter of Fred's team, I'd been terrified he'd ask for an autograph or something. Thankfully, he didn't. With Dave being that bit older and able to do proper man's stuff like unblock a U-bend or install a boiler, Fred respected him. They played off the same handicap in golf and though Fred was the professional footballer, Dave seemed to know just as much as he did about the game. Listening to them picking dream teams, I was struck by how similar the two of them sounded to when Dave was talking to Hope. The consultant had told us that Asperger syndrome was more common in males than females. Perhaps they had a touch of it themselves, I thought. Maybe we all do.

'It's a proper bromance with them two, isn't it?' said Doll, linking my arm and pointing me towards the spa entrance, where the staff handed us big fluffy robes, slippers and complimentary baskets of aromatherapy toiletries.

'It's funny,' she said, as we stripped off in the changing room. 'When you're rich, people are always giving you stuff. Chocs on your pillow, goody bags . . . you don't get that at the Travelodge, do you, even though you'd be much more grateful? Talking of which,' she delved into her pink leather tote bag, 'I got you a little something in Dubai.'

Inside the small cardboard carrier bag was a Day-Glo yellow Gucci bikini.

'You're not wrong about it being little.' I held the tiny pieces up against my robe.

'Bought one for myself,' said Doll, pulling the exact same item in Day-Glo pink out of her bag, which made me feel less guilty about her extravagance.

I couldn't help noticing that Doll had got rid of all her body hair, which was a shock because, with her petite frame, it made her look like a child again. Standing shamelessly naked in front of the mirror, she pushed her tiny breasts up to give herself a cleavage.

It must be far easier for Doll to check herself, I thought, because there was hardly any flesh to probe, nowhere for the lump you thought you'd felt to slide away and hide.

'What d'you think?' she asked. 'Fred wants me to get them done.'

'A boob job?'

'It's all right for you,' she nodded at my chest, 'but everyone else does.'

I drew my robe tighter around me. I didn't consider my breasts an advantage. Clothes never looked like they were supposed to on me, which is why fashion models are flat-chested, I guess. Until meeting Dave, I'd been such a good Catholic girl, I'd genuinely believed that letting a man touch your breasts was something you did only when a relationship was serious because men were driven by lust. It hadn't even occurred to me that I was supposed to like it too.

'You'd have to buy all new clothes,' I said.

'You're supposed to be putting me off, not encouraging me!' Doll laughed, which was a relief, because for a moment there, I'd thought she was seriously contemplating surgery, and I would have found it difficult to be neutral about that. Mum had one breast removed, and it wasn't pretty and had given her a lot of pain, so I didn't have much time for perfectly healthy women choosing to go under the knife voluntarily.

Our massage tables were side by side. The lights were low, and the soothing sound of running water was coming from somewhere, I thought probably speakers rather than an on-site waterfall.

'Is Dave into porn?' Doll asked, as our masseuses ran surprisingly strong fingers over our backs.

With the noise of the trickling water, I wasn't a hundred per cent certain that she'd said 'porn', but I couldn't think of any similar-sounding word I might have mistaken it for. I wasn't going to repeat 'Porn?' louder.

'I mean, when you first get together, you want to try everything, don't you?' Doll continued. 'But with Fred it always has to be something new, and now, as often as not, we have to film it!'

After three years of regular beauty treatments, like full body waxing or facials or having her eyebrows threaded, which for some reason was better than plucking them, Doll had become so used to people doing stuff for her that she didn't really notice them any more. She was doing that thing she'd hated her clients for at the salon.

'They talk to each other like you're not even there!' she used to cry, outraged.

I'd always been way behind Doll as far as sex was concerned, but after losing my virginity to Dave, I'd naively imagined that I'd caught up. But it seemed I was still the innocent one, because porn hadn't even crossed my mind, let alone the do-it-yourself idea.

'Not that Fred's into S and M, or anything,' Doll carried on. 'It's just, well, I'm not a bloody gymnast, know what I'm saying?'

There was a part of me that would have liked to admit that I had no idea, so she'd tell me, because it's natural to be curious about what other people get up to, isn't it? But it's funny how sex is taboo even with your best friend, so you never talk specifically about what happens 'down there' or 'behind closed doors' as Mum used to say.

Were Dave and Fred discussing X-rated fantasies on the golf course, I wondered, or worse still, comparing statistics on our performance? I didn't think so. I trusted Dave completely. He was always very patient and very gentle with me. After what Doll had just revealed, I felt even luckier to have found a man like him.

'How's work?' Doll asked, as we reclined with some special seaweed-enriched clay plastered all over our faces, and slices of cucumber on our eyelids.

The new school year had just begun. After all Doll's sex and shopping, our Victorian Day sounded pretty lame. Hope and I had dressed up as chimney sweeps, with daubs of soot on our faces, and sung 'Chim Chiminee' all the way to school, although, strictly speaking, Mary Poppins was Edwardian, but Hope was a bit frightened of *Oliver!*

When we arrived there'd been embarrassed glances from the other staff, because I'd misunderstood the instructions. The grown-ups were supposed to dress up as strict Victorian teachers. Mrs Corcoran, in full black Queen Victoria regalia with a white lace cap on her head, had ordered Hope to go and wash her face, which caused all sorts of problems because Hope hadn't understood about her being in role. I'd spent a miserable day wearing a shirt covered in smuts and a pair of Dad's old trousers held up with string.

Doll laughed so much her face mask cracked all over like a puddle in a drought.

'I miss all that, you know,' she said.

'School?' I was astonished.

'I mean work. I really miss working. How stupid is that? I

miss the goss. There's days when Fred's training when I don't talk to a soul.'

'Don't you go out with the other girls?'

'They're not like you, Tess. They're not like me, really,' she added, wistfully. 'I mean, there's a limit to the number of shoes you can buy. Will you listen to me! Those are words I never thought I'd say!'

Pores cleansed and skin exfoliated, we sat dangling our feet in a pool, with small fish chewing off the dry bits of skin. It felt slightly tickly, but not exactly unpleasant.

'What's to stop you going back to work?' I asked.

'It'd be different if I was a model or something, but junior stylist doesn't really cut it, does it?'

I remembered when almost every girl in our class had wanted to be a hairdresser. It had seemed like the ultimate in glamour back then.

'Fred says having a baby would give me something to do . . .'

I knew Doll well enough to know that the casual way she let this slip belied a deeper concern.

'What's your current thinking on that?' I asked carefully.

It's difficult with your best friend's boyfriend, isn't it, because you're never going to think that he's good enough, but there's a limit to how critical you can be in case they stay together?

'I'm only twenty-one, and Fred's just a big kid himself,' Doll replied. 'Do you think it's old-fashioned to want to be married first?'

'Not if that's what you want,' I said, thinking boob jobs, porn, baby factory, what's happening to you?

'Fred says we should have a kid and see how it goes.'

'It's not just up to Fred, though, is it?'

Doll's face broke into a smile.

'I'm so relieved you said that, Tess,' she said. 'I can pretend to be trying, can't I?'

That wasn't really what I'd been suggesting.

I couldn't help looking at Fred differently when we all got back together for our lunch. Good-looking, yes; not the sharpest knife in the box, but good-humoured enough. He'd probably make a decent enough dad, if you forgot about the porn, which I couldn't. But did the house, the cars, the clothes, the jewellery and the glamorous holidays make him the person Doll should marry? If he'd been on an average income, like Dave, would she still be with him? Who was I to judge, sitting there with my free lunch and my fish pedicure?

'I went to church with Mrs O'Neill,' Hope announced, as soon as I got in the door. 'We sang hymns.'

The warm cloak of well-being the massage had placed around my shoulders slipped straight off.

'Father Michael says it's shocking how little she goes!' said Dad. 'He says she should join the choir.'

'You could have asked me,' I muttered.

Once Hope had got into a routine, it was difficult to wean her off it.

I'd stopped taking Hope to Mass after Mum died. I thought I was doing enough without that. I knew Mum wouldn't like it, but as she said herself, you don't have to go to Mass to believe in God. Not that I was sure I still did, although I quite often found myself praying – that the other kids would pick Hope for their team in games, or that she wouldn't throw a wobbler, or even that she *would* throw a wobbler when we were doing the tests at the hospital, because with her being so well-behaved, there was the danger of them thinking I'd made it all up.

'She's my daughter, Tess!' said my father.

'Did you go along with her, then?' I demanded, knowing

full well that he hadn't. He'd gone to the pub. I could see it in his face and smell it on his clothes.

Gallivanting, Mum used to call it. I looked it up. It's a nineteenth-century word, apparently, from the French, meaning 'to go about in search of pleasure'.

In the ensuing silence, Hope said, 'Dad went to pick up Anne.'

'That's your karaoke partner, is it?' I met his glare full on.

That surprised him. The 'who the hell told you that?' look on his face gave me a little kick of triumph.

'What's Anne like then?' I asked Hope.

'Anne likes strawberry cheesecake,' she said.

To be fair, Anne was a bit of a godsend herself, as I found out the following weekend when she invited us over. She was a widow, her husband having suffered a massive heart attack at Sandown Park on the final race of a big accumulator. His horse had come in as he was taking his last breath, which meant, Anne said, that he had died happy – 'We've all got to go sometime, haven't we?' – and Anne was enjoying his winnings for both of them. She had a nice new detached house, and a little red Mazda two-seater with an open top, which she allowed my father to drive quite soon after their relationship went public (it was always a little unclear how long it had been going on beforehand, and I never tried to find out). Best of all, Anne had a jukebox in her kitchen-diner, which looked exactly like a proper one from the fifties, but played CDs.

'Hope's welcome here as often as she likes,' she said.

Of course she had no idea how literal Hope was at that point; Anne was just keen to be on the right side of my dad. I couldn't understand it, because I thought she had a lot more going for her than he did, but Dad scrubbed up well and he could be generous and charming when it suited him.

Living life to the full was Anne's philosophy, and I suppose that's exactly what Dad needed. She was certainly a striking woman, with a pile of ash-blonde hair on her head and a different tight dress every time you saw her. She claimed to be fifty-one, same as Dad. But from the look of her neck, I thought she'd probably been that age for several years, although Doll said the sun can do that to your skin. Blousy is the word that best conjured up Anne's bright pink lipstick, her full cleavage and the little roll of fat round the top of her Spanx. With her full-throttle laugh and the cloud of scent and fags that she carried into a room, she couldn't have been less like my mother.

I decided Anne was probably a good thing, and tried not to mind her attempts at flattery, placing a be-ringed hand on my arm, and telling me, in a confidential whisper, 'Your dad says he doesn't know what he would have done without you,' when I'm sure he never said any such thing.

It was Anne who found an article about Asperger syndrome in one of her magazines, which said that people thought Albert Einstein had suffered from it, and that was clever of her because it gave Dad a way of talking about it, boasting almost. Dad always liked to bring something to the party.

13

GUS

It began like any other morning, or perhaps with a little more attention to the clock, because it was at the beginning of the Integrated Clinical Care courses which we spent in hospital, behaving more like real doctors. I was pleased to be in at the deep end in A&E, seeing it as a life-or-death test for me as much as the patients. If I couldn't handle mangled people, then it was probably better to find out sooner rather than later. I'd discovered that I wasn't squeamish as I examined the crushed hand of a construction worker, and some suppurating lesions on the bottom of an old man who had been found in a dressing gown tied with string in a council flat full of newspapers and pigeons.

What neither Lucy nor I had fully anticipated was the pressure of being in the public gaze, acting like we knew what we were doing without the safety valve of black humour in coffee-bar post-mortems with our peers. That first evening we'd both arrived home exhausted and would have got a takeaway from our local Indian had Lucy not thought about our breath the following morning for our already suffering patients. So I'd made cheese on toast.

'How was it?' Lucy asked me, as we both slumped onto the sofa.

'No one died,' I told her. The cliché has a grim resonance for medical students. I was too tired to go into any detail.

To my surprise, Lucy had found Paediatric Outpatients unexpectedly challenging.

'The thing they don't teach you is it's not just about dealing with the children, it's about dealing with the parents. There was this father who threw a real wobbler at the consultant, and I'm sitting in the corridor outside with the child pretending not to hear the shouting . . . I just had no idea how to handle it. I was completely useless at it!'

'You're not useless. You're going to be a brilliant doctor.' I tried to boost her. 'Honestly, I'd put money on it.'

'Really?'

'Only a fiver, obviously.'

It was easy to make her laugh, but the next morning, I think I was the one who felt more up for work than she did.

At the junction with Euston Road, we kissed quickly, then our paths divided. As I stood waiting for the lights to change, I watched Lucy walking away, half-expecting her to swivel and wave to me before disappearing from my line of sight. But I could see from the stiffness of her gait that she was preoccupied. She didn't turn, and my arm, halfway to raised, returned quickly to my side.

It's funny how an image can stick in your mind. Now, the memory of standing there in the incessant noise of London traffic, with a slightly crisp September breeze blowing through my hair, watching my girlfriend walk away from me, seems like a turning point in my life.

A&E was constantly busy: a Japanese girl had fainted on the Tube, but there was no indication of anything more serious than her not having eaten breakfast; a toddler stung by a bee at the zoo, whose ear had swollen up alarmingly, was given anti-

184

histamine and observed, his mother instructed to go to her GP for an EpiPen in case of future stings; a courier who'd come off his bike was diagnosed with concussion, X-rayed and admitted.

On my break, I was on my way to get a breath of fresh air when I noticed an old lady sitting alone in a wheelchair near the entrance where the ambulances came in.

'I'm just waiting for the ambulance men,' she told me.

Once I'd made the mistake of asking, I found it hard to get away because she was garrulous and, like a lot of old people, eager to apologize for causing a fuss. She explained that she'd called her daughter, at work, who'd told her to dial 999. It wasn't something she'd have done herself, because it probably wasn't anything, just her arm feeling a bit funny.

'How do you mean, funny?' I asked. Was that a doctorly sort of question?

'Well, my hand's all cold. And it's not exactly freezing out, is it?'

Once you're inside a hospital, you lose all sense of time and weather, but I recalled that the sun had been shining as Lucy and I walked to work.

'When did you first notice this?' I asked.

'Must have been a couple of hours ago now? It suddenly didn't feel right. And then it went all cold. Couldn't seem to warm it up. It was my daughter who told me to call an ambulance. I felt a bit daft, you know, telling them, "Well, I've got a cold arm."'

'You did the right thing.'

'So you do think it's serious?'

My naive attempt to reassure had only alarmed her. To my relief, two ambulance men appeared. 'OK there, Mrs Collins?'

'I was just talking to this nice doctor. He thinks it might be serious.'

The ambulance men gave me the look of contempt that

proper professionals reserve for student doctors. 'We'll take you to the triage nurse now, who'll go through all the details.'

I was called away to a dance student who'd had a fall and sprained or broken her ankle and after that it was my lunch break, so by the time I saw Mrs Collins again, she must have been waiting for over an hour.

'How's the arm?'

'It's ever so white . . .'

'Have you seen a doctor?'

'Just waiting for one. It's very busy, isn't it?'

The only reason I could think of for someone having a cold, white arm was lack of blood supply. Which, in the absence of a tight sleeve or tourniquet, seemed to me to indicate a blocked artery. And the only way I could think of for an artery to be blocked was a clot. And clots weren't good.

I was wracking my brain to think of another explanation. Who was I to think I might know better than a triage nurse who'd been seeing patients for years? And yet, once the alarm had started ringing in my head, it wouldn't stop. I went to the desk and enquired what was happening with Mrs Collins, trying to imply that the old lady was badgering me. The desk nurse looked at her screen and told me that Mrs Collins was on the list for the vascular registrar.

'Has he been informed that it's urgent?'

I got a look that said I was now reaching beyond my competence, which I already knew, but having taken the decision to brand myself a troublemaker, I had already done the damage and I wasn't prepared to back down.

At school, I was never very good at not-blinking contests, and I'd never, ever managed to beat Ross, but I was determined to get the nurse to pick up the handset of her phone. She punched a number into the keypad, then handed the handset to me. 'Probably best you explain.' There was a whisper of triumph in her voice.

The vascular registrar was clearly not someone to be messed with.

'Yes?' Curt. Female.

'Hello . . . Er . . . I'm a student doctor, and I may be wrong, but I think there's someone down here you should see rather urgently . . .'

'And that's because . . . ?'

I was in the middle of describing Mrs Collins's arm, when I realized I was talking to a dead line. A smirk glimmered on the desk nurse's face.

I'd alerted the expert. It was all I could do. If it was a clot, I wasn't qualified to prescribe a blood-thinning agent anyway. And if it wasn't, and I did, there'd be a risk of haemorrhage. I wasn't even any good at getting an IV in. That had been proved pretty conclusively on several occasions when I'd had to call in a nurse to help me. Ultimately, what you find yourself thinking is: *If she dies now, it won't be my fault.*

There was nothing more I could do.

I dislike that phrase.

It sounds so worthy and sincere, a shorthand for: *We've tried everything, we've worked as hard as we could, we've really thought about the individual concerned*, but in reality, that's rarely true. Not that I'm saying doctors are lazy, or that they deliberately make mistakes, but when it's busy, things are missed or delayed. Very often, survival is just a matter of luck.

I made my way towards the ambulance entrance and stood in the diesel fumes fantasizing about taking off my white coat and walking away, a free man.

In the first year of studying Medicine, I had been determined not to let my parents down. In the second, Lucy had convinced me that everyone else had the same worries and insecurities as me. In the third, as other university students graduated and started earning, I realized that very few people really like the job they're doing. At least it was possible to earn good money as a doctor. But I'd never quite managed to silence the voice in my head that screamed, whenever I was under pressure, *I don't want to do this!*

On my way back in, I almost bumped into a very slim woman in a white doctor's coat, which, unlike most doctors, she was wearing buttoned up. Intriguingly, no other clothing was visible apart from very sheer black tights, or stockings.

'Angus?'

Nobody apart from my parents had called me that for years.

'Charlotte!'

'Dr Grant to you!'

Was it a joke, or an order? Probably a bit of both.

'Dr Grant.'

I grinned.

She didn't.

'What are you doing here?' I asked.

Clearly, she was working at the hospital, but I hadn't seen her before or noticed her name on the board in A&E.

'I'm the vascular registrar. I've just come in and some bloody student calls me down here. What about you?'

'I'm the bloody student.'

She sighed impatiently.

'OK then. Where?'

I took her to Mrs Collins's bed, stepping away as she drew the curtain around. I've never quite understood why that's the procedure, because it gives the patient a totally false sense of privacy and makes neighbours even more inclined to listen in. I hovered, hoping to learn something from Charlotte's cool, professional consultation.

'. . . right, well, Mrs Collins, what we'll do is get a nurse to put a line into your other arm to get some medication in, and we'll see if we can't get this arm better very soon.'

The curtain swept back sooner than I anticipated and I felt as if I'd been caught in the act of eavesdropping.

From her voice, I'd never have known that Charlotte considered the situation anything other than routine but her fury was obvious as she stormed towards the nurses' desk, telling them in no uncertain terms to get an IV of heparin into Mrs Collins as quickly as they could.

'Then I want her admitted to my ward, understood? Who the bloody hell was in charge of triaging this patient?'

The nurse on the desk cowered visibly. 'She's on her lunch break.'

'That's very fortunate for her!'

Again, Charlotte turned round quicker than I expected, making me feel as if I was stalking her.

'Good call, Dr Macdonald.' She gave me a little wink as she marched past.

The exotic scent of her perfume lingered for a couple of seconds after she'd disappeared down the corridor, giving fleeting relief from the usual sour odour of disinfectant that never quite masks the persistent background of sepsis and shit that pervades a busy A&E department.

The end of the school day brought in several boys with assorted football injuries, but the slight lull that often occurs in the early evening before the place starts filling up with alcohol-related conditions, didn't happen that day because there was a pile-up in which seventeen people were injured, one fatally.

At five in the afternoon I was asked if I would stay on, and only just had time to call Lucy on the new mobile phones we'd bought when we realized we would be in separate places. It's strange to remember a time when mobile phones weren't connected to the Internet, and were only carried for use in an emergency. I stood in the bit where the ambulances come in, because you weren't allowed to make calls in the hospital, as the sirens' wails got closer and closer.

When I said I wasn't squeamish, that was before I saw

people with their faces burned off. Strangely, the horror didn't make me want to walk out, because I knew I could be useful. The adrenaline keeps you going. You just do what you're supposed to do. You live in the present. I only got time for one breather between ambulances. Standing in the same spot where I'd earlier dreamed of walking away, I found myself thinking, *I love this job!*

That was the night I started smoking. You'd think doctors wouldn't, with the health risks. But it doesn't work like that. When you're witnessing how tenuous life is, you don't seem to care as much about the vague notion of future health. I'd smoked at school. You had to if you didn't want to get labelled a wuss. So when I was offered a cigarette by the male nurse who was standing beside me, it felt like a gesture of solidarity to take it.

I didn't get off until after eleven, having kept myself alert for sixteen hours. I wasn't tired, but I would have gone straight back to the flat if I hadn't run into Charlotte at the hospital entrance.

'Angus,' she said. 'Again!'

I couldn't tell whether the repeat encounter was welcome, or an irritant.

She had just finished her own shift.

'How is Mrs Collins?' I asked.

It all seemed a very long time ago. I'd lived several lives since then.

'I think we've managed to save her arm,' she said. 'It's a bit of a miracle, really, that you called when you did. My colleague hadn't been made aware of the urgency of the situation.'

I wondered if she was covering. 'So, are you enjoying it?' she asked, walking just ahead of me, inclining her head back slightly to talk. A soft grey cashmere cardigan was slung casually over a black vest and skirt that caressed her sheer black legs just above the knee. Her heels tapped the pavement.

'Enjoying is probably not the right word . . .'

'The accident?' Word had obviously travelled fast. 'Was it nasty?'

'Nasty' seemed like a child's word for the injuries I had seen.

'Pretty nasty.'

We'd come to the junction with Tottenham Court Road. She was heading south, and I was heading north.

'Do you have to be anywhere?' Charlotte suddenly asked. 'You look like you could do with a drink.'

It was more of a diagnosis than an offer. Was there some protocol about socializing with senior colleagues? This was Charlotte, I told myself. I'd known her since I was thirteen.

I glanced at my watch. It was long after the pubs had closed.

'I don't know where we'd go,' I said.

She let out a light laugh.

'We'll go to my club,' she said, throwing her arm in the air to stop a taxi I hadn't even noticed approaching.

The club was one of those chic Soho networking places with a camera entryphone and cool-looking staff on reception. It was thronging with sophisticated types in their twenties and thirties.

'It's mostly media,' Charlotte told me, as we carved a way through the throng. 'But someone I know is on the commit-tee.'

Was that someone a man or a woman? I wondered, keeping my eyes on the loose chignon of raven hair in front of me. A man, I decided. Charlotte was too intimidating, not someone I could imagine with a gaggle of women friends like Lucy. My eyes scanned the cocktail bar, the contemporary art on the walls, the kitchen counter where chefs were working, the specials chalked up on a blackboard – pumpkin ravioli with sage, slow-cooked pork belly, braised radicchio – trying to take in all the details so I'd be able to fully describe this night-time party world we didn't even know existed.

'Is it always like this?' I had to shout to be heard.

'I suppose it's slightly more *Decline and Fall of the Roman Empire* tonight,' said Charlotte.

We pushed through a room where people were watching what I initially assumed was a disaster movie on a huge plasma screen.

I stopped for a moment, realizing that the broadcast was coming from an American news channel, the same footage again and again of a plane flying over the heads of a fire patrol and straight into one of the World Trade Center towers. Then a long shot of both towers: one with smoke billowing from it, the other approached by a plane, as tiny and black as a bird, which flew straight into it.

'Holy cow!' said the reporter, as the entry point erupted.

'What's happening?'

Charlotte frowned at me as if she thought I was being facetious, then realized my bewilderment was for real.

'Oh my God, are you the only person on the planet who doesn't know? Do you think it's too cold to go outside?'

'No, let's . . .'

Charlotte led me up a narrow flight of stairs with a door at the top which opened onto a roof terrace with soft lights and luxurious garden furniture. The night air was refreshing after the sweaty heat of drinkers.

A waitress approached as we sank into the deep, linen-covered cushions of a rattan corner sofa. 'What can I get you?'

'I'll have a Grey Goose Martini, very dry, with a twist.'

'The same,' I said, when the waitress turned to me.

Grey Goose, it turned out, was vodka, no doubt an incredibly expensive brand. The sting of anxiety about who was going to pay the bill when the first round arrived was soothed by the balm of the second. The Martinis were viscously cold, the relaxation so immediate, it was the nearest thing I could imagine to mainlining morphine.

As Charlotte recounted as much as she knew about what had happened in New York, I took my second cigarette of the day. She smoked red Marlboros. I remember thinking how ballsy she was. No Silk Cut or Marlboro Lights for her. Everything about her was cool, I thought, trying not to stare at her lips.

'I'm surprised they haven't closed the airspace over London,' she said.

Our eyes followed the lights of planes dropping silently westwards across the night sky towards Heathrow.

'Do you think the world's going to end?' she asked.

I remember thinking, *What a way to go if it does!* Sipping cocktails with Charlotte, in a magical rooftop world of spires and baroque porticoes which couldn't be seen from the street. How amazed Ross would be if he could see me talking to her here, occasionally even making her laugh. And how livid . . .

'How long have you been a member here?' I asked.

She considered the question. 'I suppose a couple of years.'

Not with Ross, then.

I noticed she smoked her cigarettes no more than halfway down, then ground them out decisively, as if telling them – and herself – she didn't need any more.

'And your friend? The one on the committee?'

I was at that stage of drunk where I could hear my voice, but it was as if someone else was speaking.

She stretched like a cat along the cushions.

'You're not trying to ascertain my personal history, are you, Dr Macdonald?'

'Not at all!'

'Do you go to the theatre often?' she asked.

Such a non-sequitur, I wondered if I'd missed some important chunk of conversation.

'Never,' I said.

'Oh. It's just last time, you said you'd been to the National.'

Last time? Did she mean that first Christmas after Ross? It was nearly four years ago and it seemed longer. I'd been just a boy, all enthusiastic about what London had to offer. I couldn't believe she'd remembered.

'. . . so I assumed . . .'

'Yes, well, I still like the theatre,' I said. 'It's just I never go.'

'We should see something,' she said.

I looked at her empty Martini glass, and thought I wasn't the only one not making sense. Was she flirting with me?

'Another?' she asked.

'Why not?'

I'd reached the level of drunkenness just before oblivion sets in, when you feel absurdly in control.

I can't remember how many more we had, or how the bill was settled, or what we talked about before I found myself walking with her, past the little Tudor folly in the middle of Soho Square, across a deserted Oxford Street and along a street parallel to Tottenham Court Road which was lined with Greek restaurants and pizzerias, all closed.

'Charlotte Street . . .' I read the street sign, wondering, not for the first time, whether I was dreaming.

'Yes, perfect, isn't it?' she said, with her breezy, disparaging laugh. 'This is me.' She pointed at a door beside a newsagent.

I vaguely remembered her telling me at some point in the evening that she'd moved from Battersea to be near the hospital, but my brain took a moment to catch up.

'Are you coming up for coffee?'

*

It was a studio flat on the top floor with cupboards into the eaves and a big dormer window with French doors out onto a small roof terrace.

'Have a seat,' Charlotte instructed, as she went to put the kettle on. The tiny kitchen was too low for me to stand up in.

The only place to sit was at a small circular table with two bentwood chairs, or on the queen-size bed, which was covered in a heavy white cotton and lace bedspread. There was a chandelier dangling from the ceiling with coloured glass flowers. The style of the room was rather like one of those exclusive antique shops in the backstreets off the Boulevard Saint-Germain, the sort that don't look as if they're open to the public.

Charlotte returned with mismatched porcelain cups.

'It's not much more than a pied-à-terre, really, but come and see the view.' She brushed past me to open the French doors.

One way, the Telecom Tower, amazingly close and huge; the other, rooftops, surprisingly dark for so near the centre of London. There was an almost suburban stillness here that there hadn't been on the roof in Soho, with only the occasional distant sigh and clank of trains coupling on the mainline out of Euston, which we could hear from our flat when we had the windows open in summer.

'Look,' I said, 'I think it's probably time I went home.'

'Oh . . .'

Not OK. Just 'Oh . . .'

The roof terrace was so small, I could smell the camomile steam from her cup, mingling with a powerful blast of her perfume. Had she squirted herself with scent just now? Why would she do that? Did she like me? Of course not! Not like that. So, was this all a joke? Downstairs, my mind had been very clear. I thought I'd walked the vodka off. But now, reactivated by the hot, dark coffee, the alcohol seemed to have gained new momentum. I felt jittery, almost frightened, because I somehow sensed that if I turned towards her, even one degree, I would be in danger.

She was the one who moved, walking inside, kicking off her shoes, sitting on the bed and pointing a remote at the television.

'Jesus!' she said.

'What?' I perched on the bed beside her.

On the television were images of the towers coming down, those great, symbolic towers collapsing into ruins and people running in the street pursued by a monstrous tsunami of dust and debris, images that meant that the world would never be the same again.

We both stared silently at the screen and then Charlotte turned towards me, fear making her face even more beautiful, and I knew, suddenly, that I could. Then we were kissing, eyes tight closed as if to obliterate reality, as we tore at each other's clothes.

They were stockings, the kind that stay up on their own, with a broad band of lace around the thigh.

Fucking Charlotte was as surreal and thrilling as fucking a film star. Her pliant body, her hungry mouth, the wilful act of succumbing to temptation carried me to a place on the cusp of pleasure and exquisite pain that I'd never been to before, nor even knew existed.

I lay spreadeagled with my brother's lean and stunningly beautiful girlfriend stuck to my chest, unable to believe what had happened, unwilling to move in case the fantasy would suddenly dissolve into sticky embarrassment.

Charlotte finally lifted her face, her lips dark from kissing, her long hair falling untidily around her shoulders.

'You've certainly grown up,' she said.

I didn't dare to speak.

She rolled off me, moving my arm to allow her to lie next to me.

'You know what . . .' She took my hand and guided it between her legs. 'I think there's even more.'

Sinning is like lying. When you've done it once, it doesn't seem any more sinful to do it again.

The first time, my mind was so focused on trying to sense what she wanted, I'd kept my eyes shut. Now I saw the wonderful moment she disappeared into climax and I never wanted it to stop, my fingers wet with her, my head full of her gasps.

'Thank you,' she said afterwards.

What was I supposed to say? I said nothing.

'You've got handsome. Did you know? Definitely improved with age.'

'Like cheese?'

'Or wine,' she laughed.

I tried to think of something to say to her, but every compliment I rehearsed in my head seemed crass or underwhelming. I didn't want to be naked and disdained.

'I have to go . . .' I kissed the cute tip of her nose.

'Really?' She drew a sheet over her perfect little round breasts.

Was she slightly annoyed? Because I was going? Because I'd said it, not her?

'Really,' I said.

She watched me dress.

'I'll see you around, then,' I said.

She said nothing.

I let myself out and ran down four flights of narrow stairs.

Dawn was breaking as I walked home. I went straight to the bathroom and ran a deep bath and lay in the purifying water, unable to believe what I'd done.

It was the accident.

It was the vodka.

It was the apocalypse in New York.

It would never happen again.

So, how much, or how little, was I going to tell Lucy? It began to dawn on me that in a moment of sheer intoxication I had jeopardized my whole life. The strange thing was that I hadn't felt guilty until then because Charlotte was so separate from my life with Lucy. If I had betrayed someone, it was Ross.

Should I confess everything and get it over with? I was almost sure Lucy would forgive me, if I explained. Or would she? Why hurt her? It was never going to happen again. I hadn't encountered Charlotte until now, so it was unlikely I'd run into her again. If we did see each other, she'd behave as if nothing had happened. We both would. She was probably regretting it already. It was a blip on the timeline of our lives. A wave from the past had rolled into the present, broken with a thunderous splash, then ebbed away again.

As I towelled down, I began to work out what I'd say. Not the sex, so not the rooftop apartment, so not the club, so not Charlotte. Cupping my hands over my mouth, trying to smell my own breath, I wondered if I could get away with not mentioning the alcohol? No. In my account of events, maybe I'd put a bottle of vodka in the hands of the male nurse who had given me a cigarette. It had been a traumatic day, we'd needed a drink after work.

I lay down on the sofa in the living room and when Lucy woke me up a couple of hours later from a dead, dreamless sleep, nothing about the previous evening seemed to have any reality at all.

'It was very considerate of you to sleep in here,' she said, presenting me with a cup of hot tea. 'But I honestly wouldn't have minded being woken.'

So I didn't say anything at all.

My head felt peculiarly clear but I was jittery and a little clammy, as if sweating vodka. I guessed that the alcohol level in my bloodstream was still way above any sensible level for treating patients, but there was no way I could call in sick in my first week, so I made myself toast and scrambled eggs with lots of butter while Lucy ate a bowl of muesli.

'Isn't it awful?' she said as we listened to the news on the radio.

'Unbelievable,' I said.

For the rest of the day, my hangover was only a heartbeat away from palpitations. When my shift finished, I left immediately, walked back to the flat and was asleep long before Lucy arrived home. I woke before dawn and decided to go for a run, my first that week, and when I returned, I showered, and made pancakes for breakfast and it felt as if all the bits of me that had been blown apart were melded together again.

We spoke about going back to Lucy's parents' house in Broadstairs if the weather stayed nice for the weekend. Walking away from me at the junction with Euston Road, Lucy raised her arm and waved. The world had not ended. Everything was fine and normal. I promised myself I would never again drink Martinis, Grey Goose or any other brand.

Halfway through the afternoon, I was listening to a small boy's chest with a stethoscope, which still gave me a childish thrill, when my pager went. I ignored it while speaking to the boy's mother. His chest appeared clear, so we needed to investigate the possibility of asthma. The alarm on her face made me remember what Lucy had been saying about dealing with parents. Adults are generally far more stalwart hearing about their own diagnoses than they are listening to their children's.

My pager went again. The message said there was a call on the internal phone for me.

'Have you got five minutes, Dr Macdonald?'

Charlotte's brusque tone immediately made me think I must have done something wrong.

'I'll meet you on the top floor,' she said.

The lifts were notoriously slow so I took the stairs, which allowed me to observe her in her buttoned-up white coat and stockings for a second or two through the glass door on the landing. There was an impatience about her, as she moved from one foot to the other, checking her watch. 'Dr Grant?'

'Dr Macdonald,' she said, swivelling on her heels as I surprised her. 'There's something I'd like your opinion on. Follow me.'

She led me back through the door to the staircase, but instead of going down to the wards, we went up a flight, to another landing where there was an emergency exit onto the roof. Leaning back against the door, she took my hand, and guided it under her white coat.

I could hear the clatter of people running up and down the lower flights, and the hum and whirr of the lift. As she began to pant short, sharp breaths, I instinctively held my other hand over her mouth to stop the noise, which drove her even wilder. Ripping down my zipper, she clamped her legs round me, pinioning my buttocks with the pointed heels of her shoes, giving me no choice but to thrust and spill into her as she rode waves of climax.

I'd never done it standing up before. I'd never done it with my clothes on. I'd never done it in a hospital or on a landing against a door with a green running man in front of my eyes. It felt dirty and wrong and fantastic.

We stood, locked together, breathing against each other's necks until she nudged me away. I zipped up and watched her combing her fingers through her hair, securing her chignon, smoothing down her white coat.

'Do you ever wear anything under that?' I asked.

'I don't do this all the time, if that's what you're thinking.'

It wasn't. But now it was, and I didn't know if that made it better or worse.

'I can't do this,' I said. 'I've got a girlfriend.'

'And that's a problem because . . . ?'

'I love her,' I said.

There was just a hint of a raised eyebrow. Enough to make me feel a hypocrite.

'Well, that's a shame,' Charlotte said. 'We're good together.'

She reached up to touch my face, the caress of her hand on my cheek almost more intimate than anything else we'd done. So I had to kiss her again. She was brilliant at kissing, slow and temptingly sensual.

'You're the loveliest thing,' I said.

'You too,' she said. 'You're the best, Angus. The best ever.'

14

2002

TESS

For our third anniversary, Dave surprised me with a weekend in London. He fixed up for Hope to sleep over at Anne's, where Dad was living virtually full-time now, and he'd consulted Doll about where we should stay, all without me knowing. We caught a train full of Arsenal supporters drinking lager at nine o'clock in the morning, so Dave had a great time comparing statistics and predicting the score. When we got to London, and all the red-and-white shirts swarmed merrily towards the Tube, I knew he would have loved to follow along with them to the match.

Doll had apparently offered to book us into the Hilton, and I was relieved that Dave hadn't accepted, generous though the offer was. But the hotel he had chosen on Southampton Row was a bit shabby and impersonal, so I felt disappointed for him. Our room looked out over a grimy well in the centre of the building, where ventilation ducts from the kitchen were pumping out blasts of bacon.

'We won't be spending much time in here anyway, will we?' I tried to make the best of it. 'It's so exciting! I've never stayed a night in London before. And the flowers are beautiful!'

Dave had rung in advance to get white roses in the room, which were what he always gave me on our anniversary because they had been in the wedding marquee where we'd had our first kiss, so I'd never mentioned that we'd had white roses on Mum's coffin.

For lunch we had a sandwich and a cappuccino in Costa, still a bit of a treat in the days before every other shop had an espresso machine with a milk frother. Dave said what we did for the rest of the afternoon was up to me because I was more familiar with London.

'How about the Eye?' I suggested, knowing it was one of the things he wanted to do.

'Shame to waste the afternoon queuing . . .' he said, insisting he'd be more than happy to wander round places like Doll and I used to. But as we passed a pub on the way to the Tube station, I could see him craning his neck to catch a glimpse of the match on Sky Sports.

'Why don't we meet back at the hotel after?' I said.

'Are you sure?'

I walked straight down to Waterloo Bridge and along the riverbank to the Tate Modern.

A huge, blood-red sculpture by Anish Kapoor filled the vast space of the Turbine Hall like a jumbo jet in an aircraft hangar. To me, it looked like a giant human organ, which kind of made sense when I read that the title was *Marsyas*, a mythological figure who was flayed.

In the galleries, I spent a long time looking at a cut-out picture by Matisse called *The Snail*. The spiral of bright colours gave me such a feeling of joy I was glad Dave wasn't there making comments about painting like that when he was four which was what he always said when there was something about modern art on the news, like the record price a Picasso had fetched at auction, although I'd read that Picasso himself said he'd spent his whole life learning to paint like a child.

In the lobby outside the gallery, there was a little exhibition of a primary-school class's attempts to reproduce Matisse's *Snail* with torn coloured paper on a sheet of white A4. It was amazing how different all the pictures were. A couple of them were really good; others, even though they contained exactly the same elements, just weren't, somehow. I wondered what Picasso would make of that. I bought a postcard of the work in the gift shop, thinking Hope's class might try a similar thing in Art.

There were posters advertising free lectures in the gallery on weekday evenings. If I lived in London, I thought, I would go along and learn about art, and in summer I would queue for the Proms and learn about classical music. There was so much stuff available, even if you weren't a student.

Standing on the wobbly bridge I could see Shakespeare's Globe and the house Sir Christopher Wren lived in when he was building St Paul's and all the way down to Tower Bridge. I walked across to the north side of the river and caught a bus along Fleet Street to the Aldwych. Wending my way through Covent Garden, I paused outside the regal frontage of the Royal Opera House, its cream stucco columns flooded with golden light. Along the outside walls, there were framed advertisements for the new ballet season.

A few weeks back, Kev had sent us the programme of a triple bill. I hadn't been able to work out why – he'd been in lots of productions and never sent a programme before – until I spotted his name on the cast list. His first-ever solo role. Along with it he'd enclosed a postcard of the Empire State Building, with *When are you coming to see us?* scribbled on the back. I'd promised Hope long ago that we'd go to New York and I'd almost saved enough money when 9/11 happened, which put everyone off flying. It would be so amazing to see him performing on stage, I knew I should get up the courage while Hope was still young enough for a child's fare.

The crowd going into the Opera House matched the opulence of the foyer. Whoever it was who said that women can never be too rich or too thin was probably an opera goer. Some of the men were wearing bow ties and the women had those little bejewelled clutch bags you see in magazines and tottered on high-heeled shoes you'd never find in Clarks. I swept inside with them and up the red-carpeted staircase.

On my right was the Crush Room, where people were eating their pre-show suppers beneath sparkling crystal chandeliers that were reflected in the enormous mirror at the end of the room, making it look like an endless glittery hall; on my left, a huge conservatory-like room echoed with the hubbub of rich people drinking champagne.

I slipped through a door which took me up a red flight of stairs into a curving corridor lined with wooden doors and, daring to open one, found myself in the dark antechamber of a box, where there were hooks to hang your coats. Stepping down into the seating area, I sat and gazed up into the vast, empty auditorium, its tiers decorated with pretty little lamps and gilt curlicues, then down at the heavy crimson velvet curtains edged with gold rope and embroidered with the initials of the Queen. It must take some nerve to step out onto the stage with thousands of expectant faces watching you. No wonder Kev was highly strung.

I jumped up as the door to the box opened.

'Oh, excuse me!' said a tall man, backing out again.

'No, I'm just looking,' I mumbled, sliding past him and his female companion, my eyes lowered, as if I'd ventured into a posh shop where I couldn't afford to buy anything.

Dave wasn't keen on trying any of the Chinatown restaurants with roasted ducks and strange-looking sausages hanging in the window, so we got a window table in the Aberdeen Steak House where you know what you're eating, and there's an awful lot of it, including a big flat mushroom, onion rings, the lot.

I loved watching the different types of people hurrying past: groups of foreign teenagers carrying matching backpacks; families with whining children who'd been on their feet all day; chefs who'd stepped out of the kitchen for a quick smoke; young couples on their first date, and elderly ones who'd grown tetchy with one another.

'They've obviously missed the start of the show and she's livid because she booked the tickets months ago,' I said about a couple who were arguing just on the other side of the glass.

'Do you know them?' Dave asked.

'Course not!'

'You're weird, sometimes, you know that?' he said.

The waiter took our order and brought glasses of house white to go with the prawn cocktail.

'This is the life!' said Dave. 'Cheers!'

We clinked.

He leaned across the table. 'Can you believe it's been three years?'

People always say that women are the ones who push for commitment, but in our relationship, it was more Dave. I was always a bit flustered when he started talking about 'us' because he was my first proper boyfriend, the only man I'd had sex with, but I wasn't quite convinced that he was the soul-mate I'd envisaged sharing my life with. My romantic education had come from novels and all my favourite heroines had to suffer misunderstanding and despair in their pursuit of true love: Bathsheba Everdene and Gabriel Oak, Dorothea Brooke and Will Ladislaw, Meggie and Ralph de Bricassart – none of them were easy-going relationships like mine with Dave. Don't get me wrong – I really liked him and we had a good time

206

together. He was attractive and generous and occasionally, like this weekend, surprised me with unexpected thoughtfulness, but I just wasn't sure I was ready for the next step and I sometimes suspected that's what he was leading up to.

It's difficult to keep veering off the subject when you're sitting face to face in a booth, and he's intent on three courses. I babbled on about the passers-by and the steak – was it the quality of the meat, or the sharpness of the knife that made it so easy to cut? – and I ordered a glass of red to go with it and encouraged Dave to do the same. Since he'd been drinking lager all afternoon, he went fairly rapidly from mistily sentimental to recounting, step by step, the injustice of the penalty kick that had been awarded to his team's rivals.

When we left the restaurant, the audience was coming out of the theatre where *Mamma Mia!* was showing, laughing and singing snatches of the title song. An air of celebration mingled with the delicious sweet smell you get from those vendors cooking nuts in caramel, which I've never tried because I always think the taste's bound to be a disappointment, like proper coffee.

'Wouldn't Hope love this?'

Hope was somehow always with us, even when she wasn't.

'We could bring her up to see a musical at Christmas, if you like,' said Dave.

I wasn't sure it would be worth the money. When we'd taken her to the pantomime at the Winter Gardens, she'd sung along so loudly that the pantomime dame – a comedian famous for his ad-libbing – had invited her up on stage to sing with him. Hope was wearing a yellow summer dress with thick purple tights because she chose her own outfits in the holidays, and had a Santa hat with lights in the white trim perched on her head. The dame just about managed to tread the line between having and making fun, but it had been a struggle to get Hope to leave the stage, and had probably set a dangerous precedent. Nobody would tolerate that kind of behaviour in London.

Back in our hotel room, Dave switched on *Match of the Day* while I went into the bathroom to have a shower. We only had a bath at home, so a shower was a bit of a treat. Standing under the powerful jet with the water streaming down my back, and the wine still blurring my brain, I jumped when Dave slid open the perspex door and stepped in with me.

Even now I was still slightly shy about being naked with the lights on. Dave's body was sturdy and strong. He claimed he was five foot ten and a half which was technically taller than me, but I always felt kind of exposed standing beside him with no clothes on, as if my arms and legs were a bit too long some-how. I was never sure whether to look him appreciatively up and down like he did me. There's nothing hidden with a man, is there, and it feels so personal, somehow. Dave kissed me, first a peck. Then, with the mmms becoming longer and more intense, he pressed against me in the shower cubicle, his stiff-ening erection jabbing into my tummy button. There was a gleam in his eyes, a subtle change from affection to urgency. He wanted to do it, right there with the water streaming over us. Trying to get some purchase on the tiles with my back as he hoisted me up, I inadvertently knocked the temperature dial from warm to scalding.

'Bloody hell!' Dave slammed the dial the other way to freez-ing.

So we had to turn the water off, which killed the moment.

'It's not like it is in the movies, is it?' Dave laughed.

It was one of his phrases, and I knew it was meant to be funny and forgiving, so I laughed too, but it always made me slightly feel as if I wasn't very good at sex.

Dave wrapped me in a big white towel, and then picked me up, carried me back into the bedroom and lay down beside me. I dried myself as best I could, making a turban of the towel for my head, so my wet hair wouldn't soak the pillow.

Dave climbed on top of me, giving me another long kiss.

He was very gentle, but I was still always a bit tense as he caressed my breasts, half-expecting him to find something that I'd missed. I lay there, holding my breath, as if he was a bomb-disposal expert checking the ground for unexploded ordnance.

Dave was always keen for me to have a good time, but sometimes I wanted to say to him, 'Just get on with it, I don't mind.' Instead I'd pant and moan into his ear, like they actually did in the movies.

The bit I enjoyed most was lying in his arms afterwards, all warm and contented, knowing that I'd satisfied him.

'You know when we first met,' Dave said, propping himself up on one elbow. 'When I came back to your school on the last day of term?'

'Yup . . .'

'I told you I'd left something in the hall . . .'

I did remember, but thought it was funny to mention it now, three years later, because if it had gone into lost property, it would probably have been thrown away by now.

'It was my heart,' Dave said. 'I left my heart in that hall, Tess. I've loved you from the moment I set eyes on you.'

I couldn't think of an adequate response – I was meant to be the one who was good with words – and the silence began to feel too long, so I said, 'I love you too.'

The following afternoon, Dave's reluctance to queue for the London Eye was explained. He'd booked us tickets that fast-tracked us to the front.

We were almost at the top, and I was pointing landmarks out to him – 'Look, there's Nelson's Column, there's the Tele-com Tower' – when I became aware that the whole pod full of tourists had gone quiet. I turned round to find Dave on one knee, offering me a ring in a little blue velvet box.

'We've been together three years now, Tess . . .' He started into a speech he'd clearly rehearsed. 'It's been the best three years of my life, because you're the nicest, funniest person I've ever met.'

There was a wobble in his voice. Please God, I prayed, don't let him cry!

'I know you don't think you're beautiful . . .'

Why are you even telling everyone that?

'. . . but you are to me. I want to make a happy life for you, so, I'm sure you know what's coming next. Will you marry me?'

The crowd sighed, as if they'd collectively been holding their breath. Even if you didn't understand a word of English, it was pretty clear what had just happened. Camera lenses, which had been pointing out of the windows, were now trained on me.

'Look at the view!' I wanted to shout at them. 'We'll be down in a minute and they don't let you go round again!'

'It's been such a lovely weekend—'

Realizing it wasn't going to be a straightforward 'Yes!', Dave interrupted before I had a chance to get to 'but . . .'

'You need to think about it,' he said, adding for the benefit of any English speakers, 'She thinks a lot!'

No one responded. They were mostly Chinese, I noticed, much shorter than me, and looking up at me the way children might gaze at a dinosaur skeleton in a museum.

'Take the ring anyway,' Dave urged.

So I did, because it gave him the chance to get back up to his feet without losing face. Then we kissed quickly, and received a little round of applause.

*

'Dave didn't tell you he was going to propose, did he?' I asked Doll when she popped by on Monday evening to hear how the weekend had gone.

'No, but I guessed. He was so keen to get everything just right, bless! Let's see the ring, then,' she said.

I went upstairs and got the blue velvet box. It was a pearl, surrounded by tiny diamonds. It looked so modest compared to the bracelet of diamonds dangling from Doll's arm, I felt almost fonder of it.

'Because I was wearing pearls the first time we kissed,' I said.

'Weren't those my pearls?'

'They were.'

'So, anyway,' said Doll, impatiently, as if I was the one who'd interrupted the flow of the narrative. 'You said yes?'

'Sort of.'

'Sort of?'

'It's complicated, isn't it?' I said. 'I mean, would he move in here? His flat's not big enough for all of us. I've got to think about Hope.'

We were sitting in the kitchen because Hope had *Pop Idol* on in the living room.

'Dave is great with Hope,' Doll said.

'I know. It's just . . . I thought marriage would be different, not the same,' I finally admitted.

'You're weird, you do know that?'

'That's what Dave always says. I didn't say no. I just want to think it through.'

'If he sticks around. You want to think about that!' Doll warned. 'Dave's good-looking and he's lovely. He's a kind man, Tess! Your mum would be so happy!'

Would she, though? I didn't know if that was true. And I didn't think it was for Doll to say, to be honest.

Anyway, she'd forgotten the first bit Mum had said about

finding a man who understands who you are. I didn't doubt Dave loved me. But he didn't even know about the bit of me that wanted to live in London and learn about stuff, and discover what I liked and what I was capable of.

'Who'd have thought you'd be the first?' Doll said so sadly that we sat there in silence for a moment or two. 'Me and Fred have split up.'

So then I understood, and appreciated Doll making the effort to talk about my good news first.

'Shall I make us a cup of tea?' I asked.

The way our friendship worked, I was always more comfortable listening to her problems than having her giving me advice. Maybe it was something to do with being a big sister rather than the baby of the family.

'We had a row about me working,' Doll began. 'And I said, "Well, I've got to look out for myself, haven't I, if you're not going to marry me?" And he didn't say, "Let's get married," he just said, "Please yourself!" Four fucking years, Tess! *Please yourself!* "I will then," I told him. And that was that. Four years! Can you believe it? I don't need that shit any more. I'm sick of being on Fred's arm, like some bloody . . .'

'Appendage?'

'Whatever,' said Doll. 'What have I got to look forward to with Fred? Babies and Botox, that's what.'

If I was meant to say, 'But what about . . . ?' like she'd just done with me, I couldn't think of anything, because I hated the way that Fred had been increasingly dictating what Doll was and wasn't allowed to do.

'You're sure, then?'

'I've moved all my stuff back home.'

I knew it was selfish, but I felt pretty happy that she'd be just down the road again. 'So are you going back to the salon?'

'Not exactly . . .' Doll gave a strange little smile. 'I've seen the future, Tess, and it's nails.'

212

'Nails?'

For a moment, I was thinking metal spikes you hammer into wood, but then I noticed that Doll was proffering her hand. Each fingernail was pale glossy pink, with a diagonal flash of diamanté stones.

'Everyone needs a haircut, right?' she said. 'Now everyone needs their nails done too. Except a nail salon is cheaper to set up, because you don't need a lot of space and equipment, and you don't need people who can cut hair either.'

'Do you know how to run a business, though?'

'Tess, I've met a lot of business people through Fred, and you'd think they'd be clever and educated and stuff, but they're not. Fred's agent says there's two ways of making money. You have one big clever idea, like Bill Gates, or you have a little one and you do it over and over. So what I'm going to do is nails, and only nails, and do them well and at a price people can afford. I'll be the first in this area.'

'Isn't having your nails done just a passing fad?'

'Trust me, Tess, I'm a trained beautician. There's no going back with this one. It's like Halloween.'

I couldn't see the connection.

'When we were kids, we didn't have all the cards and presents and dressing-up and trick-or-treat, did we? You can't not, now, can you?'

She had a point. We even had a Halloween-themed week at St Cuthbert's.

'What are you going to call your business?' I asked.

'I was thinking Maria O'Nail's. What do you reckon?'

'How about The Dolls' House?' I suggested, sparking off her enthusiasm.

'That's brilliant, Tess!'

She took a pink leather notebook out of her pink Mulberry handbag and wrote it down.

'You've got the apostrophe in the wrong place,' I pointed out. 'It can either be Doll's House, that is your house, or The Dolls' House, which means for lots of dolls.'

'Sod the apostrophe!' said Doll. 'I mean, who cares? It's not like Toys R Us is grammatical, is it? Hang on, though, doesn't The Dolls House make it sound like there's only one?'

'Not that you're getting ahead of yourself, or anything!'

'The Body Shop has loads of branches, though, doesn't it?' Doll mused. 'And she started in a seaside town, didn't she? What you have to do is build a brand . . .'

Perhaps my friend *did* have what it took. She'd always had an eye for a buck. She'd got a Saturday job sweeping up in a hairdresser when she was only thirteen and was getting tips for washing the customers' hair within a few weeks. By fifteen, she was setting her mum's friends' hair for church socials at a fiver a time, and the day of our school prom she'd organized back-to-back appointments for full hair and make-up in the O'Neills' bathroom. So it kind of made sense that all this time she'd been a WAG, with nothing to do except look good in photos, she'd been taking notes.

'You need publicity, obviously, but I've got contacts in the magazines,' Doll continued. 'I've got to get a move on, though, because there's only a couple of months before "Following her split with footballing fiancé Fred, Maria O'Neill launches The Dolls House" turns into "Who?"'

'Only one problem.' I tried to inject a note of realism. 'Won't you need some start-up money?'

I noticed she hadn't given Fred the diamond bracelet back. I wondered how much that was worth.

'So, I put on my Chanel and went to the bank, didn't I?' Doll said.

'Number Five?' In my head I could hear my mother saying, 'If you marry a rich man, Tess, that's the scent he'll buy you!'

'Not the perfume, you wally. My suit! You know the little black-and-white check collarless jacket and skirt that shows just the right amount of leg? Must have looked the part, anyway, 'cause he said it shouldn't be a problem.'

I felt a bit left out, discovering that she'd already got so far in her new venture without me.

'You'll help me, won't you, Tess?' Doll asked, because she knew me well enough to see what I was thinking.

'Course I will,' I said. 'If I can.'

'You already came up with the name!'

I put a mug of tea in front of her.

'This is the life!' Doll helped herself to a Tunnock's caramel wafer. 'You know what, Tess, you think there's this whole exciting world out there, but I've been to Dubai and St Tropez and Florida and I've stayed in five-star hotels, and honestly, there's nothing quite like sitting here in your kitchen, eating a biscuit if I feel like it. Sometimes the best things are staring you right in the face, know what I mean?'

15

2003

GUS

A few weeks into our Foundation One, Lucy booked us a mini-break.

'I found this last-minute deal on the Internet. Four-star hotel in Brighton. We've got a sea view and everything,' she said, when I returned on Friday morning from an all-night shift.

'Wow!'

'We can have a proper dirty weekend,' she said.

'Isn't that a contradiction in terms?'

She laughed.

'So when are we going?' I asked.

'This evening, silly. It's last-minute! Two nights for the price of one. We'll arrive late, but we'll have the whole day tomorrow and Sunday to do exactly what we like!'

She gave me a knowing look. The dirty-weekend idea was so unlike Lucy, I felt slightly panicky.

'What?' she asked, seeing the expression on my face.

'No, nothing,' I said. 'Charlotte had tickets for the theatre, but she'll find someone else.'

'Sure?' said Lucy. It was a rhetorical question.

I gave her a quick kiss before she went off to work.

Charlotte wasn't answering her phone when I called, so I left a brief message, and when I pressed *disconnect*, felt a rush of relief. It was her birthday. She would not be pleased and that would be the end of it.

I'd decided to mention Charlotte to Lucy a few weeks after it happened, describing her as a friend of the family. To be honest, I may have made her sound rather a forlorn figure, someone who it was my duty, almost, to accompany to the occasional play or opera. If Lucy had met Charlotte, she might have been more suspicious, but, ironically, she actually welcomed the idea of my 'opera buddy', because I think she privately dreaded that I might suggest we go together.

I told myself I wasn't really lying when I said Charlotte was 'much older' than me, or that I thought she was quite a lonely person. Like cigarettes, taken up on the same day, Charlotte had become an addiction that was much harder to quit than I'd thought.

Lucy had been horrified when I ran out of excuses as to why I smelled like a pub.

'Since when?' she'd asked, when I'd confessed to smoking.

'Since 9/11,' I'd told her disingenuously. I'd become quite good at telling half-truths by then.

In the beginning, I couldn't believe it was happening; as it continued, my rationalization went something like this: Charlotte could not be seriously contemplating a relationship with me. I was five years younger than her and, more to the point, the little brother of her former boyfriend. Compared to Ross, I was callow, inexperienced and weedy, so my role in her life must simply be as a temporary plaything until a real contender came along.

I'm not trying to deny my responsibility, but to a callow,

217

inexperienced, weedy member of the male gender in his early twenties, the offer of sex with someone as out-of-your-league and up-for-it as your older brother's stunningly beautiful girl-friend was impossible to turn down.

On several occasions, I did try to stop, once managing to survive nearly two weeks by running twice a day, fast, round Regent's Park. But when I bumped into Charlotte, also running, at six in the morning, the sight of her normally smooth fringe waywardly plastered across her forehead, her perfectly sculpted shoulders glistening with sweat, was too much. We did it there, in the park, against the back of the coffee shed just near the formal gardens, her sweet stale morning breath in my ear, her long, smooth thighs clamped around mine, the silky wet readiness of her as I slid in, my forehead banging against splintery slats of wood that smelled of creosote.

I was absolutely sure that sooner or later she'd decide she'd had enough. I somehow convinced myself that in the mean-time there was no more damage to my relationship with Lucy than had already happened, so my sin was more opportunism than treachery.

By the time Lucy and I arrived on the south coast, it was late. We took a cab from the station. Small extravagances were still a novelty after so many years on a student budget and I could feel the tingle of Lucy's excitement across the fug of Christmas-tree air-freshener.

The hotel had a faded Victorian glamour. As we approached the reception desk, I whispered, 'Are we supposed to check in as Mr and Mrs Smith?'

There was a flash of enquiry in Lucy's eyes and a slightly awkward giggle. We'd been together for almost six years by then, and were on our way to earning decent salaries, but we were still skirting the question of marriage.

I threw open the French windows and stood on the balcony.

218

The breeze was fresh and salty, the pier glittering with coloured lights. Occasionally the wind carried a snatch of pop music or a distant scream from one of the rides over the soft crash of waves. I could feel the pressure of the city lifting from my shoulders.

'Do you have to smoke?' Lucy said as I lit up.

Her face was all frowny with concern for my health and made me think, as I did several times a day, how lucky I was to be with her, and what a shit I was. I stubbed out the cigarette decisively, grinding it into the concrete floor of the balcony, telling myself that was my last one, ever, but not promising out loud, because I'd done that so many times before, as Lucy would remind me, and then I'd feel like a failure and the whole cycle of need would start again.

We stood together, looking out to sea, her body fitting comfortably against mine, and I felt as fond of her as I had on the first day of our relationship, and almost as nervous about the prospect of having sex, which was the reason that we'd come here. How could I have thought that she wouldn't notice the diminishing frequency of our lovemaking, or told myself that she probably preferred it that way?

In the morning, we walked along the slatted boards on the pier, hand in hand, with Lucy chatting about the rides she'd been on at funfairs, and whether it would make her feel sick to go on a Waltzer so soon after eating a full English breakfast, and just about anything to avoid the possibility of a silence in which the question of my impotence the previous night might acquire some greater significance than me just being tired.

My mobile phone vibrated repeatedly against my thigh as Charlotte called to remonstrate. I suddenly realized that we had stopped walking and Lucy had just asked me a question.

'Sorry?'

'Have you got any change for the token machine? Honestly,

Gus, it's like you disappear sometimes! Do you think you get enough oxygen up there?'

I exchanged ten pounds and we wandered around the various rides before deciding which to go on. The Booster was the most dangerous. With four seats at each end of a high rotating arm, it made the others look like kids' stuff.

'Come on!' I grabbed Lucy's hand and pulled her towards the kiosk. 'The view from the top will be great.'

Lucy's screams, a primal mix of fear and excitement, were a bit of a turn-on because her responses were usually so measured. As the ride went faster and faster, fear diminished and pleasure increased to a peak where all we could do was laugh with sheer exhilaration. When the ride began to slow, our hysteria calmed, and I realized that I hadn't thought about Charlotte for at least five minutes.

We were lured into the amusement arcade by the air-hockey table, where Lucy won several times amid the clatter and jingle of fruit machines. Tennis was the only sport we really played together, and I had the advantage of height and speed so even though she had much better technique, she only won if I let her. Her approach to air hockey was more about angles than my stabs at power, so she beat me fair and square. As the last puck shot into my goal and the glee spread across her face, I found myself overwhelmed with affection for her.

In The Lanes, every other shop was an antique jeweller's. The windows sparkled with diamond rings. Even though Lucy said nothing, nor lingered longingly as I noticed several other women in couples doing, I suddenly wanted to make it up to her for the previous evening by going down on one knee and proposing. It sounds ludicrous to say it, but it was only a sense of honour that stopped me. I knew it wasn't fair to ask Lucy to marry me until I had finished with Charlotte once and for all.

*

I bought Charlotte a Paul Smith silk scarf from Liberty for her birthday, which she thanked me for, but did not put on.

'I've got a present for you too,' she said.

I unfolded the tissue inside the Agent Provocateur box to find shell-pink silk camiknickers, and a pair of fine-denier ivory stockings. 'This is for you, right?'

She shook her head. 'It's for you. I just wear it. Do you want me to put the stockings on, or would you like to tie me to the bed with them?'

Sometimes it crossed my mind that Charlotte should, or possibly did, have a sideline as a high-class call girl. Where did she learn this stuff?

If the sex was more mind-blowing than ever, it was because I knew it was the last time. Afterwards, I got up, showered and dressed, knowing I would feel too vulnerable trying to tell her while I was still naked.

'Here we go,' she said, as I stood by the door, rocking slightly from foot to foot.

'I know I've said it before, but this really has to be the last time,' I said.

'You haven't gone and told the wife, have you?'

'Don't call her that.'

'She's not pregnant, is she?'

'Not that I'm aware,' I said, trying to be cool but sounding like a prat.

'That would be awkward . . .'

'Why?' I bristled. If Lucy was pregnant, it was nothing to do with Charlotte. It might even be rather nice, I thought, except Lucy was far too sensible to make a mistake.

'Because I am,' said Charlotte. 'Pregnant.'

Then, after a long pause, 'Can't you look a bit happier than that?'

'How?'

'Darling, it's pre-GCSE stuff, isn't it?'

'I mean . . .' Surely she was using something?

'Polycystic ovaries. I never thought I'd conceive.'

'But you should've . . .'

'You never asked.'

How had that happened? I was a doctor, for God's sake. Why had I abandoned all the rules? Because each time felt like a once-in-a-lifetime opportunity that I could so easily mess up.

'How long?' My voice echoed in my head, as if someone else was asking the questions that had to be asked.

'I won't bore you with my menstrual cycle, or lack of it, but in the absence of the normal indicators, I appear to be at least three months, possibly getting on for four.'

Her stomach was still flat. Was this some strange kind of joke? I must have looked bewildered.

'And yes, it is,' she said.

'What?'

'Yours.'

'And you're going to . . . ?' At that point, I was still thinking of it as something to do with her and no one else.

'I've given it a lot of thought. Obviously, it's unexpected, but I'm thirty and with my ovaries it might not happen naturally again. The time I'll lose from my career now is probably less than if I make surgeon then have to go through IVF.'

'So what do you want me to do?' I asked.

'Aren't you going to offer to make an honest woman out of me?'

Was she teasing?

'You want to marry me?'

'Is it so surprising? We have the best sex ever. You're intelligent and cultured. I think you'll probably make rather a good father.'

Everything she was saying was so strange to me, I felt as if I was hallucinating, as if she was some sort of surrealist installation, lying there in pale silk underwear, her lips and nipples dark from sex, and inside her tummy, a little human being who half-belonged to me. As I stared at her body, I felt I could now see the new roundness of her belly where the tiny foetus was curled up inside.

In one of Lucy's obstetrics books, there was a chart of a baby's development, with all the stages described in terms of items of food. At four months, the baby was well beyond a kidney bean, probably not quite a grapefruit yet.

When I didn't say anything, Charlotte said, in a wistful tone I'd never heard before, 'It might be fun . . . don't you think?'

For a moment, she looked so vulnerable I wanted to hold her and reassure her that everything would be all right. And yet I still wasn't sure whether this was some sort of elaborate game, and the only question I could think of asking to find out was, 'Will you marry me, then?'

Occasionally, when we were having drinks in some theatre foyer, I'd allowed myself to fantasize that people might mistake us for a proper couple, but I'd never thought about how we might arrive at that status, and if I had, it wouldn't have been like this.

'Oh, Angus, you're so sweet!'

She knelt up on the bed, took my hand and said, solemnly, 'I will,' before rewarding me with the most tender, sensual kiss I had ever received.

How do you tell your girlfriend of six years that you've un-expectedly got engaged to a woman you've unwittingly got pregnant? A woman who happens to be the former girlfriend of your older brother, who you've never mentioned?

On my walk home from Charlotte Street, I took deep breaths, trying to compose a speech in my head, but the pyra-mid of lies I had constructed, which hadn't felt like such a big deal incrementally, now seemed unscalably huge. It began to dawn on me, for the first time, that in revealing lies that I had

223

thought were mine and mine alone, I would be demolishing Lucy's life too. I didn't know if I could do that. But I had to. There was a baby. There was Charlotte . . .

Lucy was out at the cinema with some girlfriends when I got back, and they went on to Nando's afterwards. It was too late to start explaining when she came in, because I was already in bed, pretending to be fast asleep.

I should have told her the following day, but she'd had to inform a pregnant mother that her baby's heart was no longer beating, and, after she told me that, I couldn't bring myself to say anything.

I promised myself that I would do it at the weekend, but on Thursday, my father rang to say that he and my mother had some news they wanted to give me in person.

'You're not ill?'

'No, not that.'

But it sounded more serious than, say, a decision to retire or move.

'I've got to go and see my folks,' I told Lucy.

'Can I come?'

'I don't think that's a good idea.'

She'd never been to my parents' house. Now didn't seem like the best time for a visit.

'Why?'

When I couldn't summon an immediate excuse, it occurred to me that it might actually present a way of encouraging Lucy to question our relationship before I broke my news.

My father was waiting for us at the station. 'I'll come straight out with it,' he announced, as he started the car. 'Your mother and I have decided to separate.'

'Your father's been having an affair with his dental nurse,' was the version of events my mother offered almost as soon as we were through the front door.

'Perhaps you'd rather I . . . ?' Lucy began, embarrassed because this kind of personal revelation clearly was not what she'd been expecting.

'No, you might as well hear what's in store for you when you lose your looks and your libido,' my mother snapped.

It was such an uncharacteristically forthright statement, I wondered if she'd been drinking, or watching daytime television.

'Your mother and I haven't been happy for some time—'

'How could we be after—?' asked my mother.

'—and now this chance has come along, I feel I have to try—'

'She's thirty-seven,' said my mother.

Unable to think of a suitable comment, I made the mistake of looking at my father.

'Oh, I see,' my mother rounded on me. 'You knew all along, did you?'

'Absolutely not!' I protested.

'He honestly didn't,' Lucy chimed in.

My mother stared at me. I didn't know what I was supposed to say or what she wanted me to do. Should I remonstrate with my father, or try to stop him? Was that what Ross would have done? I was aware now that Lucy had spotted the pictures of my brother on the mantelpiece. Ross in a mortarboard holding his degree certificate was right next to mine, in exactly the same pose.

The silence seemed interminable.

'So, what's going to happen?' I asked eventually.

'I'm not leaving this house,' said my mother, immediately. 'I've put my whole life into it.'

'I'll be moving out,' said my father.

'Don't make it sound like a sacrifice!' she shouted at him.

'I've put a lot into it too,' he said, rather pathetically.

225

'And now you've destroyed it all!' said my mother, then rushed from the room.

I'd heard her crying so often, but this sound was different, like a wounded animal.

'Mum will be OK financially?' I asked, feeling that someone ought to represent her interests.

'Yes, yes!' he said impatiently. 'Look, I think it's probably better if I leave you to it. I'll be in touch about the arrangements.'

'OK,' I said. And then, because I couldn't think of anything else, I held out my hand, which he seemed surprised and grateful to grasp.

'She couldn't let go,' he said, his voice uncharacteristically croaky with emotion. 'She wouldn't allow me even to want to.'

I'd seen them as a unit, bound together by grief, but we'd all been as alone as each other.

'I hope you'll be happy,' was all I could think of to say.

I could see in his eyes that he thought I was being sarcastic, but it was somehow too late to explain.

'It doesn't seem fair, does it?' Lucy said, after the automatic security gates had closed behind his Lexus. 'You couldn't really see your mother with a thirty-seven-year-old man, could you?'

She walked over to the mantelpiece to get a closer look at the photos: Ross with gaps where his baby teeth had been; Ross in his prep-school cap, blazer and shorts; Ross receiving the rugby cup; Ross with his eight, all of them holding the boat above their heads; Ross wearing mirror ski goggles with a snowy mountain behind him.

I took a deep breath.

'That's my brother,' I said. 'He was killed in a skiing accident the Christmas before I started uni. I didn't want people to cast me as a grieving person and not know what to say to me, you know?'

'Oh, Gus, I'm so sorry!'

Lucy's eyes were full of tears, which wasn't part of the scene I had written in my head.

'It must have been terrible for you . . .'

'Well, yes. But now you're doing that thing, you know?'

'Sorry.'

She wasn't the one who was supposed to be sorry. She was supposed to be upset that I'd misled her.

'What happened?' she asked gently.

A question nobody had voiced since my parents, and then the search party, and then the police all those years ago. A question I tried to avoid thinking about.

'He was skiing off-piste and hit a tree. The brain damage was so severe they decided to switch off the life support.'

'Were you there?'

'When they switched it off? No. My parents were.'

Lucy didn't say anything, but I knew that wasn't what she'd been asking.

'I don't suppose you can forgive me for not mentioning it?' As soon as the words left my mouth, I knew I'd mistimed it. I should have waited to let the implications sink in.

'But there's nothing to forgive!' Lucy exclaimed. 'I'm just so sorry I wasn't there for you!'

She turned and tried to hug me, but I couldn't put my arms around her. Her attempts to make it easy for me were making it much more difficult.

'He was very handsome,' she said, picking up the photo of him leaving with a backpack for his gap year.

'Yes. He was handsome and cool and good at everything. Everyone adored him.'

'And is this his girlfriend?'

With Freudian failure of eyesight or foresight, I hadn't spotted the picture of Charlotte and Ross dressed as Morticia and Uncle Fester.

'Yes.'

'She's very beautiful.'

'Yes.'

Lucy was very quiet for the rest of the day, although she put on a bright face when my mother came down and prepared supper for us. A chicken-and-leek pie. If my mother had been her normal self, she would have made up the guest room for Lucy, but she was so distracted she didn't think of it, so we went to bed in my old room. At first, it felt sweetly poignant to rediscover our way of lying together with me curled round her back, just like the first time in Lucy's single bed in Broadstairs, although neither of us was now in any mood for sex. After many minutes' silence I realized that she was as unable to sleep as I was.

'Are you OK?' she asked in the darkness.

'I've had better days.'

'Sorry. Crass of me.'

'No. It's fine. I'm sorry to involve you in all of this.'

'Don't be sorry. I wish you *had* involved me. It feels so strange that you didn't tell me about Ross. There's this whole important part of your life I didn't know anything about, and I thought I knew you so well.'

Another few minutes of both of us pretending to get to sleep.

'Your heart's beating really fast,' Lucy said. 'Are you sure you're OK?'

'No! I'm not!' I cried.

Suddenly I couldn't contain my panic.

I sat up. So did she. She reached to turn the light on, but I didn't know if I could say what I had to say with her looking at me.

'Don't!'

'What's the matter?'

'I'm fine. No, I'm not. I'm a shit!'

228

'Gus, calm down. It's OK. You've had a big shock. Honestly, Gus. You're having a panic attack. Just breathe. I'll get you some water.'

'I DON'T NEED WATER!'

I'd never shouted at her before. Now, the silence was loaded with hurt.

'Lucy. I'm sorry, but we've got to split up. I've been meaning to tell you all week, long before all this with my parents.'

'Don't be silly!'

'I'm serious.'

I couldn't see her face properly, but I could tell she still didn't believe me, probably thought it was a temporary insanity brought about by shock.

'I've been having an affair with somebody and I'm going to marry her.'

Coward to say it in the dark!

Now I didn't stop her from switching the bedside light on, and when she did, she could see in my face that I wasn't joking. She didn't cry, not then, not as I'd expected.

'Why?' she asked calmly.

What a good doctor she was going to make.

'She's pregnant,' I sighed. 'She wants to have the baby.'

'But do you love her?'

Sounds strange, but that question hadn't crossed my mind. I wondered if it had crossed Charlotte's. Neither of us had mentioned love. She was too cool and I was trying to be.

'Yes, I do.'

Unable to be near Lucy as I said it, I got out of bed, pulling an Arsenal dressing gown from the hook on the back of the door to hide my nakedness. It had been bought for me when I was about twelve and only just did.

I went to sit down on the edge of the bed.

'Don't!' Lucy cried, so I jumped up again, feeling exposed and stupid.

'You haven't been using precautions?' The levers in Lucy's brain were clicking into place and my crimes beginning to stack up.

'I assumed—'

'You've endangered me as well as deceiving me?'

The disease side of things hadn't even crossed my mind.

'I'm sure—'

'Just like you were sure she was on the Pill? What's her name, by the way?'

'Charlotte.'

'Not your opera buddy? Oh my God! What an imbecile I've been! I trusted you, Gus! I thought you were such a sweetie! It never crossed my mind not to trust you!'

'I know,' I said.

'Does Charlotte know about me?'

'We don't really talk about—'

'You just screw? Or do you actually go to the opera? Jesus, Gus! Have you gone mad?'

'Maybe.'

'You live with me! You can't know what it's like to live with her. This is crazy! It's crazy, Gus!'

I felt as if I'd frozen. There were no excuses. There was no explanation.

Suddenly Lucy launched herself at me, thumping my chest with her fists.

'What's wrong with you?' she screamed at me. 'What's wrong with you, Gus? It's like you're in some kind of trance!'

Getting no reaction, she sank to her knees, her mouth contorted in a silent howl of pain, before collapsing in a noisy flood of sobs.

I hated seeing her so upset and out of control, my blameless friend, my companion. She was the person who'd made me feel normal and I'd repaid her by behaving so badly, there was nothing I could say or do to comfort her.

Eventually, she took an extraordinarily long intake of breath and pulled herself together again.

'It's because of Ross, isn't it?' she said.

I thought she was talking about my attraction to Charlotte. How clever she was to see that.

An image of Charlotte in her white bikini, the day Ross brought her home to try out our hot tub, flashed across my mind. But even though she'd remarked on her beauty when she saw the photo downstairs, Lucy didn't know that Ross's girlfriend was Charlotte, I realized, and I'd never revealed the connection.

'Once you lie about something, you lose respect for the other person you're lying to,' Lucy continued, thinking out loud. 'You thought less of me because you hadn't told me that, so it made all the other lies easier, I suppose.'

That was very perceptive too.

'I should have listened to Helen,' Lucy said with a sigh of resignation. 'She never trusted all your dreamy shit.'

She looked up at me hovering impotently in my ridiculously too-small dressing gown. 'Just leave me alone, Gus.'

I went to Ross's room and lay on his bed with his shelf of trophies glinting at me, listening to the muffled murmur of my girlfriend talking on her mobile phone all through the night.

Around seven o'clock in the morning, the doorbell rang. I ran downstairs and opened the door to Nicky. Lucy walked straight past me without speaking and sat in her mother's car.

'The last thing I wanted to do was hurt her!' I faltered.

'Oh, Gus, *really*?' Nicky said, looking at me with such disappointment, I felt like I'd betrayed the whole family.

'What's happening?' My mother was standing in her dressing gown on the stairs as I turned round from closing the front door.

'I've split up with Lucy.'

'Here? Why?'

'I let her down, I'm afraid.'

'Not like your father?'

I wanted to protest. No, not like that. But what was the difference? Silence betrayed my guilt.

'Why?' my mother suddenly shouted at the ceiling, her head thrown back in imprecation.

'Ross was no angel, you know!' I said, regretting the words as soon as they left my lips.

My mother's empty stare was far more unsettling than her usual look of vague disappointment. It made me shiver with certainty that, at that moment, at least, she hated me.

'I don't know why you're here,' she said, with an impatient wave of her hand as she turned back up the stairs. 'Can you just go, please?'

On the train back to London, I could no longer locate myself. I stared at the reflection of my face in the window. The person I was had been an illusion and I felt sick with shame and self-loathing.

In our flat, I packed my clothes into a suitcase like an automaton, unsure whether it would cause more pain to leave items that had been given as gifts or take them with me, coming down on the side of leaving them.

I walked around each room one last time, unable to compute that I'd never again wake up in that bed, never again cook Lucy breakfast on that stove, never again huddle next to her on that sofa in winter, our ridiculous oversized slippers peeping out from under the duvet.

On impulse, I dialled her mobile number.

'Are you OK?'

'What do you think?' She sighed wearily.

Silence.

'Don't worry, Gus, I'm not going to do anything stupid . . .'

'I didn't think . . .'

'No.'

Another long silence.

'Don't call me again, Gus,' she said, and hung up.

I posted my key through the letter box.

For once, the lift was working.

As I wheeled my suitcase along the busy road, a different anxiety began to take over. I was swapping stability for exhilaration, but what if it had all been a wind-up? Charlotte and I hadn't spoken since the beginning of the week. It seemed an age ago now. What if she laughed in my face? Where would I go? Nash would probably let me crash on her sofa, I thought, but not before giving me a lecture about my treatment of women, and I didn't think I could bear to disappoint anyone else.

Charlotte took a while to answer the entryphone, and when she did, her voice was frosty. 'Yes?'

'It's Angus!'

She buzzed me in. I bumped the suitcase up the stairs. The door to her flat was open and she was lying on the bed in her rose lingerie.

'I was beginning to think you didn't have the balls!' She patted the space beside her.

How amazingly quickly the brain adapts: one moment standing in the street, gloomily homeless; the next, climbing on top of my lover, swamped by the delirious disbelief I imagine a EuroMillions winner feels.

People usually describe winning the Lottery as a fairy tale, forgetting that fairy tales have a dark side. For me, the frisson of foreboding was always there, like Hansel being offered candy he knew he shouldn't accept.

In the three weeks before we married, Charlotte and I discovered things about each other that you can't know without living together. Charlotte couldn't cook. I rather regretted abandoning the shallow Le Creuset casserole which doubled as a frying pan that Nicky had given me for my last birthday. Charlotte was messy. The pristine state of her attic flat, it turned out, was solely due to a cleaner who came twice a week. In the intervening days, Charlotte never hung up her clothes nor put her washing in the basket. Charlotte's justification was economic. If you could pay someone less to do the jobs than you could earn, why waste your time?

On that rationale, or because I'd worked as a waiter so long, I sometimes felt rather like a butler when I ironed Charlotte's clothes or brought her breakfast in bed. Except that butlers don't generally walk around in boxer shorts, nor, when the lady of the house has finished breakfast, do they get kissed with shiny buttery lips, or lie with her writhing on top of them, sandpapering their bare skin with toast crumbs.

We decided to marry in Marylebone Register Office. If you were allowed to do these things immediately, we'd probably have asked a couple of strangers on the street to witness our union, but you have to give notice for the bans to be read, and so we told our parents. Charlotte's were long-divorced. She hadn't seen her father for many years, and he lived in Scotland with his new family, but he sent us a card and a cheque for a thousand pounds. Her mother, who had recently moved to the Balearics with Robbie, a childhood sweetheart she'd met on Friends Reunited, insisted on flying over for the ceremony.

I decided not to invite either of my parents after their individual reactions to the news.

'But Lucy is a lovely girl . . . !' My father tried to puzzle out the sequence of events, and found it a step too far on the Lothario scale, even for him.

'Surely you don't mean Ross's Charlotte?' my mother said.

I rang Marcus, who was by then a contract lawyer for a big City firm, to ask if he'd be my best man.

'I'd be honoured,' he said. 'Let me check my diary. We're talking this year?'

'Next Wednesday,' I told him. 'Spur-of-the-moment thing.'

'Oh. Well. Congratulations! Better get working on my speech!'

'Don't worry, it's just a quick ceremony, followed by lunch at Piattini. We're flying to New York the same evening.'

'Good for you!' he said. 'The number of weddings I've been to recently that must have cost as much as a house! I'm assuming no dress code then?'

'No dress code.'

I bought a black suit from Marks & Spencer, the only off-the-peg one I could find with a thirty-five-inch inside leg. Charlotte bought herself a cream tuxedo-style jacket and a new little black dress from Liberty, because, although the pregnancy was barely visible, she had put on a little weight around the tummy. The outfit hung from the curtain pole above the French doors.

'Isn't it supposed to be bad luck for me to see your dress?' I asked, as we got into bed the night before the wedding.

'Oh, I hate all that stuff. Grown women getting trussed up like virgins in order to be given away – in the twenty-first century, for heaven's sake!'

I thought of all the months of preparation there'd been for Pippa's wedding and how I'd have had to go through the same palaver with Lucy, and how much more grown up it was like this.

The following morning, I lay watching Charlotte dress in new black underwear and stockings, wondering if I'd ever get used to the thrill of seeing clothes slide over what was underneath, a kind of reverse striptease that was almost as arousing as it was the other way round.

We took our small carry-on cases with us in the cab. We'd decided on New York for our honeymoon because it was new to both of us, and seemed like a suitably sexy place for a long weekend, which was all the holiday I could get away with so soon after starting my Foundation One year.

Marcus was standing on the register-office steps as our taxi drew up. I saw his face when Charlotte stepped out because that was the effect her arrival had on men – you couldn't *not* look at her – and then his surprise when I followed, and paid off the cab driver.

'Marcus, this is Charlotte,' I introduced them.

'Pleasure to meet you.' He shook her hand and smiled, more suave and composed than I'd ever seen him, but when he turned to me, he was unable to hide a boyish how-on-earth-have-you-managed-this? look that made me feel like the winner of a competition I hadn't even entered.

Charlotte's mother presented her with a small hand-tied posy of the palest pink roses, which contrasted sharply with the garish display of fabric blooms on the registrar's desk. We emerged onto the busy street again in a shower of rice, also provided by Charlotte's mother, which stuck to our hair and clothes and got in our mouths as we laughed. Then the four of us hailed a cab to Piattini.

I'd served hundreds of meals there, and eaten many times in the kitchen, but I had never before dined in the restaurant. Stefania had prepared a wedding breakfast of perfect buttery saffron risotto dressed with a sliver of gold leaf, followed by a *tagliata* of rare charred steak, accompanied by a rocket salad drizzled with treacly balsamic vinegar. For dessert, there was a chocolate-and-hazelnut *semifreddo,* with sheets of caramel so fine they dissolved in the mouth after the first tiny crunch. We applauded her when she came up from the kitchen to offer us her congratulations.

I noticed her slight double-take as I introduced her to Charlotte and they kissed on both cheeks in that strangely chaste way that Europeans do. Stefania and Salvatore weren't my surrogate parents, but it was a family business that I had been a part of for several years, so the relationship was closer than employee and boss. In a slight blur of Chianti, I clocked Stefania's surprise at my highly sophisticated wife. With Marcus, the same look had made me feel triumphantly validated; on Stefania's face, it was slightly disconcerting.

Charlotte had spent her father's gift on booking us into business class so there was plenty of space for me to stretch my legs. I'd already had a lot more to drink than she had because of the baby, and now there was a constant supply of champagne.

'I could get used to this,' I said drowsily, as the cabin lights were dimmed and the stewardess handed us pillows with clean cotton cases.

'Just as well,' Charlotte replied. In the darkness, I was aware of her hand seeking mine.

I'd been talking about the luxury; she was talking about us.

The simple act of holding hands felt like the most intimate thing we'd ever done.

'Come on,' she whispered against my neck.

I followed her to the toilet cubicle and we consummated our marriage at thirty thousand feet, with grains of rice skittering from our clothes.

16
2003

TESS

I think it's called the mile-high club. That's definitely what was going on, but I don't suppose it was much fun with Hope banging on the door. I'd thought the business-class toilet would have more room – I couldn't risk letting Hope go in on her own and locking herself in – but we couldn't wait, so we ended up walking all the way back through the dimmed economy section, where people were trying to sleep, with Hope loudly declaring, 'My knickers are wet!'

'Why didn't you go at the airport when I told you?'

'I didn't need to.'

It was so long since Hope had had 'an accident', I hadn't packed a change of clothes in my hand luggage and I was dreading asking the stewardess for a towel for the seat, but it got worse in the cubicle when Hope pulled down her knickers and saw the blood.

None of the books gives any advice about how to tell a mildly autistic child in an aeroplane loo that they're having their first period. Hope was only just eleven, so I hadn't expected it to happen yet, even though I knew that plumper girls sometimes got theirs before they went to big school. It's a difficult enough process to explain at the best of times, especially to someone as literal as Hope. The only upside was that by the time I got her out of there, with a wad of tissues stuffed into her knickers, Hope was so exhausted from screaming she slept the rest of the flight.

Kevin and Shaun were waiting for us in the arrivals hall with a sign saying: *Céad míle fáilte Teresa and Hope Costello.*

Which shows it's true what they say about Irish people becoming even more Irish when they're living abroad.

It's funny when you haven't seen someone for several years, because there's always a bit of awkwardness at first, when you're looking at each other wondering if they're thinking how much older you look too.

I've never quite understood why men with a fear of going bald elect to go completely bald at the first sign of losing their hair, but it can't be nice seeing a shiny dome relentlessly stretching back from your brow, even worse if it's a bit patchy. I suppose the thinking is that shaven is cooler than comb-over, and I'd have to agree with that. Did Kev have to wear a wig when he was performing, I wondered? I'd never seen a bald ballet dancer, not that I'd seen a lot of ballet dancers apart from on BBC2 on Boxing Day and the all-male swans at the end of *Billy Elliot*, and you couldn't see their heads for feathers.

I've no idea what Kevin was thinking about me. Or perhaps I have, because he and Shaun discussed the idea of getting me a 'makeover' long before Shaun suggested it later on in the holiday.

'Good flight?' Kev asked.

'Blood is coming out of my room because I'm not going to have a baby,' Hope announced.

I think even Kev had to admit at that point that Hope wasn't like most girls her age.

'She got her first period . . . Yes, on the plane . . . No, not

239

expected, obviously . . . Apart from that? Oh, fine, perfect flight, thanks.'

'Welcome to the Big Apple,' said Shaun.

He seemed like a decent, sensitive man. Although we'd only just met, I found him easier to be with in some ways than Kevin, who I'd known all my life. With Kev, there was always the defensiveness. It wasn't that I was going to make a big deal about him leaving me to do everything, but he still had to keep listing all the reasons why it had been impossible for him to come home even for the occasional visit.

We took a yellow cab into Manhattan. I was disappointed at first. New York was just like any other city on the outskirts, with scrubby nondescript buildings, dusty parking lots and advertising hoardings, although, if I'd thought about it, I should have known from *The Great Gatsby*. As soon as we caught our first glimpse of Manhattan, all lit up like the beginning of *Friends*, that changed of course. Driving over the Brooklyn Bridge and seeing the view, so familiar from television and movies, really brought it home to me that the Twin Towers were no longer there, and how the empty bit of sky must remind New Yorkers every day how the whole world would never be the same.

Kev and Shaun had a duplex loft apartment in the downtown area known as Tribeca. Shaun explained the name was short for the Triangle Below Canal Street, although it sounds more exotic than that, doesn't it, like some old Russian quarter or something. Kev told us that Robert de Niro – he called him Bob, as if he knew him – lived just round the corner. The apartment seemed quite dark when Shaun opened the door and showed us the bedrooms on the fifth floor. Hope and I had a room of our own with a view towards the Wall Street area, a big double bed and a futon unrolled on the parquet floor.

Kev and Shaun shared an enormous double bed in the other bedroom. I didn't know what Hope was going to make of

240

that. She wasn't keen on what she called 'kissy stuff' between a man and a woman and I had no idea how she'd respond to the idea of two men doing it. I kind of felt I should have prepared her, but I didn't know where to start, so I spent quite a lot of the holiday dreading the moment she would ask an embarrassing question, and it would somehow be my fault.

You entered the living room on the fifth-floor level, but the ceiling above had been knocked out and a staircase went up to an open-plan kitchen which had doors onto a roof terrace. All the glass gave it a massive, airy feeling.

'Why is the kitchen upstairs?' Hope wanted to know.

'Why not?' said Kev. Like I said, defensive.

'Tree! Why is the kitchen upstairs?'

'It's just the way Kevin and Shaun like it. It means you can eat your meals and look at the view, see?'

I could tell she was thinking, *Why would you want to do that? We* didn't look at a view at home, or in school, or any other place where we ate our meals.

'Is your house upside down?' Hope asked Shaun.

'I suppose you could say that,' he chuckled. 'But please make it your home!'

Hope wasn't good with idioms.

'Our home is the right way up.'

We wandered around the neighbourhood before eating an early supper, because it was already after midnight for us. It was the kind of area where the clothes shops look like art installations with a neon tube in the window and maybe just one pair of shoes, or a dress on a hanger, and no price tags. Shaun had booked us into a lovely restaurant, but it was wasted on people who had no idea of the difference between a flounder and a snapper (or even that they were fish) and knew pasta only as 'cheesy', 'meaty' or 'tinned'. The staff were so helpful and friendly, I think they'd have gone out and bought us a can of Heinz spaghetti if we'd demanded it, but I assured Shaun that

241

Hope would be fine with *farfalle* – although better to call them bows than butterflies – with cherry tomatoes and goat's cheese.

I couldn't help noticing that the tip Shaun left was bigger than the entire cost of any meal I'd ever eaten out. I told him on the way back to the apartment, when Kevin fell in next to Hope for the first time and Shaun and I hung back to give them some space to get to know each other, that we'd be just as happy with McDonald's or KFC.

He smiled at me. 'What would you like to do while you're here?'

'We have to see the Empire State Building. I mean go up to the top.'

You could see the actual building in the distance from their roof terrace.

'Would Hope like to see a musical?' Shaun asked. 'Kevin says she enjoys singing.'

I hesitated, because of course that was the thing she'd like most of all.

I decided to be up front about it. 'The problem is, if she knows the song, she'll try to sing along. And she knows *all* the songs.'

'Don't worry, Tess,' said Shaun. 'I spend my life dealing with high-maintenance people.'

He was a director, so he probably meant all the dancers and actors, but he definitely nodded his head in Kevin's direction, and we exchanged one of those sweet, private moments of understanding.

The following evening, Shaun got us tickets for *The Lion King*. We had four seats right in the centre of the stalls, house seats, he called them, which people in the theatre know about because they save them in case someone like George Clooney wants to come along at the last minute. Hope sat between Shaun and me, and when the lights went down and the music started, he said to her, nicely, but very firmly, 'Now, Hope,

242

you're in the audience, and the audience's job is to sit still and stay quiet, otherwise we won't be allowed watch the show any more.'

Which was a risky strategy, but clever, because it didn't give her any time to object. To my astonishment, she did exactly as she was told. It helped that Shaun was a man, I suppose, because we were used to doing what Dad told us, and there was so much for her to look at. It's amazing the way the cast move like African animals and the music makes you well up. Literally breathtaking.

Afterwards, as soon as we were on the street, Hope said, 'Can I sing now?'

And Shaun said, 'OK, now you can.'

So it was 'Hakuna Matata' all the way home, much to Kev's embarrassment, although the other passengers on the subway enjoyed it. If Kev had taken the cap off his head, I reckon we could have filled it with change that evening.

After that, Shaun took Hope and me to Broadway shows matinee and evening. *Wicked*, *Hairspray*, *Les Misérables*, and her favourite, *Mamma Mia!* Kev had a performance coming up and was rehearsing most days, so couldn't join us, and I sensed he was a bit miffed. Kev liked to be the centre of attention, and maybe he was right to be jealous, because, to be honest, I think I fell a little bit in love with Shaun. Not in a physical way, obviously – although he was a very good-looking man and wore beautiful clothes, like soft yellow cashmere sweaters with perfectly clean jeans, and he always smelled lovely – but just because he was so considerate and good at bringing out the best in everyone. Not just Hope, but me too.

Shaun was the first person I ever spoke to properly about Art. We went to MoMA together while Kev took Hope to the zoo. They have some lovely Matisses there, as well as all the Warhols, and it was great to see them in the city where they'd actually been made (I'd never said 'made' about art

243

before that, always 'painted', which wasn't the right word). He also introduced me to contemporary American literature, selecting shiny hardback novels from the shelf in their living room, which I read every night, and discussed with him the following day. My mind was like an empty vessel, thirsting for knowledge. He didn't even laugh when I said that, but instead told me I should go to school, which means university in America.

'I had a place to read English,' I told him proudly. 'At University College London. But I couldn't go because of Mum.'

'Here we go!' said Kevin, playing an imaginary violin.

We were all sitting in Central Park because it was one of those days when it's so sunny you think it's warm enough for a picnic (which we'd got in a paper carrier bag from a deli called Zabar's), although when he said that, the grassy lawn we were sitting on suddenly felt a bit too cold, the breeze a bit chilly, and we probably should have moved off.

It's not that I wanted people to think I was a martyr, or thank me all the time, but I did feel I was coping with something pretty difficult, and making some sacrifices on the way. I wasn't looking for sympathy, but because of other people's refusal to acknowledge that there was actually a problem (in case that meant they might be obliged to share the responsibility), it didn't seem fair somehow, that I wasn't allowed to get any recognition either.

So I said something of the sort and Kevin took umbrage.

'It's not as if you were going to study anything useful,' he said.

Which sounded just like Dad, when Kev's meant to be the artistic, creative one of the family.

'Like dancing's useful, you mean!' I retorted.

To which he replied, 'Why has everyone in my family always been against me dancing?'

244

'Why do you always twist things? *You* were the one saying what I wanted to do was nothing!'

How easily siblings revert to being children. You started it! No, you started it! Very soon you're so cross you can't actually remember who started it.

'I just meant it didn't stop you reading books,' Kev said. I should have recognized that as his attempt to climb down. But I was on fire by then.

'It stopped me getting a degree! I was top in our school, and now I'm not even qualified for anything!'

'But you still can be, Tess,' Shaun said. 'And you should be, shouldn't she, Kevin?'

'She should be, shouldn't she, Kevin?' echoed Hope.

That afternoon we went on the Circle Line boat which takes you all the way around Manhattan Island.

Standing out on deck, Kevin pointed. 'There's the—'

'Statue of Liberty,' Hope told him.

'How did you know that, Hope?' He looked over the top of her head at me, surprised.

'You sent us a postcard.'

I could see he was pleased as well as impressed.

He started pointing out the other sights as we chugged past: the Staten Island Ferry, South Street Seaport, the Brooklyn Bridge, the Manhattan Bridge . . .

'That building is United Nations HQ,' Hope said as we motored up the East River. 'It says so underneath people on the news.'

Where most people would probably be watching the reporter and listening to what he's saying about the latest meeting of the Security Council or whatever, Hope's paying attention to the shape of the building and reading the words in the red strip along the bottom of the screen. It's two ways of looking at the same thing. I could see it was dawning on Kevin that Hope was bright, but in a different way, and I was so pleased, because it's difficult to explain to someone; they have to get it themselves.

'What about that one?' he asked.

'Empire State Building, where the Giant Peach landed,' she said, as if he was a complete idiot for asking.

'Correct! And that one?' He pointed at the Chrysler Building.

'I don't know.'

'Well, I'll tell you, shall I . . . ?'

It almost made me cry to see Kev putting his arm around his sister and talking to her about his adopted city. I think it was the first time Kev had seen Hope as a gift instead of a problem, which sounds like something a priest would say, but is actually quite a good way of looking at her.

Shaun and I withdrew, leaving Hope and Kev out on deck, bonding.

'What are you going to do when she goes to high school?' Shaun asked me.

They didn't have teaching assistants in the same way at big school, and even if they did, I knew it wouldn't be a good idea for me to go with her. At some point, Hope had to tackle the world on her own, and it seemed like the right time to start the process. If she didn't panic in her upcoming SATs exams, she would get the required grade 4 to be in a normal form, and we now had a Statement of Medical Need, so she would have a care worker with her at least some of the time. Which was all good progress, but it raised the question, what was I going to do?

'Have you thought about training to be a teacher?' Shaun asked.

'That's what everyone says!'

It was the most logical path for me to take, given that I still had to be at home for Hope outside school hours. Dad was mainly living with Anne by then and Anne didn't want Hope full-time.

'Bad enough having Dad full-time,' Kev said the previous evening, when I'd described Anne for him and we'd smiled at each other with that shared understanding only siblings have, friends for a moment instead of rivals.

Several things were stopping me from going down the teaching route. First, I'd need to get a degree, which would mean studying in the evenings while I continued to work as a TA, and that would take at least three years. Then I'd have to do a teacher-training course, with no income coming in, for another year. But my main objection was that I didn't actually want to be one.

'I was at school, then instead of going away to university, I went back to school, and now I'm supposed to spend the rest of my bloody life in school!' I told Shaun. 'I haven't even learned anything yet!'

Shaun held up his hands, like he'd heard enough reasons.

'So do you know what you *do* want to do?'

I was on a tourist boat in a foreign country, with a man who hardly knew me, but I found myself admitting something that I'd never told anyone before, except my mum – and that was when I was ten years old, so it probably doesn't count – not Dave, nor even Doll. It was almost like it was an opportunity to try out the words, see how they sounded. If Shaun laughed, the mockery wouldn't follow me round like it would at home.

'I'd like to be a writer.'

He didn't laugh. To be honest, if I'd believed there was the slightest chance he would, I wouldn't have told him, so it wasn't that brave.

'Do you write?' he asked.

'I used to write poems at school, and I'm always making up stories. Do you think I'm crazy?'

'If you're asking if I think you can write, I can't answer that until I read something you've written. What I do know is that you're a reader and writers are always readers. And you surely have a speaking voice that's all your own, Tess. But that's all I can say. The rest of it is up to you. Write some stuff. Go to a creative-writing group . . .'

I felt like I was being given permission, which was exciting. But the question of how I was going to make my living remained.

'I could always work for Doll . . .'

'Doll?'

'My best friend.'

It was hard to believe Shaun now knew me so well without knowing about Doll, so I gave him a potted history of our friendship. Doll had been spot on in her predictions about nails, and she'd worked really hard, living back at home, spending all her time and savings on setting up The Dolls House. The business was now growing so quickly she was about to open her fourth nail bar.

'She sounds like an enterprising lady.'

I felt a tiny irrational twinge of jealousy. Doll had enough male admirers. She couldn't help being pretty, which made men go out of their way to help her, but she was ruthless about taking advantage, from the bank manager to the bloke who'd designed her logo and even Dave, who'd done a lot of work putting in sinks and stuff and only charging her at cost. I didn't want to share Shaun with Doll, even though he lived in New York, so it was unlikely they'd ever meet.

'The name was my idea,' I said.

'But you don't want to work with her?' he asked, picking up on my ambivalence.

'One, people say you shouldn't work with your friends. And two, I'm just not interested in pampering and exfoliation and all that stuff . . .'

'Maybe your work doesn't have to provide all your intellectual and emotional satisfaction? Maybe you should do

248

something that will leave you the imaginative space to write . . .'

He was actually taking my ambition seriously.

'So, what's number three?' he asked.

'I don't look right, do I?'

Shaun laughed out loud.

'Well, if that's your only problem, sweetie,' he said, 'let me tell you about what Kevin and I have been planning.'

The makeover. That probably makes it sound spookier than it was. We're not talking plastic surgery, or Botox or anything like that.

'You're a blank canvas,' Shaun said.

'Thanks a bunch.'

'I mean, my dear, that you have unrealized potential. Will you let me help you realize it?'

Hope and I both had our hair cut while Shaun instructed the stylist exactly what he wanted: a neat bob for Hope that suited the shape of her face and was easy to maintain; for me, a radical restyle that left piles of nondescript frizz on the floor of the salon, and a face I barely recognized.

I'd had longish dark brown curly hair with a centre parting since I was a child. At school I'd worn it in bunches or plaits. Since then, Doll had bought me all the hair-straighteners and serums ever invented to try to tame and smooth it, but nothing ever worked for more than a day or two. Usually I scraped it back in a big bushy ponytail, and if I wanted to look smart, pinned and sprayed it up into a bun. Whenever I did that, people said I looked like my mother, which was nice, because she was an attractive woman, but I think what they probably meant was old.

Now, when I looked in the salon mirror, I saw someone young. The frizz, when chopped, had miraculously turned into glossy curls. With my hair now short, my eyes looked much bigger. Shaun said the word was 'gamine', which the dictionary defines as an elfish tomboy.

After a session with the dance company's make-up lady, who tidied up my eyebrows and showed me how to make the most of my cheekbones, and then the department-store trip, with Shaun as my personal shopper, giving me the confidence to try on outfits I wouldn't have dreamed of considering, I felt like a different person. The American sizing probably had something to do with it; I'd never been an 8 before.

I drew the line at heels. It's different in America, where everyone's taller. Dave was going to find it difficult enough to get used to me in short A-line dresses with cropped jackets, or ankle-skimming Capri pants, without me towering over him too.

'Who's Dave?' asked Shaun.

It probably said a lot that I hadn't once mentioned my fiancé, not that we'd set a date yet.

'Dave is the Music Man,' Hope explained, as if that was the only introduction required.

That night I sat with Shaun out on the roof terrace drinking Cosmopolitans, feeling very *Sex and the City* with the glittering grid of street lights stretching way into the distance. My high-ball glass was full of ice, the lime and cranberry juice was tart and refreshing and you couldn't really taste the alcohol, so I probably drank too much too quickly.

'You're marrying this guy Dave?' Shaun asked.

'He's a lovely man and he's got his own flat in Herne Bay and a van. Everyone likes him . . .'

I stared at a nearby apartment building. Behind each of those windows, there were little dramas going on, I thought. Thousands and thousands of little dramas. I loved cities.

'But?' said Shaun, leaning over and refilling my glass.

Was it so obvious there was a but?

I sighed. 'I can't seem to get rid of this stupid idea that there should be more. I know things probably aren't as amazing out there as I think, but I want to find that out for myself. It's all right for Doll because she's lived the dream and now she's got work she loves, but why do I have to take her word for it?'

Shaun said nothing.

'Same time,' I argued with myself, 'I love Dave. Everyone does. He's like part of the family. Even Dad likes him! And Anne. And what would Hope do without him? I can't even think about that. So . . . I don't know why I can't just get on with it, and make everyone happy . . .'

If I was looking for confirmation, Shaun wasn't going to offer it.

'It's not Dave's fault, by the way,' I tried to explain. 'He loves me. But the thing is, he doesn't really know me!'

'What doesn't he know about you?' Shaun asked.

I took another long gulp of my pink cocktail. 'The first time Dave saw me, I was at work with the kids, and you know how they are, they crowd round wanting to tell you things all the time, so Dave had this vision of this caring, maternal type of person, you know? I don't think he'd even have noticed me standing on my own at a student party . . .'

Shaun stayed quiet, giving me the space to continue with thoughts I'd never voiced before.

'What Dave wants out of life is a nice little house and a family, and the thing is . . . I don't even want kids!'

Still no reaction.

'I am NEVER EVER going to bring a child into this world.'

The words seemed to reverberate in the air, like the moment after church bells cease tolling.

'Why?' Shaun said eventually.

'Because I couldn't risk dying and leaving them. I couldn't do that to anyone!'

Suddenly there were tears trickling down my face and I didn't know where they had come from.

'It's terrifying looking after a child, you know? I'm living in fear all the time because what the hell would happen to Hope if I wasn't there?'

The tears were choking me now.

'It must have been like that for Mum, mustn't it? So why the hell didn't she get herself checked? It was SO selfish of her, and I honestly can't forgive her for that. What was she thinking? What did she think was going to happen to us?'

Then crying totally took over, convulsing my body, drowning out the drone of traffic from below.

'I'm sorry, Mum! I know you didn't mean it . . . I'm so sorry!'

I felt Shaun standing beside me, gently resting a hand on my back, which made me weep even more because he was so lovely, and in two days' time we'd be home, and I wouldn't have him to talk to, and I wouldn't even have the holiday to look forward to any more.

And then, suddenly, I took a huge breath. There were no more tears.

One summer in Ireland when we were kids, we dammed up a little stream of water on the beach. When the time came to go home, the tiny trickle had become a huge lake, and we all stood there, with Dad counting one, two, three, before smashing the wall with our spades, releasing a torrent that gushed down the beach to the sea. Then suddenly the sand was flat again, the water all blended into the sea, and I'd stared at the sun going down over the horizon, feeling strangely sad, as if a little part of my life had gone.

'I should've got through the anger stage, shouldn't I?' I said.

'Grief's not a checklist, Tess, it's a process.'

'I'm not really angry with Mum,' I said. 'I loved her more than anyone. I just wish she hadn't always put everyone else first, because actually that didn't help, because Hope needed her to be there . . .'

'And you needed her?'

'But I wouldn't have needed her so much if she hadn't died!'

'Tess, sometimes you're almost as pedantic as Hope!'

When people talk about nature and nurture, I think they forget that nurture works both ways. It's obvious children copy grown-ups, but nobody ever talks about how much grown-ups copy children. Those funny little sayings that become part of a family's language, they're usually from the kids, aren't they? So if there are ways Hope and I are alike, maybe it's genetic, or she's picked stuff up from me, but maybe I've picked stuff up from her too.

'Shall we try to unpack some of this?' Shaun asked.

'Unpack' was a word he used a lot and not about suitcases.

I nodded.

'Seems to me the major issue here is your fear of dying,' he said. 'You're assuming you'll die early because your mother did?'

'And her mother did . . .'

'So, isn't there a genetic test you can have?'

'There is.' I repeated the article I'd read recently. 'But only five per cent of people get cancer because of genetics. And at the moment the guidelines are that they won't give you a test unless there's evidence that a close relation carries the mutation . . .'

I'd been to the doctor about it. The nice female GP I usually saw was on maternity leave, so I'd had to see the head of the practice, a much older man who'd known me since I was a child and still treated me like one.

'How old are you now, Tess?' he'd asked, peering at my notes. 'Twenty-four! That's far too young! Having a genetic test has all sorts of serious implications . . .'

Sometimes you don't dare ask about scary things like 'serious implications' in case by saying the words out loud you make them more likely. So instead I'd asked, 'How old do I need to be then?'

'We'll think about it again when you're in your thirties and you've had a family. Enjoy life, Teresa! Don't look so worried!'

'That's crazy,' Shaun said. 'If the test's available, I think you should go back and demand it. What does Dave think?'

'He says the doctor ought to know what he's talking about,' I said. 'Which is probably fair enough.'

He hadn't diagnosed my mother's ovarian cancer, but she hadn't gone to see him, so I couldn't blame him for that. The nice female doctor had told me that taking the Pill lessened my chances of getting that one, at least.

'Have you told Dave about not wanting kids?'

'No,' I admitted.

'Why?'

'Because I know he'd say something like, "You say that now, but . . ."'

'What if he said, "Tess, I don't want kids either. I just want to be with you?"'

'He wouldn't.'

'But if he did?' Shaun stared at me.

'I don't know,' I confessed.

But suddenly it all seemed much clearer.

On the final night, the three of us went to see Kevin perform in the ballet of *Romeo and Juliet*. He wasn't Romeo, but he was Benvolio, who has a big solo dance in the second act. Technically, Kev was on fire, but what I loved most was the natural, laddish quality he brought to acting the role, jeering and bantering with his mates Mercutio and Romeo. It took me back to him and Brendan kicking a ball about in the garden at home, and it made me want to cry, because if Dad was there, he'd see that there was nothing effeminate about the dancing at all and he'd be really proud of his eldest son. And I knew that, underneath, that's the thing Kev still wanted most in the whole world.

I tried to tell him at the after-party, but it's not the same, someone telling you, is it? Especially not your little sister.

He did wear a wig, by the way.

I'd never seen Hope so animated as when we got back and she was telling Dad and Anne about the trip. Of course, she had a different take on it from me, like the sound of the subway trains coming into a station, which I hadn't even noticed, and the way Americans pronounce 'coffee'. She sang them songs from all the musicals and Dad didn't believe her when she said we went nine times, although he should have known that Hope doesn't lie.

'Who paid for all this then?' he asked me.

'Shaun got us house seats,' I told him, knowledgeably. To be honest, I didn't know whether that meant he paid or not, but it shut Dad up.

'There's something unusual about Shaun and Kevin,' Hope suddenly said.

Just when I thought we'd managed to steer a safe course through *that* whole question.

I could feel the temperature in the room falling as my dad waited for the inevitable evidence of his youngest daughter's exposure to mortal sin. He looked at me daggers.

'They have their kitchen upstairs!' said Hope.

Dave was talking on his mobile phone outside the restaurant, so he wasn't aware of me approaching, and I saw him for a moment as someone else might see him. He was wearing a plain navy polo shirt and well-fitting jeans and he looked really masculine and kind of hot. All the certainty I'd brought back with me from New York began to waver. Was I really going to let this lovely man go on some vague hope that there was something better out there waiting for me? In New York, it was easy to dream, but this was my real life. Dave loved me and cared about me, and that suddenly seemed so precious, I couldn't think why I would gamble it away. Maybe all I'd needed was a bit of distance.

He looked up at the sound of my footsteps running towards him, and put his mobile phone in his pocket.

'Wow!' He did a double-take. 'You look different!'

'Do you like it?' I did a little twirl.

'It's great,' he said.

To be honest, I'd been expecting more than great.

We gave each other a quick, almost embarrassed, peck of a kiss. It had only been a week, but it was like we'd forgotten what to do.

At the table, I handed over the Yankees cap I'd bought him. He put it on his head, then took it off again.

'So what do you fancy?' He picked up the menu.

I wished we hadn't gone for pizza because pizza in New York was so much better, and I found myself babbling on about it, probably because of jet lag.

'Anything to start?' He beckoned the waitress over.

'No, thanks.'

It felt almost like our first date, when I'd been eager to impress but didn't know what sort of thing he'd like to talk about. I'd promised myself that I wouldn't mention my plans to get a different job and write until I'd got a bit further, but it all came tumbling out.

'A writing group?' Dave repeated.

'Just to see if I can.'

'Why do you want to do that?'

'Because I think I might find it creatively fulfilling,' I said, a little bit prickly, like Kev.

'You and your big words!'

The phrase seemed to echo between us.

'Have you been seeing a lot of Doll?' I asked, meaning, as in doing the plumbing for her new shop, but Dave had such an open face, I saw immediately that, one, he had, and two, he thought I meant much more than plumbing.

'You and Doll?' I faltered.

I'd left a message on her answerphone to say we were back, but she hadn't called immediately to get the low-down.

'I'm so sorry, Tess . . .'

'If I hadn't asked, were you actually going to tell me, or were you going to carry on behind my back?'

'It's not what you think . . .'

'How is it not what I think?'

'It's serious,' he said.

He was right, because that wasn't what I was thinking at all. I was thinking fling. I couldn't seem to work out whether that would have been better, or worse.

Everything felt a bit out-of-body, like being in a film whose script demanded that I should ask, 'How long has this been going on then?'

'Only this week. We've been working late, trying to get the new shop ready and—'

I held my hand up to stop him. I didn't want to hear the details.

'Only this week, and it's *serious*?' I imitated his earnest tone.

'Doll and I have known each other years, though, haven't we? Not that I'd ever thought it was possible . . .'

The implication being that any man in his right mind would want Doll over me. Thinking about sex, or whatever it was he was thinking about, Dave's face broke into a smile.

'For heaven's sake!' I shouted.

Then I couldn't think of anything else to say, so I scraped back my chair and walked out, leaving him to pick up the bill.

Half an hour before, I'd felt so grown up with my new hair-cut and styling, but now, as I sat on the bus home, it was as if

I'd gone right back to our first school disco, watching all the boys dare each other to ask Doll to dance as if I didn't even exist.

Doll's big blue eyes froze when she opened the door.

She'd been expecting Dave, I realized. Had they agreed that he would report back after? Were they planning to sit there analysing my reaction, or rush upstairs and screw?

'It just happened . . .' said Doll.

'How?'

'You really want to know?'

'Nooooo!'

She looked upset at the rawness of my anguish.

She touched my arm. 'Come inside and we'll talk.'

I batted her hand away.

'What's there to talk about?' I asked bitterly.

'Don't make me choose, Tess!' she whined.

'Don't you dare try to make out I'm the unreasonable one and you're the hapless victim . . .'

'Hapless?'

'Unfortunate.'

'I'm sorry,' she said. 'I knew you'd be cross but I thought—'

'What? That I'd give you my blessing?' I was suddenly furious. 'No problem, Doll, take my fiancé! Do whatever you want. You always do anyway. It's always take, take, take, with you, isn't it? I'll have this one, oh and that one, in both colours, please. Someone else'll pick up the tab . . .'

'You bloody cow!' Doll retaliated. 'What have I ever taken from you?'

'My homework, my ideas . . . my bloody fiancé!' I cried.

'You didn't *really* want him, though, did you?' said Doll.

There was no answer to that, and she knew it, and her willingness to use privileged information gleaned from knowing me so well felt like the ultimate betrayal.

'Don't go! Please, Tess!' She chased me up the road. 'You'll find your dream, I know you will . . .'

'What?' I rounded on her. 'So you can take it away from me?'

'That's not fair!'

She stopped.

I marched on, half-expecting her to continue after me. But she didn't. Nor did she come round to our house later.

We'd fallen out badly only once before, aged eight, for the summer term when Doll had suddenly announced that Cerise McQuarry was her best friend.

'I think you're better off without her,' I remembered Mum saying.

That's all very well, but I've got nobody now, I told her silently.

PART THREE

17

2005

GUS

'Would you recommend parenthood?' Marcus asked me.

We were both watching as my daughter Flora, wearing only a nappy and a pair of tiny pink jelly shoes, reached the water's edge. She squatted down, with that amazing sense of balance that toddlers acquire so soon after they've started walking, to scoop seawater into her yellow plastic bucket.

Marcus had invited us for Sunday lunch on the north Kent coast. As a weekend escape from his loft apartment in a converted mattress factory in Clerkenwell, he'd recently acquired a converted fisherman's hut in Whitstable. In line for a partnership at the big City law firm, he was able to live comfortably on his salary, while investing his eye-watering bonuses in cool properties. He was indisputably more successful than I was, or ever likely to be, but I was already a father. There was never anything hostile about our unspoken competition, but it was always there, as if we audited our lives by comparing them.

'Unreservedly,' I replied.

'Doesn't it stop you doing things?' he asked, picking up a stone and skimming it across the water. We both watched, counting silently. One, two, threefourfivesixseven.

I was tempted to say, 'We no longer have sex in the box when we go to the opera.'

But I knew that would cross the line between friendly one-upmanship and showing off.

I picked up a stone and skimmed it. Seven.

'You kind of stop thinking that way,' I said. 'Your needs aren't so important, not compared with your child's.'

'In what way?' Marcus was trained to cross-examine the evidence.

Picking up another stone, then discarding it for not being flat enough, I searched for a precise illustration.

'I always thought we'd go on holiday to Italy when I finally started earning, but it wouldn't be much fun for Flora trawling round churches. To be honest, she's as happy here as she would be in some island spa in the Maldives,' I added, which had been Charlotte's idea of a suitable holiday destination until she'd properly imagined ten hours of Flora on a plane.

'No regrets, then?' Marcus asked.

'None,' I confirmed, unsure how he'd react if I told him that my one regret was returning to work after the parental leave I'd taken in between switching my training from hospital to GP surgery.

The creation of a warm and loving home had been much more rewarding than I'd anticipated. I'd enrolled in a twice-weekly mother-and-baby group, where we sang 'The Wheels on the Bus' with our bewildered infants propped on our laps, making circles with their hands during the chorus. In the after-noons, I relished having the time to shop for fruit and vegetables as the market stalls were packing up, introducing Flora to real items the Very Hungry Caterpillar ate. I made it my routine to cook Charlotte something delicious for dinner each day, and diligently puréed organic produce for Flora when she started on solid food. When I brought along cookies that I'd baked to the mother-and-baby group, I became, in Charlotte's words, 'the darling of the yummy mummies'.

'You miss your old friends, obviously,' I conceded, wondering if that was what Marcus was getting at. This was only the second time we'd got together since Flora was born.

Nash was the only pre-baby friend I'd seen fairly regularly in the first few months because she'd had free time during the day to stroll round Battersea Park with me and the pram. But now she'd landed a role in an American medical drama series, she'd gone to live in LA.

'How's the job going?' Marcus asked.

'Fine,' I said. 'Steep learning curve, obviously.'

It had been difficult for me entrusting Flora to another person, but it would have been mad not to finally qualify after having worked so hard. We'd hired Kasia, a Polish Philosophy graduate, as our nanny. She didn't have any formal qualification in childcare, but she was intelligent, responsible and keen to practise English, so Flora was now taken to lots of new activities like baby gym and swimming. Charlotte was probably right when she said that I missed Flora much more than she missed me.

With no one else around and the lulling rhythm of waves breaking on the shingle, I was, for a moment, tempted to confide in Marcus that I hated general practice, but I decided not to out of a kind of loyalty to Charlotte. She'd mooted the idea on the plane home from New York. Wouldn't general practice be a more flexible career? Who could resist the new deal for GPs which made the salary of the average hospital doctor look like peanuts by comparison? Wouldn't it be far more cost-effective if I were the one to take parental leave? Unfortunately, the reality of having to make decisions about a relentless stream of people I'd never seen before sometimes felt like a kind of nightmare. I spent far too long with each patient, which led to queues building up in the waiting room, exasperated colleagues and longer hours than I needed or wanted to do.

Marcus skimmed another stone. Eleven, possibly twelve, bounces.

I stooped to pick up an oyster shell, smoothed by the scouring of the tide.

'Come and look at this shell, Floss.'

'Sell,' Flora repeated.

'Not in your mouth, Floss,' I warned. 'It's sharp.'

'Sarp.'

'Shall we take it back to show Mummy?'

'Bucket.'

'Good idea. We'll take a bucket of shells back to our own garden in London, shall we?'

'Mary Mary Quite Contary . . .' Flora started singing tunelessly.

'How does your garden grow?' I joined in, delighted by the spontaneous connection she'd made between shells and gardens.

Marcus looked at me as if I'd lost the plot.

'Do you have a garden in Wandsworth?' he asked.

'A very small one,' I told him.

If life in the tiny top-floor flat among the rooftops of Charlotte Street had been like floating, the house in Wandsworth grounded us. We'd chosen the neighbourhood because it was somewhere youngish, upwardly mobile, middle-class couples like us could still just about afford a house. If you sat looking out of the small bay window at the front, you'd see a constant stream of new parents running past with babies in designer three-wheeled sports buggies like ours. But the street was gloomy and the mid-terrace house was dark inside.

'Why don't you move?' Marcus asked.

'Because the areas we like are out of our price range until I start earning a full GP's salary,' I told him. 'Not a problem you'll have,' I added, guessing why he was asking all these questions.

He'd recently married Keiko, a banking economist, and I assumed that they were applying their analytical minds to the pros and cons of parenthood.

'What about sex?' Marcus said, lowering his voice to make sure he was out of Flora's earshot.

For a moment, it felt like we were back in the Lower Sixth at school, in the days when we still thought that sex was something you might be fortunate enough to be awarded by the strangely mysterious opposite sex.

Charlotte and I still had great sex. Just not as often and never outside the house. These days, if we did it while listening to *La Bohème*, it was on a CD rather than during the performance. 'It's funny, but sex doesn't matter as much either,' I said, which was a mistake because it made it sound like we had none at all.

Marcus pulled a face.

'But you're happy, you and Charlotte?' he asked.

I hesitated. 'Happy' wasn't a Charlotte kind of word. There wasn't a day when I didn't wake up feeling astonished and privileged to find her beside me, but if I'd asked her, 'Are you happy with me?' I suspected she'd laugh as if she was far too busy dealing with higher-order issues. And yet there was no doubting the unique bond of our shared love for Flora.

I know that every parent thinks their child is special, but it was an objective truth that Flora was both unusually beautiful and advanced. In the little red book the government gives all new parents to chart their child's progress, which most people forget to fill in, or lose after the first few months, Flora had reached each developmental goal well ahead of target. She had taken her first step just before her first birthday and, at eighteen months, had already acquired a large enough vocabulary to ask for most things she wanted. She had inherited her mother's raven-haired beauty and my blue eyes, a startling combination that inspired a great deal of admiring attention.

'Mummy pretty sell!' Flora shouted, as Charlotte and Keiko appeared walking back along the beach path with oysters they'd bought at the harbour.

'That's nice, darling,' said Charlotte, picking Flora up. I wished I'd had a camera to capture the two so-similar faces smiling right next to each other, dark hair blowing about in the sparkling breeze.

The fisherman's hut had been renovated and greatly extended in a contemporary minimalist style, with huge windows and an open-sided staircase that looked straight out of a magazine but was a dangerous playground for a toddler. I was dismayed to see Flora's jelly shoes leaving little clumps of wet sand on the expensive-looking rug.

'It's such a treat to be with adults who don't want to talk about potty training!' Charlotte said, accepting a glass of Taittinger from Marcus and reclining on a sofa upholstered in a pale turquoise velvet that Flora was getting dangerously close to. 'We're *so* boring these days, aren't we, Angus?'

Amusement played around Marcus's lips. In the floodlight of my wife's attention, I saw my friend not as the spotty youth he had been, but as the attractive, wealthy man he had become. Charlotte knew Marcus only as charming, successful and rich. I'd noticed the gleam of approval in her eye as I parked up beside his Porsche.

'Mummy eat sell,' said Flora, pointing at Charlotte as she tipped an oyster down her throat.

'It's called an oyster, darling,' said Charlotte.

'Sell, sell, sell!' Flora shouted, wrestling her hand from mine.

'She's clearly got a future in the Stock Exchange!' said Marcus, glossing over the slightly awkward spectacle of our daughter's insistence.

'Here, have a taste . . .' Charlotte picked up another oyster, tipping a little of the fluid into Flora's mouth.

Flora spat it out immediately, just missing the turquoise velvet upholstery.

'Sarp,' she cried.

I loved the way her brain applied the word which I'd introduced to indicate danger to a taste that was offensive to her.

I set her own little plastic chair and table up for her to eat her lunch in the kitchen while I helped Keiko prepare the grown-ups' meal.

'Is it a Japanese recipe?' I asked, as she took a sea bass out of the fridge, and I squeezed limes with a wooden reamer.

She gave me a small smile. 'Jamie Oliver.'

In the living area, the conversation continued at slightly louder volume, ostensibly to keep us included.

'Venice! You lucky things!' Charlotte was saying.

'We'll be there for the Biennale,' said Marcus.

'I've always longed to go to the Biennale!' said Charlotte. 'Angus!' she called. 'Why don't we go to the Biennale? I'm sure Kasia could manage . . .'

I couldn't imagine flying out of the country and leaving Flora, but I said nothing, because if I raised an objection Charlotte was far more likely to dig in her heels.

'Caroline would love it, Angus!' Charlotte called. 'I don't know why people are so horrid about mothers-in-law. Mine's a godsend!' she told Marcus.

My mother's hostility to our marriage had disappeared with Flora's birth. Flora looked exactly like Ross did as a baby, she told us, when she turned up at our house unannounced the day after I'd called from the hospital to inform her she was a grandmother.

'I thought that too,' Charlotte agreed.

'At least she's not ginger!' my mother remarked.

'Quite!'

'Just pretend I'm not here,' I'd said.

'It's different for a girl, Angus!' the two of them chorused.

There was no denying it was useful to have a spare baby-sitter because Kasia didn't work weekends, but however much I tried to welcome my mother's presence back into our lives, I couldn't shake off the feeling that I was in the way whenever she was around. I particularly hated her speaking about Flora in the first person plural, as if she knew what my child was thinking, especially since most of 'Flora's' thoughts seemed to coincide with her own.

'We like carrots, don't we? We don't like ratatouille, no. We think Daddy puts too much garlic in his cooking, don't we?'

'Maybe we could take Flora to Venice with us?' I called into the living room.

'Do you see what I mean?' I heard Charlotte say. 'Completely misses the point!'

'Actually, you'd have a problem getting a decent hotel now,' said Marcus, gallantly refusing to gang up on me. 'We booked months ago.'

'Do you enjoy contemporary art?' I asked Keiko, trying to establish our own alternative conversation.

'Yes.'

I wasn't sure whether she was insecure about her English, or just naturally reserved. Was there always a dominant partner in a relationship? I wondered. Would Marcus actually be able to cope with someone like Charlotte?

'Will you keep an eye on her while I get the changing stuff out of the car?' I asked Keiko.

When I returned, she was crouched down beside the chair, playing peek-a-boo from behind her curtain of glossy black hair, delighting Flora, who kept trying to grab the hair with tomatoey hands, shrieking, 'Kay Ko, Kay Ko!'

'There's a lot of paraphernalia, isn't there?' Marcus observed, as I carried Flora and the changing bag upstairs.

'With all the plastic in our house, it sometimes feels like we're single-handedly responsible for China's economic boom!' said Charlotte.

Marcus stood up and followed me.

'Want to practise?' I offered, spreading out the changing mat on the bathroom floor.

'You guessed!'

'I am a doctor.'

'Not 'til it's absolutely necessary,' my friend smiled ruefully.

'Do you think Marcus and Keiko are thinking of having a baby?' Charlotte asked, in the car on the way home.

'She's a couple of months along already,' I said.

'Really?'

I sometimes thought it was just as well that Charlotte had gone into surgery because she wasn't particularly good at reading people unless they were under anaesthetic and she'd just opened them up.

'Do you think we should have another?' she suddenly asked.

'Baby?' I asked, astonished.

'No, bottle of champagne, what did you *think* I meant?' said Charlotte, crossly.

'Wow,' I said.

I was aware of the general consensus that having just one child is unfair or somehow selfish. The first question I was always asked when I was out with Flora was, 'Is she your first?' with the assumption that there would be more. Several of the yummy mummies were already pregnant with their second, but it had never occurred to me that we would. Charlotte freely admitted that she was not very maternal, or 'mumsy' as she called it. I'd never imagined she'd want another.

Maybe I wasn't that good at reading people either.

'It would be nice for Flora to have a little friend, wouldn't it?' Charlotte wheedled.

I couldn't tell whether she was trying to elicit a positive response, or simply reassurance that Flora was perfectly all right on her own. I was confused by my own feelings of ambivalence. Having Flora was certainly the best thing that had ever happened to me, and the fact that Charlotte was proposing another meant she must be satisfied with our life together; but was it a good idea to change things just when we'd got a set-up we were all comfortable with?

I glanced in the rear-view mirror and saw that Flora had fallen asleep.

Would I be able to love a second child as much?

By the time we'd found a parking space in our road, the sun was setting. I lugged all the paraphernalia inside, including Flora sleeping in her car seat. The house was warm, Kasia was out. It felt homely, just the three of us together.

'Fancy a drink?' I asked Charlotte. 'On our terrace?'

It was the big name the estate agent had given the tiny square of decking, but it was pleasant to sit there on summer evenings and it was the one place we were allowed to smoke a cigarette, as long as Flora wasn't playing nearby.

'Vodka tonic, please,' said Charlotte, producing a packet of ten Marlboro from her handbag, giving me a wicked smile.

I filled two glasses with ice.

'We're out of vodka,' I said, looking in the cupboard.

'Gin then.'

There wasn't much gin left either. I gave it all to Charlotte, opening a fresh bottle of tonic.

The mixer cracked and fizzed over the ice.

We took our drinks outside and sat silently smoking, the tips of our cigarettes glowing in the fast-falling darkness.

'It's lonely being an only child.' Charlotte resumed our conversation.

It can be lonely as one of two, I wanted to say.

'It's pretty unlikely to happen anyway,' she added.

'Seemed to happen pretty easily last time,' I said.

My tacit agreement ignited a sexual charge like an electric current connecting across the space between us.

What I'd never experienced the first time, when conceiving was about the last thing on my mind, was how amazing sex is when you're actually trying to have a baby. Obviously we're genetically programmed to like it, but when primal instinct synchronizes with intent, it adds a new, almost spiritual, dimension.

Afterwards, I was tempted to call Marcus and tell him that sex did matter just as much after all.

18

TESS

The mobile phone was a recent-enough acquisition for me still to panic whenever I felt it vibrating in my pocket at work. I was on my break, and it was unspoken etiquette that you didn't yack away in the staffroom, so I stood up and went into the ladies' toilets to take the call.

'Hello, yes?'

The initial shudder of relief when it wasn't Hope's school turned to a muffled drumbeat in my brain when it was the receptionist at the hospital. After nearly four weeks' waiting, I'd managed to subdue the fear, but it was straight back to total immersion.

'You've got the results?' I asked, my heart rate escalating.

From her brisk manner, I could tell that she wasn't going to reveal anything over the phone. She didn't have to, because when she offered me an appointment with my counsellor at ten o'clock the following morning, I already knew the result of the test – why would I even need an appointment if it was negative?

As I pressed the button to hang up, though, my imagination immediately started inventing reasons why that needn't be the

274

case: I'd developed a good relationship with my genetics counsellor, whose name was Jane, over the chats we'd had before I
opted to have the test. Perhaps she wanted to give me the good
news in person and shake my hand before sending me on my
way? Or perhaps she wanted to remind me that at some stage,
we would need to think about Hope getting a test, and discuss
a strategy for doing that?

'You all right, Melons?' Lewis winked, as I walked back
through the store to the checkouts.

The produce manager had a bit of a thing for me. Produce
was really the worst place for him because of all the possibili-
ties for lewd innuendo – if it wasn't bananas it was cucumbers,
and what he did with a fresh fig had put most of us girls off
ever trying one – but he wasn't a bad bloke. It was all done in
good humour.

'Everything all right?' asked my supervisor, when I asked
permission to come in late the following day because I had a
doctor's appointment.

'Yes, fine, women's stuff, you know . . .'

We were quite a friendly lot – a group of us went out bowl-
ing once a month – but there was no one there I knew well
enough to confide in.

I'd been working on the checkouts at the new Waitrose
since it opened. They did ask me at the interview if I'd thought
about training for management because of my A levels, but
I told them I saw it more as a job than a career. I wanted to
have that imaginative space Shaun had talked about for writing, and it paid better than the other supermarkets because of
the bonus. We weren't just staff, but 'partners' in the business,
which sounded a lot better, not that it particularly bothered me
what I was called. What suited me was that they were prepared
to be flexible about my shifts which meant I could be around
for Hope. One of the partners who collected up the trolleys in

the car park had learning difficulties, so they understood about that sort of thing.

Not that Hope did need me so much any more. Like any teenager, she was pushing for more independence. With Hope it wasn't about hanging out in the seafront amusement arcades with her mates, because she didn't really have mates; it was more things like walking to school unaccompanied and having her own money to spend on her own CDs, and, I suspected, sweets from the One Stop.

There was an open house at school that evening. We'd had a few issues with bullying at the start, but Hope seemed to be doing OK now and managing her lessons with a bit of individual support from her teaching assistant during classes, and a lot from me with her homework.

Usually, Mrs Goode was the teacher I looked forward to seeing because Music was the subject Hope excelled in. Because of all my own stuff swirling around my head it took a little while for me to understand that she was telling me that Hope wasn't going to be allowed to continue going to choir. Apparently there had been several incidents when things had been said that weren't very kind and there'd been complaints. Mrs Goode glanced at Hope who was sitting next to me staring at the floor, and it suddenly dawned on me, horrified, that it was my sister who had been doing the bullying in this instance.

'Perhaps Hope would like to learn an individual instrument?' Mrs Goode suggested, eager to offer an alternative. 'She's drawn to the piano, aren't you, Hope?'

'I'm not sure we could afford piano lessons,' I said. 'And we haven't got a piano at home.'

'I've spoken to the head and the school would be prepared to lend Hope a keyboard. With her gifts, I'm sure she'll pick it up quite quickly. There are books you can get, then if she takes to it and finds she likes it, we can see about tuition . . .'

She mentioned the name Martin's Music, which was where

the middle-class parents at St Cuthbert's used to get their children's musical instruments. It was a dark little shop, up an alley off the main pedestrianized shopping street, opposite the place where we got our shoes re-heeled. We'd often looked in the window, but we'd never gone in because Dad didn't like the idea of Hope getting her hands on a recorder or a quarter-size violin, although she'd probably have got a better noise out of them than most kids did.

'Can we go to Martin's Music?' Hope asked as we walked home.

'It'll be closed now.'

'Can we go when it's open?'

'We can, Hope, but only if you promise to be kind.'

She said nothing. Was she capable of remorse, I wondered? Even though I'd known her all her life, I never had the slightest inkling of what was going through her mind.

'Hope, you know when those boys outside the One Stop shouted at you and called you fat?' I said. 'Did you get a funny feeling inside?'

'Not funny!'

'I mean a horrible feeling.'

I took her silence to mean yes.

'You see, Hope, when you say to Emily in choir that she's singing the wrong notes, she gets that horrible feeling too. So it's not very nice, is it?'

'Emily does sing all the wrong notes.'

Well, you're fat, I felt like saying, but you don't, do you?

I couldn't get to sleep that night, but when I finally dozed off in the early hours, I dreamed I was opening the door to the consulting room and my counsellor Jane was standing there with a bottle of champagne. As the cork shot across the room towards me, I woke with a jolt of elation that instantly returned to dread.

I looked at the alarm clock. Four hours to go. With the town still sleeping, I got up and went for a long walk along the clifftop, watching the sun rise over the water and the whole sky turning pink. Red sky in the morning. If I hadn't already known, I knew then.

Hope had no idea, obviously, and I was wearing my shop uniform as usual, so she found it peculiar and unwelcome when I gave her an extra-long hug before waving her off up the road. She walked to school on her own now, but there was never a morning when I didn't feel as if I was holding my breath until around nine, by which time I knew the school would have phoned me if she hadn't turned up.

The bus driver said, 'Cheer up, love. It may never happen!' Which I thought was a bit insensitive, given that I'd just asked for a fare to the hospital.

I tried to make my smile menacing in its insincerity, then sat down, wondering whether a woman had ever said that to a man, and what men were thinking when they said it. I mean, did they really want to brighten your day, or was it a way of saying, 'You're a miserable cow,' and getting away with it?

When I nervously opened the door to the counsellor's room, Jane said, 'Come in, Tess!' without looking up from her computer screen.

'Have a seat!' Now she was smiling at me, but I could see the little flicker of terror in her eyes.

For a split second I thought, I don't have to do this. Why don't I tell her that I've changed my mind and just leave not knowing? I'd always said that not knowing was the worst thing, but now it suddenly seemed like the attractive option. Except I did know.

'I'm afraid it is a positive result.'

I thought I'd explored all the possible feelings I might have on hearing those words – because you do that, don't you, hoping that if you really believe the worst, you'll trick it out of happening? – but it wasn't like any of those scenarios. I suppose that's why they tell you to sit down, because you feel like you're falling through a void. I'd never understood before why being seated would help.

Jane's lips were moving, but I couldn't really hear what she was saying because my brain was a blur. I'd done all the research. When we left New York, Shaun had presented me with a laptop for writing, but once I'd got the Internet at home it was like discovering an infinite library and I spent a lot of time reading, not just about cancer. I knew that when you test positive for a mutation of the BRCA 1 or 2 genes – mine, Jane was saying, was BRCA 2 – you've got two choices. You can opt for preventative surgery. First a bilateral mastectomy, then removal of the ovaries, leading to an early menopause. Or you can choose surveillance, which means you get a mammogram and MRI scan every year, so you can act quickly if anything shows up.

But it wasn't really my choice, Jane seemed to be telling me now. Even though the cancer tends to occur a little bit earlier as it passes down through the generations, they'd still be pretty reluctant to give me radical surgery at the age of twenty-five, especially since I hadn't yet had children.

'But if you're offering me yearly mammograms and MRI scans, you must think it's a possibility?' I argued.

'It's very unlikely.'

'But it was very unlikely that I'd test positive, wasn't it?'

Jane looked at her notes.

'Your grandmother died at fifty-one. Your mother was forty-eight,' she said. 'You've got time on your side.'

'But Mum was forty-three when she got cancer the first time . . . so that brings it down to forty for me . . .'

'We can't put a date on it, Tess,' said Jane. 'You may never get it. Or it may not happen till you're seventy.'

'But it could happen tomorrow!'

Jane sighed. She wasn't going to lie to me.

'If I have the surgery, then my chances of getting cancer go back to the same as everyone else's?'

'That's right.'

'So not zero, then?'

'Not zero, no,' she sighed. 'Look, Tess, it'll take a while to process this . . . you don't have to make any decisions right away. What I want you to hold on to, Tess, is that knowledge is power.'

That's what we'd agreed during the counselling. I'd been so relieved when I was eventually offered the test, I'd kind of forgotten that getting it wasn't the real battle.

Knowledge is power. As I walked back to the bus stop, I'd never felt more powerless. A random act of biology had chosen to give me a death sentence, and there was nothing that I could do to change that.

Word must have got around that I'd gone for a hospital appointment, because there was normally a bit of banter, but today my colleagues seemed quieter than usual. Maybe the fear showed on my face. I spent my shift on autopilot, with all my options repeating in my head so loudly that on several occasions I forgot to ask about cashback or give out the charity tokens.

'You all right, Tess?' my supervisor enquired, when she came to sort out a jammed till roll.

'I'm fine,' I said.

It was true, wasn't it? There was nothing wrong with me. I was a perfectly healthy woman, but it felt as if I was incubating something horrible inside me, like in *Alien*. The strange thing was that it wasn't alien at all. It was in my DNA. Like curly hair, it was part of who I was. That was the impossible bit to get my head around.

Surveillance was a peculiar word to use about the wait-and-see approach, because it felt more like the cancer was watching me than that I was watching it.

Usually, I passed the time on the checkout by making up stories in my head about the customers from their shopping. You can tell a lot about a person from the items in their trolley. I'm not just talking about whether they're having a party or they've got a cat.

Now each item moving towards me on the conveyor belt seemed to carry additional significance.

Weren't pomegranate seeds supposed to be superfoods that warded off cancer?

'What do you do with them?' I asked the young career woman, in a neat little suit from Next, because we were encouraged to build rapport with the customers.

'Anything really,' she said, distractedly. 'Scatter them on salad, that kind of thing.'

So why the diet cola? In America, it actually had a label saying that one of the ingredients was known to cause cancer in rats.

Are hot flushes as bad as they say? I wanted to ask the middle-aged woman whose basket included a packet of Menopace, a box of Tena and a jar of Options low-calorie hot chocolate.

Hadn't the bloke with three-for-the-price-of-two Doritos, a jar of dip and a four-pack of lager heard the advice about maintaining a sensible weight and eating your five-a-day?

'Evening in?'

'Wanna join me?' he said.

I pretended I hadn't heard. You'd be surprised how many offers I got.

I'd have been more tempted by the guy with Parma ham,

ciabatta and a bag of rocket in his trolley. But he was in a serious enough relationship to be picking up Lil-Lets for his partner without trying to hide them behind the toilet roll.

'You all right, Tess?' said Lewis as I walked through the racks of fruit and veg at the end of my shift.

Would he still fancy me with a flat chest? I wondered.

Since I didn't currently have a boyfriend, wouldn't now be the ideal time to get the operation done? Or would it be the worst time? If the purpose of surgery was to live happily ever after, wouldn't having it ruin my chances of doing that?

I walked home, thinking that time alone would help sort out all the questions in my head, but it didn't really.

Even if I had the surgery, I might die of something else. The mutation of the BRCA gene increased your chances of pancreatic cancer, and they couldn't usually detect that until it was too late.

When would I fit in an operation anyway?

And wasn't there a risk to surgery? With my luck, I'd die on the operating table. And where would that leave Hope?

If I insisted on having the surgery, there'd be no going back; but if I left it, they might even find a cure.

'When you don't know what to do, do nothing,' Mum used to say.

But look where that had got her.

That's the problem with imaginative space. It gives you too much time to think.

Passing the O'Neills' house, I was half-tempted to ring the bell and have a chat at the kitchen table with a cup of tea, just like we used to do after school. But Mrs O'Neill would only tell me that God has his reasons. It wasn't her I needed to talk to anyway. Doll was the person who had always been the counterbalance to my tendency to dwell on things, and she didn't live there any more.

Doll got her wedding and Dave got his wife. That sounds jealous, which I wasn't really, because in my heart of hearts I knew that they'd be great together. There was a picture of the two of them in the local paper, in the country hotel with the Jacuzzis. Ironically, it appeared on the same day as the headline *Fred Out* because Fred had sustained a cruciate ligament injury and wouldn't play again for the rest of the season.

I'd thought about sending them a card, but I couldn't find the words because I was still smarting over the things she'd said and the things I'd said. I'd sounded like I'd hated her, which wasn't true, but it still wasn't on, what she'd done, and we couldn't just pretend it hadn't happened. If I'd had a self-righteous notion that denying Doll my friendship would be her punishment, though, that was an own goal, because I was the one who'd lost out on companionship and fun.

Sometimes, I wished Doll would just turn up at my checkout and we'd go for a coffee in my break and it wouldn't be such a big deal. But people are loyal to their own supermarket, and The Dolls House was growing all the time, so she probably didn't have time for shopping.

Or maybe someone had told her where I worked, and she was deliberately avoiding me?

You'd think with someone you'd known all your life, you'd be able to imagine what they'd say in a given situation even if they weren't there, but Doll always had her own take on things. She was a cup-half-full person whereas I'd become a bit cup-half-empty since Mum. Now, I thought, there was probably a no-cups-needed kind of joke waiting for one of us to say. We'd been through all the watershed moments together – first day at school, First Communion, first period, first kiss, first parent dying, first serious boyfriend – so it seemed strange that she wouldn't even know about first serious health dilemma.

I still believed that if I rang her up and told her about the test, she'd be straight over with a bottle of Pinot Grigio, or, these days, probably something pricier like Sancerre that the posh customers bought to go with their sea-bass fillets. But, being married, she'd then go home and tell Dave, and I couldn't bear the thought of the two of them lying in their king-size bed, after a bout of gymnastic sex, saying, 'Poor old Tess!'

When I got in, I rang Shaun. He'd encouraged me all the way through the counselling and the test, so I was dismayed to hear a stunned silence. I realized he'd also been banking on a negative, so now it wasn't just the shock, it was as if he somehow felt responsible.

I found myself having to reassure him. 'Knowledge is power, Shaun. That's what we have to hold onto . . .'

But as Kev's partner, Shaun's concern was no longer solely for me. 'Is it possible Kevin's inherited the bad gene too?'

'I suppose it must be a fifty-fifty chance,' I said, slightly irritated. I couldn't bear my brother making it his problem right now.

'Please don't tell Kev,' I pleaded.

'I think I have to, Tess,' Shaun said.

Which felt like another door closing.

I felt so miserable, I was going to skip my writing class. Then Hope arrived home with the promised keyboard on a special little trolley and immediately started experimenting, and I was sure I'd go mad if I stayed home.

The creative-writing class was part of the Adult Education Programme at the local tertiary college and Leo, our tutor, was a university professor with longish salt-and-pepper hair swept back from his face and designer stubble. There were five of us students. Liz had an idea for a romcom set on a cruise liner; Violet was a pensioner whose grandchildren wanted her to write down some of the stories she told them about the war;

Ashley was a teenage computer geek who was writing a fantasy novel with characters called Snork and Godroon.

We were all different, but we gelled together – and then there was Derek, a retired policeman, who considered himself above the rest of us because he had self-published a crime novel. One evening, he'd collared me on the way to the bus stop, saying we were kindred artistic spirits and would I like to go for an Indian, but I told him that I felt it might disturb the creative dynamic. I know policemen retire early, but fifty was still nearly twice my age, and, to be honest, I was a bit disturbed by his lurid descriptions of murdered women.

It wasn't just about reading out our writing. Leo set us exercises to build up our skills, like getting us to invent characters for people in old photos he'd bring in, which was a bit like me and Mum making up stuff about people in cafes. The technical term is backstory.

Another week, we'd have to tell three anecdotes about things that had happened in our lives, two true and one false, and see if the class guessed. It was a way of practising storytelling skills.

I worked out that the trick was to set the scene. No point in saying that you'd met George Clooney unless you gave all the details, like you were walking through Leicester Square and there was this big crowd of people outside the cinema waiting for stars to arrive on the red carpet, and you suddenly realized that you'd inadvertently got yourself onto the wrong side of the cordon, when this limo drew up beside you and all these photographers closed in, so you couldn't move. Then this man got out, straightening his tie, buttoning and unbuttoning his jacket, like men do when they're on chat shows – I think it's a nervous thing, but maybe it's something to do with creasing – and he was so close you could smell his aftershave, and he looked at you, and gave you this, like, 'You don't quite realize who I am, do you? Wait! Now you do!' kind of smile, before moving on in a blizzard of motor drive.

They were all fooled by that one.

For our homework, Leo would give us a word, like 'greed', or 'winter', it could be anything, and we had to write something: a description, a bit of dialogue, a poem, a story, whatever we wanted. But it was important to do it.

'What do writers do?' he'd ask, if anyone turned up with excuses.

'They write,' we'd chorus.

I loved learning a new skill. I suppose it was escapism. When I sat at my computer, everything beyond the Word document just disappeared. Usually I wrote far too much and Leo's advice to me was to throw away the dictionary and keep it simple.

He had a wide vocabulary though, and was always dropping words like 'contextualize' and 'Kafkaesque' into the lessons. He was also incredibly well-read. Whenever he mentioned an author he admired, I'd make a note and order their books from the library – Nabokov, Kundera, Grass – for me it was more like doing a course in European Literature than Creative Writing, because I'd be thinking, these authors are so amazing, why am I even bothering? But Leo said we weren't there to become great writers, we were there to become better writers.

'Write about what you know,' he said.

'Who wants to read about a supermarket?'

Somehow I'd become the joker in the class, which I never was at school. You can be different in a place where nobody knows you, can't you? More yourself, somehow, or the person you'd like to be.

'Who wants to read about a small-town housewife?' Leo countered.

'I'm not a housewife,' I said.

'No, but Emma Bovary was.'

286

Occasionally, Leo gave me this amused smile, which wasn't patronizing, or avuncular. I'm not sure of the word for it.

'I'm not Flaubert,' I said.

'No,' said Leo, simply, making me wish I hadn't tried to show off.

He had this ability to make you feel really intelligent or really stupid and the tension between the two was simultaneously scary and exhilarating. 'Tension' was a very Leo word.

The class usually went to the pub afterwards, and sometimes Leo would come along too and keep us rapt with anecdotes and quotations. The thing about him I liked most was his voice, which was melodic and a tiny bit Welsh, like Anthony Hopkins' or Michael Sheen's, with an actor's range from whisper to bellow.

Once, he mentioned the novel he'd written and how the publisher had put a terrible cover on it and mucked up the publicity, which was the reason you couldn't find it in a bookshop.

'They do say that those who can't, teach,' said Derek, when Leo was up at the bar, which the rest of us thought was incredibly arrogant and ungenerous.

I ordered Leo's novel from the library. *Of Academic Interest* was a dark comedy about an English lecturer on a university campus in the eighties. I read it straight away. The tone reminded me a little bit of a novel I'd read by the American author John Updike. When I said that, Leo's eyes lit up, so I didn't tell him I wasn't that big a fan of that type of writing.

The class took my mind off my test result for a couple of hours, but as soon as I left, it all started rushing back. Standing at the bus stop, I was so preoccupied I didn't even notice the car pulling up beside me until Leo wound down the window and leaned across the passenger seat.

'Hop in!' he said. 'I'll give you a lift.'

'No, you're all right. It's too far . . .'

'Please!' he said. 'I'd like to.'

So then it seemed ruder to refuse.

For the first few minutes, I just sat staring through the windscreen, aware of him occasionally glancing across at me when he slowed down at traffic lights.

'Are you going to say what the problem is, Tess?' he finally asked. 'You don't seem your usual effervescent self.'

'It's a long story,' I said.

'Why don't you tell me it?'

He made it sound like an assignment, and at first I thought, *No*, and then I thought, *What's to lose? We've got at least half an hour and we can't just sit here in silence*, so I started in with my mother dying of cancer and the cloud hanging over me and how I'd used all my powers of persuasion to get a genetic test and how the irony was that I now wished I hadn't.

'But you haven't got cancer?' Leo asked, his voice gentle and tentative like Anthony Hopkins' – in *Shadowlands*, not *Silence of the Lambs*, obviously.

'No,' I said. 'But it's likely I will get it, at some point.'

Somehow it helped to say it all out loud to someone intelligent and sympathetic, especially after Shaun not being much help.

'There are steps I can take to prevent it, but they're pretty drastic and I can't get my head around them . . .' I went on.

'Do you have to decide right now?'

'I won't stop thinking about it unless I do. That's just the way I am.'

Leo said nothing for the last few miles, but when he stopped outside our house, he switched off the engine and turned to face me, looking into my eyes very seriously.

'On my desk,' he said, 'I have a tray marked "In" and a tray marked "Out", but I also have a tray marked "Pending". And when I'm not sure what to do about something, I'll put it in the "Pending" tray, and then I've done something with it, you see?'

He had this way of approaching things from a different angle. You'd think he was simply giving you information, and then you'd realize it was a metaphor.

'You're saying I could make a decision not to make a decision for the moment?' I clarified.

Rewarded with the amused smile, I found myself wondering how he kept his stubble the same length. It was definitely more than a five-o'clock shadow, so he probably shaved every two or three days. But if that was the case, with seven days in a week, you'd expect that on some Thursdays, there would be more growth than others. Perhaps he shaved just once, on Monday morning, and that way we always caught him at the same point. By Sunday night, he was probably approaching a beard, which he'd then shave off in the morning, starting the whole cycle again.

I realized I was staring at his mouth.

'Why don't you ever write about any of this?' he asked softly.

'It's a bit personal, isn't it?' I said, suddenly aware of being physically much closer to him than I'd ever been.

In the distance, I could hear Hope on her keyboard. She had already managed to pick out the notes of 'Is This the Way to Amarillo?' which was everywhere because of Comic Relief.

'Graham Greene said that writers have a chip of ice in their hearts,' Leo said. 'What do you think he meant?'

'That they look at things in a detached way?' I guessed.

'Exactly!' he said. 'Writers see everything that happens as material.'

His eyes held mine for a moment longer and for a split second I was sure he was going to kiss me, then he leaned right across my body to open the passenger door to let me out, and drove off without saying another word. Of course he wasn't going to kiss me! I told myself, standing on the pavement, feeling slightly light-headed. He was married. His wife worked at the university. But my body still felt trembly inside, and his voice remained in my head all the time I was trying to get Hope to stop playing and go to bed.

I sat down at my laptop. The word Leo had given us to write about was 'holiday'.

I found myself thinking about the best holiday we'd ever had as a family. It must have been the summer of 1995, ironically, the year when the BRCA 2 gene was identified. I remembered it as such a happy time, with Hope still a toddler, and a bit more room in the house because of the boys leaving home. I'd done really well in my GCSEs and Mum had finished the chemo so Dad splashed out on a package to Tenerife to celebrate. He'd won a trophy at the Irish pub in Playa de los Cristianos for the best Elvis Presley impersonation with his rendition of 'The Wonder of You', and Mum bought the painted plate that stood next to it on the knick-knack shelf in the kitchen. And all that time, in a lab somewhere, scientists in white coats and masks were using those pipette things they always show on the news when there's a breakthrough in genetics to squirt coloured liquid into test tubes and discover things that would spell disaster for all of us. Not that it was the scientists' fault, obviously.

I found myself writing about a family by a pool in the Canaries. It was curiously comforting putting myself in my Mum's shoes, imagining how she must have felt lying in her one-piece swimsuit with the padded cups, with the sky all blue above her and not a cloud in sight.

I wasn't sure whether it was the beginning of a story, or even a poem, but I gave it the title, 'Today is the First Day of the Rest of Your Life'.

At the next class, I was more nervous than I'd ever been reading my homework out, because it mattered, somehow.

There was a long silence when I finished.

'That's the sound of people wanting more,' Leo said, eventually. 'And it's so much better than the sound of people wanting less,' he added, somehow managing to wink privately at me and nod in Derek's general direction at the same time.

19

GUS

Maybe, when things are going well, you shouldn't tempt fate by trying to make them better.

Our second daughter endured a trickier start to her life than Flora had. During the pregnancy, Charlotte suffered badly from morning sickness. Then the baby was late, which upset the timetable.

As Charlotte was keen to return to work as soon as she could, I negotiated a month's paternity leave in lieu of holiday. We'd decided in advance that this would be a good opportunity for Kasia's annual trip back to Poland to see her family. Since the due date coincided almost exactly with the start of Flora's new term at nursery, the timing looked perfect. We hadn't even considered the notion that the baby might not slot into our carefully planned schedule.

The birth was difficult because the baby's head wasn't curled into her chest but tilted back, as if she wanted to see where she was going. We had decided on Bella as a name for a girl, but even the most doting parent could not have called her a beautiful newborn, with her face bruised from the forceps and her scarecrow head of red hair.

It's easy to believe, when you have a baby who sleeps as Flora always had, that you're a naturally relaxed and competent parent. I'd allowed myself that secret thought when overhearing the yummy mummies moaning about sleep deprivation. Bella was the retribution for my smugness. With Charlotte back at work after just a fortnight, and Flora less than delighted by a screaming infant grabbing all the attention that had previously been hers, I found myself regularly driving round South London in the small hours with Bella in the baby seat next to me sleeping fitfully between traffic lights.

Since training to be a GP, I'd lost the hospital doctor's habit of long, irregular hours, so I now existed in a zombie-like state of limited consciousness, my eyelids jerkily fluttering like the wings of a dying bird the moment I sat down, my consumption of espresso driving my pulse to a level where it sometimes felt like my heart was the only muscle in my body still capable of movement.

Charlotte was open about the fact that she didn't really 'do' the baby stuff, as if it was a choice that we could all elect to make. If I was exhausted, that's what I'd signed up for. Instead, Charlotte took on the role of making sure that Flora didn't feel neglected, spending a lot of time reading with her in the evenings, and, at weekends, taking her to ballet matinees and butterfly houses. Flora grew more like her mother each day, from her use of expressions – 'Honestly!' – to her choice of clothes. Charlotte loved to tell the story of how, when trying on a pink ballerina party dress in Selfridges, Flora had asked the assistant, 'Do you have it in black?'

At six weeks old, Bella started developing eczema. For the first few days, I persuaded myself that the patches of colour on her cheeks were a rosy sign of health, but when it started spreading all over her tiny body, I could no longer avoid the diagnosis.

Eczema isn't a condition that elicits much sympathy. It's not usually life-threatening, unless it is allowed to develop a staph infection, but it is itchy and miserable for the child, and ugly to look at. When you have a healthy baby, you don't realize how often well-meaning strangers peer into the pram to make a cheery comment; when you have a baby with eczema, you are acutely aware of the smile sinking from their faces as they see the crusty, weeping rash.

I rued the times when desperate mothers had brought their eczematous children to the surgery and I had blithely doled out hydrocortisone cream, assuring them that their children would grow out of it. How little I'd known of their worry and how ignorant I'd been of the care required to minimize the suffering of the child. Most children do grow out of the condition by the age of two, but when your baby's only six weeks old, that feels like a life sentence. And the likelihood is that the child will develop asthma after the eczema disappears.

I spent any downtime at work searching the Internet for support organizations, which proved far more helpful than any of my GP colleagues at providing practical tips. Kasia sewed little cotton mittens onto the sleeves of Bella's Babygros to minimize the damage from scratching.

If it's your own child, you find the energy, even when you're working full-time, to get up in the middle of the night when the only thing that soothes her is being held and rocked gently. If you're just an employee, you don't have those reserves of parental love to draw on. Kasia did her best to share the load for a couple of months, but she'd found a boyfriend who was keen for her to return to Poland and help with his online business, and there was no reason for her to stay in England.

When she handed in her notice, I must have looked so desperate, she promised to wait until we found someone we liked. But it was difficult. Both Charlotte and I were back at work. The only candidate who we both thought might do came for interview on a day when Bella's skin was particularly angry, and visibly recoiled when we tried to introduce her.

Although there's no real doubt about eczema being an allergic disease, Charlotte developed the theory that it, and Kasia's departure, and any other problem we had, were due to the Wandsworth house.

'It's so low-lying and dark here. I'm sure the air is full of particulates,' she sighed, so frequently that I eventually twigged what was expected of me and asked, 'Do you think we should move?'

I assumed that she was thinking of getting a place further out of London in the cleaner air of Surrey, where we'd both spent our childhoods, but the house she had set her heart on was situated in one of the white stucco-fronted crescents off Ladbroke Grove. It was tall, elegant and way out of our price range.

'Don't say anything until you've seen inside,' she whispered, as we followed the estate agent up the steps to the front door.

There were four storeys including the basement. 'And potential to go into the roof,' he pointed out obligingly.

He was only about my age, but exuded the confidence of someone who drove a red sports car and wore his short black hair spiked up with gel.

'A lot of people also decide to go down these days,' he said, giving Charlotte a wink at the double entendre.

She rewarded him with a breath of insincere laughter.

An old lady had lived in the property and it hadn't been modernized, I guessed, since at least the fifties. The kitchen, with its stand-alone cooker and yellowing cupboards, had the look of a stage set for a John Osborne play. The whole place reeked of cats.

'It's way too big for us,' I whispered to Charlotte.

'Exactly,' she said. 'I'm thinking we could create two flats, one in the basement, one on the top floor, and still have a nice house in between.'

I guessed the only reason Charlotte had been able to get us through the door was that the property was practically derelict, or in the vocabulary of television estate agents, 'a project'. One of the disadvantages of having two small children is that you're so tired you'll watch anything on TV.

'The people in the top-floor flat would have to walk through our bit,' I said, wondering why I was even entertaining the proposal. Charlotte was one of the least practical people I knew, and I'd never even put up a shelf. We were unlikely property developers. The only person I could think of who might be able to help us was my father. But we'd fallen out of touch with him and his new wife, through lack of effort on both sides, and perhaps out of loyalty to my mother, who we saw rather too often for my liking.

Charlotte dismissed this objection before I'd voiced it. 'Kasia knows lots of builders. Just wait until you see the garden . . .'

The garden itself was fairly small and overgrown, but at the bottom, there was a gate leading into a small private park, which was shared with the other properties backing onto it. Even on a bleak late-November day, it felt like a secret oasis in the heart of the city. One of the large, well-established deciduous trees had a swing attached to its lower branches, another had a treehouse built into its sturdy trunk. The plaintive cooing of a wood pigeon made me aware of how peaceful it was. You could hardly hear the traffic.

'Wouldn't the girls love it?' Charlotte slipped her arm through mine.

We stood there imagining ourselves sitting in this leafy Eden on summer evenings, watching our children play, with a glass of chilled Sancerre, maybe, and the smell of barbecues drifting from our neighbours' gardens.

'Saturday mornings in Portobello Market.' Charlotte knew exactly which buttons to push. 'All the museums just a walk across the park . . .'

'Quite a long walk,' I pointed out.

She frowned at me for spoiling her fun.

'Thoughts?' said the estate agent, without looking up from his mobile phone.

'We've got a bit of talking to do.'

'It's a probate sale, as you know, so they're eager to sell, but I've got people queuing up to see it,' he said. 'So, if you're interested, don't *talk* for too long.'

He addressed this all to Charlotte, as we walked back through the hall, then shook our hands and pointed his keys at the red sports car which bleeped obediently.

'Wait,' Charlotte said, a ventriloquist through her forced smile, as I took our car key from my pocket.

'OK,' she said, when the estate agent had turned onto Ladbroke Grove. 'I didn't want him to think we were the type of people who drove a Picasso.'

'We are, though,' I said.

'Well, I don't see myself in that way,' she retorted.

Charlotte saw herself as the type of person who drove a much swankier car, and lived in a beautiful stucco-fronted house in Notting Hill. She had every right to, I suppose, because she was now a consultant, earning a good salary, and should have been married to someone who was earning as much, if not more, than she was.

'When I get my first partnership,' I promised, 'we'll look in this area.'

'That'll be too late,' she said firmly, as we sat in traffic. 'Don't you see this is our one chance, Angus? It'll be out of our reach in a matter of months. There's a slight lull because it's coming up to Christmas, but as soon as spring gets going, the market will take off again. We've only got a look-in because it requires modernization.'

'That means more money on top of the money we can't afford!' I countered.

'But we'd be adding value. We'd make it all back and more by selling one of the flats!'

'I see the logic,' I said, trying not to sound negative. 'But I don't see the deposit.'

'Well, actually, there is a way,' said Charlotte. 'If your mother sold her house and if we sold Wandsworth, we'd have enough for a deposit, and my salary would cover the remaining mortgage. The lower-ground floor has its own front door. It would be a completely independent flat.'

I finally realized where she was going. 'Have my mother move in with us?'

'She'd love it, Angus.'

'You've dreamed up the idea with my mother?'

'Not at all,' said Charlotte. Then, slightly sheepishly, 'She did say, with Kasia leaving, and us in a spot, she wouldn't mind looking after the girls full-time. I don't see how that would work unless she was living with us.'

From her refusal to look me in the eye, I suspected that negotiations had progressed to a more advanced stage.

The traffic started moving again. We inched forward.

'It would make things much easier all round,' said Charlotte, leaving a few diplomatic moments to let her proposal sink in. 'And she's so good with Bella. It's logical, Angus!'

My mother had been a dental nurse. When she came up to babysit at weekends she was scrupulously hygienic with Bella's bathing and moisturizing regime. If she was really volunteering to take over from Kasia full-time, I knew I should be overwhelmed with gratitude, and yet every fibre of my being resisted it.

Sitting serenely in the passenger seat, Charlotte said nothing for the rest of the journey home, while my instincts wrestled with my intelligence, trying and failing to formulate a rational argument as to why my mother living with us would be such a bad idea.

'We'd hardly see her, you know.' Charlotte broke the silence just at the moment my mind had run out of excuses. She should really have been a professional poker player because she knew exactly when to sit tight and when to up the stakes. 'I'm sure she values her independence as much as we do.'

'We'd share a garden . . .'

'But what a garden!'

Sometimes you can let yourself believe that if you just change one thing in your life then everything else will fall into place. Picturing our family in that leafy tranquil place, I allowed myself to imagine that our lives there would be magically transformed. When I finally qualified as a GP, I would get a job in a surgery nearby, because there was no way I could commute from north of the river to the practice in Croydon. Maybe I'd like it better at a different place; it would be a fresh start where my colleagues would think of me as an experienced family man rather than a student who'd mucked up; I'd be earning a good salary so Charlotte wouldn't have to work so hard; the girls could safely learn to ride bikes in the garden; on Sunday mornings, the four of us would go to the Natural History Museum or rowing on the Serpentine and be a happy family together.

It was getting dark as we turned into our street, making Wandsworth's low red-brick terraces seem even more oppressive after the airy white villas of Notting Hill.

'All right then, let's see what she says,' I said as we pulled up outside the house.

By the time my mother arrived the following weekend, it

was apparent that the proposition had already been discussed at some length.

'Don't you think you ought to see it first?' I asked her. 'It's in a terrible state.'

'Oh, most of that's cosmetic.' My mother flushed as she realized she'd let the cat out of the bag.

The following Monday morning, Charlotte made an offer which was accepted subject to contract and my mother's house and Wandsworth went on the market. A week later, when Kasia departed, I felt a jittery mix of terror and excitement. We'd committed ourselves to unexplored territory and there was no going back.

My mother moved into Kasia's old bedroom from Sunday to Thursday nights, returning to her house on Friday evening to spend the weekends clearing and packing up. For a couple of weeks, the arrangement worked amazingly well. I was able to drive to work instead of getting the train because my mother had her own car to ferry the children around. Bella almost immediately began sleeping through the night. At weekends, she tended to be a little more fractious, bearing out Charlotte's view that I pandered to her demands too much.

My mother and I were careful around each other. I fought back the silent scream in my head when she said things that annoyed me; she dutifully disappeared after dinner each evening to watch television in her own room. On one occasion, late at night, when she'd clearly fallen asleep with the telly still on, I tried to slip in to turn it off, but found her door locked.

'You're the one who wants her to be independent,' said Charlotte, when I got back into bed grumbling about the noise.

Since Flora's birth, my mother had spent Christmases with us. It was a time of year I think we both dreaded. With snow twinkling over each channel ident on television, ski weather reports after the news, and happy extended families sitting down for banquets together during every ad break, I sometimes felt as if Ross's ghost had managed to track us down to our living room.

However patient and solicitous a son I tried to be, I was sure my presence was an unwelcome reminder for my mother, so my solution was to hide in the kitchen for most of the day, pretending I needed to baste the bird or stir the sauces. Occasionally, I would poke my head round the door of the living room to ask if anyone would like a cup of tea or a refill of champagne, and glimpse my mother, wife and daughter doing Christmassy things together, almost as if they were someone else's family.

Curiously, with the prospect of us moving in together in the New Year, our last Christmas in Wandsworth felt less fraught, perhaps because we were all making a conscious effort to look to the future. My mother arrived on Christmas Eve with a side of smoked salmon and an expensive Yule log from Waitrose. She stood in the kitchen with a gin and tonic talking to me instead of scuttling off immediately to chat to Charlotte, asking how my job was, and whether I'd decided on turkey or goose.

In turn, I praised the presents she had chosen for Flora and Bella. It was almost as if we had each privately decided to forgive the complaints we had against each other. Perhaps there was a statute of limitations on resentment, I thought, realizing, almost with surprise, that it was the tenth Christmas since Ross's death.

On Christmas Day, when I saw my mother helping Flora to thread beads onto ribbon to make a necklace, I felt a rush of pride that she had been able to find joy with her grandchildren.

Flora wriggled down from her lap and ran over to me.

'Daddy, next year, we're going to have a very tall Christmas tree!' she said. 'So tall, we'll need a stepladder to put the star on the top!'

'That's right!' I said, imagining the high-ceilinged living room of our prospective house all painted white.

301

'What is a stepladder, Daddy?'

'It's a ladder that stands on its own.'

'Can you draw it for me in my notebook, please?'

Flora had a fascination with words so I'd bought her a notebook with a bright plastic cover from Paperchase in which I wrote new vocabulary down for her, often drawing an illustration. Next to the word *Stepladder*, I sketched a Christmas tree standing in a bay window like the one on the upper-ground floor of the Notting Hill house, with a stepladder beside it and a little girl on the top rung, stretching out with a star in her hands.

I handed the notebook back to Flora.

'St-e-p l-a-dd-er,' she said, sounding out the syllables, with her finger following the letters.

'Reading at four years old!' said Charlotte proudly.

'Ross was an early reader,' said my mother. 'And Angus wasn't far behind,' she added quickly.

'Granny may even have her own tree downstairs,' Flora said, clearly repeating something my mother had said. 'So we'll have two trees!'

'There are lots of trees in the garden, too,' I said, joining in with the plans. 'So maybe we'll be able to string some coloured lights on those!'

Now Charlotte was smiling at me. She had Bella sitting on her lap, who was holding a soft little elephant with one ear that crackled and one ear that squeaked and a bell inside that tinkled when she shook it. Bella's skin was having a good day, and with her halo of orange curls, she looked positively cherubic.

In my mind, I tried to capture the softly sparkling image of the three generations of women in my family, knowing that if I brought out the camera, their poses would stiffen, and the glow of contentment around them would be lost.

'Why don't you come and sit with us?' Charlotte said. 'You've been working so hard all morning . . .'

'Make a bracelet with me, Daddy,' said Flora.

The turkey was resting, the gravy was made. If the vegetables were a little overcooked, what did it matter?

Still wearing the navy-and-white striped apron, which had been her present to me, I sat down on the sofa next to my mother, and she handed me a tray of assorted beads. Flora clambered onto my lap.

In the grate, the flames of the coal-effect gas fire flickered. As the light outside the bay window faded, the coloured lights on our tree seemed to glow brighter. I found myself thinking that if someone were looking in from outside, they would see a perfectly happy, harmonious family.

20

2007

TESS

Anyone would think the UK population doubled over the Christmas period. I don't know how people find the room in their fridges for all those ceramic pots of chicken parfait with shiny jelly and a cranberry on top. And if Stilton's so delicious, why don't we eat it all year round? How come families can survive quite happily with a single packet of Jacob's Cream Crackers for the rest of the year, but suddenly, everyone has to have this great big tin of 'Biscuits for Cheese'? Who is daft enough to fork out twelve pounds for a chocolate Swiss roll with some fancy icing on it? Does anyone in the country actually *like* Christmas pudding? And, on that subject, why pay more for one with an orange in the middle, when, at that time of year, you can get two nets of Navelinas for three pounds?

There's not a lot of seasonal goodwill in a supermarket, with the crowds and the queues and the expense. I'd been promoted to supervisor, so I spent most of my time on the customer service desk dealing with relentless moaning and occasional incidents of pudding rage.

'Miss Costello to Aisle Four, please.'

Next to the bakery counter, two men were arguing over the last box.

'Why do you have the bloody television adverts if you're going to sell out?' the loser shouted at me, his face alarmingly pink.

Is it worth the high blood pressure, I wanted to ask him? You'll give yourself a heart attack before you've even started on the brandy butter.

'Could I offer you a complimentary stollen with our apologies for your disappointment?'

'Do I get one too?' his opponent demanded.

'If you're willing to hand your pudding over to this gentleman . . .'

Not a sentence I'd have ever imagined myself saying.

I'd discovered that the most efficient method of dealing with problems was to grovel and offer compensation wherever possible.

'It defuses the situation,' I explained to the deputy manager, who was more inclined to justify than hand out freebies. 'This way, they go away with a free cake and something nice to tell their family and friends. So they'll come back to us instead of seeing what M and S Simply Food has to offer.'

'You should really be thinking about marketing,' he said.

I was reluctant to take up the career-development opportunities offered partly because I suspected they'd find out that I didn't really possess 'people skills' or 'leadership qualities' or anything other than a bit of common sense. I didn't see my future in a supermarket, although as time ticked by, I sometimes wondered what I was waiting for. I'd given up any mad idea I'd had of writing for a living when a short story I'd written about a shop assistant who makes up lives for customers from the contents of their trolleys hadn't even been acknowledged by the magazine I'd sent it to. Perhaps I should just accept that it wasn't going to get any better than retail. Sometimes, the best things are staring you right in the face, Doll used to say.

It had worked for her. She was on the local news switching on the town's Christmas lights.

'Maria Newbury, North Kent's entrepreneur of the year!' said the reporter shoving a microphone in her face. 'Or should I say, *entrepreneuse*?'

'I don't know, should you?' said Doll, flirty as ever.

'There's a lot of talk about glass ceilings for women in business. How have you managed to break through?'

'At The Dolls House, there's no glass ceiling,' Doll told him. 'Because it's like, well, I'm sitting on the roof, aren't I?'

He'd loved that.

'Maria Newbury, founder of The Dolls House,' he turned to camera. 'Where the sky's the limit!'

When I asked Hope what she wanted for Christmas, she said a grand piano, because Martin had one in his flat above the shop.

She and Martin – technically Martin Junior, because his dad who owned Martin's Music had Parkinson's and had gone into one of the residential care homes on the Esplanade – had developed a sort of rapport. It was a bit like the friendship she'd had with Dave, based on having similar library-like brains as far as music was concerned, and I was really pleased about it because I suspected Hope missed Dave.

'I don't like Doll,' she'd said, when she'd seen the wedding photo in the paper.

At twenty-one, Martin was pretty young to be running the business on his own, because it wasn't just the shop – there was also a workshop out back where he repaired clarinets and re-strung guitars and stuff like that. He'd initially given the appearance of being cross with us for disturbing him when we went in to buy Hope a Teach Yourself Keyboard book, but I think it was more social isolation than deliberate rudeness. His mum had run away with a jazz saxophonist when he was a child, so that probably accounted for a lot. And when we kept returning for more and more advanced books, he was so impressed with Hope's talent that he gave her the occasional lesson for free.

It was just me and Hope for Christmas because Dad and Anne had gone to Anne's timeshare on the Algarve, and I'd had to work right up 'til the store closed on Christmas Eve. We spent the morning in our pyjamas, eating chocolates. Hope seemed pleased with the full-size keyboard that I'd bought and hidden under Dad's bed. She immediately wanted to start on the book of classical pieces that Martin advised me would be the right level for her. The keyboard had a much better tone than the school one, and sounded just like a proper piano, or organ, or harpsichord, whichever mode Hope chose, as she hesitantly picked out tunes you hear all your life on adverts without knowing their names, like 'Für Elise' and the 'Moonlight Sonata'.

It was nice just to relax with her, knowing that our dinner was only going to take four minutes to cook whenever we felt like it, because I'd bought us microwaveable Christmas ready meals with turkey, veg, chipolata sausages, the lot.

'Why are there three?' Hope asked, when she looked at the packets in the fridge.

Knowing Hope's appetite, I'd thought she might like a second, and it was Christmas after all, but I wasn't going to tell her that up front.

'They were on three-for-two,' I lied.

'Can we invite Martin?'

It was nearly four o'clock in the afternoon by then and already dark outside.

'I expect Martin's got plans of his own,' I said.

'He's seeing his dad,' said Hope. 'Then nothing.'

'If you want to invite him, you'll have to give him a call,'

I told her, amazed when she went straight to do it, because Hope never liked using the phone. I think the uncertainty of the process disturbed her.

In my heart of hearts, I'd have preferred not to have to go upstairs and get dressed and tidy up the wrapping paper, but I was thrilled at the idea of Hope having a friend to the house, even if it had more to do with the asymmetry of three ready meals in the fridge than her thinking about Martin being on his own on Christmas Day.

He turned up half an hour later with a present for her: a music book called *Songs from the Musicals*, unwrapped, because he'd obviously picked it from the rack on his way out of the shop.

I sat on the sofa watching him play and Hope sing, with the silver tinsel tree behind them, thinking it was a bit like Christmas in a Victorian novel when families used to entertain themselves round the piano.

When Hope sang 'Defying Gravity', Martin said, 'She should have singing lessons. She's a coloratura soprano.'

I didn't know exactly what that was, but I mentioned it to Dad when he rang up to say Happy Christmas.

'Singing lessons? She can already sing, can't she?' he shouted above the noise of the bar.

I'd bought a box of the most expensive crackers because they were practically giving them away on Christmas Eve afternoon, so Hope, Martin and I sat at the kitchen table with gold crowns on our heads. I noticed that eating was something Martin did very solemnly, as if it was an end in itself, not just a means to an end, exactly the same as Hope. We had a raspberry pavlova for our dessert, which was still a bit icy because I hadn't taken it out of the freezer in time, but instead of asking for seconds, Hope sprang straight up when she'd finished and went back to the keyboard.

Listening to the two of them as I washed up, I suddenly

thought of a solution to a problem that had been preoccupying me. All the pupils at Hope's school had to do 'work experience' for two weeks in Year Ten. Most of her peers chose to help out in the old people's homes, but nobody could see Hope being much good at that. Other kids, who were thinking about a career in teaching, did theirs at primary schools.

Hope's tantrums were few and far between nowadays, but you never quite knew what was going to set her off, so even if a school had taken her, they'd probably have to have someone looking after her, and that wasn't exactly the point of work experience, was it? It had been looking like Hope would have to spend two weeks at home, but what harm could she do in Martin's Music? She would know the location of every piece of sheet music and every book within a morning of working there, and it would save Martin the hassle of putting down his cloths and waxes and screwdrivers to serve customers.

'Do I have to pay her?' Martin asked, when I floated the idea as he was leaving.

'No,' I said.

'OK then.'

After Hope had gone to bed, I sat in the living room staring at the lights on the tree, thinking how happy Mum would be to see Hope with a friend. It suddenly struck me that it was our tenth Christmas without her. Ten years was twice as long as Hope had known Mum. In that time she had gone from a little girl to a young woman. But everything else, even the twinkling tinsel tree, had stayed the same.

I never took Hope to the grave when she was little, because I knew the idea of Mum in the box underground would frighten her, and Mum wouldn't want that, but I decided we'd go on Boxing Day, buying a bunch of glitter-dipped carnations from the petrol station we walked past on the way to the cemetery.

'"Devoted wife to James and beloved mother of Kevin,

Brendan, Teresa and Hope,"' Hope read out the inscription on the headstone. 'Who's James?'

'It's Dad's full name.'

'Is Dad still married to Mum?'

'Well, yes . . .'

'Mum'll never stop loving us, Tree.'

'No.'

'I don't remember Mum, Tree.'

'Sssh,' I whispered. 'Don't say that here.'

Not that I really believed Mum could hear us.

I left Hope standing behind the counter with Mozart playing through the speakers and Martin whistling along in his workshop. As I opened the door on my way out, the bell jangled and Hope did a kind of shooing motion with her hand, as if to say, 'Go! I don't need you any more!'

It was one of those January days with almost blinding bright sunshine and a bitter edge to the wind. That's probably why my eyes were smarting as I walked down to the seafront, because there was no reason at all to cry. I was actually incredibly relieved because it suddenly seemed possible that Hope would find her path in life. Wasn't it great that she had found a niche for herself? There was nothing I wanted more than Hope to be self-sufficient.

Sometimes happiness does make you cry though, doesn't it? Like when Mum was smiling and waving and crying all at the same time when we saw Kev off at Heathrow.

Wasn't enabling Hope to be independent what the last ten years had all been about?

But, I couldn't help thinking, what was the purpose of me now?

New Year is normally an optimistic time with the days getting longer and the shops full of Valentine's cards and heart-shaped chocolates and Prosecco with pink labels, but I couldn't seem to cheer up. The ten-years thing seemed so significant somehow, which was ridiculous because it was only a few days different from nine years, and I'd been all right with that.

I felt so low, I decided to give the first writing class of the new term a miss, but the following Monday evening, Leo appeared in the store. I noticed the contents of his trolley first. Dog food was on buy-one-get-one-free but sometimes the promotions didn't register at the tills.

'Can I help you, sir?'

'I certainly hope so!'

The voice, then the face, clean-shaven, bearing out my shaving theory.

'I didn't know you had a dog,' I said.

'I like to maintain some semblance of mystery,' he whispered, flirtatiously.

'Sometimes there's a blip in the software,' I told him, concentrating on pressing buttons on the till, hoping he wouldn't notice the blushing. 'If you give me your receipt, I'll sort out a refund.'

'That's not the problem,' he said. 'Look, when do you get off work? I need to ask you a favour.'

For the fifteen minutes until I finished, my brain invented all sorts of stories to explain his request, none of which turned out to be accurate.

In Caffè Nero, Leo paid for his espresso and my latte and brought them over to the table.

'I've got a bit of a problem because I've got tickets for *Much Ado About Nothing* at the National next Friday. My wife was supposed to be coming, but she forgot to write in the diary that it's her departmental dinner . . .'

I nodded.

'. . . so she said, "Why don't you take that girl you're always talking about in your creative-writing class?"'

It took a moment for it to dawn, because I was thinking that he really was going to ask me a favour, that this was his charming way of offering a treat.

'Me?' I asked, and was rewarded with the full amused smile.

When I got home, I put all my nice clothes out on the bed and tried on outfits. Smart-casual was how I thought Doll would describe the occasion. Eventually, I decided on a duck-egg blue cardigan from the fifties that I'd bought from the Oxfam shop but never found an occasion to wear. It was embroidered with beaded flowers in pastel colours and lined with silk. Teamed with new skinny jeans, I felt it struck exactly the right balance of glamorous enough for the theatre, but practical for sitting on a train. Catching myself pouting at the mirror, I gave myself a talking-to: this was not a date; Leo was just a wonderful teacher who took an interest in his students. And he was a married man. Any attraction I sensed between us was purely in my head and I must not make a fool of myself. But I still couldn't quite quash my excitement.

You'd think being in the south of England, the weather would be milder than the rest of the country, but for some reason if there's snow forecast, it usually falls in Kent. The weather meant Hope's bus was delayed coming home from Martin's Music, so I was worried about her, and shouted at her when she finally got in, which was unfair because it wasn't her fault, but I was sure I was going to be late.

'Why are you carrying on like this?' Hope said, which is what I said to her when she had one of her tantrums. So that made me feel bad.

'I had to wait for Hope . . .' I apologized breathlessly to Leo for almost making us miss the train.

'Hope?'

312

'My sister.'

I'd never mentioned Hope in class, which now felt a bit disloyal, but it was really more to do with having a corner of my life that wasn't defined by her.

'She has Asperger syndrome.'

'Isn't that the thing in that novel?' Leo asked.

'*Curious Incident of the Dog in the Night-time*? Yes.'

A lot of people had heard of it now because of that.

'Have you ever thought of writing from Hope's point of view?' Leo asked.

I laughed. 'I've spent a lot of my life trying to see things through the prism of Hope's mind, and I've never got anywhere close,' I said. 'I don't know what it's like to be Hope any more than I know what it's like to be you!'

'It might be interesting to try . . .'

'Maybe I will one day. At the moment, I'm trying to find out what it's like to be *me*!'

The snow was falling heavily by the time we arrived in town, the air thick with snowflakes dancing in the orange aura of the lamps along the South Bank.

'It's like being in one of those Monet paintings of the Houses of Parliament,' I said, trying to demonstrate a knowledge of culture. 'Except with snow, instead of fog, obviously.'

Leo gave me the amused look.

'Did you know that Monet was actually in exile here in London, because of the Prussian war in France?' I continued.

'I didn't,' said Leo.

'You can get a lot from art-gallery websites.'

'Is that so?'

'Isn't it amazing that nobody liked the Impressionists when they started?' I asked.

'A true artist isn't concerned about his popularity.' Leo finally shut me up.

We got to the National Theatre in time for a drink before the curtain went up and sat, with gin and tonics, listening to the jazz band that was playing in the foyer. My outfit was fine. Some of the women were in dresses and heels, but some of them were just in jeans. The blizzard outside made everyone look a bit windswept and blotchily pink, however much time or money they'd spent on their make-up.

Although I'd seen the film of *Romeo and Juliet* and we'd read *Othello* for A level and watched the DVD, I'd never been to a live Shakespeare play before. As the lights went down, my pulse quickened. I'm not sure whether the nerves were for me or the actors, but I needn't have worried because they looked like they were really enjoying themselves. I'd expected it to be a more formal and reverential experience, but it was really funny, not just nod-at-each-other-and-smile-smugly funny, but laugh-out-loud hilarious.

During the interval, while Leo went to the toilet, I leaned against a wall with my second gin and tonic, trying not to look like I was eavesdropping on the conversations going on around me. I noticed London theatregoers talked much louder than people coming out of the multiplex, almost like they *wanted* people to hear their opinions.

Next to me, two middle-aged men and a woman were standing with a younger woman, who was very much the centre of attention. The clever comments she offered about the play made me think that she might be an actress herself. She was beautiful enough, with long, dark hair and a way of holding herself like she should be at a cocktail party with a cigarette in a long holder, even though she was only wearing plain black tailored trousers and a black cardigan, probably cashmere, I thought. One of the men was particularly attentive. He had a slight foreign accent and was talking about a recent production he'd seen.

'You never have been to the Salzburg Festival?' he asked, surprised. 'Mountains and opera, you know. It's quite special.'

'Sounds blissful,' said the woman, her green eyes shining at him.

Maybe it was a blind date set up by the other two? He seemed rather old for her. Old but rich. Definitely rich. You wouldn't wear a black polo neck under a light brown tweed jacket unless you were.

'Shall we go back in?' their host asked as the ten-minute bell rang.

'Such a shame my husband's missing this . . .' said the beautiful woman.

'So lucky for me,' said her admirer, in a low whisper. His hand hovered a fraction of an inch from the small of her back as he stood aside to let her go first.

'Ready?' said Leo, reappearing.

'Yes,' I said, snapping back into my own narrative as I followed him back into the auditorium.

Outside, the snow had turned into a blizzard. We managed to trudge through the drifts along the river and up over the Charing Cross footbridge, but, by the time we reached the station, all trains back to Kent had been cancelled.

I was anxious about Hope spending the night on her own, but when I rang Anne, she'd already gone across and collected her.

'What will you do?' she asked.

In my imagination, a film was running about a young woman and her professor stuck for one magical night in the sparkling city, reciting lines from *Much Ado About Nothing* on the steps of the National Gallery, making snow angels in pristine white drifts in the parks . . .

'Shall we try the Premier Inn?' said Leo.

They didn't have any single rooms left and no twin rooms

either; in fact we got the last double. I negotiated a folding toothbrush and tiny toothpaste from the reception desk and when I came out of the bathroom, Leo was already in bed. My jeans were wet from the snow and the beaded cardigan was too fragile to sleep in, so I made the decision to sit on the bed, strip down to my knickers, vest and bra, then duck straight under the duvet, without ever looking at him. I turned off the light on my side.

'Shall I place a pillow between us?' Leo breathed gin and tonic against the back of my neck.

'No need,' I giggled. 'I'm not going to pounce on you!'

I meant it as a joke, to show I wasn't even thinking about that, but it came out sounding more like an invitation.

'Not even if I do this?' he asked, planting a feather-light kiss on the nape of my neck, sending a current down my spine that made my whole body spasm.

I didn't dare turn, in case he was joking, and I'd find my nose an inch away from his amused face.

'Or this?' he asked, slipping the heel of his palm under my arm and gently cupping my breast.

Then I turned and he was looking at me with great seriousness. We kissed, tentatively, then ravenously. The stubble was scratchier against my skin than I'd imagined.

Leo said I possessed the earnest innocence of Audrey Hepburn in the body of Claudia Cardinale. I treasured the description even more after googling her. I was constantly aware of the contours of my body under my shop uniform, as if the very top layer had been ripped from my skin, exposing my nerve endings to the slight catch of the polyester fabric. I stood at the customer service desk staring down the frozen-food aisle, with his voice slowly repeating the four syllables of the word 'voluptuous' in my head. I kept my mobile phone in my top pocket, so when he texted, it vibrated next to my heart.

After work most evenings, Leo took me to country pubs where no one would recognize us and talked to me about poetry and made love to me in the car after.

'You're a breath of fresh air,' he said. 'And I can't get enough of your body.'

I listened to his compliments, silent and passive, unable to find evocative-enough vocabulary to describe the overwhelming feeling that I had been waiting for him all my life.

I told no one about our affair. I didn't want Shaun's opinion. I didn't allow myself to consider what Mum would think. The memory of her face blended with the features of the painted statue of Our Lady the two of us had prayed in front of when I was a little girl, her skin smooth and radiant, her lips pursed in a little strawberry smile, her eyes gazing distantly beyond me. She wasn't there, so it didn't matter what she thought.

Secrecy strengthened the delicious illusion that Leo belonged only to me.

I think I must have persuaded myself that his wife had tacitly instigated the relationship. Although he rarely mentioned her, I assumed she'd gone off sex with the menopause. I fell on every crumb of information like a scavenging seagull.

The two of them had met as students at Oxford playing opposite each other in a garden production of *Look Back in Anger*.

I ordered the play on Amazon and was dismayed by Jimmy Porter's tirades.

'Were you an Angry Young Man?' I asked Leo.

'I was a working-class Welsh boy who had stumbled over enemy lines into the territory of the middle classes,' he replied. 'I shared his existential despair.'

'But you're middle class now . . .' I said.

'You consider that an improvement, do you?' He frowned at me, then suddenly laughed, flipping irritation to indulgence.

His unpredictability was exciting. I constantly felt as if I was

317

tiptoeing along a tightrope of adoration in peril of plunging to disfavour, but I'd always known that real love would be terrifying and precipitous. Weren't all great love affairs, from *Doctor Zhivago* to *The English Patient*, about stolen moments of agonizing ecstasy? Wasn't suffering what the word 'passion' actually meant?

If Leo was a romantic hero from literature, he was Mr Rochester. Not just because of his age and marital status – not that his wife was insane or he locked her up, obviously – but because there was a dark, brooding side to him. His creativity had been stifled by the compromises of work and family obligation. I told myself we were soulmates. Just as his love completed me, mine would complete him. As Jane Eyre found, the challenge of cheering a troubled soul is compelling, each fleeting smile worth a hundred hours of a lesser suitor's happiness.

One afternoon, when I'd worked the early shift, Leo drove me to Whitstable. We walked along the concrete path beside the beach. As the sun faded, the silver surface of the sea dulled to pewter; the wind blowing across the water was bitterly cold.

'Close your eyes,' he suddenly ordered.

As his footsteps receded, I began to tremble with an irrational fear that he was going to abandon me there.

'Don't look!'

I heard metal scraping on metal, the click of a padlock, then footsteps returning towards me, a warm hand taking mine, and guiding me, still obediently blind.

'Down these steps! Duck your head!'

A door closed behind us. Lobster pots and creosote and the stale, almost sweet, smell of damp towels.

'You can look now.'

We were in a hut. Surrounded by boxes of books and bits of broken furniture, two canvas chairs and a table were set up with a candle, two stemmed glasses, a bottle of Rioja and a small dish of almonds.

'Bought this place with my first advance,' Leo told me. 'A space to write, you know? Never got round to doing it up. I'm told they're worth a fortune now . . .'

'Do you write here?' I asked.

'Too bloody cold. But perhaps, now you're here . . .'

I was overjoyed by the idea of being his muse. The wine was soft and warming, like blackberries in summer, the almonds sweet and salty. Leo took my hand and we climbed up a splintery ladder into the cramped roof space where he undressed me carefully, staring at my pale skin in the light of the guttering candle, as I lay on the cold, damp mattress.

'You are my odalisque,' he whispered. 'And now I'm going to fuck you so hard, you'll feel me for days.'

He climbed on top of me, entering me straight away and riding me until our bodies smacked together with sweat and I was obliterated by his need. Spent and satiated, we flung apart, chests heaving as we stared up at the bare wooden boards of the pitched roof. Then, he put an arm around me and drew me roughly against his chest, stroking my face with infinite tenderness.

When the candle died, we felt our way down the ladder, locked the door behind us, then stumbled back to his car in the darkness, my burning skin stinging in the freezing air.

21

GUS

They were forecasting snow on the radio.

From the moment I woke up, a sense of foreboding hung around me. I'd been up several times in the night because Bella was developing a cold – not a sniffle, but a chesty infection that sent anguish through my body every time she coughed.

I dithered over my cereal. Charlotte had already gone to work, a piece of toast clamped between her teeth as she closed the front door. My mother was chatting to Flora at the kitchen table. I went upstairs and took Bella's temperature again, almost hoping it would be high enough to give me the excuse to stay off work, but it was only just above normal.

'Make sure she gets lots of fluids,' I told my mother, as I slid my thick winter coat on over my suit.

'I have had two children of my own, you know.' Her eyes stared blankly for just a moment, before she pulled herself back to the present.

'Call me if she gets any worse, won't you?' I said, as I stepped out onto the gloomy Wandsworth street. The sky was ominously grey and overcast. 'Perhaps Floss should skip nursery today, so you don't have to take Bella out in this?'

'She'll be perfectly all right,' said my mother. 'We don't want to miss nursery school, do we, Flora?'

The traffic was lighter than usual, probably because of the weather warnings, so I arrived at work early, which made the morning drag with a seemingly endless procession of young children with nasty coughs similar to my daughter's. I gave the same advice about fluids and Calpol for a raised temperature, soothing words about viruses not responding to antibiotics re-iterated as reassurance to myself as much as to the mothers.

At lunchtime, the snow finally arrived, soft, thickly falling flakes bringing their own white light to the small square of garden outside my surgery window. I gazed out, in a trance-like memory of the wonder I'd felt as a child, when the arrival of snow had presaged only fun. I imagined Flora's delight at seeing it for the first time. At the weekend, we would build a snowman together. Perhaps I should call in at Toys R Us on the way home and buy her a sledge? I pictured Flora and her little friends' excited faces pressed against the window of the nur-sery school, waiting to be let out onto a soft white carpet that crumped under the soles of their wellies. When my phone rang and it was the nursery, it felt almost as if I'd willed the call.

'We were wondering if someone is coming to pick Flora up . . .' the nursery teacher said.

'I'm sorry?'

'She's been waiting twenty minutes.'

'My mother's probably stuck in the snow.'

My brain went straight into overdrive, picturing my mother slipping on an icy pavement and smashing her head. In the flurries outside my window, Ross's face loomed, his teeth white, his eyes hidden behind mirror ski goggles.

'It's not snowing here,' said the teacher.

'Have you called her?'

'On the mobile and the landline, twice,' she said.

I imagined my mother slumped on the kitchen floor in cardiac arrest.

Or perhaps Bella had taken a turn for the worse? Now I saw them sitting anxiously in the GP's waiting room.

I knew I shouldn't have come to work.

'Could you possibly keep Flora there?' I said, trying to control the whirr of hypotheses and think of a practical plan of action. 'I'll come as soon as I can.'

'Flora can stay for the afternoon session if you like? We can give her lunch?'

I'd forgotten there was an afternoon session.

'Yes! Good idea. Thank you. I'll pick her up from that.'

I hung up and pressed the speed dial for home, my hand shaking. There was no reply.

The senior partner was eating a sandwich at her desk when I explained the situation to her, feeling like a truanting child in front of the headmistress.

'Of course you can go, Angus,' she said in a bored voice. 'But it'll probably be nothing. It usually is.'

My colleagues' professional duty to assess what was in front of them coolly and without emotion seemed to permeate their personalities. Or maybe people who wanted to be GPs were just like that naturally and I wasn't made of the right stuff.

My mother's car was still parked outside the house when I got back. The weather couldn't seem to decide whether it was snowing or raining. When I opened the door, the television was blaring so loudly, I wondered if the problem was simply that she hadn't heard the telephone. Was she becoming deaf? Perhaps I should suggest a hearing test?

I found her in the front room, fast asleep, a glass of water balanced precariously on the arm of the chair. I switched off the television. Upstairs I found Bella in her cot, also sleeping. Her forehead felt hot, but although I could still hear a slight rattle in her chest, her breathing was less shallow than it had been that morning. No one died. My heartbeat levelled as I walked back downstairs to the kitchen.

I filled the kettle, alarmed to notice on the draining board an almost empty bottle of Tesco's own-brand vodka.

Charlotte always bought Grey Goose.

An image of Charlotte pouring herself a vodka tonic, just a few days before, flitted across my mind.

'Are you trying to tell me I've got a drink problem or something?' she'd asked me.

'What?'

'Have you watered my vodka?'

'Of course not!'

She'd sniffed the glass.

'I'm sure it's not as strong as it used to be!'

'Perhaps you *have* got a problem, then!' I said.

We'd laughed about it.

I stared at the vodka bottle, then remembered the glass on my mother's chair. There had been occasions recently where her alcohol consumption had slightly concerned me. Three glasses of champagne before Christmas lunch followed by wine during the meal and several refills of her brandy 'nightcap'. I hadn't said anything. It was Christmas, after all.

Surely she wasn't drinking every day? Not during the day? Not while she was in charge of our children? Surely not when she was going to drive?

I picked up the bottle and walked back down the corridor to the front room.

My mother's eyes opened slowly and locked onto the bottle in my hand.

'Only the tiniest drop,' she stammered, sitting up quickly, knocking the glass onto the floor. I picked it up and sniffed it.

'I think it's probably more than that,' I said.

'Helpss her ssleep,' she said, slurring a little.

A beat. I realized she was talking about Bella.

Running back into the kitchen, I sniffed the half-empty baby's bottle on the table and, unscrewing the teat, sipped a little of the fluid. Formula laced with alcohol. A baby white Russian. No wonder she was sleeping so well!

My mother was behind me now, summoning excuses. 'She gets herself so hot and bothered with all this crying!'

'She's a baby!'

'You were the same, of course. Very colicky.'

'Did you drug me then?' I asked, expecting her to scoff at the suggestion.

'A little bit of gas on occasion, when we lived above the surgery.'

'Bloody hell! No wonder my head was in the clouds!'

My mother looked confused, as if she suddenly couldn't compute why I was at home.

'Can you tell me how much you've had today?' I asked, trying to keep my voice level and doctorly.

'Just a glass. No more than a unit or two.'

When you ask patients how much alcohol they drink, the ones with a problem always know the recommended quantities, and admit to just below that figure, casually, as if they've never really given it a thought.

'I don't usually,' my mother was saying. 'Jussh today . . .'

She stared out of the window where snowflakes were now falling past the orange street lights.

'Because of the snow?' I asked.

She beamed an insanely gratified smile at me as if I'd finally understood her.

'So, how many of these do you get through a week?' I picked up the bottle, trying to keep my tone matter-of-fact.

'One at the most,' she said.

A glance at the ceiling.

'I'll just go and check on Bella, shall I?' she said, but I was up the stairs before she'd got to the first step.

She had forgotten to lock the door to her bedroom. There were two empty vodka bottles in her suitcase. She'd arrived on Sunday evening. She was drinking half a bottle of vodka a day on top of the wine she always had at dinner, and we hadn't noticed.

Bella started coughing. I picked her up. Her nose was blocked with yellow gunk, and her nappy was full, but she didn't seem any worse than she had that morning.

'There she is, the little darling!' said my mother as I brought her down, as if she'd already forgotten our race for the stairs. 'I'll just go and get Flora, shall I?'

'No!'

'I'm fine to drive.'

'Of course you're not!'

I put Bella in a snowsuit and took her in the car with me.

Flora was thrilled to have done a whole day like the older children and was full of chatter about the snowman they'd built in the playground. I bought her a Happy Meal in the drive-thru for being such a good girl, and sat in the stationary car, with the snow now falling thickly around us, wondering what on earth we were going to do.

Charlotte was already in a bad mood when she called because I hadn't answered her texts about where we should meet before the show. We'd been invited to the National Theatre by her head of department.

'Something's happened and I can't come,' I said.

'But you know how important this is to me! Are the girls OK?'

'They're fine.'

'So?'

'I really can't explain now. We're all fine.'

'Is Caroline there? Well, why on earth . . . ?'

'Apologize on my behalf. Say I've got a cold, or something nastily contagious if it makes it better. Do you think you'll be able to get home?'

'Oh, for God's sake!' said Charlotte.

She arrived back, after midnight, slightly flushed and goading me about how marvellous the play was. She'd got a taxi on Waterloo Bridge with no trouble at all.

'I don't know what's wrong with this bloody country,' she said, slipping into bed beside me. 'An inch of snow and everything stops. I mean, it's not as if we don't get snow. London's at the same latitude as Moscow, for God's sake. In Switzerland, the snowploughs come out and everything goes on as usual. Sorry, did I wake you up?'

'No, I was awake. I wanted to explain.'

'Explain' was probably the wrong word to choose because it made me sound apologetic.

'Yes, what is the great mystery?'

'You know Bella has been sleeping so well since my mother arrived? Well, today I discovered the reason. She's been dosing her bottle with vodka.'

I was expecting at least 'Oh my God!'

'I remember my grandmother saying they sometimes used to do that,' Charlotte mused. 'It obviously works!'

'You're not suggesting it's OK?'

'Oh, relax, Angus, for God's sake! She's perfectly fine, isn't she? I don't expect it's done much harm.'

'I really can't see any way a doctor can approve, even tacitly approve, of giving alcohol to a baby.'

'All right, all right. I do agree, if that makes you any happier.' Charlotte yawned and turned over, as if the subject was closed.

'My mother's an alcoholic.'

The word was difficult to say. I wondered if I was experiencing something of what people felt going to AA for the first time.

'Don't be absurd!' Charlotte murmured.

'Remember you were worried how much you were drinking? Well, it turns out you weren't, but she was. That's where the vodka was going and she's been bringing her own secretly. I found two empty bottles in her suitcase, Charlotte! The nursery called me because she hadn't picked up Flora and when I got here, she was passed out, completely pissed, but still thought she could drive when I woke her up.'

Charlotte suddenly sat up and turned on the bedside light.

'Are you sure?'

'She's a danger to the children and to herself.'

'Well, we'll have to get her some help.'

'Yes, but in the meantime . . .'

'What?' Charlotte asked.

'We'll have to find someone else. Or I'll have to look after them . . .'

'You can't be serious!' Charlotte shrieked. 'We're exchanging contracts on the house next week.'

'We won't be able to.'

'Think about it, Angus. Our sale will fall through, Caroline's sale will fall through. If we lose that house, we'll never move. Prices are literally going up every day!'

'We'll just have to stay put then,' I said.

Charlotte stared at me.

'What is more important?' I persisted. 'The girls' safety, or moving upmarket?'

'God, you're so fucking pious!' Charlotte screamed, then got out of bed, taking the duvet with her, went downstairs and slammed the living-room door.

In the morning, I woke up to find her sitting at her dressing table applying make-up.

'Are you in work today?' I asked, surprised.

She didn't reply to my question, but, staring at my reflection in the mirror, simply stated, 'I'm not sleeping on the sofa again.'

'Good,' I said, blearily.

'You're the one who can do that from now on. Or perhaps you could have the nanny's room since your mother's gone.'

'Gone?' I sat up.

'She says she knows she's never been welcome here and she's driven off on an icy road, so I hope you're satisfied!'

'But that's crazy. It's not my fault. I want to help her . . .'

'She says you've blown everything completely out of proportion, as usual.'

'And is that what you think?'

'I'm not prepared to live in Wandsworth all my life!' Charlotte yelled, then, as if surprised by the noise she'd made, picked up her handbag and went out for the day.

It wasn't so much the sex, because it hadn't been frequent since Bella's birth. Initially I'd been afraid of hurting Charlotte after the stitches, and then we always seemed to be so tired. But I missed the companionship of sharing a bed, the familiar rhythm of my wife's breathing, even her huffing and pulling the duvet over her head when I got out of bed to tend to our daughter.

Curiously, the financial meltdown provided a ray of hope for us. For a couple of months, London house prices plummeted. Suddenly it was a buyer's market and when we made a low offer for a little house at the top of Portobello Road, it was accepted. Even Charlotte had to admit that it was a much more suitably sized property for us. Paradoxically, it was my mother's absence that made it possible. I'd taken a few weeks of unpaid leave which stretched on to what the head of the GP surgery in Croydon called 'a mutual parting of the ways'. With no childcare or redecoration costs, and interest rates going down, we

328

had just about enough money and I had the time to search out the best mortgage deal and organize the packing. The girls thrived and Charlotte was freed to do the things she needed to promote her brilliant career, like working late and flying to conferences in glamorous destinations like Monte Carlo and Doha.

When we'd settled in, we invited my mother to visit, but she claimed she was too upset by my accusation. I thought the problem was more that she didn't think she'd get through the weekend without alcohol, and eventually Charlotte, who took the girls to see her every couple of months, conceded that was probably the case. There's not much you can do to help someone who won't admit they have a problem.

At weekends, Portobello Road is an impassable throng of tourists, but during the week, especially early in the morning, it's virtually empty. On fine days, after dropping Flora off at school, Bella and I usually walked all the way down the street looking for Paddington Bear in the windows of antique shops, trying to guess which one was Mr Gruber's. We'd read the Paddington books so many times that the pages were falling out of our copies. I was almost disappointed when, one day, Bella pointed excitedly at a life-size toy bear, complete with duffle coat, sou'wester and wellington boots, standing on a chaise longue deep inside one of the shops. But the following day he had gone, perhaps proving more attractive to customers than the second-hand furniture. So our quest continued.

By the time the antique shops petered out, and the street became a food and clothes market, Bella had usually fallen asleep and I often whiled away the morning reading the newspaper with a coffee and one of the delicious little custard tarts with a glaze of burnt sugar that they served in our favourite cafe. One spring day, as I was manoeuvring the buggy through the door, I heard someone shouting, 'Gus! Gus!'

Nobody had called me Gus for years, so it took a moment to register Nash waving across the road at me. I hadn't seen her in person since Flora was a baby, but I had occasionally watched her on television because the American medical drama series she starred in had become a huge hit in the UK too. With her hair dyed a deep crimson colour, she looked much sleeker and smarter than before, and as we pushed through to the back of the cafe where there was a table with room for the buggy, I was aware that other customers were nudging each other as they recognized her face.

'How long are you back for?' I asked.

'Indefinitely, I'm afraid. I was in a motorbike accident,' she informed me.

'Are you OK?'

'No, actually I died,' said Nash. 'Oh, wait a minute, you're only on series two over here, aren't you? It's what happens to ballsy female leads. We get tamed or we perish . . .'

'What a shame,' I said, adding quickly, 'Everyone thinks you're great.'

'Really?' said Nash.

I caught a glimpse of her old endearing neediness beneath the immaculately groomed exterior.

'Even Charlotte,' I told her. 'And she's a real consultant herself now.'

'Wow!' said Nash, flicking her gleaming curtain of hair back over her shoulder. 'So, what are you up to these days?'

'Still looking after the kids. It's a long story. This is Bella, by the way.'

'Cute,' said Nash, glancing at my sleeping child, then giving me a long, appraising look. 'I could never see you as a doctor . . .'

'How come?' Now I was the needy one.

'Too insecure. You need to have a certain confidence in

330

your decision-making skills . . . I did a lot of research for the role . . .'

'Obviously,' I said.

'So what *are* you going to do, Gus?' she asked.

The perennial London question. In a thriving capital city, your job defines you.

'I haven't thought that far,' I said, as Bella began to stir. 'Look, why don't you come back to ours for some lunch?'

Our front door opened straight into one big room which served as the living room, dining room, and kitchen. I had fastened felt boards to the walls to display the girls' art along with a few of my sketches of them.

Nash looked at the drawings as I prepared a simple lunch of pasta with cherry tomatoes and basil. 'Who did these?'

'I did.'

'They're good, Gus. I always knew you must have a hidden talent!'

'Perhaps that's something I could do . . . you know, in Covent Garden, those people who draw the tourists?'

Nash stared at me. 'Jesus, Gus, only you could be thirty years old and thinking of a career as a street artist!'

I put a steaming bowl of pasta down in front of her.

'How about becoming a children's portrait artist?' She blew on a hot forkful. 'There must be some loaded parents round here?'

'A couple of people have asked me, you know, when they've picked their kids up from play dates, but I've never thought of charging . . .'

'God, Gus, you haven't changed!' Nash laughed.

'Why do you say that?'

'You're so – I don't know what the right word is – fey, maybe? Unworldly. Dreamy.'

'Sorry.'

'Don't be sorry. The quality I'm talking about – it's not un-attractive.'

'Charlotte thinks it is.'

I said it without thinking.

'Does she?' said Nash, intrigued.

I always believed that things would improve between Charlotte and me. In the new house, we usually slept in separate bed-rooms, but there were still occasions, like after the children's birthdays, when all our tiny guests had departed, goody bags in hand, and our daughters had gone to bed hugging their new toys, that we would open a bottle of champagne to toast another milestone on the journey we were on together. A goodnight kiss would turn into something more intimate, and our bodies knew each other so well, the physical imperative would take over.

I was sure that there would come a time, perhaps when we were on holiday, when everything would magically revert to how it used to be. We did rent a cottage for a week on the north coast of Cornwall. On the beach, we looked like the sort of family you'd see in a Boden catalogue, casually well dressed, smiling in the sunshine, and oh-so middle class. For the chil-dren, Charlotte and I always put on a united front, agreeing on table manners, limiting high-sugar snacks, listening to what they told us, encouraging them to explore rock pools and create pictures with seaweed. Charlotte wasn't as down and dirty with the digging as I was, but she was competitive; so suggest a game of rounders, or a race to build the best sandcastle, and she'd throw herself into the challenge. We even enjoyed ourselves on the rainy days, visiting the Eden Project and Tate St Ives, buying big net bags of imported shells to make our own art with UPVC glue and sugar paper spread out on the kitchen table.

It was only after we'd kissed the girls goodnight and switched off the light in their room that our relationship also shut down. Charlotte had a book; I did the washing-up. We might mention something the kids had said that had amused us, but otherwise an unnavigable gulf of silence stretched between us. I went to bed first and pretended to be asleep when Charlotte got in beside me. And then I'd lie still and anxious until sleep blotted out the sadness and a new morning brought the glorious chaos of small children clambering into the bed and creating the energy for another day.

'Why don't you and Mummy have one big bed at home?' Flora once asked.

I looked at Charlotte for an answer. She was always better at finding the words to say nothing than I was.

'Daddy snores so loudly, Mummy can't sleep, and Mummy has to go to work,' she said.

And so I obliged by closing my eyes and snoring as loud as I possibly could with my girls' laughter pealing around us.

22

TESS

Anne was all for organizing a meal in a posh restaurant with a tasting menu; I thought Hope would be happier with Pizza Express, but it was Dad who came up with the perfect suggestion. 'It's Hope's eighteenth. What do you do when you're eighteen? You go to the pub!'

We were on the point of objecting, when he added, 'And Thursday's karaoke night!'

So we booked a table for an early supper because they did a carvery, and there was also a salad wagon, depending on how hungry you were. Then Hope said, 'Can Martin come?'

Hope now worked full-time at Martin's Music. After her work experience, he had asked her to come in on Saturdays, paying her minimum wage, because, as she told me proudly, 'I'm useful, Tree.'

So it seemed like a natural extension when he'd offered her a full-time job after her GCSEs.

When customers came in, Hope was marginally less rude than Martin was, and the arrangement allowed him to take on more of the lucrative instrument repair work, so it suited them both.

*

334

Pushing open the heavy door of the pub, I felt a kind of draught, as if someone else had come in behind me. I turned round.

Mum was wearing the navy dress and jacket she wore for weddings.

'Oh my God! You're here!' I cried.

'I wouldn't miss this for the world, would I?' she said, smiling at me.

I woke up, the fizz of elation suddenly flat in the chilly morning air. I lay with my eyes closed, trying to summon back the feeling of her presence, telling her, 'Hope's eighteen, Mum. And she's fine, you know. You'd be so proud of her!'

I wanted to add, '. . . and of me!'

But, as a single tear rolled a ribbon of coolness down my cheek, I wasn't so sure about that bit.

They gave us a rectangular table for six, so it was Dad and Anne, Martin and Hope and me opposite an empty chair. For Mum, I thought, still disorientated from seeing her so clearly that morning.

I felt like a maiden aunt, sitting at the end of the table, but at least I was out of range of Anne's be-ringed fingers gripping my arm and her Silk Cut breath reassuring me, as she often did, that it was never too late for love, and 'The One' could come along at any time.

None of them knew that I was in love. Just recently, though, I'd occasionally caught myself wondering if it was only a pre-tend relationship, the dilapidated hut a kind of grown-up Wendy house where we role-played being a proper couple. Instead of a kitchen we had a single Calor gas burner; instead of a bedroom we had an old mattress; instead of watching telly together we read musty-smelling orange Penguins, their pages brown with age, and I fussed around, making mugs of tea and anxiously hoping to inspire Leo. Did we fool the City couple,

Marcus and Keiko, in the converted hut next door, all glass and Porcelanosa, who came down from London for weekends with their cute half-English, half-Japanese children? Was it obvious that I was Leo's mistress?

I'd been so swept up in the romantic impossibility of our love, believing our time together more piquant than other couples', that the question of why it had to be like this hadn't really occurred to me before. Now that Hope was growing up and Leo's kids had left home – one was doing a Masters at Stanford University in California, one was earning a fortune as City actuary, a job that Leo claimed to despise, but often boasted about to Marcus – why shouldn't we begin to think about our future, or at least do something together like a normal couple?

I'd floated the idea of going to Glastonbury.

There would be bands from all eras . . .

'And mud,' Leo said.

'But don't you think it would be just amazing to experience the energy in that huge sea of people?'

'Sweet Tess! How do you manage to stay so relentlessly optimistic?'

These days, his compliments increasingly transformed to critique if I dwelled on them.

And yet there was always a tantalizing promise that things would be different one day.

Like last time, after sex, when Leo had asked me, 'Shall we elope to a finca in Spain, Tess? Shall we lunch in the shade of an olive tree and drink good wine and grow oranges and fuck like there's no tomorrow?'

'Or Italy?' I'd suggested, unsure what a finca was. 'I've always wanted to go back.'

He gave me such an amused look I felt like a fool for failing to understand that the offer was only another of his metaphors, as insubstantial as a wish.

And yet, I told myself, even a metaphor must mean that at some level he wanted it too?

Martin was talking to me. Not talking, exactly, more making an announcement.

'Hope wants to have singing lessons,' he said. 'Now she's eighteen, she can do what she likes.'

'Good idea!' I agreed.

'You can't stop me!' Hope chimed in. 'I'm eighteen!'

With everyone at the table looking at me, I wondered how long I'd been in Leo world and whether I'd missed something.

'I've never tried to stop you!' I laughed.

'You wouldn't allow her to have music lessons,' Martin pressed.

'Hang on,' I protested. 'I've never stopped Hope doing anything!'

Wasn't I the one who'd bought her the keyboard? Wasn't I the one who'd listened to her singing all these years?

'You said lessons are too expensive,' said Hope.

'Well, yes, that was piano lessons and it was a long time ago, wasn't it? Nobody said anything about singing.'

'Martin did.'

'Yes, but . . .' I'd thought it was just him being nice.

I looked to Dad and Anne for support.

'You should have said,' Anne now joined in. 'You only had to ask.'

Dad appeared poised to come to my rescue, when Martin added, 'What about the church choir? Hope says you wouldn't let her go . . .'

'Now, she has a point there, Tess,' said Dad. 'Weren't you always dead set against her going to church?'

Inside I was screaming, *How dare you? Didn't I do enough?*

I remembered telling Mum she should stick up for herself more, and now I was staying silent just like she always did.

Trouble was, I couldn't think of a way without it sounding like Hope was a burden and I didn't want to do that and I expect that's why Mum didn't either.

My eyes blurred as I stared down at the grey slices of lamb and the bullets of roast potato in the puddle of gravy on my plate. Mum always said that we mustn't cry on birthdays because it would bring bad luck.

'I've got a bit of a headache,' I said quietly, pushing back my chair. 'I think I'll leave you to it.'

None of them said, 'Don't be silly!' or 'Of course you can't go!'

In fact, as I glanced back at them from the door, Dad picked up the menu and asked, 'Now, Hope, will it be the black cherry cheesecake or the banoffee pie?'

I stood on the street just outside the pub door for a few minutes, wondering whether I was being oversensitive and should go back in. I was half-waiting for one of them to come out and get me. When it was clear that wasn't going to happen, I started walking towards the seafront in a bit of a daze. I didn't feel like going back to a house all decorated with bunting and balloons; I couldn't call Leo because he was attending a graduation ceremony with his wife, and he'd hardly welcome his phone going off in Canterbury Cathedral.

I stood, staring down the coast, the dark outline of the land against the pale apricot light of dusk, the sea breeze making my tears taste even saltier.

All this time, when I thought I was the one making the sacrifices, had I really been preventing Hope from doing the things she wanted? Had I expected too little of her and stopped her from becoming the person she wanted to be? I was so shocked by what Hope had said, I couldn't even be sure whether Mum would have had any comfort to offer me. I think I felt more desolate than at any time since she died.

There was only one person in the world who I knew would

be able to tell me, one person who'd been there from the start. I found myself dialling a number I hadn't used in a long time.

The phone was answered on the first ring, giving me no time to rethink.

'It's Tess,' I said. 'Can I talk to you?'

'Where are you?' Doll asked, instantly recognizing the despair in my voice. 'Stay there, Tess! Stay there! I'm sending a taxi for you.'

The gates opened automatically as the cab approached Doll and Dave's house and I fumbled in my bag for my purse.

'Fare's paid,' the driver told me. 'Mrs Newbury has an account.'

Mrs Newbury. Maria Newbury was a celebrity, who regularly appeared on *South Today* or *Meridian* to give her opinion about all-female shortlists or the importance of apprenticeships. Mrs Newbury had a big house and a thriving business; I had nothing to show for all the time we'd spent apart. We spoke a different language now and we wouldn't have anything to say to each other. Why had I even called her?

The door opened as I went to press the bell.

'I like your hair like that,' Doll said.

She stepped forward and hugged me so hard it felt like she was trying to transfer all her regret and apology straight into me, and I hugged her back until we were both shaking with tears and laughter.

The living room had one completely glass wall. As we sat there, a big white leather sofa each, the light outside faded and the window was dark like a giant television screen with the two of us reflected in it.

Doll listened without ever interrupting me, but when I paused, she said, 'I'm so relieved, Tess, because I thought it must be cancer when you called, you know, with your mum getting it young? Sorry. Not helping. I mean, obviously, this is bad in a different way . . .'

339

'Do you think Martin's right?' I asked her. 'All of them obviously thought so.'

'First of all, Tess, I'm not being offensive or anything, but your dad was always a bastard who'd say anything to put himself in the right, and Anne's the daft bitch who shacked up with him.'

'What would you say if you *were* being offensive?' I asked.

'And Hope, well, she says things, doesn't she, but she doesn't put all the meaning in like you do,' Doll continued.

'Subtext,' I said, using one of Leo's favourite words.

'Whatever,' said Doll. 'You know Hope doesn't mean to be unkind. Hope doesn't really do kind, does she? And this Martin guy sounds a bit on the spectrum himself. They're obviously well suited.'

'It's not that sort of relationship!' I protested.

'No?'

'Hope doesn't have a romantic bone in her body!'

'How do you know?'

'I just know!'

'You didn't know you were stopping her doing things.'

That was a bit harsh, but it was why I'd come.

'But not . . . surely?'

I'd never even considered Hope having a relationship with Martin. And yet, now I came to think about it, I'd noticed him taking her jacket and hanging it up for her like a real gentleman. Surely they weren't . . . ?

'Isn't this what every parent of every teenager goes through?' said Doll. 'You have to learn to let go.'

'Easy to say, but who picks up the pieces if it goes wrong?'

'True,' Doll conceded.

'Maybe I was overprotective. Maybe I didn't get everything right,' I admitted.

'Nobody in the world could say you didn't do your best.'

'Did I, though? Maybe I should have taken her to Mass.'

'And have Father Michael terrifying her with all his warn-ings about—'

'—the pleasures of the flesh!' we both said together, mim-icking his ominous tone.

I glanced around nervously as if the elderly priest might be lurking, listening in the shadows.

'Fred said the football team never got changed as fast as when Father Michael was refereeing,' Doll confided.

'Was Father Michael why you didn't marry in church?' I asked.

'It nearly killed my mum. She still thinks Dave and I are going straight to hell!'

Once Dave's name had been spoken, it sort of hung between us.

'I'm sorry about Dave, Tess,' Doll said eventually.

'Oh, it's so long ago, I've kind of forgotten how to be cross about it,' I told her. 'Or even why I was, really.'

'I was sure he was The One for you, Tess,' Doll said. 'Honest I was, but then, when he and I got together, it was like there'd been this blip in destiny and really he was The One for me.'

'Do you really believe in destiny?' I said. 'Isn't it more that you had the opportunity to see that Dave was reliable and romantic and handy with a plunger, which you wouldn't have known if you'd bumped into him at a disco . . .'

Doll stared at me. 'God, I've missed you SO much, Tess! You never let me get away with anything!'

'Me you same!' I said.

My mind kept going back to Hope.

'You did what you did,' said Doll. 'Doesn't every parent go through these feelings? Nobody can do more than their best, can they?'

The way she kept saying 'parent' when I wasn't actually sounded almost like she'd been thinking about the challenges

341

of parenthood herself, which, I guessed, could only mean one thing. 'Are you pregnant?'

She stared at me. 'Jesus. Does it show?' She smoothed her hand over the flat front of her white jeans.

'No!'

'How did you know, then?'

'Because I know you,' I said.

'We've been trying so long, we thought it would never happen. But it's almost twelve weeks now. I just went for my first scan and when you phoned, I was sure it was Dave calling to see how it went. He was meant to get back from a trade fair last night but his flight was delayed. Anyway, I'm glad it was you,' Doll said. 'Because you're the first person that knows. It's the big moments I've missed you most, Tess.'

'Me too,' I said.

Doll pointed a remote at the window and a white blind rolled down.

'So what about you and your fella?' She tucked her knees up on her sofa in anticipation of a girlie chat.

'What fella's that?' I asked.

'Come on! I saw you a couple of weeks ago!'

'Where?'

'I was having lunch at the Oysterage in Whitstable. I sometimes take the franchisees there. So anyway, there I am, sitting on the decking, pretending I'm listening to sales figures and stuff, when suddenly I see you like fifty yards away reading in a deckchair . . .'

'What *are* you talking about?' I laughed, still thinking I could get away with it.

'So this bloke pulls you to your feet and gives you this massive snog, and you're practically undressing each other walking back up the beach, not that you've got a lot on, just the neon-yellow Gucci bikini I brought you back from Dubai, remember that time I went with Fred?'

342

'What did you think, then?' I asked. It was actually a relief finally to admit it to someone.

'He's quite mature, isn't he?'

'He's a professor,' I said.

'Figures,' said Doll.

'How's that?'

'Jo and the old professor bloke in *Little Women*!'

'You wanted to be Amy . . .'

'Because she was pretty. And, she got nice Laurie.'

Of course she did.

We both sat in silence for a few moments.

'You've got to go back and see Hope sing, Tess,' Doll said. 'I'd come with you, only I want to be here to show Dave the first photo, you know, that they do with the ultrasound?'

She came with me to the door, but just as I was reaching for the handle, it opened, and Dave was standing a foot away from me. He was wearing a well-cut grey suit and his hair was a little longer. He had the type of all-round tan that rich people have, but his smile was just the same, perhaps slightly whiter.

'All right, Tess?' he said.

'All right,' I said.

'Great stuff!'

I stepped back to let him pull his suitcase inside and we gave each other a quick, embarrassed kiss on the cheek.

'How's the writing going?' he asked.

'Writing?'

'You said, you know, last time . . . you were going to a writing group?'

I was amazed that he'd remembered.

'I started,' I told him. 'Then I stopped.'

We all laughed, dissolving the tension.

With Leo, all my imaginative space seemed to be taken up with our relationship. And I suppose the stakes were higher, because if I'd given him something to read and he'd torn into it, I'd have been devastated. I'd never gone back to his class, because I knew Liz and Vi would see what was going on. Occasionally I wondered if they ever mentioned me, but I didn't ask, in case Leo would think I was being silly.

'I work in Human Resources now,' I said. 'At Waitrose.'

'That's a good company that,' said Dave.

Which is what everyone said, except Leo, who couldn't understand why I would want to work in a shop, although technically, since my promotion I wasn't *in* the shop any more, but upstairs. Being from the academic world, Leo didn't understand how difficult it was to get a good job, any job, in the middle of a world recession. When we'd advertised for a shelf-filler recently, we'd got seventy applications for the one post. And you'd have thought we were looking for the chief executive from the interviewing process the candidates had to go through, like building a tower from spaghetti and marshmallows, saying what they'd be if they were a food, that sort of thing.

'I'm head of department,' I said.

'You'll be managing the store next,' said Doll.

I suddenly remembered how nice it was when somebody thought you were clever.

They were both smiling at me.

'Look, I'd better run. I'm going to watch Hope sing.'

'Say hello from me,' Dave said.

'I will. She'd like that.'

'You should let us know when she's singing again,' said Doll.

'It's just the karaoke.'

'We'd like to see her, wouldn't we, Dave?'

'We would,' he said, going inside and leaving us to say our goodbyes, as if he'd sensed I was starting to feel a bit awkward with all those 'we's.

Doll gave me another really tight hug.

'Good luck!' she said. 'I'll call you tomorrow, shall I? See how it went?'

'Yeah, speak tomorrow,' I said, same as we used to.

I pushed open the pub door just in time to see Hope being led onto the stage by my dad, who'd always fancied himself as a bit of a Louis Walsh, not knowing the rumours about him being gay, obviously.

'Now, listen up,' Dad said, tapping the mic. 'Because this here girl's got a voice. Her name is Hope Costello and you heard it here first!'

Hope stood there. Anne had loaned her a black dress with three-quarter sleeves, which Hope had chosen to accessorize with a maroon hoody from Gap and trainers. Holding the mic, she looked straight ahead, which happened to be directly at me, but I don't think she could see me through the nerves.

The intro to 'Crazy' started playing. Hope missed the first cue. A sigh of sympathetic embarrassment rippled round the room. My hands were clenched by my sides, my heart beating really fast, and inside my head, my voice was urging her, *Come on, come on, Hope, please, you can do it!*

Shutting her eyes, as if to block out the crowd, Hope came in for the second verse on exactly the right note.

If you'd closed your eyes, you'd have thought you were in the room with Patsy Cline herself. I think Martin must have picked the song. Country's probably the nearest thing you get to classical on a karaoke machine. He certainly knew what suited her voice.

When Hope sang the final line and stepped back from the mic for the last few bars of instrumental, there was a stunned silence for about a millisecond. And then the roof came off.

A month later, Hope told me she wanted to move into Martin's flat above the shop. I don't think it occurred to either of them

345

that I would feel anything about it. Hope had never done sad, lonely or totally-at-a-loss.

I didn't know how to approach Hope about the nature of their relationship. Neither of them seemed very interested in physical contact, but who knows what goes on behind closed doors? Hope had never liked 'the kissy stuff'. If you hugged her, she'd stand stiff as a board, enduring it until you'd finished. Over the years, whenever I'd tried to initiate chats about reproduction or contraception, Hope informed me that they'd done it in Personal, Health and Social.

I'd been putting off the inevitable talk we'd have to have about genetic testing as well, assuming the right moment would emerge, maybe when I decided to have the surgery myself, because Hope wasn't very good with hypotheticals. Now, anxious not to be accused of letting her down again, I took her to see the nice female GP and sat outside while she explained about the reasons for being on the Pill, and was relieved when she came out holding a prescription.

'Do you take these Pills, Tree?'

'Yes.'

'It's a good idea if you're not ready to look after a baby.'

'Yes.'

It was about as close to a woman-to-woman chat as we ever got.

The great thing about Martin is that he never saw Hope as being any different from anyone else. As Doll said, he's probably on the spectrum himself. Maybe we all are, to an extent. Isn't that what 'spectrum' means?

Neither of them knew about the tenancy of our council house, of course. Dad wasn't prepared to remain liable for the rent when it was just me there. Why should he? I was a grown woman earning wages, and it was about time I sorted out my own living arrangements. I did hang on as long as I could, just because Hope was such a creature of habit, I was worried she wouldn't adjust to everything being different. But, as she said, whenever we met for a milkshake on the seafront together, 'It's much more convenient for work.'

Martin's flat extended over all three floors above the shop. The loft was a music room, with a big window looking out over the rooftops towards the sea. If you walked down the High Street in the evenings, when it was quiet because the shops were all closed, you could sometimes hear them up there with Martin playing the piano and Hope singing. Occasionally, you'd hear laughter too, if Martin hit a wrong chord, or Hope forgot the words, and then they'd start up again.

It certainly sounded like they were happy.

Not that I was stalking Hope, or anything. It's just tough to stop worrying, when you've worried for so long. Maybe it was me who'd become the creature of habit?

My salary stretched to renting a one-bedroom flat, with its own little garden. I wanted a bit of outside space because of Leo's dog, Ebony, an old black Labrador who sometimes came to the hut with us. Being honest, I did assume that once I had a place of my own, we would spend some of our time there, but I wasn't necessarily thinking that Leo and I would set up home together. Or perhaps I'm kidding myself, and that's why I asked him with me to IKEA, although I said it was about having the car to bring stuff back. I could tell straight away that he wasn't keen on the idea and the Friday before, he called and asked me to meet him in Whitstable. I had a sense that something was wrong, but as I hurried along the concrete path by the beach and saw the door of the hut open, my heartbeat quickened with excitement, as it always did, at the prospect of seeing him.

The woman's hair was long, dark and streaked with grey. She was wearing one of those quilted cotton jackets made out of Indian fabric in a pink-and-orange pattern, a smart-casual bohemian kind of look. I couldn't help noticing, because she'd kicked off her orange Birkenstocks, that her toenails were painted the exact same deep pink colour of the jacket, which made me wonder, fleetingly, if she was one of Doll's customers. There was something about the outfit that said two words, 'middle class'.

'You must be Tess,' she said, looking up at me standing on the path.

I almost said, 'Teresa', because I didn't know her, and, as far as I was concerned, she was sitting in *my* chair.

'I don't understand,' I said.

'Oh, I think you do. All good things must come to an end as I'm sure your mother told you!'

'My mother's dead,' I said. 'And she never said that in her life.'

The supercilious mask slipped.

'Oh, I'm sorry,' she said.

'That's OK. You had no way of knowing.'

She looked different from the way I had imagined his wife. I'd always clothed her in a dark suit with a round-neck jersey top in a muted colour. The only brightness I'd granted was a silk scarf. My version of her wore shoes with a bit of a heel that tapped as she hurried down the university corridors to her next lecture.

'You're not the first, you know,' she said. 'I don't suppose he told you that he had to resign from the university after his last conquest complained of sexual harassment.'

'This isn't sexual harassment!' I said.

She gave me a wry smile. 'I don't know what it is you all see in him!'

'Why are you with him then?' I countered.

She sighed, wearily, just like Leo did when I said something that displayed my lack of education.

'Leonard and I have been together nearly forty years,' she said. 'We're old mates. We enjoy each other's company.'

'Leonard?' I echoed.

'Oh, he's not doing that *Leo* thing again, is he?' She chuckled. 'I don't know why he thinks Leo is any better.'

I did. Leo sounded like a writer. It was the name on his novel. Leo sounded like it was short for Leopold or Leonardo or something. Not Leonard. Leonard just sounded like a bloke in the pub, or someone who played bowls in a flat white cap, someone old.

It was beginning to drizzle.

'Does he know you're here?' I asked.

She stared at me.

'You're sweet, you really are. I should have insisted he did his own dirty work.'

'I'm not sweet,' I said.

But then I couldn't think how to prove it, short of smashing the coffee mugs or throwing pebbles at her, so I just stood there, with scenes from our affair flashing through my mind.

'You *told* him to take me out!' I said.

'I'm sorry?'

'The ticket you couldn't use, for the National Theatre. *Much Ado about Nothing* . . .'

Still, she looked blank.

'When we got stuck in London in the snow,' I added, trying to jog her memory.

'Oh, it's been *that* long, has it?'

Now she was the one looking ruffled. I was stung with momentary guilt for dumping him in it with her. How was I supposed to know what story he'd told?

'Why now?' I heard myself asking.

'It's only natural for someone of your age to want children . . .'

'But I don't!'

Leo knew that, didn't he? Hadn't the decision I was going to have to make about surgery been hanging over us all this time? Didn't it contribute to the exquisite poignancy that laced the silences after sex? Weren't we in a metaphorical 'Pending' tray waiting till one of us had the courage to face dealing with the inevitable? Surely he hadn't forgotten the first time we talked, properly talked? Surely I hadn't been alone in thinking that was the bond that made our love uniquely profound?

It was raining now, drenching my hair and soaking through my uniform blouse to my skin.

'You were asking him to choose,' Leo's wife said. 'Like most men, he's lazy. It's too much effort even to think about leaving his nice comfortable house. However much he likes to think he's still an Angry Young Man, he's got used to his en-suite bathroom and the four-star hotels his wife pays for. He's not going to go back to camping and bedsits at sixty-one, is he?'

'Sixty-one?'

A small smile played around her lips.

'Why are you telling me?' I asked, still clinging to the mad hope that this wasn't actually happening. Perhaps he didn't know she was here? Perhaps it was her attempt to break us up, which would actually backfire as soon as he arrived? I glanced over my shoulder. There was no sign of him.

'So long, Tess,' he'd said on the phone. He'd never used that expression before.

'For your information,' I said, trying to hold myself with dignity, 'I never asked him to choose. He's invented that.'

'Well, he is a writer,' she said.

I suddenly realized why the situation I was in, standing there in front of her with the rain plastering my hair to my forehead and dripping down my face, felt so weird but some-how familiar. In Leo's novel, *Of Academic Interest*, there was a scene where the main character's wife tells a female student

350

that the affair is over, except it's not a fisherman's hut, it's a gazebo at a faculty garden party.

Writers see everything that happens as material.

'What a fucking coward!' said Doll.

'I'm as angry with myself as I am with him,' I told her.

How could I have been so stupid? He'd told me his favourite novel in English was *The End of the Affair*. Shouldn't I have known, from that and everything else I'd ever read, that things never turn out well for adulteresses?

'And now I've got nothing,' I said.

'You could see it like that,' Doll said. 'Or you could make it the opportunity to do what you've always wanted.'

23

GUS

Nash was always on some dietary fad or other and she said I was the only person in the world who could make lentils delicious, so lunch at our house had become a regular event.

'You should go on *Masterchef*,' she said, ever eager to plot a new career for me.

'Do people really do that?'

'I was joking!'

Nash was finding it difficult to get work herself. She'd commanded such a huge salary in America that the roles that might now be big enough for her seemed few and far between. I think she was probably difficult to work with because she was always saying outrageous things about other actors. She enjoyed gossiping to someone who was completely outside her world and had nobody to tell. I learned more about her encounters with men than I wanted to know or she should have told me. 'Too much information?' was one of her favourite phrases.

Occasionally in the afternoons, after I'd picked Flora up from school, Nash would accompany us to Kensington Gardens, where we'd sit on a bench chatting while the girls played in the Peter Pan park.

One Friday, an argument between my children broke out on the pirate ship.

Flora was always Wendy, while Bella took the role of Michael, who needed Wendy to look after him. Usually, the arrangement worked very well. But this time Bella had decided she wanted to be Tinkerbell.

'Well, I'm sorry, but you can't!' Flora told her, crisply, sounding uncomfortably like Charlotte.

'Why can't?' Bella asked, not unreasonably.

'Girls,' I intervened. 'Why don't you take it in turns?'

Nash suddenly stood up.

'I've had it with you being such a bloody pain, Flora! You be Peter Pan and Bell be Tinkerbell for a change!'

I don't know if it was the swear word that shocked my elder daughter, or just the novelty of someone telling her off, but she drew back, chastened, and Bella was allowed to whizz around ding-a-linging until she became quite breathless.

'Flora has too much of it,' Nash said.

I felt I'd been reprimanded.

'And Bell's got to learn to stick up for herself,' she added.

'Yes. You're right.'

'You don't want her getting bullied when she goes to nursery, do you?'

'No.'

Was this how bullying started, I thought, with the parents' tacit permission? I needed to be more aware of it.

'What will you do then?' Nash asked.

'I'm not sure,' I said.

'God, you're hopeless! Do you mind if I make a suggestion? Go to cookery school.'

'They cost the earth.'

'Well then, get a job in a restaurant for the lunch service, or something. There's a Michelin-starred restaurant just down the road from you. Why don't you talk to the chef? I'm sure you could come up with some sort of quid-pro-quo arrangement, like a kind of apprentice. You used to be a waiter, didn't you?'

'Charlotte couldn't cope with me waiting tables.'

'Oh, for God's sake!' said Nash, exasperated. 'You always give the impression that your wife's disappointed in you!'

I wasn't aware that I gave any impression of Charlotte. I avoided talking about my marriage with Nash.

'She *is* disappointed in me,' I said.

'So what are you two doing together?' Nash demanded. 'I just can't see it. What do you have in common?'

'We both put our children's interests first,' I said. I'd always had the tendency to sound pompous when cornered. 'You'd understand if you had kids of your own,' I added, making it worse.

'Oh, don't give me that shit! I know perfectly well what it's like to be the child of parents who hate each other, thank you very much. '

'Sorry,' I said.

'Don't always be sorry,' said Nash. 'Hangdog is one of your least attractive looks.'

'Charlotte and I don't hate each other, by the way.'

It was ironic that I said it on the very day that Charlotte informed me she was having an affair.

I'd suspected something because her conference weekends had become increasingly frequent. For some reason I'd envis-aged him as younger than her, another student doctor, possibly, in a leather jacket, with longish hair, oozing sexual energy. I was, as usual, completely wrong, because he was considerably older than Charlotte, bald and big in pharmaceuticals. His name was Robert.

'Where did you meet?' I asked.

Charlotte was sitting on the opposite sofa in our downstairs room studiously avoiding eye contact.

'At the theatre. He stepped in that snowy night you let me down,' she said. 'Obviously, it didn't start straight away.' She finally looked at me.

How long *had* it taken? I felt it would be ungentlemanly, somehow, to ask.

'So, why are you telling me now?'

'Well,' said Charlotte, as casually as if she were outlining her plans for the day, 'the thing is, Robert wants us to go and live in Switzerland with him.'

'Us?' For a moment, I crazily thought that she was including me in this arrangement.

'The girls like him. He likes the girls.'

'Hang on! The girls don't even know him!'

'They do, actually.'

Now Charlotte stared down at the floor.

'That week in Majorca,' she mumbled.

Charlotte had taken the girls to see her mother in Majorca by herself, claiming that it was so rare for her to spend quality time with them. I'd stayed at home to redecorate the children's bathroom, which was becoming a little mouldy and wasn't good for Bella's asthma. When the girls came back full of the things they'd done with Robert, I'd assumed that they meant Charlotte's stepfather Robbie. How very convenient for Charlotte that the names were so similar.

Had she brought him along on their trips to see my mother too? Had Charlotte asked them to lie to me?

'That's the only time,' Charlotte said, as if reading my thoughts. 'I'm sorry I lied, but it was the only way I could think of testing the arrangement without raising the emotional stakes.'

'Quite right. Couldn't have anyone getting emotional,' I said.

'Sarcasm doesn't suit you,' Charlotte replied.

'So your mother's given this Robert her stamp of approval,

has she?' Somehow it was more humiliating to know that other people had been in on the conspiracy.

'Yes, she has. Not that that particularly matters to me.'

What did matter to her? What had ever mattered to her? I stared at my wife, as if seeing her for the first time: a very attractive woman in her mid-thirties, at the peak of her career. I was no closer to knowing what was going on in her head than I had been the day we first made love in her attic room in the rooftops. Had it all been a sham? Or just the last couple of years?

'Well, I'm sorry to upset your carefully worked-out, emotion-free plans, but I won't agree to it,' I told her. 'I won't allow you to take the girls away!'

'I don't actually see that you have a choice,' said Charlotte. 'How would you look after them on your own?'

'I'll get a job!'

'And an au pair, because you'd have to work all the hours God sends to keep up the mortgage payments? That's if anywhere will have you, with your work record!'

'We'll have to downsize.'

'I don't know if you've noticed, but prices are going up.'

'We'll have to live somewhere outside London, then. People do, you know.'

I could hear myself speaking as if I was another person listening to me, and everything I said sounded lame.

'You might be prepared to let the girls descend to your reduced circumstances, but I'm not. And I'm their mother. Who do you think the courts will back?'

'You'd be prepared to put them through a custody battle, would you?' I desperately tried to regain the moral high-ground.

'If you choose to fight me, you'll be the one doing that,' she countered.

I found myself thinking that she could have been a lawyer.

She had the cool, analytical brain for it. And then it dawned on me that she must have already talked to one. Robert probably had a legal team at his disposal. Charlotte had rehearsed every argument and I was at a total disadvantage. Perhaps I should ask for time out to prepare my own defence? I would call Marcus. In our unspoken competition, I'd now be the first cuckold, the first to get a divorce, the first to fight a custody battle.

'If we'd been a normal family, you wouldn't have seen them so much during the week, would you?' Charlotte reasoned, moderating the sharpness of her tone.

A normal family. That's what I'd wanted us to be. Had I let everyone down?

'Where in Switzerland?' I asked.

'Geneva,' she said. 'Robert has a house with a view of the lake.'

About six months ago, there had been a conference there, I remembered. Or had there? Was that another convenient coincidence, or another lie?

'Have you got a job there?' I wanted to know.

'I've had various offers, but I'm not in a hurry. The girls will be my first priority.'

'That'll make a change,' I said, acidly.

'I haven't really had a choice, have I?' she snapped.

'I can't see the advantage for the girls,' I said, realizing that the only argument I had a chance of winning was one about their future.

'There's an international school just a block away. Bella won't know any different. Flora is very adaptable, as we know.'

I took this to be a reference to the fact that Flora attended a state school rather than a private one, which Charlotte would have preferred if we could have afforded it.

'It's a good time for them to move,' she added.

That was inarguable. If they were going to move, better

when they were young, before they had established relationships with friends and teachers.

'Geneva's a fantastic place to grow up. They'll speak several
languages, meet fascinating people. Robert's a count, actually,
though he doesn't really use his title.'

'I thought Switzerland was a republic?'

Charlotte stiffened.

'He also has a chalet in Austria,' she said.

'You're not thinking of letting them ski?'

'You can't stop them having a full life just because of your
guilt,' Charlotte said. The ghost of a smile swept across her face,
as if she tasted victory.

'It's not guilt, it's rational fear – skiing's dangerous, remember!'

I pictured my brother hurtling through the whiteness, glancing back over his shoulder to see if I was catching him up.

It was fear. But it *was* guilt too. We both knew it, although
we'd never mentioned it in all the years we'd been together.
Did Charlotte hold me responsible like my mother did? Had
she been holding a knife behind her back all this time, waiting
for the moment to stick it into my gut?

Is this your revenge, Ross?

How had I ever imagined that I would get away with taking
his girlfriend? How could I have thought that I deserved my
beautiful daughters?

'Nobody *has* to ski,' I said moronically.

And then suddenly I started crying. I hadn't cried since I
was thirteen. In my first term at public school, I'd learned how
to keep it back because crying was for wusses. Now I was choking with tears, as if the reservoir of emotion that I'd dammed
up for so long was all pouring out of my eyes and nose and
mouth in a great, wet, drowning flood.

At one point, I felt a soft, tentative pat on my back and

I shouted 'Get off!' so violently, Charlotte snatched her hand back, as if from a live wire.

She waited until my shoulders finally stopped heaving, then handed me a tissue.

'You'll still see them,' she said, emollient now, as if collapse signalled my defeat. 'Geneva's only an hour and a half's flight. It really won't be very different, except you'll be the one who has them at weekends . . .'

'Don't be ridiculous!' I said, snorting back the tears, suddenly coldly determined. 'They're far too young to fly to London every weekend.'

'Well, once a month, then,' she said.

The terms were already worsening.

'Don't you think we ought to see how the girls feel about this?' I suddenly asked.

Charlotte was visibly taken aback, as if I'd lobbed a fast ball at her head. I could tell it was a scenario she hadn't anticipated and I could almost see her brain racing through the calculations, acknowledging it would be unreasonable to deny them a say.

'Let's speak to them in the morning,' I pressed. 'They'll have the whole weekend to ask questions.'

'OK, but we must all be together,' said Charlotte, anxious to get the ground rules established. 'And we have to keep it simple, no pressure . . . we'll say something like "Mummy and Daddy don't love each other any more, but—"'

'But that's not true, not for me . . .' I interrupted.

Charlotte looked at me impatiently, as if I was unnecessarily trying to complicate things.

So I missed the opportunity to ask if, as her words had implied, she'd once loved me too, and tormented by that, and by all the questions Flora and Bell might come up with, I stayed awake most of the night until eventually succumbing to sleep in the pale chill of dawn.

I was woken by the smell of toast. Charlotte and the girls were already sitting at the table when I raced downstairs bleary and dishevelled.

'Morning, sleepyhead,' said Charlotte, making the girls giggle.

'Shall we have pancakes?' I said, attempting to recover lost ground, adding, when Charlotte shot me a glance, 'We often have pancakes at weekends when you're away.'

How unusual it was for the four of us to be together, I thought, my brain still raw and hollow from crying. Was Charlotte's claim that it wouldn't be so very different actually right? I poured myself a cup of coffee from the cafetière.

'We have something to tell you,' Charlotte said brightly, then looked at me.

I tried to remember the exact wording we'd agreed.

'Mummy is going to live with her friend Robert,' I began.

'One of the reasons is that I want to spend more time with you two,' Charlotte interjected, which sounded like pressure to me.

'The thing is, we both love you so much that we both want you to live with us,' I said, hating the speed at which it was all coming out. I looked across the table, expecting tears, but the children appeared only slightly curious as they spooned their cereal.

'Are you getting divorced?' asked Flora. It was a condition she was quite familiar with because several of her friends' parents were separated.

I looked at Charlotte.

'In due course,' she said.

What were a seven- and three-year-old supposed to take from that?

'You can stay living here with me just as we are now, if you like,' I said.

'Or live with me in Robert's house,' said Charlotte, glaring at me.

'I want to stay with Daddy!' shouted Bella immediately, as if it was some lovely sleepover we were talking about.

My heart felt as if it would burst with love, and a smile broke over my face like sunshine.

'What's Robert's house like?' asked Flora coolly.

'Well, it's very big and it's got a swimming pool,' said Charlotte.

'That's not fair,' I muttered.

'Would you prefer me to lie?' Charlotte asked.

'Does it have a garden?' Flora wanted to know.

'An enormous garden.'

'Has it got swings?' Bella now chimed in.

'It's not as good as Kensington Gardens . . .' I countered, desperately.

'Why can't you take it in turns?' Flora suddenly beamed, as if she'd hit on the obvious solution.

'We *will* be taking it in turns,' said Charlotte, her brain more alert than mine to the possibility of breaking the impasse. 'The only thing we need to decide is which place you'll go to school. Bella will be starting school soon, won't you, darling?'

'Will you take me to school, Mummy?' Bella asked.

'Yes, I will. Won't that be fun?'

Marcus put me in touch with a female divorce lawyer who was fierce but offered little hope. She intimated that it would be less damaging for the girls if I behaved as if I thought the whole thing was a good idea. To my surprise, Nash concurred, saying that the worst thing about having separated parents was the strain of pretending to each one that you were happier with them than the other. I think I'd secretly been hoping that she would insist on me putting up more of a fight.

'But going to court won't restore the status quo, will it?'

361

said Nash, making me understand that what I wanted was impossible.

My decision not to contest at least ensured that I would have the girls every other weekend and every holiday.

I met Robert, choosing Kew Gardens as the venue. I'm not sure why, because I'd never been there in my life, but I thought it would be somewhere we could walk undisturbed and he wouldn't be able to dodge any difficult questions. It's actually a wonderful place with amazing Victorian glasshouses, but I doubt I'll ever go there again.

As I parked on Kew Green outside the big wrought-iron gates, I noticed a man a few cars along pointing his key fob at a little green G-Wiz electric car, and thought how silly and toy-like it was for someone so tall and distinguished. Never imagining that Charlotte's lover would drive anything less flashy than a convertible white Audi, I walked behind him all the way to the Orangery cafeteria, our agreed meeting place.

After a couple of minutes standing awkwardly by the cutlery island, Robert was the one who dared to approach me with eyebrows raised, smiling and offering a firm handshake, as if we were about to start a business meeting,

'Angus?'

'Robert?'

My first reaction was a strange sense of relief, because he was so much older than me that people were bound to mistake him for my children's grandfather. Perhaps because of the age difference, I couldn't seem to feel much anger towards him. Ultimately, it was Charlotte who had decided to leave me; Robert couldn't have enticed or persuaded her against her will. If wealthy and well-preserved was what she wanted, I was never going to be able to compete. Clearly a rich and powerful man, Robert sat on the board of an arts foundation and an opera company, and although he was wearing jeans and a coral Ralph Lauren polo shirt on the day we met, I could easily picture him in formal dress at the Salzburg Festival, with Charlotte beside him in a fabulously expensive ballgown.

He was open about his history as we strolled down the Broad Walk towards the lake. Amicably divorced from his first wife, with whom he had a son who held some post in Brussels, he clearly had no desire to take my place in Flora and Bella's lives, but he said perceptive things about them to demonstrate that he was sensitive to their needs.

'If your daughters would be living with us, it would be an honour for you to visit my house,' he promised.

I couldn't quite work out how it was that I was the one who would appear uncivilized if I turned the offer down.

'We don't say that,' I heard myself saying.

'Excuse me?'

'In English, we say, "if your daughters were living with us . . ."' I told him, feeling a tiny, idiotic fillip of triumph as momentary embarrassment furrowed his assured Eurocrat brow.

'Also, I will ask Flora and Bella to correct my English!' he laughed, smoothly re-establishing his composure.

When we parted at the gates a couple of hours later and he raised his hand in a friendly wave, I felt almost sorry for him taking on the icy presence of Charlotte, although I was sure he would know exactly how to deal with her. And when things with Charlotte were going well, I remembered dismally, she wasn't cold at all.

Charlotte took the girls to say goodbye to my mother, because I was still smarting from her response, when I phoned to tell her the news.

'I'm astonished it's lasted as long as it has.'

At the ages of seven and three, the girls couldn't really imagine how different their lives were going to be, and it didn't occur to them to be sad. I tried not to show them how miserable

I was, but I didn't want them to think of me as uncaring when they came to realize that the arrangement wouldn't be as equal as they'd been led to believe. During our last few days together, we did our favourite things, and they were astonished to be allowed all the sweets and ice creams they asked for. I hugged them a lot, and said things like, 'I will miss you very much!' and 'Remember that you can always call me, or Skype me. Mummy and Robert both know how to do that, so just ask them to help you!' and even, a little melodramatically, 'I love you so much and my life won't be the same without you!'

To which Flora responded, 'But you'll still be in our house, won't you, Daddy? And our room will be the same? And we'll come for weekends and holidays just like Harry and Hermione and Ron do from Hogwarts?'

On the last evening, I cooked a family meal of their favourite *tricolore* salad and pasta *alla carbonara* with strawberries and ice cream for dessert, and, after they had eaten, and smashed me at tennis on the Wii, they went up to bed and were asleep within seconds of me closing the last page of *A Bear called Paddington*.

I sat in the dark for a few moments, inhaling the indescribably comforting smell of just-bathed children, listening to the peaceful stillness of them sleeping, with fat wet tears rolling down my cheeks.

Charlotte was still sitting at the table when I went downstairs.

'That was more carbs than I've eaten in a year,' she said, stretching back on the sofa.

Automatically, I began to collect up the plates.

'Don't,' she said, pointing at the ceiling. 'You'll wake them.'

I sat down opposite her, wiping my nose with the back of my hand, like a child who's forgotten to bring a handkerchief to school.

'I'm sorry it's so hard for you, Angus,' she said.

'Are you?'

The last thing I wanted to be was petulant after being so decent about everything, but all the defences I'd erected were collapsing around me.

'I tried, Angus. I tried so hard. I really did . . .'

Suddenly I realized she was crying too. I couldn't remember seeing her cry before. Not since Ross's funeral.

'The thing is, you'd never give an inch, never compromise,' she choked.

I couldn't believe what I was hearing. Me? Me? She was turning it all the wrong way round. We'd always done what *she* wanted, not what *I* wanted.

'. . . the pressure of being the only one who's earning . . . of looking after everyone . . . it just didn't seem to occur to you . . . you just didn't get it! Did you ever for one minute think whether I'd like to spend time with my children? I didn't want to be a full-time mumsy mum, no, but most people get a little balance!'

'But I thought—' I'd assumed that her career was the most important thing to her. She always seemed pleased to be freed from the day-to-day grind of keeping house.

'Did you, though? Did you ever actually think?'

Clearly not as much as I should have done.

Charlotte took a deep breath. 'I know you were trying to exorcize Ross, when we first . . .'

His name jolted because it had always been a taboo word for us.

'. . . but didn't it ever occur to you that I was too? I was going to marry him, Angus, and my whole life was turned upside down. I had to learn to look after myself. I didn't know how to talk to people without being this tragic figure. When I went out with men, I dreaded the moment they'd ask, "Why is someone as pretty as you still single?" With you, I didn't have to say anything.'

365

I stared at my soon-to-be ex-wife. I was about to face a future without her, and now it was as if the past had happened without her too. I'd always seen her as coldly, sexily controlling, like the vampire in the photo on the mantelpiece. Now I wondered if she'd dressed as an angel that day, in a white dress with wings, would I have thought of her differently?

'Sex with you was the nearest I got to oblivion,' she said.

'Thanks,' I said.

'No, I mean in a good way. It was like a drug. And when I fell pregnant, it seemed like, I don't know . . . I couldn't not keep the child . . . could I?'

'No!'

A world without Flora was unimaginable.

'We muddled through, for a while,' Charlotte said. 'Didn't we?'

I hadn't looked after her. She'd needed looking after. She'd used the expression twice. And I'd thought I was good at looking after people.

An image of Charlotte kneeling on her bed in shell-pink Agent Provocateur lingerie on the night she told me she was pregnant flashed across my mind.

'Can't you look a bit happier than that?' she'd said, and, then, in a small, wistful voice I'd never heard before or since, 'It might be fun, don't you think?'

'Couldn't we still?' I now stammered. 'Isn't there a chance? For the girls? I'd do anything—'

'Oh, grow up, Angus, for God's sake!'

She'd found someone to look after her now, and we both knew he'd do it so much better than I ever could.

The silence extended until I finally said, 'I could do with a drink. Would you like one?'

She granted me a wry smile. 'I thought you'd never ask.'

There was a bottle of champagne in the fridge left over from some more convivial occasion. We clinked glasses.

'Truce?' Charlotte suggested the toast.

'Truce,' I echoed, though, typically, I wasn't sure exactly what I was agreeing to.

'I knew it was never meant to be,' I said.

'Are things meant to be?' Charlotte asked. 'If we lived our lives on that basis we'd never accept any responsibility.'

'I love my children,' I said.

'They're still yours,' she said.

'We'll have to find a way of making it work. For them.' I tried to sound grown up and responsible.

'I'll drink to that.' Charlotte clinked my glass again, in comradely fashion, before retiring to her room.

The following afternoon, when I returned to the silent, empty house and noticed her half-full glass still standing on the dining table, I did wonder if it had all been a way of prepping me for not making a scene at the airport.

PART FOUR

24

2012

TESS

Candyfloss-blossom trees, yellow daffodils, lime-green grass; a paintbox row of houses, blue, pink, aquamarine; pyramids of orange, red and purple fruit. My key in the door, a steep wooden staircase in front of me . . .

Each morning I woke up with a thump of disappointment; then, getting out of bed, bare wooden boards under my feet, walked to the window, pulled back the blind a fraction and looked out. In the street below, market stallholders were calling to each other as they set up their pitches, poles clanking, a dustbin lorry reversing, joggers bouncing past, a well-dressed woman dragging a small, yawning child in school uniform along the pavement, the sweet waft of croissants filtering up from the cafe next door, all confirming it wasn't a dream.

I took up running because in London everyone does some kind of exercise, not like at home where you sign up to a Zumba class and start making excuses after a couple of weeks, like it's raining, or you're tired, or *Scott & Bailey* is on the telly. In London, you have to have an answer when people ask you how you stay in shape, especially during the Olympics when everyone was pumped up with healthy resolution. Most of our clients went to the gym, but being indoors most of the day, I preferred to exercise outside. It had started off as a walk each morning, but since it took a good fifteen minutes to get to the park, I bought a pair of running shoes and a sports bra, and built up my speed gradually until I could do about six miles in an hour. I'd never run before, but once my legs had got the idea of what was expected of them, it became a bit of an addiction.

People always say that they like New York because it's exactly how it is in the movies. I love London for the opposite reason. No movie I've seen captures London's variety: the serene elegance of the white stucco terraces; the improbable red-brick Christmas cake of the Royal Albert Hall, golden Albert glinting in the sunshine; horses galloping on Rotten Row; crazy swimmers diving into the Serpentine; and, near Hyde Park Corner, where I turned back for home, gardens with luscious herbaceous borders and pergolas of roses, planted and tended for no other reason than to give people colour to look at.

Sometimes I'd find myself listing the flowers, like Hope and I used to do on our walks to school: red-hot poker, lavender, Sweet William, acanthus lily, the names repeating in my head until I reached a rhythm where I'd travel hundreds of yards with no memory of doing so, before returning to the busy immediacy of the Bayswater Road.

I always slowed to a walk at the top of the Portobello Road, wondering whether the people who lived in the terrace of brightly painted houses woke up each morning with the exhilaration I did, in my flat at the other end of the street.

I say my flat. Really it's Doll's. She says it was a business decision, but it was a pretty big coincidence that she decided to open her first London store in the exact place I'd always dreamed of living.

For a while, after Leo, it was like I lost interest in things. I don't know what I would have done without Doll coming round every week with a takeaway and a DVD just like she used to.

When she said I should think of my new freedom as an opportunity, I thought she meant university, but since they'd raised the tuition fees, that was never going to happen. The theory was that you earned more as a graduate, so you could pay back your student loan, but graduates were finding it just as difficult to get work as anyone else. And I was disillusioned with professors. I'd hung on Leo's every word, but I wasn't sure it'd be worth paying nine thousand pounds a year to listen to him, and that's before accommodation, bills and food.

'I'm not talking about university,' said Doll. 'I'm talking about living in London like we always planned . . .'

'London's expensive, Doll. The sort of job I'd be able to get wouldn't even cover the rent.'

'That's where I come in.'

'I'm not taking money from you,' I said immediately.

Doll was very generous, but she was over the top. The charm bracelet she bought Hope for her eighteenth was gold and must have cost a fortune, and it went straight into a drawer just like the one we'd bought all those years before on the Ponte Vecchio, never to be looked at again.

'I'm not offering to give you money – I have a business proposition,' Doll said. 'I've bought this property in West London, a little shop with a flat upstairs. It's all taking off up there now, what with the Euro in crisis and capital flying out of Europe. London's thought of as a safe haven, and then there's all the oligarchs. If I don't get in now, I never will.'

It was amazing how Doll had taught herself about business and economics if you'd seen her GCSE results.

'There's no way, with the baby coming, I'll be able to over-see things up there as well—'

'I don't know anything about nails,' I interrupted, because

373

you shouldn't work for friends, everyone says that, and I wasn't going to risk losing her as a friend again.

'But you do have transferable skills,' Doll continued, unfazed. 'You know about taking on staff, health-and-safety, managing rotas, all that HR stuff. And you're clever, so it wouldn't take you more than an afternoon to learn about the ordering and the health regs.'

I opened my mouth to contradict her, then realized she was giving me exactly the sort of pep talk I was always giving middle-aged women who wanted to come back to work after having kids but had lost their confidence and couldn't believe anyone would want to employ them.

'I need someone I can trust, because there's a lot riding on this. And I know you won't fuck up.'

'Just like I haven't fucked up anything else in my life?' I said despondently.

Now Doll looked impatient. I felt a bit like a candidate on *The Apprentice* about to get a dressing-down. Maria Newbury didn't tolerate whingeing, so if I wanted this opportunity I was going to have to pull myself together and grab it, best friend or not.

'Where is this shop?' I asked.

'So, here's the thing,' said Doll. 'It's on the Portobello Road.'

I was worried that Doll was overreaching in a recession, but the way she put it was: having your nails done is like buying a caramel latte. When you don't have a lot of cash to spare, you'll cut back on spa days and restaurant meals, but you still deserve a little bit of a treat.

Mum used to say that if you do something with a happy heart it will bring you joy. And who wouldn't be happy stepping out each morning into Portobello Road, popping into a Portuguese cafe for a cappuccino and an almond croissant? Before I became manager of The Dolls House, Portobello, I'd never once painted my nails, let alone had anyone else to do it for me. Like the running, it's surprising how quickly you get addicted. If you'd have told me once that I'd ever express a desire for turquoise toenails to match the colour of a new swimsuit, I'd have bet my life against it. Now I saw potential new nail designs everywhere I looked: the pink pompom flowers of a cherry blossom against the azure sky went down well with our Japanese customers; a silver-and-black Art Deco pattern echoed the mirrored interior of the Wolseley, where a lot of our businesswomen clients had breakfast meetings; a single tiny gold-leaf star on midnight blue was very popular at Christmas. Ours was the first nail parlour to reproduce the London 2012 logo, until we received a warning about copyright infringement.

It was me who noticed that the only other shops that seemed to be thriving in the midst of austerity were tattoo parlours. I'd never dare to have a tattoo myself and thought there must be others like me, so I managed to source some beautiful temporary tattoos made of organic vegetable dyes, which looked cool, didn't hurt and stayed on your skin for a few showers if you didn't go at them too vigorously with a loofah. Doll was delighted that I was 'adding value' to the business.

I joined a writing class at the City Lit. Not fiction. I'd had enough of fiction with Leo. This was called Life Writing and it attracted a flotsam and jetsam of oddballs, like me, who'd come to a watershed in their lives.

Sarah had been married to a very rich guy who traded her in for a younger model, literally, because she had been a model too, and she was still thin and walked with her legs crossing over each step, but anxiety had etched itself in lines on her once-smooth face.

Lorcan was a motorbike courier who was trying to reconstruct his memory after suffering severe head injuries in a near-fatal road accident. We were very different people but we got comfortable quite quickly because of trusting each other with a lot of personal information.

And then an Australian set designer called Gayle turned up. When she read out a funny piece about her fascination with her ex-lover's growth of designer stubble, I knew we'd be friends. She'd had a six-year affair with her former boss in Melbourne. Apparently he'd suffered from 'existential despair' just like Leo. 'Mid-life crisis,' Gayle called it.

She and I often went for a drink or a movie together after class, and on Sundays in the summer, queued for the Proms or the free gigs in Hyde Park. It was nice having a female friend my own age to do things with. Being a teaching assistant and at Waitrose, I'd always ended up with middle-aged female friends, apart from Doll, and Doll had never done culture.

'Your creativity's finally been unleashed,' said Shaun when he and Kev came over for a holiday.

They stayed at a boutique hotel in Fitzrovia and I met up with them most evenings, feeling quite sophisticated because I now knew which restaurants were in vogue and which were the must-see plays. We did the touristy things too, like tea at Fortnum & Mason, and cocktails in the American Bar at the Savoy, even though the prices were ridiculous if you allowed yourself to think about how many mojitos you could get from a bottle of Havana Club, a net of limes and a packet of fresh mint from Waitrose.

'How *are* you?' Shaun asked the day we spent alone together, when Kev went down to visit Dad and Hope.

We were at the David Hockney exhibition in the Royal Academy. I loved that exhibition so much I went back five times. Most of the paintings were of trees, and even though I've seen trees all my life, those paintings changed the way I look at them. Some of Hockney's colours are so bright they seem almost crude and artificial, but when you really look at new leaves with spring sunshine on them, or red twigs in a winter hedgerow, you see they are that vivid. For me, that exhibition literally made the world more colourful.

We were in a room with giant canvases showing the same coppice in the four different seasons.

'I'm happy,' I told him. 'And I've decided that I'm going to have the surgery. There's a process you have to go through, with counselling to see if you're ready psychologically, then consultations with the surgeon, so it may take a year or more . . .'

Shaun nodded. I couldn't tell if he thought it was a good idea or not.

'Even when you get a date, it's not fixed because they'll postpone you if someone needs it more urgently,' I continued. 'But I am on the pathway now and I'm feeling very positive about it.'

We moved on into a room full of paintings of white hawthorn blossom.

'Before, it always felt like I would be giving up on life if I had everything removed, but now it feels as if I'm embracing life.' I paused. 'And you won't believe this, but I've decided to get reconstruction too. At first I thought, that's just not me, but then I thought, why not? They offer it free. It's not like silicone implants because they take tissue from your thighs or tummy so that it ages with you . . .'

'Doesn't look like there's much to take,' Shaun said, looking at my newly toned legs.

I managed a grin. 'I've always wanted smaller breasts.'

Shaun smiled at me. He did approve, I thought. And actually, it didn't matter whether he did or he didn't, because I knew it was right for me.

We went for a walk in Green Park afterwards. Sunshine was filtering through the big shady trees making random dots of bright white light on the tarmac that danced as the branches swayed in the breeze.

'Seems like you're in a good place,' Shaun said.

377

'Being in a good place,' was one of those phrases that Doll used a lot too.

Yes, I always felt like saying. *I'm in London!*

'And is there a new man in your life?' Shaun asked.

'No,' I said.

Everyone else seemed to know how to have a relationship – Doll, Dad, even Hope, for God's sake! – but I didn't.

Gayle was a serial Internet dater. She was signed up with Match.com and eHarmony and all the rest of them, and she was always telling me I should give it a go, but, to be honest, the string of funny stories she told about her encounters put me off. Sometimes I even suspected she was going on the dates simply to write about them.

One evening, when we were sitting with a bottle of Sauvignon Blanc waiting to watch *L'Elisir d'Amore* relayed live to the piazza outside the Opera House in Covent Garden, she got me to ask her questions to practise for a speed-dating event. I asked her some of the interview questions we used in HR, like, 'How would your friends describe you in three words?' and, 'If you were a vegetable, what would you be?'

'An onion?' said Gayle.

'Why?'

'Because it's got lots of layers . . .'

'But the smell lasts all day on your hands and it makes you cry,' I pointed out.

'OK. I'll say a tomato.'

'Technically, that's a fruit.'

'You'd be hopeless at speed dating,' said Gayle.

'I know,' I said.

'How do you envisage meeting someone?' Gayle asked.

'I think it'll have to be more spontaneous,' I replied.

What put me off about all the new ways was that it was like you were sitting with a sign over your head saying, 'I want a boyfriend.' I had the standard Richard-Curtis-movie type of fantasy, where a stranger would bump into me spilling my latte and we'd look into each other's eyes and know.

'So, there's this new app you should try, called Tinder,' said Gayle. 'It shows you photos of people in the area who are also using it. So, if you like the look of someone, you just swipe yes, and if they swipe back, it's a match and you can message each other. It's a bit like when you catch someone's eye on the Tube, you know? But you're doing something about it.'

She got out her iPhone and demonstrated. There were seven men in the vicinity using the app. Were some of them in this crowd, I wondered? Or even inside the Opera House? It was kind of spooky. Gayle swiped yes to two of them. One was a match. *What U doing?* he messaged. *Watching the opera*, she tapped. He didn't reply.

'Saves a lot of time,' said Gayle.

'Have you actually met anyone?' I asked.

'Three guys. Two losers. The third, a pistol between the sheets. You should try it.'

'You had sex with a stranger?' I asked, in what Doll always called my 'nun's voice', just as the crowd fell silent for the beginning of the overture.

'What's to lose?' Doll asked when we met for our fortnightly business meeting.

'My dignity?' I said.

'No big deal, then.'

We both sprayed crumbs across the table laughing.

We usually had our lunch in the Michelin-starred restaurant down the road, but sometimes Doll brought Elsie, my goddaughter, along with her, so we were eating baguettes in my flat while Elsie cooked a wooden lunch with the toy kitchen I'd bought for when she visited.

'Come on,' said Doll. 'Let's sign you up before you change your mind.'

I was slightly alarmed by her vicarious enthusiasm for the project, remembering how much she nagged me to get engaged to Dave, when subconsciously she was the one who'd wanted to.

We got as far as selecting a photo from my Facebook page when Doll suddenly called a halt.

'No,' she said. 'Nobody's going to swipe that.'

'Thanks.'

'Only because you take a rotten photo,' she said. 'If you're trying to look sexy, you look fed up; when the camera catches you unawares, you can look a bit mad, which isn't you in real life, promise. What we need is a professional head shot. It'll be tax-deductible for publicity purposes.'

So I spent an afternoon in a photographer's studio with a hair and make-up artist and came out with a series of sultry photos that looked nothing like me at all. Which was actually a good thing, I thought, because if nobody swiped me, I wouldn't take it personally.

Gayle bought me a packet of condoms, because the one thing you couldn't do was have unprotected sex with a stranger, and a courgette from the vegetable stall in case I needed to practise rolling it on.

'Bloody hell!' I said, when I saw the size of it.

'If you were a vegetable . . .' Her eyes twinkled. 'What was Leo like then?'

'More of a gherkin,' I said wickedly, thinking how he'd hate me saying that.

However much you tell yourself that it's just a bit of a laugh and you're not going to worry one way or another, unreciprocated swiping isn't a good feeling. I only persevered because Gayle and Doll kept texting me for updates.

On Sunday morning, sitting behind my *Observer* in the cafe next door, I jumped as my phone vibrated a match. Carl. He and I shared Lorcan as a Facebook friend, which was a tiny bit reassuring.

Thomas Hardy or David Nicholls? he messaged, which I thought was clever because one wrote *Tess of the D'Urbervilles* and the other wrote *One Day*, which has a quote from *Tess* at the front.

Both, I messaged back.

Coffee?

Drinking one right now.

Where?

Carl was there in less than the ten minutes he said it would take him, so I didn't have the chance to change my mind. He was reasonably tall with broad shoulders, floppy blond hair, and about twenty-one. There was a really horrible moment when he looked around the cafe, his eyes travelling straight past me, but then he smiled, eyebrows raised, and I smiled back.

'Tess?'

I wasn't sure whether to get up, or stay sitting or air-kiss or what, so I just said, 'Have a seat,' as if he'd come for a job interview.

He was wearing jeans and a grey T-shirt that was quite clingy so you could see the contours of his chest and he carried around him the warm, slightly animal, smell of a man who'd just woken up. I imagined him sprawled across a big double bed, phone on the pillow, opening a bleary eye to look at my photo and failing to register I was at least ten years older than him.

'Can I get you something?' I asked.

'I could murder a bacon sandwich,' he said.

I got myself another latte and a little custard tart.

He told me he was a student doing a degree in English Literature and Icelandic because his mother was from Iceland. For some reason, I told him that I had studied English

381

Literature too, and we talked about books we had read recently, and when he asked me what I did, I said I was a writer.

'Wow!' he said, staring at my mouth.

'What?' I asked.

'You've got a flake of pastry . . . no, other side.'

The conversation seemed to have come to a natural close. Perhaps he didn't believe I was a writer, or perhaps being so young and beautiful, writing was the last thing on his mind.

'So, what shall we do now?' he asked, holding my eyes with his.

'We could go for a walk?' I suggested. 'It's a lovely day. But I'll need to get different shoes.' I was wearing flip-flops. 'My flat's next door.'

'Right,' he said, standing up with me.

I didn't mean that. I wasn't sure that was what I wanted. What if he was a strangler? But now it would sound rude to say, 'No, you just sit here and wait.' And he'd probably be gone when I got back.

'I didn't actually mean, you know . . .' I stammered.

He smiled slowly. 'But is it such a terrible idea?'

Ten years younger, but far more grown up than me.

This was new territory. Casual sex with a toyboy I would never see again. He might be a murderer, but the truth was probably more that he woke up with a hard-on.

'OK then,' I said.

My flat is really one large room with the kitchen units and table at one end and a double bed in the front bit near the sash windows looking over the street. I immediately went to the sink and filled the kettle, but when I swung round and said, 'Coffee?' he'd already taken off his T-shirt. His torso was like a sculpture.

'Do you wax?' I asked him out of professional curiosity.

'I don't need to,' he said.

So young he hadn't even grown body hair.

'I don't do this sort of thing,' I said. 'So I've really no idea what the procedure is.'

He laughed gently.

'Just relax,' he said, walking towards me, taking the kettle from my hands and putting it down on the table.

I raised my arms obligingly as he lifted the loose silk shirt I was wearing over my head, removed my bra and cupped my breasts as if he was weighing them, then kissed each one. He unbuttoned my jeans. I stepped out of them. Taking my hand, he pulled me to the bed, lay down next to me, his fingers finding places no other man had found. I began to lose myself to tingles of pleasure so unexpected I started laughing.

'What?' He drew back.

'No, don't stop, it's lovely!'

'Do you want me to wear a condom?'

'Of course,' I said.

Carl took the condom from me and carefully rolled it on – which was a relief because, even after practising on the courgette, I still didn't feel very confident – then he gave me another slow smile.

There was something a little odd about taking instructions from a stranger, but I found it empowering looking down at his beautiful face relaxing as I got it right.

'That's good. Now do this . . . yes . . . like that . . . oh, yes!'

I'd been in love with Leo, but we'd never talked during sex. I didn't even know this guy and yet he felt about a hundred times more involved.

Afterwards, I lay on his chest, his sculpted pecs against my breasts, our bodies breathing in sync. Then he withdrew carefully, and wrapped the condom in a tissue.

'A lot of women your age want a baby,' he said.

After what we'd just done, I felt it was slightly ungallant of him to refer to my age.

383

'And you do that?' I asked, primly. 'Aren't you afraid you might have kids all over the place?'

'Is that such a terrible idea?'

Jesus!

He started getting dressed. I remained in bed, under the duvet, oddly embarrassed now to be naked in front of him.

Carl.

For some reason, that ad that used to be everywhere flashed across my mind. I began to laugh again. He looked at me, perplexed.

'Carling refreshes the places other beers cannot reach!'

('Can you believe he was too young to know that ad?' I asked Doll, when I called her straight after he'd gone.

'Wasn't it Heineken?' she said.)

'So, what are you supposed to say after one of these encounters?' I asked him as he tied his laces.

'I had a good time,' he said, leaning over the bed to give me a final kiss.

'Me too,' I squeaked, pulling the duvet right up to my chin.

He opened the door and looked at me. I waved my fingers over the top of the duvet and then the door closed, he was gone, and the flat felt very silent. I thought for a moment that I might cry, but my mind was perfectly clear and happy; my body tingled all over as if it had been reawakened. *The pleasures of the flesh*, I thought, giddily, touching myself again down there where it still felt warm and fluttery with one hand, running the other ever so lightly over my breasts, feeling my nipples pucker up beneath the tips of my fingers. I stopped, lifted my hand away, then touched again, pushing a little harder.

The lump was right behind the nipple, not round the edges of the breast, where I'd always imagined finding it.

('Oh shit,' said Doll.)

*

The trouble with embracing life is you forget to fear the worst. It had only been six months since my annual MRI scan and a consultant had examined me in preparation for surgery since then, and I'd checked myself, but clearly not as rigorously as I should have because the lump was already the size of a hazel-nut.

If you were a nut, what would you be?

The locum GP said it was probably a cyst, because it was incredibly rare for someone of my age to get breast cancer.

'Look at my notes,' I said.

His face changed. And I knew then, for sure.

People talk about waiting lists on the NHS, but when it's cancer, everything moves very fast. You're going along with your life, having casual sex with a Nordic student, then two weeks later, you're lying in one of those hospital gowns waiting to go down to the operating theatre, and you're thinking, *What if I hadn't met Carl? Would I now be running round Hyde Park as normal? How big would the lump have had to get? How long would I have gone on feeling fine?*

My dad and Anne came to see me with Hope.

'First my wife, now my daughter!' Dad started, before Anne ordered him to go outside and get some air.

'You're strong, Tess,' she said, gripping my hand, big gold rings digging into the undersides of my fingers. 'You've got what it takes to fight this thing off.'

But I knew it didn't work like that. My mother was a strong woman. Quiet, but strong. Nobody just surrenders, do they?

'Do you have a pink diamond?' Hope asked.

'Pink diamond?' I echoed.

'Doll got a pink diamond against breast cancer,' said Hope.

The nurse asked me if I was ready for my pre-med.

Anne gave me a kiss, then left me with Hope. I thought for a moment that my sister was going to follow suit and kiss me too, but she didn't. She just stood there. Suddenly, I really needed to feel Hope's awkward, ungiving weight against my chest and smell the familiar scent of L'Oréal Kids strawberry shampoo I'd washed her hair in so many times and which she still used because it wouldn't occur to her to try anything else.

I'd always loved Hope unconditionally, but just this once I *so* wanted to be loved back.

Feeling myself drifting, I stretched my hand towards her, but still she stood just out of reach.

'You're not going to die, Tree,' she suddenly announced.

In my woozy state, I could picture the conversation that had gone on, when Hope, hearing the word 'cancer', would have asked, 'Is Tree going to die?'

And Anne and my father would have looked at each other awkwardly, not knowing quite how to respond, and, just before the silence got too long, one of them, probably Anne, would have said, 'No. She's not going to die.'

Because we'd all learned over the years that Hope didn't do 'probably' or 'yet'. What she needed was an answer to her question.

Just like the rest of us, really.

A wave of blissful relief, knowing that I meant something to her, washed through my body. Maybe it was just the drugs.

'Are you asleep?' Hope asked.

'Almost,' I whispered.

'Shall I sing you?'

'Yes, please.'

So I was lulled into anaesthesia by her pitch-perfect cover of ABBA's 'I Have a Dream'.

25

2013

GUS

In a leafy road just five minutes' walk from the hospital where I was working, I looked up and down the street before pressing the doorbell, checking that no one could see me, as if my appointment was somehow secret, or shameful.

There was no chaise longue for me to lie on, just two comfortable chairs. Dorothy was more homely and less intellectual than I'd imagined she would be. After going over my history, she asked me to talk her through the accident.

'It's like a loop of film running in my brain,' I said.

'What's on the film?'

Ross's face glancing back at me through the thickly falling snow, his teeth white, his eyes hidden behind mirror ski goggles, flakes settling on his dark, swept-back hair.

'He's in front of me,' I said. 'Skiing at speed, and he glances back to see if I'm there and then there's this tree and he's missed the split second he needed to avoid it . . .'

'But you weren't there?'

'No, but we'd raced a hundred times. It's what he did.'

'OK, so let's say that *is* what happened, even though you

don't know it is. If you'd been there, behind him, how would that have made a difference?'

I never got beyond the glance, the tree, the smash, the consuming panic.

I didn't have an answer to her question.

We sat in silence for what seemed like forever.

'The injuries Ross sustained,' she eventually said. 'Could you have saved him, if you had been there?'

'No.'

'Even if you'd been an A&E doctor?'

I smiled. Was that perhaps why I'd ended up in A&E?

'No. The brain damage was catastrophic.'

'And yet you believe, in some way, that you caused his death?'

'I should have been with him!'

'Why? You knew it was dangerous. You tried to stop him.'

I heard myself saying, 'Maybe I didn't try hard enough . . .'

It was the admission I'd promised myself I would never make. Not to my parents, or to the rescue party, or to the police. I should have tried harder. But I walked away.

My eyes filled with tears. Dorothy let me cry.

'How did it feel walking away from him?' she gently asked.

'It felt good,' I sniffed. 'Like I'd given up caring if he liked me any more.'

'So you left him powerless?'

'Yes.' I began to weep again.

'And that's why it happened?'

It sounded so ridiculous spoken out loud.

'Did you feel relieved when your brother died?' she asked. 'Did you think that his bullying would stop?'

'I couldn't seem to feel anything. It was a kind of deadening, interspersed with moments of panic, not relief at all,' I said.

'Because the bullying didn't really stop, did it?' she said, gently. 'You were so used to being bullied, it carried on without him.'

Strange how one sentence can make sense of sixteen years.

It was Nash who'd persuaded me to talk to someone after I'd finally explained about what happened to Ross.

'I had a patient with similar indications in series three,' she said. 'I'm pretty sure you're suffering from post-traumatic stress disorder.'

I wondered why in all the years of studying Medicine that had never occurred to me.

'Because you never told anyone, maybe?' Nash said.

We were drinking in her club, not the one Charlotte and I had been to on that fateful day in 2001, but a similarly exclusive private members' place on Shaftesbury Avenue.

'I leave my left-wing credentials in the cloakroom,' Nash breezily informed me, pre-empting any sarcastic remark I might think of making when she signed us in.

The club backed onto another of those secret gardens you find behind the most unlikely streets in London. Nash was a defiant smoker. I still pretended I wasn't, despite occasionally buying a packet of ten, lighting one and taking a couple of drags before stubbing it out with the heel of my shoe. So we were on the terrace, companionably silent, almost as if unwilling to move on to another topic.

Finally, Nash said, 'You know I've always liked you.'

'And I've always liked you,' I said.

'I don't suppose you're interested in becoming a casualty of my torrid and disastrous love life?' she asked.

The panic started in my stomach, then ripped up my throat to my brain. Nash had been my rock since the girls left, lending me the money for the few months I needed to complete my training, supporting me through the first exhausting weeks back at work, sympathizing about the difficulty of diagnosing deep vein thrombosis and the horror of dealing with an acid attack from her on-screen experience of emergency admissions. Nash knew all my worst bits and I knew hers, but it just wasn't there for me, and I knew it would have to be all or nothing with her.

What I wanted to say was, 'Please don't stop being my friend!'

But she had bravely asked the question and I knew I had to get up the courage to answer it truthfully.

'No,' I said. 'I'm sorry.'

I couldn't do the 'I'm not ready' excuse with Nash. And I was sure she'd get annoyed if I started on the 'You're a great person, but . . .' thing.

There was a long, vacant pause before she drained her glass, and replaced it carefully on the table. I was sure she was going to get up and walk out of my life. Instead, she lit another cigarette.

'Well, that's cleared the air,' she said, blowing a tempting cloud of smoke across the table.

I was determined to keep the house for the girls to return to if they ever tired of the novelty of living with Charlotte. I don't think she thought I'd manage to keep up with the mortgage payments, but I did, finding strange solace in my work, as I always had done in the hectic world that is an Accident and Emergency department, because you have to exist entirely in the present. As I'd feared, weekends with the girls grew further and further apart, because I didn't want to insist on the custody arrangements, forcing them to upset the new lives they were establishing.

I started running again. The quickest way to reach the park was through the busy bottleneck of Notting Hill Gate and straight along the Bayswater Road to the first gate. On summer evenings, the pavements were hot, the air full of noise and reeking with the smell of cheap cooking fat; on winter mornings, when I'd finished a night shift, I sometimes felt like the only person awake in the city, my footsteps pounding the concrete pavement, darkness surreptitiously giving way to cold, grey light.

With no set time of day, I never established passing acquaintance with other runners as I had done in Regent's Park, where people I recognized by their silhouette or the colour of their tracksuit would nod or say 'good morning'. *The loneliness of the long-distance runner*, I sometimes thought, wondering if my father had been more perceptive about me than I'd given him credit for, and whether he'd appreciate me getting in touch, but never quite finding the impetus to take the idea further than that.

On my days off, I'd shower after my run and walk down the Portobello Road to our favourite cafe, never tiring of the shell of burnt sugar over the creamy deliciousness of their custard tarts. The Portuguese cafe owner and I exchanged words about the weather. I sat on a stool by the window with a newspaper, watching the world go by. Occasionally, I'd spot one of the mothers who used to stand outside the gates of Flora's school, and we'd wave, but friendship between adults was not what we'd signed up for. All we had in common was our children. Without the girls, I wasn't a single father, I was just single.

When a senior oncologist appeared in A&E to examine a patient presenting with a large lump in his thigh, I recognized him as my chess-playing fellow medic, Jonathan. Recently married to a theatre producer, he didn't yet have children and could find the time for a drink more easily than Marcus, who now had a boy and a girl of his own.

In a blatant attempt to matchmake, Jonathan and Miriam invited me to a dinner party with one of her colleagues, Gayle, who regaled us with her adventures in the world of Internet dating. She was much more attractive than I'd assumed the candidates on dating sites would be. As we walked to the Tube together, I tentatively suggested having a drink sometime, but she said I had too much baggage for her, and she'd learned to save a lot of time by being honest upfront.

Out of curiosity more than pressing need, I signed up for a month's free trial and found Lucy's sister Pippa looking for love. Weighing embarrassment against the possible pleasure of seeing her again, I decided to send her a message. There followed a flurry of emails in which I learned that Lucy had married Toby and had three kids with a fourth on the way, but that Pippa was now divorced, childless and living in Strawberry Hill. We arranged to meet up one Saturday afternoon outside the Friends' Room on the fifth floor of the Tate Modern which has one of the best views in London.

Pippa was as thin and brittle as she had been on her wedding day, when I had worried that giant Canadian would swamp her with his bulk and his bonhomie.

'What was I thinking?' she said, pushing a brownie around her plate with a fork. 'He was so decent and nice and normal, for heaven's sake! Screw-ups are much more fun, don't you think?'

I could tell she wasn't interested in seeing the Paul Klee exhibition, though she said she'd be happy to if I was desperate. We wandered eastwards along the riverbank and had too much Rioja in a tapas bar in Borough Market. As we walked back towards the setting sun, Pippa kept bumping into me unsteadily, and we ended up arm in arm, trying to piece together the lyrics of the Kinks' song, 'Waterloo Sunset'.

At the station, my tentative move towards her cheek resulted in a lingering snog, full of regret and promise. Her body was sinuous and lithe under her flimsy summer dress.

'Are we mad enough?' she whispered, her lips raspberry-red from kissing.

The territory we were entering felt dangerous and sinful and sexy.

'What are you looking for?' I asked.

'I'm looking for my for-ever person.'

I thought of Nicky's face. *Really, Gus?*

'I don't think I can be that,' I said.

'No. I don't suppose you can.'

'We'll keep in touch?'

'Of course!'

We kissed chastely on both cheeks and I waved her down the platform, knowing that I'd never see her again.

'I still think you should train to be a chef,' Nash said one day in July, just before the girls arrived for their summer holiday.

We'd seen a film at the Gate and she'd come back for supper. She was on the Dukan diet to lose weight for a big audition, so I made us a hot Thai-style salad of tofu on top of radishes, cucumber and spring onions.

'It's about as realistic as daydreaming about what I'd do if I won the Lottery,' I said, shaking up a citrussy dressing of lime juice, finely sliced ginger and chilli in a jam jar.

'Do you do the Lottery?' Nash asked.

'No! That's my point.'

She took another forkful of her salad.

'Actually, you don't have to have a lot of money, these days – you just get people to come to your home. You call it a Supper Club, you get a reputation on social media, it becomes the coolest thing, and you charge what you like!'

'But you have to know people,' I said.

'Honestly, Gus, you are A FUCKING NIGHTMARE!' Nash suddenly screeched. 'No wonder Charlotte bolted! You've got an excuse for everything. Why can't you ever just launch in?'

'I'm not making excuses!' I protested. 'I *don't* know many people!'

393

'But I do, don't I?' said Nash. 'I've got fifty thousand followers on Twitter. You've got a bijou house in the coolest part of town, with a great big kitchen table which is ideal for supper parties, and you're a great cook!'

'And I've got a full-time job, and a very small repertoire of dishes.'

'OK,' said Nash, pushing back her chair. 'I give up. I actually give up, and I won't mention it again in case I end up killing you.'

'Are you going?' I asked.

'Yes. I'm fed up with you, Gus.'

'But you will come and see the girls?'

I was suddenly nervous that they'd be bored. Nash always took them to Primark, which seemed to be one of the biggest attractions of London now.

'I'll see how I feel,' Nash said. 'At the moment, I just want to strangle you.'

Charlotte was getting jittery about the London property boom.

'I keep seeing articles calling it a bubble,' she said when she delivered the girls from the airport. 'And bubbles pop!'

London was in the midst of a heatwave, so I'd set up the paddling pool in our garden. In the past, Flora would have stripped off and thrown herself straight in, but at nine she was more self-conscious. In the three months since I'd seen her, her face had lengthened in the process of changing from the pretty child she had been to the beautiful woman she was going to be. Bella had also shot up, but she was still a freckly imp with cascades of ginger curls. I gave them hugs and they went upstairs to see if they could find their old swimming costumes. I was surprised that Charlotte had accepted my invitation to stay for a coffee, which I'd issued only as a formality. Perched on the edge of the sofa, she sipped iced water, while I put on the espresso machine.

Apparently, she and Robert were prepared to offer me a deal. If I sold the house, after the mortgage loan was repaid, they would offer me half the equity, which at current prices was probably just over half a million pounds and considerably more than the share I'd put in.

The look on her face told me that she expected gratitude for this generous offer.

'I'd probably be entitled to that anyway,' I told her coolly. 'Given the length of time we were married and my contribution to the girls' upbringing.'

One of Charlotte's eyebrows arched in surprise.

'Anyway, I'm not selling,' I said.

Now, Charlotte's eyebrows flattened and the bridge of her nose puckered into a frown.

'Don't you think three years as wronged husband is long enough?' she asked wearily.

'Haven't you imposed enough disruption on their lives?' I countered.

I should have known that I would pay for the buzz I got from that little exchange. It would have been far smarter to tell her that I'd think about it and wait until the last day of the holiday to give her my decision.

What I hadn't anticipated was her willingness to manipulate the girls, although I had no proof that she had put words into their mouths.

'It's such a big house just for you, Daddy,' sighed Flora, almost the moment we'd waved Mummy off down the street.

'Aren't you lonely here all by yourself?' asked Bell.

In the past, they had played in their old bedroom with shrieks of delighted rediscovery; now their reaction was muted.

'At home, we have our own rooms,' Flora informed me.

'I've got Hello Kitty wallpaper,' said Bell.

They were growing up, and I was happy that they were

happy in their new lives. There's a saying, isn't there, that you're as happy as your unhappiest child?

I handed them both glasses of pink lemonade I'd made.

'Sarp!' said Bell.

I liked the fact she still used the family word we'd all adopted for something we didn't quite like the taste of.

'If you want, we can redecorate your room while you're here?' I suggested. 'You can choose the colours and the curtains and everything.'

When that didn't elicit a reaction, I upped the offer.

'You could have a room each? We'll turn Mummy's old bedroom into a room for Bell . . .'

'Is there much point when we're only here for a week?' Flora asked.

'A week?'

'I'm sure I mentioned it,' Charlotte said, when I called her mobile to protest. 'The girls were so keen to go to summer camp with their friends. I didn't think for a minute that you'd want to stop them.'

I wondered whether I'd have got my three weeks if I'd agreed to Charlotte's deal, but it was too late now to clarify the rules.

At least there was no danger of us getting bored with each other, although my daughters weren't as easy to communicate with as they used to be. We Skyped regularly, but it was hard to remember the names and nationalities of best friends I would never meet, especially since at that age they changed so frequently.

Flora was now more interested in looking at the tattoo designs in the window of a shop next door to the cafe than she was in the custard tarts.

'You're much too young for a tattoo!' I said.

'But these ones wash off, Daddy!'

The thought of Charlotte's horror when she caught sight of her daughters inked was irresistible.

Flora had a dolphin transferred onto her shoulder and Bella a star on her tiny wrist.

'We've been all the way down to Greenwich on a boat, we've been on the cable car over the river, we've been to Christ Church College, Oxford, to see where *Harry Potter* was filmed,' I told Nash, when I spoke to her on the phone. 'But mostly they just want to WhatsApp their friends.'

'Stop treating them like tourists,' Nash advised. 'They probably just want to spend some normal time with you. It's lovely weather. Take them to Brighton for the day and get them to leave their phones at home. Tell them phones and sand don't mix!'

'Brighton beach is pebbles, isn't it?'

'Oh, for God's sake, somewhere else then!'

I knew a place where the sand was soft and golden. As I no longer had a car, we took the train to Lymington, changing at Brockenhurst in the New Forest.

'Where are we going?' Flora asked.

'Across the sea!'

In Yarmouth, we ate sandwiches in a pub garden looking out over the Solent, where the little yachts and giant cruise liners were like mismatched children's toys in a bath of perfectly blue water.

Maybe it's because it's an island that the Isle of Wight feels like a bit of a time warp. The shops still sell buckets and spades and little paper flags to stick in your sandcastle, and coconut ice and boxes of fudge with scenic views on, and ninety-nines with chocolate flakes that always taste just slightly stale. It had hardly changed since my own childhood.

As I hadn't thought to bring towels and the good beaches were a bus ride away, we bought lines and a packet of streaky bacon and spent the afternoon crouched on the little jetty near the pub, pulling unsuspecting crabs out of the water until our bucket was half full.

'What do we do with them now?' Flora asked.

'We let them race back to the sea,' I said.

'How do you know which one is yours?'

'You keep your eyes on your own crab! No cheating allowed!'

Unless you're a parent. Every time Flora got ahead, I made sure that my winning crab somehow became Bell's. The final score was Flora and Bell on six each and Daddy on three.

'Who did you race with when you were little, Daddy?' Bella asked.

She was a thoughtful child. I sometimes wondered if her early troubles had made her a more empathetic soul than her sister.

'With my big brother, Ross.'

'Uncle Ross who died?' Flora asked.

'Who told you about Uncle Ross?' I tried to keep my tone light and neutral.

'Granny did. He was supposed to marry Mummy, but he died, so Mummy had to marry you instead, so really we're like his daughters as well,' Flora said.

I felt the habitual rise of bile in my stomach.

It's a beautiful day and you're with your children, I thought. *Let it go.*

'How old was Uncle Ross when he died?' asked Bella.

'He was twenty-two,' I said.

Her little face puckered.

'How old are people usually when they die?' she asked.

'Ross was very young. People die at all different ages, but mostly when they are very old.'

'How old are you, Daddy?'

'I'm thirty-four.'

398

'That's not very old for a grown-up, is it?'

'No, my darling, it's not very old for a grown-up,' I re-assured her.

'I'm sad about Uncle Ross,' said Bell.

'You can't spend your life being sad,' said Flora. I could hear Charlotte's brisk voice.

'Why?' I asked.

'Because it makes other people around you sad.'

'When are you sad?' I asked her, gently.

'Sometimes after I talk to you on Skype,' Flora admitted.

'I'm usually a bit sad then too,' I said.

'It's OK to be sad,' Flora said. 'As long as you're happy most of the time.'

'Quite right,' I said.

The angle of the sun made the surface of the water pearly white; the air was gentle.

'I like the Island of Wight,' said Bell. 'Can we come back here every holiday?'

We managed to get a table on the train home, and for a while the girls amused themselves with the puzzle magazines we'd bought at the station while I read a newspaper that someone had left. When it went quiet, I looked across the table to see that Bell had fallen asleep against Flora, who was still reading, her arm protectively round her sister's shoulder. She put her finger to her lips when she saw me looking, taking her older-sister duties very seriously.

I texted Nash. *On train back from seaside. Brilliant suggestion. Are you on for shopping tomorrow?*

A message pinged back immediately. *OK, but early. Major date with hairdresser 2pm. Final audition in LA!*

Congrats! I texted back.

Not holding breath.

The part she was auditioning for was Princess Margaret in a

film about the romance with Group Captain Peter Townsend, called *The Choice*. It was perfect for her. Not only did she possess the slightly blowsy sexiness of the Princess, but she also had a real talent for conveying the vulnerable side of arrogant or difficult people. It was the kind of role – royal, biopic, period costumes – that often wins an Oscar. I didn't say that, though. With Nash, you always have to tread a careful line between complimenting and tempting fate.

'When are you leaving?' I asked, when we met up the next morning outside Primark at Marble Arch.

'Tonight. I have to miss the Stones,' she said.

'Still, how exciting!' I tried to put more enthusiasm into my voice than I felt.

I'd taken three weeks off work. Now, after just one, my girls were leaving and my friend wasn't going to be there to hang out with.

We emerged from the store with big brown-paper carrier bags stuffed with so many dresses, tops, leggings, bags, pots of glittery stuff and hair ornaments, I was grimly optimistic that Charlotte would have to fork out for excess baggage on the return flight. The pavement was heaving with shoppers and Nash was already late for her appointment, so we didn't have time for a proper farewell. I gave her a hug and wished her luck, and she set off running, then suddenly, remembering something, delved about in her bag, and raced back with an envelope for me.

'Enjoy!' she said, and then she was off again.

'Is Nash your girlfriend, Daddy?' Bell asked.

'Not my girlfriend. She's a good friend.'

'Is she your best friend?' asked Flora.

'Yes, I suppose she is,' I said, looking fondly at the disappearing figure negotiating cracked London pavements in her heels.

'I'm hungry!' said Bell.

Looking around for inspiration I found myself staring at the familiar columns of Selfridges.

'I know just the place for lunch,' I said.

The Brass Rail had barely changed since my father used to take us there for salt-beef sandwiches when we came up to see the Christmas lights, but it was far too sweltering a day for fatty slabs of brisket sandwiched between thick slices of rye bread. Instead, we sat on high stools in YO! Sushi, picking dishes we liked the look of as they passed on the conveyor belt. Afterwards, I let the girls choose a cupcake each for dessert, and, since they insisted (and I knew there was almost nothing Charlotte would like less), a particularly garish rose-and-violet one with a towering swirl of pink-and-purple icing to take back for Mummy.

In the cool, air-conditioned perfumery department, I encouraged the girls to test different colours of nail polish on their fingernails, and to spray themselves liberally with scent, delivering them back to their mother on a sugar high in a cloud of Katy Perry's *Purr*.

Charlotte had arranged tickets for *Matilda*, not including me because she didn't think I'd want to come with my mother. Flora and Bella were to spend the final night at the hotel there because they were on an early flight and Charlotte wouldn't tolerate the stress of me bringing them to the airport. On their last visit, through no fault of my own, we'd encountered delays on the Piccadilly line and I'd only just got them to Terminal 2 in time, where Charlotte was spitting fire because mobiles don't work underground and she hadn't been able to contact me.

When the girls realized that I wouldn't be spending the evening with them, they kicked up a gratifying fuss.

I bent down to give each of them a hug.

'Thank you for all the clothes,' said Flora.

'I don't want you to go, Daddy,' Bell started sniffing.

401

I hugged her delicate little frame to my chest, her sad face damp against my cheek.

'I'll see you tomorrow at the airport,' I promised.

'If the Tube's working,' said Charlotte.

'Why do you have to be such a bitch?' I whispered in her ear, as we exchanged steely air-kisses for the benefit of the children.

Her expression went from furious to fair-enough in an instant. The thing about Charlotte is that she can give it out but she can take it too. I don't know why I always forgot that and tried to get what I wanted by being nice instead of nasty.

Hyde Park was submerged under a swarm of Rolling Stones fans. Straining to recognize the song, as I headed back home, I decided it must still be the warm-up band playing. There were big fences around the ticketed area but the crowds were packed ten deep against the narrow gaps to steal a free show. The sun had been shining all day and the meltingly hot air seemed to quiver with expectation.

'I've never been a big Stones fan,' I'd told Nash when she'd mooted the idea of getting tickets earlier in the year. 'My father is. Won't it be full of sixty-somethings doing their Mick Jagger?'

'It's a bucket-list thing, isn't it, seeing a Stones concert?' she'd said.

'Bucket list?'

'Oh, do keep up, Gus! Things to do before you die.'

It had said in the paper that the gigs sold out in less than three minutes.

Now the atmosphere was so charged, I almost regretted my reluctance.

I took a side street, and was alone within a couple of hundred metres. I love the way London changes from frantic to peaceful. It's something I've never experienced in other big cities. In London, even a densely populated street can be as sleepily silent as the countryside.

Back at the house, I decided to freshen up with a shower.

Nash's envelope fell from a pocket as I stepped out of my shorts.

The first ticket was for the Stones concert which she'd bought for herself after I'd been so unenthusiastic.

The second was for a holiday, booked in my name that morning, for a two-week cookery course in Tuscany starting in two days' time.

The note she had scrawled on the printout of the booking read: *Even you can manage to check-in online?*

I called her immediately, but her mobile was switched off, so I guessed she must already be in the air. In a way I was glad, because it's hard to find the right words when you're over-whelmed, and I didn't want to sound like a prat again.

By the time I arrived at the gig, the sun was beginning to go down and the Stones had started their set. The stage was a long way off, but there was a catwalk for Mick Jagger to strut along, giving the impression that he was surfing the crowd. Huge screens showed video art moving with the music, interspersed with live close-ups of the band's deeply etched faces.

Halfway through 'Honky Tonk Women', I realized I was sing-ing, my mouth forming the words as automatically as nursery rhymes. The communality of the experience was liberating, like being part of something much bigger than just you. I'd never been to Glastonbury, or any other festival, but on a hot sum-mer's evening, in a crowd of a hundred and fifty thousand, I suddenly understood what people loved about it. For the length of a song you could forget everything that had gone before and everything that might come, and live in the gloriously sunny present. When each song ended, everyone cheered and shouted and smiled at each other, strangers united in the moment.

Darkness fell without me really noticing and as the band started playing 'Miss You', giant white butterflies appeared on the shimmering LED screens, giving the illusion of fluttering over the crowds, briefly lighting up individual faces.

About six people in front of me, I noticed a tall woman tracking the ephemeral silvery-white image as it floated over her head, her expression as innocently delighted as a child gazing up at a circus trapeze artist, her lips syncing with the words of the song. Almost as if she had sensed me watching her, our eyes met, her mouth stopped moving and time stood still. Then the butterfly flew away and her face merged back into the darkness.

The sensation of déjà vu was so strong, the moment of recognition so tantalizingly brief, I couldn't tell if she was someone I'd met or someone famous. Blinded by bursts of pyrotechnics whooshing up from the stage, my eyes scoured the crowd for her in vain.

The encore of 'Satisfaction' went on so long, it was beginning to feel as if we were in a perpetual cycle of the chorus and then, quite suddenly, it was over. The applause peaked, continued optimistically, then died with the realization that the band had already been whisked out of the park. People started moving towards the exits, exhausted and subdued, like children after a birthday party.

The flow of the crowd was fairly orderly until someone collapsed a few yards in front of me and security guards had to step in to stem the tide of moving bodies.

Amid feverish whispers, a cry went out that I'd only ever heard in movies.

'Is there a doctor here?'

'I'm a doctor!'

The crowd parted to let me through.

Several people were kneeling around an unconscious woman, debating the correct first-aid procedure.

'Shouldn't you get her head between her knees?'

'Put her in the recovery position?'

One security guard was trying to keep the crowd back, another was fanning the patient with his hat. Their walkie-talkies occasionally hissed and splurged incomprehensible messages through the hum of anxiety.

There was no obvious head wound visible; she did not appear to be having a fit; she had not swallowed her tongue. She was wearing a vest, cut-off jeans and flip-flops, so there was no clothing to loosen. Kneeling down beside her, I asked a security guard to sit with his back to her, then draped her long legs over his shoulders to get the blood supply moving towards her brain. She was breathing, but she had a fairly slow and uneven pulse.

Around me, I could hear the murmur of amateur diagnoses.

'She's had a bit too much to drink, I reckon.'

'It's probably just the heat.'

'You've called an ambulance, right?' I checked with the security guard.

As if in answer to my question, a distant siren began to wail.

'Is she going to be OK, Doc?' he asked.

Her face was deathly pale.

'Come on, wake up,' I heard myself urging. 'Wake up now!'

Suddenly, she opened both eyes and looked straight at me.

The butterfly woman!

'Do I know you?' she asked.

'I'm Gus,' I said.

I could hear the paramedics pushing through the crowd. 'Step aside. Give her some room, folks!'

The woman was sitting up now. The crowd began to move again with a slight air of disappointment that the drama was over.

'We're just going to take you to A&E, love,' the paramedic said.

'I'm OK, honestly,' she was saying. 'I'll be fine.'

'What's your name, love?'

'Tess. Look, you really don't need to—'

'We just want to get you checked out, Tess,' the paramedic continued. 'Do you want us to stretcher you, or do you think you can walk?'

'I can walk!' she said, scrambling to her feet, then swaying slightly.

I stepped forward to catch her, but a paramedic got there first.

'Let's get you into the van, love,' he said.

The bright face suddenly saddened. As our eyes met again, she made a silent plea for help, then, as if accepting defeat, sat obediently on the stretcher.

As the doors to the ambulance closed, she gave me a little wave.

The driver went round to the front. I chased him. 'Can I go with her?'

'Are you her partner?'

'No!'

'Relation?'

'No,' I admitted. 'But I am a doctor.'

He gave me the kind of dismissive look I hadn't seen since I was a callow medical student, then slammed the driver's door, his big hairy arm resting on the edge of the open window.

The ambulance started moving. I stood frozen with indecision, then, as it began to pick up speed, my legs suddenly started running.

'Where are you taking her?' I shouted.

If the lights hadn't turned red, I wouldn't have caught up. The driver stared at me defiantly, then, as they changed to green, took pity.

'St Thomas's, mate.'

He turned on his siren and stepped on the accelerator. I had to jump backwards to avoid the rear wheels running over my feet.

The main body of the crowd was heading along Piccadilly. I cut down the road that runs past the walls of Buckingham Palace, then along the south side of St James's Park to Westminster. Parliament Square was virtually deserted; the floodlights on Westminster Abbey made it look strangely two-dimensional, like a giant piece of stage scenery. Halfway across the bridge, with St Thomas's Hospital a couple of hundred yards in front of me, I slowed to a standstill, sweat trickling down my back.

An intriguing woman called Tess had fainted in front of me. Now she was in good hands. My tiny role in the story of her life was over, my compulsion to see her again irrational. It would just be weird to turn up at the hospital.

Leaning on the bridge, I looked down. The lights on the water made it look thick and black, like oil.

I heard Nash's voice. *Why can't you ever just launch in?*

I set off again, running as fast as I could.

A&E on Saturday night in the middle of a heatwave was packed with bright pink people suffering from sunstroke. There was no sign of a very thin woman with a gamine haircut and a scintillating smile.

'I'm looking for a woman who came in, maybe half an hour ago, by ambulance,' I told the receptionist.

'Name?' she asked.

'Tess. She fainted after the Stones concert. I just wanted to check she was OK. I'm actually a doctor.'

'Surname?'

'I don't know,' I admitted.

'If you're a doctor, you'll know that I can't give out any information about patients.'

'Of course. Sorry!'

I turned to go, then stopped.

'Could I just ask if she's here?'

'I can't give you any information.'

'If I left a note, could you give it to her?'

The woman hesitated.

'I honestly am a doctor . . .'

'You're not like any doctor I've ever come across,' she said.

'Please . . .'

Not a word doctors often use with junior staff.

'If you leave a note, I'll try to pass it on,' she finally agreed.

'You haven't got a piece of paper I could borrow?'

She shook her head in disbelief, then passed a notepad advertising a brand of antidepressant.

'I expect you need something to write with as well?' She rolled a biro across the desk.

'Actually, no. It's fine,' I said.

It was a crazy idea. Maybe I was the one who'd had too much sun.

The receptionist now looked almost disappointed. She sighed and took back her pen.

'Sorry,' I said, lowering my eyes in the belated hope that she wouldn't recognize me if I ever found myself working at the hospital.

The air was still stiflingly hot outside, and my mouth was parched. Remembering there were food outlets open late in Waterloo station, I headed across the road. I bought a bottle of cold mineral water, and stood in a line for the till gazing at the buckets of fresh flowers by the exit.

Why can't you ever just launch in?

It was crazy, wasn't it, to think of giving flowers to a stranger?

'Please go to cashier nine,' a disembodied voice instructed.

I sensed the person behind me in the queue huff-puffing as I hesitated. 'Sorry. Do you mind if I just get one more thing?'

*

408

There was a different receptionist at A&E when I walked up to the desk carrying a bouquet of purple stocks and pink roses.

'Are those for me?' she asked, with a bit of a twinkle. 'Don't they smell gorgeous?'

She was friendlier than the first receptionist, less of a fire-breathing dragon at the gate of the castle where the princess was imprisoned.

'I was wondering if I could leave them for a patient?'

'Name?'

'Tess.'

'Hang on. Are you the one who . . . ?'

I nodded.

'So romantic!' She smiled at me.

'Can I wait?' I looked around for a spare seat in the crowded waiting room.

'I think they're keeping her in overnight for observation.'

'I'll come back first thing in the morning, shall I?'

'I can't promise anything!'

I remembered I was seeing the girls off on the eight o'clock flight.

'Actually, I can't,' I said. 'I've got to see my kids.'

The friendly look disappeared. I wanted to say, *It's not what you're thinking*. It was all getting too complicated.

'Would you just do me a favour and give her the flowers, OK?' I thrust the bouquet at her.

'And you're Dr . . . ?'

'Gus. Just Gus,' I said, and fled.

I was at the Stones concert, except it wasn't the Stones concert, it was Pippa's wedding but the organist was playing 'You Can't Always Get What You Want'. I'd run all the way to the church and the sweat was sticking my shirt to my back . . . In the front pew, there was a tall woman with short curly hair, and I knew I had to get to her, so I started tiptoeing up the aisle hoping

409

nobody would notice me, but when she turned, it was Lucy's mother, Nicky . . . I was dancing in the marquee and the disco ball was flashing spots of light around the tent, lighting up faces for a second, then moving on and I wanted it to stop, so I could see the faces properly, but they kept eluding me. I ran out into the garden and lay down on the swing seat and the marquee opened, throwing a triangle of light across the lawn and a tall, thin woman stepped out and the triangle closed again. In the darkness, I wasn't even sure I could see her shadowy outline and . . .

I woke up with a jolt, more exhausted than when I'd fallen asleep. I just made it to the airport, only to find that the flight was delayed. Airports are such soulless places, it didn't feel like proper time with my girls, just a frustrating, endless limbo. There were only so many retail outlets where Charlotte could skulk, pretending not to watch us eating white-chocolate-and-raspberry muffins in Costa. By the time they had to head for the departures hall, we'd run out of things to say. Flora was WhatsApping and Bell was playing Fruit Ninja.

Neither of them looked back as I stood on tiptoe on my side of the gate to get a last glimpse of them going through security. As I turned and walked away, my eyes filled, but it was nothing like the ferocious flood that used to cause me to divert to the observation deck and wave at random aeroplanes taking off before wandering gloomily back to the Tube.

We were all becoming used to separation. I couldn't decide whether that was a good thing or a bad one.

Instead of getting off the Piccadilly line at South Kensington and walking home through the park, I stayed on and changed to the Jubilee line at Green Park.

There was a different receptionist at St Thomas's A&E. I was about to speak when I noticed, through the open door of the admin office behind her, the bouquet of purple stocks and pink roses, still in their cellophane and tissue, standing in a hospital water jug on the desk.

'Can I help you?'

'The flowers.' I pointed. 'I left them here for someone yesterday evening.'

'*You're* the one?' she asked.

I was the subject of the current gossip, probably an object of ridicule.

'We did try to give them to her, but she said they'd probably be better staying here to cheer people up.'

'She wasn't admitted then?'

'The doctors wanted to keep her in, but your friend was having none of it.'

I knew I wouldn't get anywhere by asking if she had left a forwarding address.

'Very nice of you, though,' said the woman, in a kind, motherly voice, as if trying to make things better. 'The scent's a lovely change from, well, you'll know, won't you – someone said you were a doctor?'

'Did she ask who left them?'

'We did tell her Gus.'

From the receptionist's tone, I could see that Tess hadn't responded.

Do I know you?

I'm Gus.

She had just been coming round from a faint.

My name had meant nothing to her. The receptionist and I both knew it. We looked at each other.

And then I turned and walked away.

PART FIVE

26

July 2013

TESS

When Doll really likes something she says she's died and gone to heaven. That's exactly how it feels lying in my room looking up at the ceiling. There are cherubs festooning garlands around a pale turquoise sky. The chandelier droplets cast tiny rainbows on the walls. The bed is so huge I can stretch my arms and legs out into a star and still not touch the corners, and the sheets are pure white cotton and reassuringly heavy. It's too warm for a blanket, but with the air conditioning, it has become quite chilly in the night.

The tiled floor is cold against the soles of my bare feet as I walk to the window and push open the shutters to see rolling hills, smudged with grey-green olive groves, and dark cypress trees spiking the blue sky. In the distance, I can just make out the terracotta roofs of a little town, which I think must be Vinci, where Leonardo was born.

An infinity pool was one of the features on the website that attracted Doll. As I lower myself into the cool mirror of water and push off into a silent breaststroke, conscious that my fellow guests are still sleeping close by, I feel as if I could swim for ever into the sky. Dragonflies dart across the mercury surface; the air is fragrant with jasmine and the first wafts of coffee from the kitchen.

The only rule of the Villa Vinciana is that guests, who have come to follow individual artistic pursuits, have to eat meals together. The idea is to give a communal feeling, although on the first day, us new ones don't really mix with those who've been here a while and already formed into friendship groups. A buffet breakfast is laid out on trestle tables beside the eating area: platters of prosciutto and cheese, melon fans, and baskets of tiny pastries filled with jam, custard or marzipan – you can't tell until you bite – all delicious.

It's not all singles. Some people have come with their partners, but they're the quiet ones because they're used to seeing each other in the morning. Those of us who arrived in the minibus from Pisa airport last night ask each another cautious questions about why we're here, careful at this early stage not to intrude or reveal too much. As well as Creative Writing, the Villa Vinciana offers courses on Italian Cuisine, Stone Carving – although that takes place at a converted olive press a few miles away, because of the noise – Yoga, and Art and Culture.

After breakfast the director of studies, whose name is Lucrezia, outlines the programme and excursions. You can understand her English, but she doesn't always use the right words. For the artistic participants, mornings are for lonely work, before the sun gets so hot, and when our creativity is very big. Then there is the long lunch, one recreational time, followed by the group seminar at six o'clock. Dinner is a buffet something light. You can eat pizza from the fire.

Sitting at a little wooden desk in front of my open window, I'm so excited at being in this magical place, I'm dying to email Doll to tell her that the room with a view was totally worth the extra cost, but I haven't got the password for the Wi-Fi and I'm a little bit afraid of Lucrezia. She seems quite strict. I suppose you have to be to organize forty or so people with all their dif-

416

ferent needs. Anyway, Doll might be cross if she thinks I'm wasting time describing the place to her, when the whole point is that I'm supposed to be writing my book.

After an hour, I'm still staring at a blank screen. It just feels a bit strange trying to conjure up life on a council estate in a run-down English seaside town when I'm sitting in a Tuscan palazzo.

I want to finish my book, but does it actually matter if I do? Sometimes, I think I'm scared of finishing it, because what happens after that? I wonder if every writer has moments like this.

I decide to explore my surroundings. If I bump into Lucrezia, I can pretend that I'm composing in my head or something. I push back my chair and stand up, slowly, because I don't want to faint again, not on this hard, ceramic floor. I apply Factor 20 sunscreen to my arms and legs and put on my big straw hat.

The *agriturismo* comprises the substantial villa where my room is, a building that looks like a church but doesn't have a cross on the roof, and a few one-storey outbuildings, which were probably stables before it was all converted into an Artistic Retreat and Cultural Centre. It's situated on quite a steep hill, which is how the infinity pool works because it's built out onto a terrace. Just beneath the high stone wall that supports it, there's a decked area with a canopy where the yoga people are practising. A steep, stony path leads down to another terrace, where there are vines with orange, green and red fruit which I suddenly realize are those tiny, expensive tomatoes you get in Waitrose. Tomatoes on the vine! I've never seen a tomato growing before. I'm reaching out to pick one, when a white butterfly lands momentarily on a leaf right beside my hand. I track it as it flutters and lands randomly along the row, until I'm suddenly aware that there's a guy in a khaki T-shirt and cut-off jeans with a trug over his arm looking at me.

'*Buongiorno!*'

I lose my footing, and slide on my bottom down the dusty

path to the next terrace, stopping my descent with the heels of my palms.

'Are you OK?' says the voice from the terrace above.

'Fine, thanks . . .' I'm too embarrassed to look round.

In fact, my hands are grazed and stinging, but it's only superficial. I stand straight up and walk on with as much dignity as my damaged pride and flip-flops will allow.

GUS

I can't see her face properly because she has this big hat on, then she slides away.

I stand on tiptoe to see over the top of the vine, and she's sitting on the dusty path, one terrace down. She leaps up quickly, all legs and elbows, and continues walking, unaware of the big patch of clay-brown dust on the back of her white shorts.

The sun is high in the sky and blindingly bright. It's almost midday and I should probably have a hat on myself because the heat's playing tricks with my mind.

I return to the kitchen with the *ciliegini* and I'm washing them at the big stainless-steel sink by the window, when the hat walks past, holding her arm at the wrist, her palm turned up, like a child who's fallen in the playground.

'Goos!' the chef calls.

'*Si?*'

'*Facciamo la pasta?*'

Shall we make the pasta?

'*Certo!*'

I bought a phrasebook at the airport this morning, with a CD that I played while driving my hire car to the *agriturismo*. It was a mistake to choose Italian on the satnav with only a couple of hours' knowledge of the language, but I found the place eventually.

There are only three of us on the cookery course helping the two chefs prepare lunch. One of my fellow students is a bear of a German with a gut bulging over the strings of his apron; the other an American divorcee in her mid-forties who speaks a different culinary English to mine – eggplant, broil, skillet. Kurt is sweating over the *osso buco*; Nancy is in the final stages of preparing the vegetarian dish of *melanzane farcite*; I, as the latecomer, have been put in charge of spaghetti *al pomodoro*, whose simple ingredients must be prepared and then added just before serving, so I'm at a bit of a loose end, until Chef points at the fresh fruit and demonstrates how he wants it cut up.

The business of serving forty people spaghetti is hotter work than I imagined, especially in a white chef's jacket, but it's more satisfying too, and as I'm doling out the last portions, I become aware of comments from the tables where people are eating.

'So fresh!'

'Pasta cooked just right!'

'Do they sell this olive oil, do you think? I've got to take some home!'

'What's the green bits?' says a voice that's like an echo in my head.

I look up. It's her. It *is* her! The butterfly woman!

She has taken off her hat, but sweat has flattened her short hair around the crown and the fine, damp curls look like a baby's hair in the bath. She's peering suspiciously at the last strands of spaghetti.

'Basil,' I hear myself saying, through the muffling nervousness that has engulfed my brain.

'Does it taste like spinach?' The voice has that slight twang, not Essex, but not far off.

419

'Not really.'

'Go on then!'

My hand is shaking so much as I deposit a portion in the bowl she is proffering, I accidently splash her thumb with tomatoey olive oil.

'I'm so sorry!' I grab the tea towel that's draped over my shoulder, but she's already put her thumb to her mouth to lick it off and in doing so, tipped some of the sauce down the front of her T-shirt.

'Shit,' she says. 'That's two today.' She turns her hand over to show me a big plaster on her palm. 'They say bad things come in threes, don't they?' she says. 'Not that anything could really be that bad in a place like this, could it?'

Her face breaks into that ridiculously familiar smile that makes me feel we've known each other for ever and sends my pulse rate soaring.

'Goos!' the chef is calling.

'*Si, Chef. Vengo!*'

I'm coming. Is that right? Or does it have the same other meaning in Italian as it does in English?

'*La frutta!*' he says crossly.

There are strawberries to be hulled and doused with juice from oranges I still have to squeeze. And then there is the clearing-up.

By the time I emerge from the kitchen again, most of the guests have left the dining area to take their coffee in the small shaded bar at the other end of the site, but my heart leaps when I see the hat still sitting there, alone, scribbling in her notebook.

Why can't you ever just launch in?

Because it's going to look weird, isn't it? She obviously doesn't recognize me and even though it is a complete coincidence, she's never going to believe that, especially after the flowers. She'll probably think I'm stalking her.

She gets up, walks towards me, flip-flops slapping against the decking.

'Very nice,' she says, handing me her plate. 'Being totally honest, I prefer it without the basil.'

'I'll remember that.'

'Did you make it?'

'I'm doing the cookery course. I prepared the fruit as well.'

'The fruit was brilliant,' she says. 'Especially the watermelon. Normally, it's full of pips.'

'There's a certain way you cut it up.'

'You'll have to show me. Not that I'm ever likely to buy a whole watermelon in England, am I? You'd get sick of it after a few days, wouldn't you? Doesn't taste the same in England anyway, does it? More like cucumber. I'm hopeless at cooking. Can't even do a barbecue without burning everything!'

'Everyone burns things on a barbecue.'

'Honestly?'

I nod and am rewarded with the smile.

'And you're . . . ?'

'Writing,' she says. 'Supposed to be, anyway. I should be getting back to it, otherwise I'll be in trouble.'

I can't think of a way of stopping her from leaving.

'See you later, maybe?' I say.

'Bound to, aren't we?'

TESS

Wish I didn't gabble on when I'm nervous. He's very polite, but there's a limit, isn't there? He's got one of those faces that changes completely depending on what he's doing. When he's listening, it's serious and intense, but if you make him laugh, he's like a boy, with nothing to hide. There's a kind of freckly look, like the actor who was Marius in *Les Mis*, that's boyish,

421

but still really sexy. He's a bit like that. Except taller. He's very tall.

Is he with someone here? Or alone? Escaping some traumatic event? His eyes are blue, but they're kind of gold as well, flickering between fun and anxiety.

Way out of my league, obviously, with his public-school accent and everything. Anyway. That's not what I'm here for.

Completing your first draft.
New writers often find it difficult to finish their first draft . . .

The rubric at the top of the course timetable is the same as the website advert that attracted Doll. She was thinking Tuscany because I'd always said I wanted to go back, but she thought I might be lonely on my own, seeing as she couldn't come with me, what with Elsie and being seven months pregnant again.

. . . Let us show you the way. The Villa Vinciana, situated in the rolling Tuscan hills above Vinci, where one of the world's creative geniuses was born, is a haven of tranquil creativity. Each air-conditioned, en-suite room is furnished with a desk for you to work during the day. In the evening, group seminars, led by our expert tutors, will provide opportunities for discussion of literary techniques, expert critique, and supportive feedback.

Day 1
Participants will present themselves and their work to the group.

We meet in the shaded area below the pool where I saw the yoga people this morning. There are only five of us, including Geraldine, the course leader. I calculate that yoga is by far the most popular course because there are at least twenty of them, and before we've even started I'm wondering whether I should ask to swap, even though I've never fancied yoga before.

I didn't get the greatest first impression of two of my fellow students – a middle-aged husband-and-wife combo – on the flight out. It wasn't the air steward's fault that the tortilla chips had run out, and, if you're going on Ryanair, you'd be mad to count on a range of snacks. The third time they called him back, I almost turned round and said, 'You should've eaten at the airport, shouldn't you?'

Just as well I didn't, because it was them I found myself squashed up against in the minibus.

There's a bit of a competitive vibe straight away. 'How long's your draft?' type of thing. The middle-aged couple, Graeme and Sue, are both geography teachers. He's writing an action thriller set on a field trip; she's writing a romcom about two teachers. She asks us to guess the title from her description. It's obvious that none of us feels comfortable doing so.

'Why don't you tell us?' says Geraldine pleasantly.

'*Staffroom Shenanigans!*' says Sue triumphantly.

'That's so cool!' says Erica, who's a very large American woman.

She's writing a vampire novel for teens, which, she assures us, is nothing like *Twilight*. I'd be happier if she'd said it was exactly like *Twilight* because I really enjoyed the whole series.

Now they're all looking at me. It's hard to tell Erica's age, but I think I'm probably the youngest in the group.

'Mine's not a novel,' I begin.

'Interesting,' says Erica.

I notice Sue and Graeme exchanging knowing looks, as if I'm a naughty schoolgirl who hasn't read the exam question carefully.

Geraldine, who I'm sure is a lovely woman, but looks quite like Leo's wife, with her long hair streaked with grey and her kaftan-type of dress, gives me an encouraging smile.

'It's called *Living with Hope*, and it's kind of about my mother and my sister, who has Asperger syndrome.'

'So it's an autobiography?' says Sue, in a bit of a patronizing tone.

'More of a memoir,' I tell her.

Graeme laughs into his hand, as if I'm stupid. Maybe there isn't a distinction? Maybe memoir just sounds better.

'There's a name for those kind of books, isn't there?' says Erica, squeezing her already piggy eyes in her effort to remember.

Geraldine steps in. 'Let's not get too bogged down with categorization.'

'My sister's called Hope, you see . . .'

'That's so cool,' says Erica.

Geraldine lays out a few ground rules for the course, about how we have to respect each other and try to be positive, all stuff I already know from City Lit. Then she asks us to sit in silence looking at the physical features of our surroundings, and listening to the sounds around us, and write what she calls a global description setting the scene, gradually zooming in on a group of characters.

The peaceful moment of contemplation is broken by Graeme. '"The sun was setting over the Tuscan hills, and the crickets were singing . . ." Is that the sort of thing you're looking for?'

'You've got the idea,' says Geraldine.

'Well, I've done mine then,' says Graeme, as if there's a prize for finishing first.

A slight breeze, charcoal-scented with pizza, rustles the canopy above us.

I can't believe I'm hungry again.

'If you complete the exercise in your own time, we'll read them tomorrow. Then we'll discuss some techniques to hone your critiquing skills,' says Geraldine, bringing the session to a close.

'Misery memoir!' Erica suddenly shrieks.

424

Everyone looks at her.

She points at me. 'That's the book you're writing!'

'No, it's not,' I say.

'Yes, that's what they're called!' she insists.

I'm about to say, 'There's nothing miserable about it.' But I realize that I don't want her, or any of these other people, knowing anything more. They're not like my class at City Lit and I don't want my chapters to be pulled apart by them, however 'constructively' they do it. In fact, I'm not prepared to share it with them.

Back in my room I feel bad, because Doll's paid so much money, and it was such a thoughtful idea, and I don't want to let her down.

I'm still going to enjoy it, I tell her on the phone, because it's a beautiful place and the infinity pool is great, and there are excursions in the minibus every day. Maybe I'll join the Culture class, or maybe I'll just do the culture bit myself.

Doll says, 'You do whatever you want! It's supposed to be a holiday!'

So that's a relief.

'Any fit men?'

'I haven't been here a whole day yet!'

'I seeeeee,' she says.

He's on duty at the wood-fired pizza oven, cutting up the huge discs with a pizza wheel.

There's a savoury one with tomato sauce, dots of floppy mozzarella and a different herb, which he says is oregano, that gives the typical Italian taste. You get it dried in England, but this is fresh from the villa's garden. If you like you can have anchovies, or bits of *salsiccia*, which is a kind of sausage. They put the circles of raw dough on a huge flat shovel and push them into the furnace for only a minute or so, because it's that hot.

His face is really pink from standing next to the oven, or maybe from the sun because red-haired people burn easily. He's friendly, but there's a limit to how long we can chat with a queue of hungry people behind me.

I avoid sitting with the writing group, but everyone else seems to have teamed up with their classmates and nobody looks very inclined to budge up and let me sit down with them. The stone carvers who arrived back late are covered in a ghostly dusting of white powder; the yoga group stare aghast at the sausage on top of my pizza because they're all vegetarians, so I perch at the end of a table on my own, watching him serving. I don't think he's here with anyone because he keeps glancing over, and I keep having to pretend that I was just staring into space, composing my book or something.

After we've all had a savoury pizza, we can go up again and get one with fresh fruit and sugar on top. I didn't know pizza could be sweet.

'It tastes like an apricot Danish!' I exclaim. Then, feeling like an idiot, 'Except peach.'

'And Italian?' he says.

But in a nice way. Not how Sue or Graeme would say it.

'Do you fancy a coffee when I get off work?' he asks.

'I can't drink coffee at night. Maybe I'll have a soft drink?' I add quickly.

'Rendezvous in the bar when we've cleared up?'

Rendezvous!

It's only when I open the wardrobe door that I catch a view of the back of my shorts reflected in the mirror on the wall. By the time I've changed, washed my face, deliberated about putting on make-up, decided against, and squirted myself with duty-free Chanel Nº5, the bar has packed up and the villa is shrouded in darkness and the profound stillness you only get in the countryside.

426

GUS

I understand that restaurant kitchens have to be spotlessly clean, but this is a holiday that Nash paid money for, and it seems a bit of a con that the villa only employs two chefs and a kitchen porter, and the people on the cookery course have to do most of the preparation, cooking and clearing-up. By the time I'm through, the cafe's deserted and the butterfly woman has given up and gone to bed.

In my room next to the pool, I lie awake listening to the cicadas and the occasional untimely crowing of a cockerel on a distant farm, smiling in the darkness at the thought of her sleeping somewhere nearby.

I wake from a dreamless sleep to the clatter of cutlery and the buttery-sweet smell of warm croissants.

As I wander towards the terrace for breakfast, I notice that there's a minibus waiting on the gravel outside the main door of the house. Her face stares at me through the window as it pulls away. She waves, just as she did from the back of the ambulance, then suddenly frowns, as if she's just remembered something.

'Where's the minibus going?' I ask the course director, Lucrezia.

'A cultural tour of Firenze.'

'And they're coming back . . . ?'

'Tonight, yes.'

TESS

Outside the railway station where the bus drops us, a guide with a red umbrella is waiting to take the Culture group on a tour. I tell her that I'm going shopping, in case it sounds rude to say that I want to follow my own itinerary.

In my memory, the other stops on our Interrail holiday are like postcards: the floodlit amphitheatre in Verona against a navy-blue sky; the bay of Naples; the view across the lagoon to San Giorgio, Venice; but that last, carefree day Doll and I spent in Florence, the day before my life changed, I can remember hour by hour, footstep by footstep almost, and, for sentimental reasons, I want to retrace it.

I take the bus to Fiesole, standing by the open window, feeling the movement of air on my face. When the bus deposits me at its final stop, belching a cloud of diesel as it turns around to return to the city, the square is suddenly peaceful and a whisper of mountain breeze cools my bare arms. In the Roman amphitheatre, I sit on one of the warm stone tiers, my memory so acute I can almost hear my younger self shouting, 'Tomorrow and tomorrow and tomorrow!' from the stage.

I take a photo and send it to Doll with the message. *Miss you!*

In the cafe, I sit under a shady vine, drinking sparkling mineral water. I eat spaghetti *al pomodoro* without basil while gazing at Florence, a miniature city in the distance, like the background of a Leonardo painting.

GUS

The chef is teaching me how to make *vitello tonnato*, which is a dish I've never tried because I've always thought it would taste strange. I'm not crazy about veal or tuna, but together? How is that ever going to work? Chef assures me that it will be *buono* if I follow his recipe carefully.

First, I have to roast the joints of veal, making sure that they are cooked but not dry. And then they must rest and cool, because the dish is served cold. Next I make a mayonnaise

428

from egg yolks, lemon juice and olive oil, and flavour it with capers, diced very fine, and with a small amount of chopped chervil and chives from the garden. To this I add a few pounded, salted anchovies, and a drained, mashed tin of tuna. Then I slice the cooled veal on the machine and layer it with the flavoured mayonnaise. It doesn't look promising, but it tastes divine.

'*Perfetto!*' says Chef, with a little nod of approval.

Kurt, who has been on the pasta and desserts, has the kitchen cleaned much more quickly and efficiently than me, and at three o'clock I find myself with a free afternoon ahead.

The pool is fairly crowded, and as my skin is not designed for sunbathing, I decide to explore the area in my hire car.

The first sign I see says that Florence is only fifty kilometres away so I take the slip road on to the Fi-Pi-Li motorway and arrive in the unpromising outskirts of the city in less than forty minutes. Signposts direct me to Parking at Piazzale Michelangelo. As the Fiat Panda climbs the zigzag road to the top of the hill, I begin to recognize where I am.

The heat hits like a blast furnace as I step out of the air-conditioned car into what must be the most beautiful car park in the world. The view of the Duomo against a vivid blue sky is so much like a postcard, it looks unreal. I head to one of the souvenir stalls loaded with football shirts and plastic replicas of Michelangelo's *David*, and buy a bottle of Factor 50 and a map, which I don't really need because I can see exactly the route I ran up from the city through incongruously rural landscape when I was last in this place.

First, just a little way along the shady main road, I seem to remember that there will be steps leading to the jewel of a church that I spotted from the rooftop pool of our hotel all those years ago.

429

TESS

There must be a bus to San Miniato al Monte, but people keep telling me different stops, or I don't understand their directions, so I decide to do what Doll would do if she were here and take a taxi. The road swirls through suburbs that look like those of any other town, then up a wooded hillside dotted with elegant villas standing coolly aloof from the jumble of medieval streets in the *centro storico*. The taxi drops me at the foot of the stone staircase that leads up to the church. I am the only person mad enough to be climbing steep flights of steps in boiling sunshine. I have to stop twice to get my breath, but I don't allow myself to look around until I reach the top terrace.

The view is so shockingly beautiful, my eyes brim with tears, just like they did all those years ago. I don't know what my problem was then, with my whole life in front of me, and no inkling yet of what was to come. I remember thinking it would be a great place to get married, which is peculiar because I wasn't one of those girls who pictured themselves in a white dress.

Inside the church, it's so dark after the bright sunlight, I can't see anything at all for a moment. Even when I've taken off my hat and raked back my sunglasses, my eyes take a little time to adjust. I walk up the steps to the raised chancel, acutely aware of the irreverent flap of my sandals, and drop a euro coin into the slot machine which floods the apse with golden light.

Staring at the huge, judgemental face of Christ, I have a powerful urge to say sorry to Him.

'It's not that I don't believe in You,' I tell Him silently. 'It's the Church I don't like, and to be honest, I don't think You would Yourself, if You were around today.'

The light goes off with a sudden clunk, punishing me for heretical thoughts.

But, after the briefest pause, it comes on again, and I spin round.

The tall guy from the Villa Vinciana is standing beside the machine. In the golden light, his hair is the colour of amber.

We stare at each other for a couple of seconds, and then we both exclaim, simultaneously, 'You're the one!'

'I *thought* I recognized you from somewhere!' I cry. 'You were here, the day I got my A-level results!'

'You were here. And then you spoke to me on the Ponte Vecchio!' he says.

'You took that photo of me and Doll. We were just looking at it the other day!'

'You told me about the Gelateria dei Neri,' he says.

'Did I?'

An image stored deep in my memory suddenly clicks open. We were on our way to catch the overnight train to Paris when I spotted him standing in the queue for the rip-off ice-cream place beside the bridge. I don't know what possessed me.

And Doll said, 'What are you like?' as we walked on, because usually she was the flirty one.

'Did you go?' I ask.

It's an odd conversation to be having in church.

'Twice,' he replies.

The light timer goes off again. He puts another euro coin in.

We stand beside each other gazing reverently at the solemn face of Christ, and then he says, 'Do you think it's still there?'

'What?'

'The *gelateria*.'

GUS

The marble terrace is radiantly white after the dim interior of the church.

My companion strolls over to the balustrade and leans against it, staring distantly at the view. There's an aura of wistfulness around her.

'That day I was here before,' she says, quietly. 'I vowed I'd come back, you know, like you do when you're eighteen?'

'I promised myself that too,' I confide. 'I thought it would be impossible to be unhappy surrounded by such beauty.'

She turns and gives me a smile that makes me want to throw away caution and tell her how beautiful *she* is, but the only word that comes out of my mouth is, 'Ready?'

The marble is slippery smooth. I offer her my hand as we walk down together, careful not to press too hard on the big plaster covering her palm.

'I fell over yesterday,' she says, her flip-flops clapping loudly against each step.

'I saw you.'

'It was you hiding in the tomatoes?'

'Yes. I wasn't hiding, by the way.'

At the bottom, we both cast a glance back up at the basilica, then, no longer needing my steadying hand, she lets go. We amble along the road, which is now busy with late-afternoon traffic. As we pass the entrance to the campsite, she says, 'This is where we were. Where did you stay?'

'A hotel. In Piazza Santa Maria Novella. I was with my parents. I'd have preferred to stay in a villa with a view of rolling hills.'

'Like the Villa Vinciana?'

'I suppose so!'

She smiles that transformative smile of hers, like the sun coming out from behind a cloud, and I can leave it no longer.

'You're Tess, aren't you?'

'I am,' she says. 'How d'you know my name?'

'Guess . . .'

Her nose crinkles with concentration.

'You saw it on Lucrezia's register?' she suggests, as we start walking down shallow steps that will take us back into the city.

'Wrong!'

'How many guesses do I get?'

I pick a number out of the air. 'Five!'

'You heard me telling someone at breakfast?'

'I wasn't at breakfast! Three left.'

'You saw it on the front of my notebook?'

She stops and takes an exercise book out of her shoulder bag, pointing at the panel where she has written, in looping letters. *Teresa Mary Costello. If found, please call* . . . then puts it back before I have a chance to memorize the mobile number.

'No! Two left!'

I wish I'd given her more guesses. I should have made it ten, or twenty, or as many as there are steps down to the city, because I don't want this to end.

'Hang on, how do I know you're telling the truth?' she suddenly demands.

'Trust me, I'm a doctor!'

As if the word has triggered a distant memory, she looks at me with an intense curiosity.

'What's your name, then?' she asks.

I hesitate.

'I'm Gus.'

We both stop in the shade of a tree.

'Gus?' she repeats.

'Look, I know it's a bit strange, but I was at the Stones

concert on Saturday, and you passed out, and I am actually a doctor.'

'You're the Gus who came to see if I was OK and brought me pink and blue flowers?' she asks, incredulously.

I nod.

'I'm so sorry but I had to leave them at the hospital because of getting my flight out here. In thirty-four years, I've never got a bouquet. And the one time I do, I can't even . . . wait a minute . . . but they were white roses . . .' She stops herself and looks earnestly into my eyes. 'Thank you, Gus. They smelled gorgeous.'

She believes that it's a coincidence that we are both here. Which, after all, it is.

I smile back at her, and then we both look quickly away, returning to the awkwardness of people who have just met. The air between us dances with silent questions.

'So, you're a Stones fan, are you?' she finally asks as we start walking again.

'Not especially,' I say.

I remember Nash's phrase.

'It's one of those bucket-list things, isn't it?'

'You're not about to die, are you?'

'I hope not!' I say. 'What about you?'

The crinkly frown.

'I wanted to feel what it was like to be in one big crowd all singing along,' she finally says.

'Amazing energy, wasn't it?'

'It was,' she agrees.

The sunshine is a little more clement now, and the road down to the city half in shade.

'Why were you unhappy?' she says. 'The last time you were here?'

'How d'you know I was?'

'Back there!' She points up the hill. 'You said you wanted to live here because it would be impossible to be unhappy. I just thought . . .'

We walk a couple more paces.

'My brother had died a few months before, in a skiing accident.'

'Oh, I'm sorry.' She touches my arm for just a second, but the tenderness of the gesture lingers on my skin.

'We were all raw with grief, but, in our very English way, trying not to let it spoil the holiday. Ridiculous, really.'

I've spent so much of my life not telling people, but now, with a stranger, the words begin to flow. 'There's such a taboo about death, isn't there?'

Great chat-up line! I can almost hear Nash screaming at me.

'Did you know that in Italy, families visit their relatives' graves on Christmas Day?' Tess says. 'The flower stalls outside cemeteries do a roaring trade.'

'What a nice idea. I love the way of life here.'

'Me too,' says Tess.

The Gelateria dei Neri no longer exists. We walk several times up and down the stretch of Via dei Neri where it used to be. My disappointment is less about the ice cream than that something we have in common has gone, our connection unravelling. But as we go on towards Santa Croce, we both spot the queue at the same moment. The Gelateria dei Neri has moved premises, and it's much bigger now.

Tess chooses a cone with three flavours: raspberry, melon and mango. After some indecision, I opt for blueberry, mandarin and passionfruit. The flavours capture the sharpness as well as the sweetness of the fruit like no other sorbet I've ever tasted. We don't know each other well enough to offer a lick and after a few moments of mmming appreciatively as we walk back towards the main square, Tess suddenly stops. 'We forgot the two-flavour rule!'

435

'What's the two-flavour rule?'

'If you get three flavours, for some reason, you only end up tasting two of them, so Doll and I worked out it would be better to have two flavours, three times a day, not three flavours twice.'

She's right. My first taste of *mirtillo* was like eating the pure distillation of blueberry, but I cannot now tell the difference between the mandarin and passionfruit.

'Let's finish these,' I suggest. 'Have a glass of water to refresh our palates, then go back.'

'You're my kind of guy!' she laughs.

Do you mean it? Are you feeling what I'm feeling? I keep getting little rushes of excitement, tiny bursts of adrenaline zinging through my limbs, making me light-headed with happiness and nerves all at the same time.

'I never got to see the Uffizi,' Tess says, as we walk past the entrance to the gallery. 'There was such a queue, and my friend could only stand so much art in a day.'

I look at my watch.

'We have time to see one painting.'

'Botticelli's *Primavera*?'

I point. 'There's no queue.'

The ticket office is closing. I thrust a couple of twenty-euro notes at the bewildered attendant, and we run up the stairs to the room where I remember the Botticellis hang.

'Oh my God! The ceilings!' says Tess, as we dash along the corridor. 'Nobody even tells you about the ceilings!'

We find the room containing two of the most famous paintings in the world and a disconsolate attendant who thought he was finished for the day.

'There's so much going on in this painting, you could look at it all day and still see things,' says Tess, stepping as close as she can to the *Primavera*.

'There are five hundred species of plant and over a hundred different flowers,' I remember.

'You counted them?'

I laugh. 'No, I read it!'

'It's so huge!' she says. 'I had no idea it was this big. I've got the poster, but it's only about a metre wide. The colours are not like other paintings, are they? There's so much green. It's like a religious painting and a pagan painting all at the same time, don't you think? If you think of Venus as Our Lady, these gods are like the saints . . . Honestly, you could look at it for a month, couldn't you? Hey, what's this?'

She moves on to *The Birth of Venus* on the adjacent wall, fascinated by the small bas-relief in front of the picture. 'This must be for blind people to see the painting with,' she says. 'Like a Braille painting. Isn't that cool?'

We take turns to close our eyes and feel.

'When blind people imagine the painting this way, do you think their brains make pictures, like our brains do when we're asleep, even though we have our eyes closed?' Tess asks.

With her commentary, I feel as if I am seeing everything for the first time.

'Do you think we'll ever know what it's like to be someone else?' She asks questions that most people of our age have grown too jaded to think about.

The attendant clears his throat for the umpteenth time.

'I think we know that he wants to go home,' I whisper.

We leave the room and walk along the empty gallery to the windows at the far end that overlook the river.

'I suppose that's what writers try to do.' Tess continues her theme. 'Be inside someone else . . .'

'And portrait painters,' I say.

'Did you know that there's a passageway full of portraits of artists that runs along the side of the Ponte Vecchio?' Tess

437

gestures towards the bridge. 'It's called the Vasari corridor. I read about it on one of the websites.'

She points to a row of square windows above the shops that I never noticed before.

'It leads from here to the Palazzo Pitti, so the Florentine lords and ladies didn't have to mix with the hoi polloi, I suppose.'

'Is it open to the public?'

'I think you have to book months in advance,' she says.

'I'd love to do that.'

'Me too!'

Is she thinking, as I am, that there is something going on between us that's bigger than here, now, today?

Under the colonnade outside, street artists are sketching tourists.

'Have you ever been tempted?' I ask Tess, as we stop for a moment to watch.

'No way! When I see myself in the mirror I think I'm OK, but in photos I always look terrible, and the camera never lies, does it? This would be worse!'

'I'd love to draw you.'

'Can you draw?' She gives me a sceptical look.

'A bit.'

'A man of many talents!' she says. 'Cooking, drawing! Gus, you could make a fortune here! What you should do is move to Italy, set up a restaurant and draw people, like Van Gogh did. There was this exhibition of his letters at the Royal Academy. Did you see it? I mean, I don't think Van Gogh cooked the food, but he painted all the people in the bar. It would make a brilliant TV series, wouldn't it? You could call it *The Art of Italian Cooking*, or has there already been one called that?'

A busker is playing jazz clarinet on the Ponte Vecchio and the cobbles are packed with tourists.

'Let's do a selfie,' says Tess. 'And send it to Doll and see if she guesses who you are!'

She puts one arm around me, her face close to mine, holds her phone as far away as she can.

'Say cheese!'

'*Formaggio!*'

In the photo, our eyes are closed because we're laughing, so we have to do another one, and as we're checking it, her arm stays around my back, and when we look up from the screen, our eyes meet and I badly want to kiss her.

'Do you think that's enough time?' she says.

'Time?'

'Before our next *gelato*?'

I love that she says 'next', as if we have a whole evening of eating ice cream ahead of us.

I freeze.

'What?' she asks.

'I'm meant to be cooking supper!'

Tess looks at her watch. 'I've only gone and missed the minibus!'

'OK,' I say, 'so, we have a choice: a) we can take a cab up to Piazzale Michelangelo and drive like Italians to arrive back late for supper? or b) we can spend a relaxed evening wandering around the city . . .'

With phones and cameras clicking all around us, this moment will appear in the background of a thousand Instagram feeds.

'I think we should probably let them know where we are,' Tess says.

My momentary disappointment that she hasn't said b) turns to joy when I realize she has.

I struggle through a difficult conversation with Lucrezia by pretending to understand less of her broken English than I do, and when I hang up, Tess looks at me anxiously.

'Chef is very crazy,' I tell her. 'The Culture group do not enjoy waiting one hour in a bus very hot. Everyone is interesting for our safety . . . however, we pay our money . . .'

'So we can do what we like!' says Tess. 'It's supposed to be a holiday, isn't it?'

Apparently, Doll would love to hear that we're sitting in Piazza Signoria drinking Aperol Spritzes.

'She thinks it tastes better if you've paid more,' Tess says.

We send Doll another selfie, from the cafe table. And I'm trying to imagine this woman, who is so important to Tess, but I can't remember at all, and hoping that she likes the look of me as these pictures ping into her inbox.

'You know,' I say, taking a sip, 'I think Doll's right!'

It's so easy to make Tess smile, and yet each time it's like an unexpected gift.

I keep wanting to say something like, 'Do you know how gorgeous you are?' and I have to keep telling myself that I'm thirty-four years old, not a teenager.

'Do you have a pencil?' I ask her.

She burrows about in her bag and then produces a stub of one.

I take a paper napkin from the holder on the table and start sketching.

She runs her fingers through her fine curls, tries to hold a serious face.

I'm finding it impossible to capture her. I remember sketching Lucy, seeing her as a doll whose expression never changed, but the essence of Tess's beauty is in her vitality. It's why she doesn't take a good photo. But the camera does lie.

'Stay still!' I tell her.

Perhaps it's my parental tone that makes her suddenly ask, 'Are you married?'

'No,' I say, then, not wanting to deceive with a half-truth,

'I'm divorced. My ex lives in Geneva with my two girls. It's a long story.'

'Oh, I'm sorry,' says Tess, picking up her neon-orange drink and taking a slurp through her straw.

'What about you?'

'Me? No. It's quite a short story in that department.' She leans over the table, trying to see how the sketch is going.

'Is that really how I look?'

'Not exactly.'

'Told you!' she says. 'Can I keep it?'

'Of course!'

'I'm going to put it in my notebook,' she says. 'Otherwise, knowing me, I'll be fishing around in my bag for a tissue and I'll blow my nose on it or something!'

She puts the napkin carefully between the centre pages.

'What are you writing?' I ask.

'Kind of a memoir,' she says. 'But I seem to have come to a bit of a standstill.'

'Do you have a deadline?'

'Not a real one,' she says, then excuses herself to go to the toilet.

I watch her weaving towards the cafe, ducking her head under the yellow parasols.

I call the waiter over and ask him to recommend a good restaurant, trying to indicate, in a man-to-man kind of way, that I want to impress, but sounding like a dodgy character from *The Godfather*.

'*Una persona molto importante, capisce?*'

When I produce a twenty-euro note, he suddenly remembers the best restaurant in Florence, and makes a personal mobile phone call to reserve a table.

As Tess walks back towards us, he says, '*Bellissima, la signorina!*' and winks at me.

'To be honest, after all that ice cream, I'd be just as happy

441

wandering round with a slice of pizza,' says Tess. 'It's a shame to sit in a restaurant, isn't it, when you're somewhere like this?'

My plan to impress her with a good bottle of Chianti and a rare Florentine steak so enormous they charge for it by the kilo vanishes so quickly I can't think why I even considered trapping her at a candlelit table with a disapproving waiter shaking a linen napkin over her long, bare legs.

We amble aimlessly together along cobbled streets on the other, less touristy, side of the Arno, where old women dressed in black sit on kitchen chairs outside their doors, chatting to their neighbours. The air is full of the smell and sizzle of frying garlic and the clink and clank of unseen mothers preparing the family supper.

'We never discovered this bit,' Tess says, as we enter a square with a little park in the centre. She gazes up at the floodlit facade of the church, with the same look of wonder on her face that I saw at the Stones concert at the weekend, and in San Miniato al Monte this afternoon, and half our lives ago.

'I think it's the student area,' I tell her.

There is a tiny merry-go-round for toddlers under the plane trees and a slow procession of young couples with prams, and older women linking arms for the evening *passegiata*. The air is balmy, the mood mellow.

We sit down at a table outside a little pizzeria. The waiter lights the candle on our table, brings us a cylindrical pot of grissini, and takes our order.

'Last time I was here, I was going to be a student,' Tess tells me, breaking a bread stick in half as she stares at the group of young people gathered on the church steps around a guitarist. 'I had my room booked in hall and my poster of Botticelli's *Primavera* all ready to stick on the wall.'

'What happened?' I ask, as the waiter brings us a quarto of

red wine and pizzas twice as large as the boards they are served on.

'When I got home, everything changed.'

The food remains virtually untouched as she tells me about her mother dying and having to look after her little sister. She pauses after describing her mother's funeral in a way that's funny and sad at the same time, and says, 'You'll know how it is, with your brother dying young. You never get over it, do you, whatever people say? You get used to it, but the missing never stops.'

I stare at the flickering candle, wondering if I am as honest as she is. I know that I have to tell her the truth, because this attraction, this connection, whatever it is that draws me to her, will not allow me to dissemble.

'The thing is, I didn't like my brother much. I didn't want him to die, obviously, but I couldn't seem to feel much, except guilt.'

Tess is quiet for so long I'm convinced that I have ruined everything.

'I think it was probably worse for you, Gus,' she finally says. 'Not that it's a competition or anything. I mean, I wish Mum hadn't died, but I always knew that she loved me, and she knew that I loved her. But now you're left with thinking you hated him, and he hated you, because that's how brothers are – I've got two myself – and you never got the chance to become men together, and find out if you could be friends.'

Would Ross and I ever have been friends? The idea's never occurred to me.

'Everyone who's left behind feels guilty,' says Tess. 'I loved my mum to bits, but I still tortured myself with all the stuff I could have done to change things. If only I'd recognized the signs, if only I hadn't been away, if only I hadn't been so wrapped up in going to bloody university as if that was the most important thing in the world. But you can't live your life thinking *if only*, can you? That's easy to say.'

I stare down at the table and Tess leans towards me, her face tilted slightly sideways, as if she's trying to get under my line of sight and make me look up, like you do if you want to get a smile out of a grumpy child.

'Two words?' she says.

'Another *gelato*?'

TESS

One minute, we're chatting away as if we've known each other all our lives, the next, silent as if we've just met. Both of those are true, I suppose. As we retrace our route, I feel very aware of his physical presence beside me, our hands almost, but not quite, touching.

'So where did you go to medical school?' I ask him.

'University College.'

'But that's where I was going!' I yell, as if he's snatched something that was mine. 'Where did you live?' I ask, more politely.

He tells me about arriving in hall with his parents, wanting to create a new identity for himself and about meeting his friend Nash, who got the room next door due to a last-minute cancellation.

'Do you think that was my room?' I ask, as we step onto the Ponte Vecchio again.

'That would be weird, wouldn't it?'

The shops are boarded up now, the buskers have gone home. We lean against the wall beneath the arches that support the Vasari corridor where powerful people used to stroll along above and unseen by the common folk.

'Do you think we'd have got on then?' Gus stares down at the Arno.

It looks better at night, more romantic. During the day it's muddy brown, but now it's oily black with shimmering reflections of the lamps along the riverbank.

My instinct is probably not, if I'm honest. He was a public-school boy with middle-class parents. He'd have seen me as a chav, and I'd have been chippy, thinking I wasn't good enough for him, which maybe I'm not. All we had in common then was a love of art and ice cream. Would that have been enough?

'Mum used to say that you can't step in the same river twice,' I tell him. 'And I was never sure what that meant, but maybe it's that if we'd met then, we wouldn't have been here together now. You wouldn't even have been "Gus" without Nash!'

'Like chaos theory.' He turns to look at me. 'If a single butterfly flaps its wings on the other side of the planet, it sets in motion a chain of events that could lead to a thunderstorm . . .'

'Or a rainbow,' I say, because it doesn't have to be something bad.

There's a moment of silence, then we straighten up, our bodies so close and trembly it's like there's an electric current zinging between us. He stares into my eyes, then his hands cup my face as if it's a precious and delicate vase and his lips touch mine for a fraction of a second before drawing away. He looks at me for what feels like forever, and then he kisses me deeply, eyes closed, as if he's giving himself to me in prayer, and his lips are so gentle and expert that my body is warm candlewax melting onto him.

He takes my hand as we walk from the bridge, both of us grinning all over our faces.

The streets are surprisingly empty, the restaurants closed. We arrive at the Gelateria dei Neri just as the proprietor is winding down the shutters for the night. Gus chooses *nocciola* and lemon, and it's *fior di latte* and pear for me. We wend our way back to the Duomo square. The floodlights make the facade of the cathedral look flat, like a giant stage set with nothing behind. There is no one else around and it feels as if the lights are on just for us, as if we've been granted a private VIP visit.

When I say this, Gus kisses me again. I keep my eyes open, because I want to fix an image in my memory of his face with the pastel stripes of the Campanile behind.

A couple of teenagers on skateboards appear from nowhere, circling us and jeering what I assume is the Italian for 'Get a room!' Then they're gone.

'The hotel where we stayed,' Gus points. 'It's just down there.'

'Nice.'

There's a moment when I know we're both thinking the same thing.

'We should probably go back to Vinci . . . ?' he says, like it's a question.

'We probably should,' I say.

It's the same taxi journey that I took up to Piazzale Michelangelo six hours ago, but the axis of my life has shifted, my quiet hymn of nostalgia replaced by a crescendo of anticipation that thrills and scares me, in case l accidentally jinx what might be happening by believing it.

In the car park, as we stand looking at the floodlit Duomo, now distant against the black sky, I suddenly shiver with a kind of presentiment that I must capture every precise detail in my mind because I'll never see this view again.

'I don't want to leave!' My voice wobbles.

Gus throws a protective arm around me, pulling me close. I love the way my head rests against his shoulder because he's so tall.

'We can always come back,' he says.

'Can we?'

'Every day, if you like. Or we can visit other places. We've got the car. We can use the Villa Vinciana as our base.'

'A bit like camping,' I say. 'Without the stones in your back and the walk to the loo, obviously . . .'

I can almost hear Doll shouting, 'What are you like?'

'I want to know more about Hope,' Gus says, as he starts the car.

So I tell him about what a funny, obstinate little girl she was, and how I never knew if I was doing right by her, and how living with her made me aware of all the lies everyone tells all the time just to make the world go round, and how difficult she could be, and how musical she was, and that leads me on to Dave.

So then Gus tells me about Lucy, and how she made him feel more secure and helped him stay the course, and how he didn't tell her about his brother, and that leads him on to Charlotte.

Gus is concentrating on the motorway, which is two lanes only, with a concrete wall instead of a central reservation, but sometimes it's easier to talk when you're not looking at the other person's face. He takes the slip road off at Empoli Est, and we drive around a deserted town for a while, before he admits that he thinks he's taken the wrong exit, and now we're lost. He stops the car in a side street, and tries to switch on the satnav, managing to change it from Italian to some other language, we think maybe Russian, but instead of finding it funny, he is agitated and grabs my hand, staring at me with such intensity, I'm almost frightened.

'Do you hate me now?' he demands.

'Why would I hate you?'

447

'Because you're such an honest person, and I behaved so badly!'

'I don't hate you,' I say. Then, 'I'm not always honest.'

I tell him about Leo, as we drive around the one-way system again and again, until, eventually, Gus spots the sign to Vinci and we climb up out of the town into hills with no light, on a road with steep, unexpected bends.

When the headlights catch the hand-painted sign to the Villa Vinciana, a part of me is relieved that we've found our way back, but mostly I wish he would drive on past, because the inside of the car feels almost like a confessional, where we can say anything to each other and there is no escape from the truth. But we haven't quite reached the end of our stories.

The car bounces down the unmade track, and we swerve into the car park with a spattering of gravel. Gus pulls up the handbrake and switches off the headlights, leaving us in total darkness. The silence seems charged with all the questions we might have asked while driving along but now feel too personal.

'So you became a writer?' he says.

'Only in my spare time. For years everyone kept saying, when Hope settles, but nobody ever thought it would happen, so when it did, I felt I hadn't done anything, and that's when I started writing this book. To give my life a kind of validity. And I suppose part of me thinks that it will be nice for Hope to have a record, if she ever wants to know about her past, although, to be honest, it would be so unlike her . . .'

There's a long silence, and I'm wondering whether he has understood the subtext.

'So you became a doctor, after all?' I ask.

'Yes. I have to keep up payments on our house, so it can be the girls' home for as long as they want. Although, this last visit, I wasn't sure they did any more. Which is probably a good thing, like you say. You have to find it in yourself to let people you love be independent of you.' He laughs ruefully. 'I just wish it hadn't happened so soon.'

'Where is your house?' I ask.

'Portobello Road.'

'Portobello Road?'

'At the top, near the Sun in Splendour.'

'One of those little houses all painted different colours?'

'Yes!' he says. 'Do you know Portobello Road?'

GUS

My girls had tattoo transfers applied in the shop she manages; she slows down each time she runs past my house; we have had coffee in the same cafe almost every morning for two years, but somehow she has never bumped into me, spilling her latte.

'I had to pass out to get you to notice me, for heaven's sake!'

In London there's so much light you can never see the stars, but here it is so dark, the sky is a black-velvet canopy studded with myriad diamonds.

'Do you think,' Tess asks, as we stand gazing up at it, 'that if we all had a kind of tracker device, a tiny light that you could see from space, then everyone's paths would loop and inter-twine as ours have?'

'No. I think this is m . . . mysterious.'

I was going to say that it is meant to be, but I heard Char-lotte's supercilious voice saying, 'Are things really meant to be?' and she has no place here.

'Mysterious?'

'Miraculous?' I offer instead.

'"Miraculous" is a lovely word,' says Tess.

We are both trembling as we kiss because it feels like there

449

is so much more at stake now we know all of each other's hopes and transgressions.

Tess tastes of pears and cream and when I close my eyes, her smile stays in my vision like the moment when a rainbow fades, but you still think it is there.

Not far away, an owl hoots.

'Can I hold your hand?' Tess asks, as we pick our way across the uneven ground.

'Those bloody flip-flops!'

'I forgot to pack shoes, which is unlike me, but I was in such a rush not to miss my plane.'

If she had missed it, would we be here now? Would she have taken the next flight? Would we have arrived at San Miniato al Monte at the same moment? The connection between us feels inevitable, and yet so fragile.

We kiss again on the stone staircase up to her room, and as we break for breath and I tug her up the steps, she loses a flip-flop. We watch it bouncing down, and then we hear footsteps approaching, so we dash along the landing, spilling Tess's keys, then rattling them incompetently in the old iron lock before finally bursting in, just in time to shut the door decisively behind us before we are discovered. With our backs against the door, we hold our breath like escaped prisoners on the run, until the footsteps pass by.

In the darkness, my hands find Tess's hands; my mouth her mouth, my skin her skin. Our desire is so frenzied, it feels as if we are trying to climb inside each other's bodies, as if we are surrendering ourselves completely to one another, as if it is the last thing we will ever do.

When I wake up, the room is dimly lit by splinters of sunshine piercing the slats of the shutters. Tess is asleep beside me, dark curls against the white pillow. It is strange to see her features so still and peaceful; almost more intimate to watch her sleeping than to kiss her awake.

Carefully, I slide out from under the sheet, and pulling on my shorts, tiptoe to the door, letting myself out without a sound.

The terrace is still silent and deserted, but the breakfast buffet is laid out. I fill my pockets with pastries and fruit. Chef collars me at the coffee machine.

'*Mi dispiace,*' I say. '*Non posso lavorare . . . una cosa molto importante . . .*'

I'm sorry, I can't work . . . a very important thing.

It would probably have been better to say it in English.

Chef looks at the two tiny cups I am filling, then winks at me. '*Amore!*'

He is Italian. He understands about important things.

On my way back to the room, I pick up Tess's flip-flop at the bottom of the stairs.

I realize I should have taken the key, because I'm going to have to wake her anyway.

I tap softly on the door.

'Who is it?'

She sounds anxious. Surely she didn't think I would sneak out and leave her?

'It's me!'

'Password!' she demands, with a nervous giggle in her voice.

'Breakfast.'

She unlocks the ancient wooden door, then dashes back to bed, pulling the sheet right up to cover her naked body.

With the espresso cups balanced on the sole of the flip-flop like a miniature breakfast tray, I place one on each side of the bed, then feed Tess a strawberry, and bend to kiss her strawberry-wet mouth. As she smiles up at me, words that have been fizzing like champagne bubbles in my body ever

451

since I stood beside her in the sunshine outside San Miniato al Monte suddenly whoosh to my lips.

'I think I love you!'

Her response is beautiful, innocent disbelief, like a child on Christmas morning.

'I don't just think I love you! I do love you! I love you!' It makes me madly happy to say it. 'You have the most amazing mind, the most gorgeous body . . .'

'No!' Suddenly, she holds up her hand and turns away, staring beyond the shuttered window, as if looking at a distant view.

'Tess?'

'My breasts aren't real!'

'I know.'

She whips round to face me.

'You *knew* I had breast cancer?'

You're writing a memoir and you're only thirty-four!

'Last night . . .' I falter. 'I could feel the scarring . . . and with your family history . . .'

The heavenly room has become a GP surgery. I try to take her hand, but she snatches it away, then, her eyes fixed on mine, lets the sheet drop.

In the thin stripes of sunlight falling across her chest, the incision lines are a little pinker and shinier than her natural skin tone. If there is a right thing to say, I don't know what it is. I long to reassure her that it doesn't make any difference, but I suspect that might make it sound like it does, so I just refuse to look away.

'They do look real, don't they?' she finally asks. 'Under a T-shirt?'

'Yes.'

'They're much smaller than my original ones. I was always a bit top heavy, to be honest. A swimmer's build, you know?'

I nod.

452

'So, is it OK if I love you?' I ask.

She thinks for a moment.

'I suppose it must be,' she smiles, and sinks back into the pillows, her eyes now sparkling with invitation.

I lie on the bed beside her, propping myself up on an elbow.

'I love you, Tess.' I stroke her face. 'I've never said that to anyone and known what it means.'

'I love you, too, Gus. And I have said it to two people, and I did mean it, but that was before yesterday . . . before I found you.'

I kiss her quickly.

'It's funny, isn't it?' she says. 'We have dictionaries full of amazing words, and yet the only phrase human beings have come up with to express their singular and infinite passion is three tiny, inadequate syllables?'

'Singular and infinite passion' is nine syllables, I think.

She reaches up to me with open arms, and as we kiss lingeringly it feels as if our souls are meeting and making solemn promises. I clasp her very tightly, trying to gather the very essence of her into me, and we begin to make love again, noiselessly – aware of other guests passing our door on their way down to breakfast – speaking without words, staring into each other's eyes, touching with silent, excruciating tenderness. I love feeling every millimetre of her long, lean body pressed against mine, I love that when she's close to orgasm she suddenly laughs with the joy of it. I love that we reach beyond the sensual oblivion of pleasure, to a paradise place of pure, ecstatic happiness.

We both suddenly freeze as we register the sharp, regular tap of heels approaching.

There is a knock at the door.

Fused together, we hold our breath.

'Signorina Costello?' Lucrezia's stern voice.

'Yes?' Tess answers guiltily.

'Do you know where is Mister Goos? His car she block the miniboos.'

Neither of us replies because we're stuffing the sheet into our mouths to stifle the laughter.

TESS

If there's one place in the world you should go to on the day you fall in love, it's Pisa.

We approach it through a stretch of souvenir market that looks like a hundred other tourist spots. There's this big fortified wall, so we can't see anything until we walk through the arch, but then it's like a vision of brilliant white marble, on flat green lawns, against a cerulean sky. I thought it was just the Leaning Tower, because that's all you see in the photos, but there's a cathedral and baptistry and cloisters, a whole amazing square of beauty. The colours are so luminous they look computer generated, and then you think about the people who built it, all those hundreds of years ago, before there was electricity or cranes or anything like that. That must be why it's called the Campo dei Miracoli. The Field of Miracles.

The Leaning Tower looks as if it's peeping round the side of the cathedral. The notice which gives you the history says that when it was first built it was considered such a failure of architecture that nobody wanted to claim it as theirs. So we don't even know the name of the person who created something that millions of visitors come to see each year.

There's a line of tourists taking photographs of their friends striking poses to make it look as if they're holding the tower up.

'Let's do one!'

I stand with my hand in the air and Gus lines up the shot. I'm about to send it to Doll, when he says, 'Why don't we take one of all these people from the other side, without the tower in it, and see if she guesses where we are?'

Which is a great idea, and she doesn't reply, so that's probably got her wondering.

We sit on the grass, like hundreds of others, although the signs say not to.

A white butterfly flits randomly from one small blade to another. I try to take a photo of it, white against the green grass, white against the blue sky, but it never settles for long enough.

A couple of backpackers approach us, holding out their camera to request a snap in front of the cathedral. The marble is as white and lacy as a wedding dress, and the tiers are like an intricately iced cake. At the apex of the roof, there is a golden statue of the Virgin Mary with baby Jesus in her arms.

The couple smile their thanks as I hand them back the camera.

'Do you think people can get married here?' I pull Gus to his feet to take a selfie of us with the Duomo.

I honestly don't mean anything by it.

'Shall we?' he says.

We look at the selfie. The cathedral is perfectly framed, and I've managed to get all of the golden statue, but only the tops of our heads.

So we do another one and I'm about to send it to Doll when Gus asks, 'Tess, did you hear what I just said?'

I pretend to be concentrating on the message when he gently prises the phone from my hand.

'Will you marry me?' he says.

'I can't!'

'Do you want me to go down on one knee?'

'No, please don't! I like you being tall!'

And I can't bear the idea of this moment appearing in the background of other people's photos.

455

'We've only known each other two days . . .'

'No, Tess,' he says, very seriously. 'We met when we were eighteen, but there was this tiny shift in fate and we kept missing each other. I know that sounds cheesy, but I can't think of another way of putting it. All I know is these last twenty-four hours have felt like a whole lifetime of how life should be. I've never been sure of anything, Tess, but I am certain about this.'

I try to focus on the purity of the white against the clarity of the blue in order to hold back the tears that are blurring my vision. But, when I speak, my voice is steady, because I'm not going to lie, and I'm not going to feel sorry for myself either, because this is actually the best day of my life.

'The thing is,' I begin. 'The thing is, they got rid of my breast cancer, but I've had a couple of dizzy spells recently, so they want to scan my brain to see if there's a secondary tumour, and that's why I'm here in Italy now, because when I get back, that's what's happening, and believe me, you do not want to be around for chemotherapy, and the likelihood is I'm going to go bonkers, then die!'

'No,' he says firmly. 'There are lots of reasons you could have fainted. It was hot at that concert. You're still very thin and weak after your op. Look, I've got a friend who's a brilliant oncologist and he will see you straight away. He'll make sure you have the best treatment. And I will look after you. Whatever happens. I promise I will look after you.'

I squeeze his hand very hard, trying to impress the reality on him.

'Mum died. She got a scan every year, but she still died.'

'But you may not,' he says.

I'm not sure whether he's talking about probability or whether he's forbidding it, but I love it that he doesn't tell me that I'll be fine if I fight hard enough.

'This is our beginning, Tess,' he says.

456

'It's not that I've given up,' I tell him. 'But the thing is, the cancer doesn't actually take any notice of that . . .'

He smiles at me, his blue-and-gold eyes shining with compassion.

'Marry me!' he says. 'Or if you don't want marriage, just be with me. "Come live with me and be my love!" Let's move to Italy! What's to stop us? I'll put the house on the market! It'll sell in a day. The girls can visit just as easily. And Hope, too, if she'd like that. I'll cook good, healthy food. Maybe even start a supper club!'

'Or we could stay in the Portobello Road?' I say.

'Or we could stay in the Portobello Road,' he agrees.

'I don't want it to feel like we're running away . . .'

'We won't run away.'

'But we may not have much time,' I say.

'Nobody knows how much time they have, do they?' he says.

I look up at the golden statue of Our Lady, and I suddenly think of how Mum must have felt after her first cancer, with Hope just a baby. And even though the title I've given my book is *Living with Hope*, I've never known before why Mum gave my sister that name. I always assumed it was because there was something different about Hope, and Mum was worried about her, but I realize now that she couldn't have seen that then, not when Hope was a newborn. It's suddenly radiantly clear to me that 'hope' was all about not allowing cancer to cast a shadow over living.

I'm standing in glorious sunshine on the Field of Miracles and I have this powerful feeling that my mum is close and she's smiling because I've finally got it.

'I've found myself a kind man, Mum, a man who understands who I am,' I tell her silently, as a white butterfly flits around us, like confetti dancing on the air.

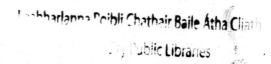

There are many charitable organizations offering information and support around the medical issues involved in the book. The following do invaluable work and were particularly useful during my research:

The National Autistic Society **www.autism.org.uk**
Breast Cancer Care **www.breastcancercare.org.uk**
Cancer Research UK **www.cancerresearchuk.org**
Macmillan Cancer Support **www.macmillan.org.uk**